WHERE NO SHADOW STAYS

SARA HASHEM

WHERE NO SHADOW STAYS

HOLIDAY HOUSE NEW YORK

Chapter heading art by marukopum/Shutterstock.com

Printed and bound in January 2026 at Sheridan, Chelsea, MI, USA.
www.holidayhouse.com
First Edition
ISBN: 978-0-8234-5700-7 | 1 3 5 7 9 10 8 6 4 2 (hardcover)
ISBN: 978-0-8234-6471-5 | 1 3 5 7 9 10 8 6 4 2 (paperback)

Library of Congress Cataloging-in-Publication Data is available.

EU Authorized Representative:
HackettFlynn Ltd, 36 Cloch Choirneal, Balrothery, Co. Dublin, K32 C942, Ireland.
EU@walkerpublishinggroup.com

To Mama and Baba, who never doubted me. Every achievement, every honor, every dream come true has your names written on it.

There I had fixed
Mine eyes till now, and pined with vain desire,
Had not a voice thus warned me: "What thou seest,
What there thou seest, fair creature, is thyself;
With thee it came and goes: but follow me,
And I will bring thee where no shadow stays."

—John Milton, *Paradise Lost*

CHAPTER ONE
PRESENT DAY

No one has tried to kill me yet today.

I add a tally in my journal. If I can go another seven hours, it'll officially be three days since the last attack.

My pen hovers over the page. I cross out *attack*. What do you call a gas station attendant who douses you in gasoline and raises a lighter?

Luck alone kept me from becoming Mina flambé. The attendant had already emptied his lighter before the thing possessed him. It never produced a spark. I managed to get in my car and screech out of the parking lot before the orange-eyed man could find another way to burn me alive.

It's getting creative. Too creative.

People stream around my tree, their backpacks slung over their shoulders and laughter ringing in the quad. It's a beautiful day in a town where beautiful days are one in a hundred. Sunshine promises a weekend of bonfires by Lake Lasem, and the prospect of spending time outdoors has put everyone in a good mood.

Lake Lasem. If I close my eyes, I can hear shrieks as someone squeezes the twelve-dollar bottle of charcoal lighter fluid—likely sold out by now at the general store—and accidentally sends the fire roaring to twice its size. I can smell bits of paper and wood burning. Feel the warmth against my toes. Taste the gooey, half-charred marshmallow melting on my tongue.

I exhale, tracing the edge of the journal.

The problem is that I can't close my eyes. I can't lose myself to imagination, because although no one has tried to kill me yet today, it's only noon.

A gaggle of freshmen emerge from the admin hall. I recognize one of the girls from the dance team. Yesenia. I approved her membership to the team myself. Someone nudges Yesenia, and she glances over. I lift my hand in a wave.

She gives me a cool once-over and keeps walking.

Right. I lower my arm, swallowing my sigh. To avoid drowning in my own self-pity, I've devised a couple of non-negotiable rules. One of them includes not sighing more than four times a day. I've already used up three. I need to save number four for a special occasion, and Yesenia brushing me off isn't special. In fact, it is exactly what I expected. I should count myself lucky she didn't hurl her backpack at my head.

Three weeks ago, a beautiful morning like this would have sent me on a picnic-planning craze. I would have been sprinting to the general store to beg for the last bottle of lighter fluid the second the bell rang. With my Polaroid in hand, I'd cajole my friends into taking at least fifteen photos by the lake in increasingly ridiculous poses. Despite the crowd, we would claim the best spot, right under the big maple tree, because Rainie would cut one path with her glare and Alex another with his smile. Charcuterie boards, little baskets of grapes, glass bottles of juice with condensation running down the sides... yeah. It would have been a great day.

Across the quad, my friends sneak glances over at me from our—their—table. Rainie catches me staring and flips me off. Lucia looks sad, and Aida squints like she's not sure where she's seen me before.

Alex is the only one who keeps his gaze averted. My heart aches, and Sigh #4 nearly breaks free. Breaking up with my boyfriend of three years was bad enough, but not even being able to explain why?

I'd learned the hard way that guilt, if given something to latch onto, can chew you to the bone.

I try to force my mind away from Alex and my friends. It won't do any good—I've already worn the tracks thin running around the same mental circles.

For now, it has to be this way.

A platoon of ants march in the grass, lining up to lay siege to my untouched mayo and egg sandwich.

"Lay down your arms, soldiers." I break off a piece of the pita and place it near the ant army. Someone should get to enjoy my meal, since I won't.

I'm startled from my silent conversation with the lead ant when shouts erupt by the theater building. Two of the theater kids wrestle on the stairs, cursing and crying as the others try to break them apart. The lunch monitors ignore them. Unless someone draws blood, those squabbles are usually a marketing maneuver to get us intrigued enough to buy tickets to their plays. *Antigone* this time, I think, continuing from *Oedipus* last week. I only know that because Miss Diaz offered ten points of extra credit to anyone who went, so I chose the busiest time and watched it from a seat in the back row, wedged between a couple enthusiastically making out and a guy who fell asleep in the first fifteen minutes.

One of the drama kids is flailing his arm around like a snake getting electrocuted, and he clocks the other guy across the jaw. Indignation breaks out on the injured guy's face, and the fight takes a turn for the ugly. Uh-oh. The monitors remain occupied with a red-eyed, giggling freshman.

Me and the ants are watching with concern—one of them has the other in a headlock—when a figure materializes between the brawling duo. A figure with broad shoulders encased in a leather jacket a size too big, a lean, corded frame covered in a T-shirt with the name of a band nobody recognizes, and a pair of black work boots with the flap turned out.

Jesse Talbot grabs the back of the drama kids' shirts and yanks them apart.

The school's resident loner looms over the boys with his patented doomsday scowl. He says something I can't make out, and the theater guys go still. They probably hadn't expected to *actually* get beat up, and with Jesse, it is a much higher possibility. After a minute, he releases them, returning to his table at the edge of the quad. The theater group elbows each other, and I can't help but share their surprise.

Jesse Talbot is notorious for keeping to himself. Aggressively solitary doesn't even begin to cover it. He hangs in the shadows of every room he walks into, like each moment is a new debate about whether it's worth stepping into the light. Dark crescents curve under eyes blacker than an eclipse, framed beneath wavy black hair a few inches past his ears. An undeniably attractive guy. Not that it matters—most girls brave enough to venture his way run straight into the barbed wire of his hostility.

Eventually, the theater kids retreat to their building. Jesse's stiff shoulders loosen.

Ah. "They got too close to his table." I share my revelation with the ants, only remembering I'm audible to more than just my army when a teacher glances over.

Her proximity startles me. Way too close. Killing close.

Dropping the last of my lunch for the ants, I hoist my backpack over my shoulder and follow a large group of lacrosse players into the building.

I have tallies to maintain.

Backpacks smack into my shoulders as I trudge down the hall, eyes on my feet and mind on my plans. After class, I'll go home and spend another afternoon hunting through Baba's office library for books about possession or missing memory. The answer is out there—I know it is.

I have to believe I'm getting closer to finding a solution and not just slowly running out of options.

Mr. Clay, deep in conversation with another teacher, shoots me a saccharine smile as he passes. I don't return it.

Not all my teachers have given up trying to coax me back into my Before self, but Mr. Clay never tried to begin with. To be fair, the behavior lines up pretty neatly for Canyon High's most despicable history teacher. Mr. Clay disliked me the moment he saw my name on the class roster freshman year. Yasmina "Mina" Mansour. Arab. Egyptian, to be exact.

Trying to win him over was my singular goal in AP Euro. I practically memorized the Bolshevik and French Revolutions to impress him, but he couldn't have cared less. It took too long for me to understand that no grade would ever be high enough. Participation credits, haunting his office hours—none of it mattered. His opinion of me had nothing to do with *me*, and he'd formed it before he even looked up from that roster.

Now, his detachment is a blessing. Mr. Clay pretends to tolerate me, and I happily return the favor. It means I don't have to worry about another well-intentioned lecture on "how things are at home" or why I left in December a decently normal, well-adjusted girl and returned a recluse.

Perfume and sweat cling together in the air. Too focused on not flat-tiring the girl ahead of me, I bump into another student. "Sorry," I mumble, raising my head with an apologetic grimace.

A flash of leather and dark eyes confront me.

"I'll live," Jesse Talbot says. He gives me a passing nod before striding away, maneuvering through the crowd with ease. I stare at his back for a long beat. The impulse to follow him comes out of nowhere, momentarily clearing the lethargic haze that's hung over me for weeks.

If anyone can teach me how to be alone, it's Jesse Talbot.

CHAPTER TWO
PRESENT DAY

I wasn't always like this.

I used to be studious, attentive. The list of my extracurriculars would make any college admissions committee weep. I split my time between my friends, dance, and Alex.

Alex. I couldn't remember a time I had kept a secret from him. Why would I need to? In a town like Ward, where people cherish a good love story, Alex and I had the best.

Fate had already laid it out for us, just waiting for someone to turn the first page. Me, the popular captain of the dance team. Him, the handsome and beloved basketball star. An alignment of the stars over a poorly lit auditorium on a Wednesday afternoon our freshman year.

My dance team was performing a complicated routine, some nightmare of choreography that was going well until they tossed me in the air. One of the lifters at the bottom broke formation, and my falling body hit the girls at the wrong angle. We scattered like bowling pins.

The lights shone around Alex as he bent over me, a fluorescent halo ringing his golden head. He'd carried me and my broken ankle all the way to the nurse's office, despite his coach shouting at him to get his ass back to the court. He held my hand until Baba arrived. For the next three months, he bought my lunch and carried it to the table so I wouldn't have to maneuver on my crutches.

By the end of month one, I'd fallen in love with him. I told him at the end of month two. By month three, we were us. Mina and Alex. He came to my performances, and I learned how to style a jersey under a cardigan for his games.

When I ended it, Alex received two measly texts.

I can't be with you anymore.

I'm sorry.

I wish I'd handled it better. Come up with a good lie, maybe faked feelings for some college guy from out of town. Any explanation would've been kinder than none.

But I tried to tell him the truth—I really did. The first week back from the trip, I asked him to meet me at the Grease & Grind. I chose a time right in the middle of the dinner rush. On the way there, I drove at a snail's pace, rehearsing my speech.

In November, I found out my mother had a sister. My aunt. She reached out and asked me to come visit my mother's childhood home in El Agamy. Baba would have never let me meet her on my own, so I lied about where I was during spring break. When I came back from that house, something came back with me. If I'm alone with someone, it'll find me. It always does.

The crowded twenty-four-hour diner seemed like the perfect place to confess. I'd had it all planned out.

Or so I thought.

Alex was already waiting for me in the parking lot when I pulled in. A quick scan of the lot turned my heart to lead. The only people near us were a mom wrangling her kids into a minivan and a jogger.

"Let's go," I said, grabbing his arm. "I made a reservation for us."

"Hey." Alex captured my wrist, clearly worried. "Are you okay?"

"I'm fine. Please, come on. We'll lose the table."

"Mina, the Grease & Grind doesn't take reservations."

The mom started her car and reversed out of the parking lot. "We have to go inside," I hissed. "Now!"

"Mina, hold on. It's too crowded in there. I'll drive us to Espresso Yourself. They have a discount on the raspberry white mochas you like."

The jogger rounded the corner, leaving the parking lot empty.

And I smelled it. The pungent odor of sewage and rot.

It was coming. Any second now, Alex's eyes would turn a cold and hateful orange, and he would try to kill me.

Panic stole away my senses. I yanked out of Alex's hold, nearly punching him in the process, and sprinted into the diner. Alex stood outside for ten minutes, waiting for me to come out and apologize, before shaking his head and storming away.

I haven't tried a second time.

I sink lower in the seat, attention switching between the world's slowest clock and my dog-eared copy of *Jane Eyre*.

English is my hardest hour of the day. Miss Diaz wears a feathered cap to talk about *Hamlet*, hangs posters of Isabel Allende's stories around the cramped classroom, reads Mahmoud Darwish poems every time it rains. Students who aren't in her class seek her out for advice. The ones who are try twice as hard to put in the effort, even though it's the last semester of senior year and they've spiritually exited the building.

If Canyon High has a heart, its name is Miss Diaz.

"Alright folks, one more weekend of *Jane Eyre* before we move on to our next unit! Look alive, look alive." Miss Diaz rubs her hands together. Brown curls overpower the book-shaped clip in her hair and bounce around her round face. "We've talked a lot about tragedy in *Jane Eyre*. I want to go over joy today. Joy is why we endure when all the obstacles are stacked against us. Where does our heroine find her joy?"

Definitely not anywhere in this book.

I run my thumb over the crinkled page of my school-issued copy. Dozens of seniors have held this copy of *Jane Eyre* in their hands. Their names litter the front page, joined by mine in tiny letters at the bottom.

I trace a drawing of a sunset etched in the corner of the page. Books are like clay, Baba always says. Every owner leaves an imprint behind. A little sadness, a little hope, soaked into the pages of an old story. Keeping it alive for the next person.

What imprint am I leaving behind?

"Mina!" Miss Diaz startles me, and I find her standing at the edge of my desk. There's a mixture of frustration and concern in her gaze. "Hon, are you alright? I've been calling your name."

"Sorry." The word comes out hoarse. It's the first time I've talked out loud to anyone other than the ants all day. I clear my throat. "Sorry. I was going over my notes on the reading."

"Alright," Miss Diaz says. I can tell she doesn't believe me. "Come up with anything good?"

I flip the page. Pretend my notes aren't doodles of prom dresses. "I don't really see what could be joyful about her life. Her parents are dead, her aunt abuses her, her best friend dies, and then her love interest turns out to be married." Frankly, it's a miracle Jane didn't flee into the woods earlier.

"Spoiler much?" someone calls.

"You should have read that last week, Tyler." Miss Diaz tsks and pivots on her booted heel. "Mina's right. There *is* a lot of hopelessness in Jane's tale. But if that's the case, why does she go back? Once she becomes a rich woman and finds a suitable match in St. John, what drives Jane to return to Thornfield?"

Miss Diaz is still looking at me. I blasted through the end of the book during fourth period. The only parts I retained are Mr. Rochester losing his vision and the other dude dying. "Because she hears his voice calling for her in the wind?"

"Not quite." She flashes an encouraging smile. "But you're on the right track. This weekend, I want you all to consider Jane Eyre's journey in its entirety. From her aunt's house to St. John's, ask yourselves this: What parts of herself does Jane leave behind, and what ties them all together?" She raps her knuckles on the podium. "Answers in two double-spaced paragraphs, please."

Backpack zippers cut through the groans. Conversation breaks out for the last minute of class. Miss Diaz crouches by my desk. "Can you hang back after the bell?" she asks quietly.

My chest tightens. Miss Diaz hasn't quit trying to catch me for a one-on-one in weeks.

"I can't today. My dad is picking me up." A bald-faced lie. Baba teaches a seminar on Friday evenings, and he heads to the university library early to get work done. He is there so often that if he didn't have the social skills of a six-hundred-year-old turtle, I would wonder if he was dating the librarian.

"I'm sure he wouldn't mind waiting a few extra minutes. Please, Mina."

I barely hear the bell over my burgeoning terror. The students start to filter out. The certainty of danger creeps over me, as persistent and pervasive as the weeds coiled around the quad. If they all leave, it'll happen again. I know it will.

It'll find me.

I clutch my binder to my chest. My heart thumps frantically against the front cover. *Not Miss Diaz. Please, please, not Miss Diaz.* "Can I come in early Monday morning instead?" Only ten stragglers left, chatting or texting by their desks.

Please let some of them wait to ask Miss Diaz a question. Please don't leave me alone with her.

"You said that last time," Miss Diaz says. She hops onto the desk next to me and crosses her ankle boots, the metal buckles clicking with the movement. "Have I done something to offend you, Mina? You can tell me. I promise I won't be upset."

The forlorn note in her voice makes me want to weep. This is the woman I've pestered for four years about everything from the merits of a peplum top to whether a classmate asking if my parents had ridden to school on a camel qualified as a microaggression. Things I couldn't ask Baba, because he would just tell me to mind my business and focus on my studies.

People like that are weeds, habibti, he'd say. *They want to tangle you up, make you as small as them. Otherwise, they know you will grow higher than they ever could.*

Good advice. Ninety-nine percent of the time, I followed it.

For the other one percent, I went to Miss Diaz.

"You haven't done anything wrong." My first bit of honesty today. I trace the outer edge of the binder with my pinkie. "I've just been busy."

The room empties. I shoot out of my chair. Dread drips in my belly, forming a pool of fear somewhere deep and dark. Miss Diaz watches me retreat with a puzzled frown. "What's keeping you so busy? Is it anything I can help with?"

We're alone, and she hasn't changed. It hasn't taken her.

Silence hangs like a guillotine in the empty room. "Just some personal stuff. But . . . if you want to meet in the quad during lunch on Monday, I can be there."

Still nothing but warm brown eyes, flooding with joy at my weak invitation.

Hope blooms inside me. What if it's over?

Miss Diaz leaps to her feet. "You've got yourself a deal. Let me write a quick Post-it so I don't forget. Ugh, Mina. I'm getting sixteen emails a day about the Spirit Week schedule. My hair turns a shade grayer every time I check my inbox."

I watch her closely, looking for any signs. Nothing. Just a long stream of complaints about block scheduling and class-separated assemblies.

The hope grows into a wildfire. A hope that's been brutalized over the course of three awful weeks. Lunch with Miss Diaz. Monday!

She bends her head to write at her desk, pen moving rapidly over the bright pink Post-it. "Done!" Miss Diaz circles the board, searching for an empty spot to stick the reminder. "Why do they need to extend study hall by fourteen minutes and shorten lunch by twenty? Just to confuse the kids?" she mutters, scanning her flurry of pastel stickers.

"There's free space next to the science fair flyer," I offer.

Lunch should be safe, right? Out in the open, with plenty of people around us? To be extra safe, we won't sit under my tree, since it's set apart from the crowd. I'll find a table smack-dab in the middle of the quad. The ants won't be happy.

I will be, though. I'll be so freaking happy I might expire on the spot, and wouldn't that be ironic?

Miss Diaz still hasn't put up the sticker. I walk to the board, tapping my finger against the rectangle of free space. "Do you want me to put it up?"

The Post-it flutters to the ground between us.

The seconds pass in centuries. The hairs on the back of my neck stand at attention. I stare at the Post-it. At the marker stains in the creases of Miss Diaz's fingers and the dirty brown carpet beneath it.

Wetness gathers under my lashes as I look up and meet cold orange eyes.

No. Not her. Not her.

"Get out of here," I whisper. I've never addressed the thing directly before. I rarely have the chance. All I ever see is the orange of a bloody dawn rising in the faces of those unfortunate enough to be left alone with me. The foul smell leaking like an open sore. Rot and ash, the odor of unbearable heat beneath a desiccating body.

Miss Diaz slaps me across the face. I stumble back, slamming my hip against the corner of her desk. Her pencil holder goes flying, sending pens and highlighters rolling on the floor.

I don't get a chance to recover before she shoves me to the ground. My elbow bangs against a desk leg as I try to rise, but the thing is moving too fast, taking a fistful of my hair and slamming my head against the carpet. Miss Diaz's hands reach for my throat.

If this had happened three weeks ago, I probably would have blacked out. I might have even tried to wrestle her politely, the way you would a friend with a habit of starting the fight but then tattling to their mom if you won.

I have the scars to speak for what I've learned since the first time I saw orange eyes.

I dig my teeth into her wrist until she hisses. Twisting, I toss her to the side and crawl backward on my palms, struggling to grab something to hoist myself to my feet. My sweaty palms slip around a chair's metal legs.

This is Miss Diaz. I don't want to hurt her. I don't even want to scream. If someone comes in and sees her accosting a student, her career is over.

I should have known better than to hope. I did know better, but hope is its own violence.

"Miss Diaz, stop," I plead. "If you can hear me, I don't want to hurt you."

Her lips part into a gruesome grin. She grabs my shoe, dragging me toward her. Black sludge coats her tongue, drips from the roof of her mouth. Bile burns in my throat. It never speaks, never answers me. I don't even know if it understands what I say.

But desperation is a universal language, even between man and myth, and it relishes mine.

I hurl my backpack at her head, temporarily knocking her grip on my leg loose. She releases me with a groan. Lurching upright, I topple as many desks as I can into her path and make a break for the door. If I can just get far enough, it'll leave her. She'll blink and be Miss Diaz again, baffled at the state of her classroom and her unexplainable headache.

As soon as I throw the door open, something sharp spears into my arm. I shriek, falling against the door and grabbing my elbow. A pair of small red scissors protrude from my upper arm. My sleeve darkens around the tear, sticking hot against my skin.

She threw *scissors* at me?

Before I can pull it out, a book the size of a brick crashes next to my head. The thing hurls them at me like missiles. Miss Diaz's beloved books. Books she's collected over a lifetime, lovingly preserved in first and second editions.

Hitting the ground, I yank the scissors out of my arm with a pained gasp. I'll have to crawl. Once I get out of the room, she'll be okay.

I make the mistake of glancing down at the scissors. The vivid red of my blood on the blades sends the world spinning. I glance away quickly. Absolutely *not* the time to let my ridiculous aversion to blood knock me out.

I've crawled hallway out the door when a book collides with the side of my head. My vision blurs a second time, and I slap a palm against the carpet to keep from going flat. The book drops open next to my hand.

How Not to Drown in a Glass of Water, by Angie Cruz.

I turn onto my back as more objects come flying, holding up the book to shield myself against the onslaught. A mug, protein bars, pencils, notebooks. Almost impressive, how many items it manages to hurl my way.

I glance to the side. With a mixture of relief and despair, I realize the hallway is empty. No one will see Miss Diaz try to kill me.

No one will see her succeed.

A weight lands on my stomach, and I drop the book in time for thin fingers to close around my throat. I scratch at her hands, writhing as I try to buck her off.

Orange spots blossom in my vision. The color of the beach in El Agamy at dusk, of the sun burning behind a gauzy film of clouds. My breath rattles in my chest as it strangles me with Miss Diaz's hands, and all I can think about is Baba. He can't lose me like we lost Mama. He won't survive another death.

An arm encased in leather punches Miss Diaz in the face. She flies off me, hitting the door with a sickening thud.

I cough violently as air rushes into my lungs. A passing touch to my throat confirms the presence of finger-shaped bruises.

Jesse Talbot stands wide-eyed above me. "Holy crap."

Miss Diaz stirs. I've grown quite scientific about analyzing when this thing manifests, and curiosity nearly edges out my instincts. Will Jesse's presence strip the thing out of her immediately? Or will it fade?

"We have to go," I croak. I'm not strong enough to test either theory. With my non-bleeding arm, I push to my feet and grab Jesse's jacket. "Run!"

To his credit, Jesse doesn't hang around to question me. We sprint down the deserted hall, not stopping until we shove through the double doors and stumble outside.

Sweet, sweet air. I barely remember to check Jesse and I aren't alone in the quad before I grab the rim of a garbage can and try to breathe through my battered throat. I don't need to prod it to know she did real damage.

Maybe I can ransack Baba's closet for a few of his turtlenecks. He owns about a million of them; he definitely wouldn't notice a few missing.

Before I can devise a plan to rob my father, a harsh voice slaps me back into reality.

"What the hell just happened?"

CHAPTER THREE
PRESENT DAY

For a supposed loner, Jesse Talbot is surprisingly clingy.

"You aren't gonna shake me, Mansour. We're neighbors," Jesse says. I absently open my mouth to correct him before realizing I don't need to. He pronounced my last name without any trouble. *Mun-soor.*

Jesse matches my clip down the street. I glare at his long legs, pumping mine in retaliation. Five foot four is a perfectly decent height. I haven't had a problem with it until now, when it's forcing me to linger next to a six-foot-two pile of questions I can't answer.

Under normal circumstances, I would probably be too shocked by the sheer novelty of Jesse acknowledging my existence to care about the context. After all, this is the guy who spent four years crossing his driveway every morning to avoid saying hello to me. I called out a good morning to him once, and he cringed like a dog was lifting its leg over his shoe.

"Oh, now you care that we're neighbors?" I double-check the street. Thanks to the nearby middle school, a long line of impatient parents usually clogs up this road around three, waiting to pick up their kids. I don't have to worry about accidentally finding myself alone with a random pedestrian.

A traffic guard in a bright yellow vest marches past me and Jesse on the crosswalk, a gaggle of tiny kids trailing behind her.

"Sorry, did I miss the deadline?" Jesse sounds mildly amused, which is more emotion than I've observed from him in close to half a decade.

I ignore the sarcasm. "Yeah, you did. Four years is a little past the expiration date for friendly small talk, don't you think?"

One of the kids to our right holds out his palms, showing off the melted marshmallow of a Rice Krispies treat to his friend. Jesse eyes him distrustfully. "Aren't we getting a little off topic here? Miss Diaz just tried to kill you."

I shush him immediately. "Don't worry about it."

If you had asked me when I woke up this morning whether it was more likely Miss Diaz would use my head for target practice or Jesse Talbot would trap me in conversation, I would have painted a bull's-eye on my forehead.

We finally turn onto our street, where dusty, two-story houses face each other across a pothole-riddled road. A knot at the base of my neck relaxes. Almost home.

Bits of splattered fig stick to the bottom of my shoe as we pass the yellow house at the corner. Per unspoken custom, each house in our little neighborhood maintains a fruit tree in its front yard. The Millers planted figs; the Ahmads, tangerines.

At our old house, an exceptionally eager Baba planted a pomegranate tree in our yard before he'd even set up the electricity. Mama used to tend to it, but the task fell to me after she died.

I could barely keep a fish alive, let alone a fruit tree. I researched everything there was to know about pomegranates. Watered and weeded and sprayed for bugs. When we moved one block down and replanted it, I'd done my best to keep it alive and kicking.

Not because I cared about the pomegranates. I never understood the appeal of eating a fruit that tastes like it's trying to eat you back. But Mama was in her best mood with a bowl of pomegranate seeds on her lap.

She'd dip a spoon in honey and coat it in sugar for me. "Come, Mina. I made the spoon sweet, so you won't even taste how bitter the seeds are. You won't say no to your mama, will you? Ashan khatri."

As soon as she whipped out the "ashan khatri," I was done for. No good daughter disappoints her mother's khatir, even if it means eating a fruit you can barely stomach. Her hands would be stained a reddish pink for days from peeling the pomegranates as fast they were dropping from the tree. It broke my heart to see her studiously stripping away the white spongy bits around the seeds, spooning in the honey she'd driven down to San Francisco to buy. The least I could do was shut up and take the bowl.

Nowadays, when the tree swells heavy in the spring, I collect the pomegranates and give them to our neighbors. I can't eat them, but I also can't bear to watch them pile up on the grass and wither.

Meanwhile, nothing ever ripens on the Talbots' land; it only rots.

The paint peels in gray strips around their house, leaving flakes of white dandruff circling the property like the chalk outline at a crime scene. Dead grass creeps from their gate to the rickety porch steps. Metal bars stripe the windows, pinning the shutters closed. No matter how many times I watch Jesse work on the porch, hammering at the molding old wood, the front steps always groan. Low and mournful, as though the house is using its last breaths to warn others away.

None of the houses in Ward are getting featured in *Architectural Digest*, but the Talbot house . . . I've watched strangers cross the street rather than pass in front of it.

We stop at the gate separating Jesse's barren front yard from the sidewalk. Jesse shoves his hands into his jacket pockets, eyeing me warily. "If Diaz is dangerous, we need to tell someone."

"Miss Diaz wouldn't hurt a fly!" One measly little murder attempt while under the influence of a supernatural force doesn't mean anything.

Jesse arched a brow. "No, apparently she only hurts cheerleaders with a chip on their shoulder."

"I'm not a cheerleader," I snap. "I was captain of the dance team."

Exasperated, Jesse runs his knuckles across his jaw. "You're killing me, Mansour."

"I'd like to," I say, and immediately slam my mouth shut. Horror washes over me. I glance down at myself without an ounce of recognition. My hands are balled into fists. My nails form red crescents on my palm from where I've dug them into my skin.

Who *is* this?

The Mina from before wasn't quick to anger. The other Mina was kind, forgiving. She would have tried to invite Jesse to the lakeside picnic and laughed off his caustic remarks. She wouldn't be standing here wondering whether to push him into the street or ask the Rice Krispies kid to smear his hands on Jesse's jacket.

How strange. I'm jealous of who I used to be.

"Leave it alone, okay? Go back to your regularly scheduled seclusion." I swivel on my heel, intent on my own yard. Jesse catches my arm. I gasp as his hand closes around my wound, sending another gush of hot blood trickling down my sleeve.

Jesse swears, removing his grip instantly. "I knew you weren't angling your arm right. She stabbed you with those scissors on the floor, didn't she?"

"Just a tiny bit," I pant. I steadfastly avoid looking at the blood. The last thing I need is to faint in front of him.

"My dad has supplies inside. Come on, I'll bandage you up."

Before I can stop myself, I back away. Jesse's reputation is nothing compared to his father's. Ward's resident mortician is the monster story parents use to scare kids into doing their homework and eating their veggies.

The long black hearse comes to the Talbot house to collect its due. Listen, learn, or next time, it will come for you.

Like hell am I going anywhere near Mr. Talbot's lair.

Jesse's gaze hardens. "He's not home."

"It doesn't matter. I can't go inside with you. We can't be alone."

Jesse spreads his arms wide, encompassing the whole of the street. "Take a look around, Mansour. We're alone right now."

"No, the kids—"

—are gone. Everyone's gone.

How long have we been the only two standing in the street? Mentally slapping myself for letting him distract me, I break into a sprint toward my house. Jesse calls after me, but he doesn't try to follow.

Good. Jesse is significantly taller and stronger than anyone the thing has possessed. In my current condition, I have no faith in my ability to fend him off. He's an asshole, but he doesn't deserve to get stuck with a murder charge.

I close the front door behind me, bolting the lock. "Baba?" I call.

The house stays silent. Still at the university, then.

Releasing a sigh of relief, I wander into the kitchen and wash my hands. Water tinted red swirls into the drain. I don't feel any cleaner. I'm not sure I'll ever feel clean again.

I fill a glass of water from the tap. Only after I've had three refills do I finally breathe. My shoulders slump, and I bring a hand to my face.

So much for my tallies.

When I feel confident that I can move without sinking into a ball on the kitchen floor, I sprinkle some Comet inside the sink and double check I've locked the front door.

Every day after school, my system goes on high alert for the sound of a car pulling up or a key jingling in the lock. I've been paranoid about running into Baba every time I leave my room. If he meanders in for a snack or goes to find his glasses while I'm down here . . . the thought sends a shiver through me. Baba is a pacifist by nature. He's never so much as slapped my wrist.

To see his eyes burn orange, to smell the rot on his skin. It would be more than I could bear.

So I stay away, and I pretend it doesn't sting that he hasn't noticed.

After taking stock of my injuries, I come to the unfortunate conclusion that I've developed all the classic symptoms of being a giant baby.

Sure, every bone in my body hurts and my clothes are ruined, but it isn't as though my organs are spilling onto the ground or anything.

Lifting my shirt over my head is a no go. My arm protests any movement. I grab a pair of scissors and the first-aid kit from the medicine cabinet, where I've been a frequent flier for the last few weeks. If Baba wonders why our dusty first-aid kit is suddenly well-stocked, he doesn't let on.

I settle on the couch, arranging a few throw pillows on the carpet in case the sight of blood gets the better of me. Baba's twenty pairs of glasses clutter the coffee table and TV stand, tossed around haphazardly so at least one is always within reach. I push them to the corner and set up my tools.

Some nineties show plays on the first channel I flip to. Loud and abrasive, good for pushing out my thoughts. I force myself to focus on the canned laugh track instead of the moist, heavy fabric sticking to my right arm.

The scissors glide through the seams at my shoulder. Bracing myself, I peel off the sleeve. The squelch of the blood-heavy fabric makes me queasy, and I rush to drop the sleeve in an empty grocery bag. Red spots spatter the plastic.

The sight of my blood smeared over the logo of my favorite grocery store disorients me. It prods at the iron fist clamped around my chest, threatening to loosen it. I don't know what would happen if my chest loosened enough for me draw in a full breath of air. I might use it to start screaming, and I doubt I'd ever stop.

I drag my hair over my right shoulder and off my overheating neck, trying to regulate my body's temperature. Our house has the insulation of tissue paper. Usually that means I spend every winter sporting a runny nose and wearing holes in the big toe of my socks, but at this precise moment, I couldn't be more grateful for the chill. My body always reacts to stress by turning into a furnace—the weeks after Mama died, I could only sleep while curled beneath an open window—but I thought it would stop eventually.

It did not. In fact, it made some new friends called shortness of breath and lethargy.

The nineties show ends, and a documentary on the Saqqara Tomb replaces it. The camera pans over the pyramids and the crowded streets of Cairo. Mystical music plays in the background. I roll my eyes, groping around the couch for where I'd dropped the remote.

"One of the oldest civilizations in the world, Egypt contains secrets beyond our wildest imaginations," narrates the British presenter. "In Egypt, or 'Masr,' knowledge works in reverse. The more our archeologists learn, the less we understand about the history of this mighty, mystifying nation. Nobody, however, can dispute the importance of the Nile in every period of Egypt's history. Sacrifices were made to the Nile in hopes of bountiful crop yields and seasonal floods." The river comes into view, sloshing against the banks of a Nubian village, stretching past the Saqqara Tomb. "Think of the secrets lost to this timeless river. If the Nile could speak, what would it tell us?"

I finally hunt down the remote. With my uninjured arm, I mute the television in time to avoid audio for the next clip, where a bunch of British archeologists dressed in white and beige suits hold ceremonial shovels inside a tomb while a couple of actual diggers wearing galabiyas maneuver around them.

To think just a month or two ago, I would have turned up the volume on this ridiculous documentary and spent the rest of the afternoon ignoring my homework to watch it. I had been so focused on soaking up all the media on my home country that I could find; I didn't even notice how strange or off-putting some of it was. Though, not for lack of warning. Baba had a habit of assessing the names in the opening credits of any documentary about Masr. If it didn't pass his inspection, he would refuse to watch it with me.

Truthfully, convincing Baba to sit down and watch anything with me was tough. To rip him away from his grading, I'd turn on a Masri show—if Ahmed El Sakka, Mohamed Henedi, or Hanan Turk is involved, Baba won't even check his emails.

Still, he never lingers past an episode or two. The documentaries irritate him, but I think the shows hurt his heart.

I only swoon a little wiping my arm clean. Progress. Who knows? Constantly sopping up blood might cure me of my phobia once and for all.

I'm all about the silver linings these days.

After I finish wrapping gauze around my upper arm, I put away the rest of the supplies and head for the fridge. I pour myself a bowl of stale cereal and climb the stairs to my bedroom. A roll of thunder shakes the house as soon as the door closes behind me.

"Ugh." I leave my bowl on the dresser and run back downstairs, grabbing the rain buckets from the garage. Ward is no stranger to storms, especially in February. Rattling, raging sheets of rain and wind lay siege to the county, flooding the lake and making the roads unusable.

Our roof may as well be Swiss cheese for all the leaks it springs. I stick buckets in strategic locations around the living room.

I switch on all the lights, fervently hoping Baba doesn't walk into the house distracted. I've lost count of how many times I've heard the muted cry of him tripping over a bucket.

The roof creaks, the wood furrowing like a stern brow under the onslaught.

I itch to grab my phone and text Rainie. I imagine the conversation would go as a million before it had.

Me:

WW Alert!! Grab your laptop, it's my turn to pick the movie

Rainie:

Not a WW. This is practically sunbathing weather. stop trying to force me to watch *Howl's Moving Castle*

Me:

you don't understand. he has silver hair and a long black coat

and he FLIES

Rainie:

He's a cartoon

Me:

. . .

you're killing me. like actual physical pain KILLING ME

Now, Rainie would probably recommend I meander out into the street with a lightning rod just for giggles. She certainly wouldn't speculate over whether we had an actual Ward Wailer on our hands.

The Talbots' rusted awning rattles in the wind, nearly louder than the rain pelting the windows. A car alarm goes off in the distance, and I resign myself to napping with headphones on.

I check my phone, but there's no alert yet. Good. Ward Wailers have the power to bring the county—and its gridline—to its knees. I hate it when Baba is out of the house during one.

I push my curtain to the side. Sure enough, dark gray clouds hover low over our street. So much for a sunny Friday by the lake. Everyone at Canyon will be home today, too. Despondently watching their plans for the rest of the afternoon disappear in the blue afterglow of a lightning strike.

Instead of feeling smug, the thought of everyone else stuck inside only depresses me further.

Spooning cereal into my mouth, I grab my journal from my backpack. I've documented every attack, every bizarre incident since I left Masr. The first ten pages of the journal remain blank. Waiting for me to fill them with the details of what happened on the trip.

But I can't. The fear refuses to let me condense it, to make it small enough to fit into words.

After I add a couple of hesitant lines about the encounter with Miss Diaz, I toss the journal, picking up the much rattier leather one I lifted from Baba's study. It contains only two entries: my mother's maiden name on the first page, written in her trademark slanted script, and a photo of her and Baba in their early twenties.

Baba and Mama smile up at me from a two-by-two photo of them posing in front of the Stanley Bridge in Alexandria. Baba has his arm around Mama, his square glasses slipping down the long line of his nose. A nest of curly hair sits on top of his head, and he's wearing a truly horrific pair of bellbottom jeans.

He's also smiling wider than I've ever seen him smile in Ward.

Mama barely takes up space at his side. Much more reserved than Baba, her hands rest in front of her skirt, lips turned up at the corners. Coils of black hair cascade in spirals around her frame. I wind one of my own curls around my finger.

Nadine Haikal and Hatem Mansour met at the University of Cairo two years into Baba's position as a faculty lecturer. Nadine had taken a series of long buses from El Agamy, a rural area on the outskirts of Alexandria, to visit a friend on campus. She ended up wandering around, lost, until Baba happened upon her.

I love hearing the story, drawing it around me like a warm and well-worn blanket, but Baba turns puce anytime I try to talk about Mama. I resent it, sometimes, how Baba hoards those memories of her. I was only nine when she went to her hometown for her first and last visit.

It's almost as if he thinks by withholding stories about Mama or Masr, I'll be a blank slate for America to fill in. A girl with an Etch A Sketch identity.

Outside, the rain howls, unleashing its wrath on Ward.

My hands tighten around the journal. I went to Masr to learn about who I am, where I come from. But also for answers, because here is my darkest, quietest secret: I don't believe them about how my mother died.

NADINE HAIKAL
EL AGAMY, ALEXANDRIA
1977

The school bus was late, which meant today was the day the hairstylist's daughter would die.

Eleven-year-old Nadine peeled the plastic around her feeno sandwich, the oven-warm bread sliced down the middle and filled with scrambled eggs and feta cheese. She sat on a dusty curb, the empty lot behind her piled high with garbage and fetid animal carcasses. A fly swooped around her sandwich. Soon, the pack of stray dogs that patrolled this road would amble by. If she didn't want new scratches, she needed to scarf down the sandwich *quick*.

Still, Nadine waited. She had a schedule to follow.

On cue, the hairstylist's door opened across the barren dirt road. A haggard man wearing layers of dirt-caked coats slept outside the salon's door, and Nadine watched curiously as the hairstylist offered him a cup of tea. According to Janna, the hairstylist's blabbermouth daughter, their family barely had anything to spare as it was. Janna always eagerly ate the half of feeno Nadine offered her every morning, and Nadine had noticed the bruises under mother and daughter's eyes growing with hunger as the drought lengthened. Stupid to offer tea to a random vagrant, who'd likely come back to the dim-wittedly charitable hairstylist's door.

No matter. Soon, the hairstylist would only have one mouth left to feed.

Janna didn't bother glancing both ways before she shot across the wide dirt road. A car hadn't passed through in the thirty minutes Nadine had been waiting. Tucked in a desolate corner of Alexandria, El Agamy was a decrepit, forgotten cluster of half-constructed buildings and empty roads. When Nadine was younger, she had loved having the run of the entire town. Her mother wouldn't bat an eye at Nadine disappearing for hours to play with the housekeeper's daughters until well past dinner. She had only interceded once, when Nadine's speech became accented with what her mother called "balady."

"Anyone who hears you speak like that will never truly hear a word you say," Mama said. "As soon as they hear a falaha, they won't need to hear anything more."

Nadine didn't know what was so wrong with a falaha—most of Masr was falaheen. They were the farmers who fed them, who climbed the towering date trees in the Haikals' garden with nothing but a piece of rope, a basket, and their bare feet. What did it matter if they spoke a little differently?

It wasn't an answer Mama liked. She forbade Nadine from seeing the girls for weeks and doubled Nadine's tutoring sessions until the accent disappeared.

The emptiness of El Agamy offered Nadine far less entertainment nowadays. Sometimes, if she walked down the right road or the sun slanted a certain way, she could almost see what her mother and grandmother meant when they said El Agamy had been beautiful. She could imagine that this had once been a place where Abdel Halim Hafiz had come to summer, where rich families had built grand, stately properties from here to Hannoville and sunbathed by the glittering beach.

Maybe she would still feel a sense of wonder about their neighborhood if she hadn't seen what else was out there. Admiring the rest of Alexandria didn't require as much effort from Nadine's imagination. She had gone to Manshiya and Sidi Bishr with her grandmother, and Nadine had been breathless as they drove around the glamorous city to Teta's favorite shopping center. Towering, colorful buildings had lined asphalt streets. Fruit vendors meandered along the paved roads, peddling their wares without fear of the honking yellow cabs winding around them. Men in shiny suits sipped coffee at outdoor cafés, a deck of cards split between them. Women linked their arms and laughed as they ducked into bustling shops.

Next to it all, the glittering Mediterranean coast stretched in a curve from the Citadel of Qaitbay to the Montaza, like the entire city was sitting on the ocean's smile.

"Teta, can we move here? Please?" Nadine had said from her seat by a store window, unable to peel her gaze away from the sheer volume of *life* happening around her. This was what a city should look like. Not the dry, lifeless corner where the Haikal family had lived for generations.

Her grandmother had pinched her ear and dragged her from the store. She threw a crying Nadine into the car and pointed a knobby finger in her face. "Don't you ever say anything so foolish to me again."

And Nadine hadn't. Not ever again.

"Salam Nadine!" Janna chirped. Like many people in Egypt, Janna was Muslim. Today happened to be Quran recital day at her public school, so she wore a bright blue one-piece hijab for the occasion. The loose buttons on her uniform had been lovingly sewn back on.

Nadine herself went to a secular private school, where they were only faithful to the number of zeros in her mother's check.

"Salam Janna." Across the street, the hairstylist watched the pair for another minute, chewing her lip worriedly. The rash of missing children had put the parents in El Agamy on edge, which is why Nadine had played the long game with Janna Elshenaway.

All it took was one moment of a lowered guard. As Nadine watched, the hairstylist shook her head slightly and retreated into her salon. The door swung shut behind her.

Nadine stood. Time to go.

"Do you want my sandwich?"

Janna's brown eyes went wide. "The whole sandwich? Are you sure?"

In answer, Nadine put the feeno in the girl's calloused little hands. Nadine's own hands were smooth. In a few years, when Nadine would start to keep a journal of her private horrors, she would joke that blood made a good moisturizer. Her hands never wrinkled, never cracked.

"Do you want to come back to my house? I don't think the bus is coming today. My mom can drive us."

Janna stopped chewing. "Oh. I should tell Mama first, though. Right?"

The last word told Nadine all she needed. She had Janna in the palm of her supple hand, and she would do whatever Nadine said.

These girls, these soft girls, they weren't a challenge. Their parents loved too hard. Protected them more than they should. Any instincts Janna might've had, instincts about girls like Nadine, never had a chance to develop. "My mom will let her know after she drops us off. Come on, we're going to be late."

Janna held Nadine's hand all the way to the ivy-wrapped iron gates around Nadine's two-story villa. The young girl shrank a little as they entered the estate, her curious gaze roving over grandiose pillars supporting delicately carved buttresses and balconies the size of some apartments.

At school, Nadine learned about a creature called an anglerfish. A hideous, ordinary fish except for one detail: the glowing fin dangling right in front of its mouth. In the darkness, the fin shone terribly bright, entrancing the anglerfish's prey. They wouldn't see the sharp, hungry teeth lying in wait. Wouldn't hear the snap of its jaws until they were already between them.

These painted walls were the Haikal family's glowing fin. And Nadine had grown up between its teeth.

Janna didn't let go of Nadine's hand past the living room, up the stairs to the second floor. It wasn't until they reached the waiting steps to the third-floor door that Janna's hand twitched in hers.

"I didn't know you had a third floor," Janna murmured. "Is your mom in there?"

An orange light spilled under the door, the rays crawling toward their dusty shoes. A soundless hum wove through the air. No matter how many times Nadine heard the sound, it never stopped raising the hair on the back of her neck.

The first fissure of fear broke open in Janna. She tugged free of Nadine, but it was too late. The shadows slithered from the walls, blots of black dancing toward them. They snuck beneath Janna's feet, slunk around her crooked hijab. Sound erupted from the shadows. Voices rang around them, and Nadine guided her gaze away from the snatches of color flitting across the dark surface.

Pockets of forever, Mama called these shadows. Moments, memories, that time saw fit to save.

But time only moved forward for a reason. Whatever imprints those shadows stored, Nadine wanted no part of it.

The door swung open. Nadine threw herself to the ground, covering her face in the nick of time. Janna's bloodcurdling scream pierced her ears, ringing in her head, and the orange glow momentarily brightened behind Nadine's closed eyelids.

Janna's screams abruptly cut off. Nadine waited for the click of the door to raise her head.

The orange light receded. All that remained from where Janna Elshenaway had once stood was a half-eaten feeno sandwich.

CHAPTER FOUR
PRESENT DAY

The next morning, the sound of a buzzing saw rouses me from a marathon night of terrible sleep.

A bleary glance from my window identifies the culprit: none other than Mister When-I-Wake-Up-We-All-Wake-Up Talbot.

I yank my robe over my pajamas and wait until I hear Baba's car leaving the driveway to creep out of my room. Strings of pain stretch inside my head, strumming between my temples. The sun barely peeks through the blanket of clouds, but its presence means the threat of a Ward Wailer is gone. My mother's journal sits on my bedside table, open to one of its many blank pages.

I shove my feet into the yard Crocs, slapping the screen door open. A rickety wooden gate separates our backyard from the Talbots'. As I approach, I spot Jesse moving through the gaps in the boards. The morning frost seeps into my pajamas, wringing a shiver from me.

"Hey!" I shout through one of the gaps. "Quit it!"

Nothing. The sawing continues, yanking at the strings in my head. The headache grows, my temper with it. I circle the yard for a way to stick my head over the gates, narrowing in on a cracked plastic chair by the fire pit. I almost forgot we had a fire pit. Baba had big plans to grill corn, potatoes, and yams, but they had long since rusted along with most of his extracurricular plans.

Slamming the chair against the gates, I climb up, ignoring the warning squeak of the cracked plastic leg. Jesse wears protective goggles and ear protectors as he brings the saw down against a hollowed-out tree log. Containers of bleach, charcoal garden soil, and compost stack the bench behind him. A blue tarp flutters beneath the containers.

Oookay, that's not suspicious at all. What the hell is he doing?

Nothing I do succeeds in grabbing Jesse's attention. I call, I wave, I whistle. Zilch. The guy is totally tuned to his own station.

Frustrated, I lower my arms. I would wonder how his dad sleeps through this racket if I didn't already have an inkling. More likely than not, Mr. Talbot is locked away in their basement. His basement, which also happens to be the town mortuary.

I try to avoid the Ward gossip mill, I really do, but it's impossible not to hear the rumors about the Talbot family. Four years ago, Elias Talbot swept into Ward with a single black suitcase and his surly teenage son to replace Mr. Whitely as the town mortician. The solemn Mr. Talbot was nothing like our previous mortician, who drove a bright green Jeep and hummed Top 50 pop songs in the grocery line. No one could believe it when Jesse's dad refused Mr. Whitley's facilities and built his own mortuary, right in the basement of his house. The motto on our street is *mind your business*, so nobody bugged Elias about pesky things like permits and zoning ordinances, although I had the pleasure of hearing Baba mutter about it under his breath for two weeks straight my freshman year.

As for Mrs. Talbot . . . not even our super sleuths can find any dirt on her. Some people think Elias murdered her—that he invented a fake story for the police after he embalmed her and stored her in his basement mortuary. Others think she's in jail for committing an unspeakable crime and the Talbots had to flee town after her arrest.

In any case, not the sort of family you want to cross. Unfortunately, I'm sleep-deprived and operating at the mercy of a single brain cell. I find a pair of beaten dance shoes Baba was supposed to throw away behind the garbage bins and climb onto the chair again. Strategy is of the essence here. Throwing the shoe too hard might startle Jesse into sawing himself in half. Throwing it too gently won't catch his eye, which means he'll keep sawing, which means I'll lose it and do something ill-advised like run into the Talbot house and cut the wires of all his power tools.

The first shoe sails wide, over the grill and straight through their open kitchen door.

Whoops.

I squint one eye shut, zeroing in like I've seen in the movies. Rearing my arm as far back as it'll go, I keep a stabilizing hand on the gate. The chair squeaks.

A shadow passes over me, a wisp of darkness smaller than a bird in flight.

The shoe flies, and several things happen in rapid-fire sequence. The chair's leg collapses, sending me flailing backward. Jesse's head jerks up, and I fall into a shadow.

The world vanishes. Filth splashes around my ankles. I struggle to sit up, gagging against the odors battering my nose. Vomit, excrement. Blood and oozing decay.

I can't see, but I could never forget this smell. The sewers carrying this putrid muck only break open in one street. A street thousands of miles away.

The nothingness at my feet wavers. From the void, a small body bubbles to the surface. Facedown and unnaturally still.

My heart freezes.

It's not real. It's not real. I screw my eyes shut and pinch my nose. Slow, shallow sips of air filter into my mouth. *I left the Haikal villa three weeks ago.*

The darkness presses close, and my hold on calm begins to rapidly unravel. The darkness knows my name. It's the darkness that pressed against me as I slept in El Agamy. That throbs in the split second before my hand finds a light switch. The most dangerous mistake is letting my gaze linger on these shadows. Once they start to change, there's no going back. They'll follow me into the light.

"Mansour!" My head snaps back as someone shakes me. The fog of terror temporarily lifts, and I take a tentative sniff of the air. Wood shavings and jasmine. The sweet, moldy tang of the Ahmads' tangerines squashed on the street.

I force my eyelids to lift. My knees are damp from kneeling on the grass. My palms lie open, facing the sky.

A position of submission. Of surrender.

A chill that has nothing to do with the temperature spreads down my spine.

At the sight of Jesse's ear protectors dangling around his neck, I latch onto the remnants of my irritation. Irritation is safer than the fear surging through me, souring in my stomach.

"Who uses *power tools* at eight in the morning on a Saturday?" I demand. I hope he can't hear the quiver in my voice.

"Power tools?" Jesse sits back on his haunches, work boots sinking into the grass. Dark eyes examine my features as though they might unveil the answers to the universe. "What the *fuck* just happened to you?"

Two slats from the gate lie in pieces beside me. Sawed off, it seems. I'd worry about explaining to Baba why the neighbor's son hacked his way onto our property, if Baba ventured out here more than once every fifty years.

"I have a headache," I say. It emerges more pitifully than I intended. A headache making me hallucinate foul smells and faraway streets and floating children.

Down the road, a door slams shut, and the rest of my fog clears. I'm alone with Jesse. Sure, his eyes are still brown, and I think Mr. Olson's smoking on his porch next door, but *still.* The thing could take him at any moment. Getting sawed into chunks isn't on my list of top ten ways to get killed.

I skirt around Jesse and throw open the screen door. "Sleep in for once, would you?" I call over my shoulder. The screen slams shut behind me.

By late afternoon, I've successfully repressed my memories of the morning, prepared and packaged dinner, organized my closet, and cleaned every corner of the house.

I purse my lips at the pile of books on my desk. I've descended into levels of boredom where even stats homework would hit the spot.

A sharp tap rings from the roof. I flinch, whipping my head toward the ceiling.

Another tap, this one directly over my bed. Rain trickles from the clear panes of the window, pooling at the sill.

No hail. So what's on my roof?

A dozen taps slam overhead.

I reach for the handle of a side door that leads to the roof and hesitate. I haven't gone up to the roof in years.

The metal side door in the corner of my room opens to a set of four steps in a claustrophobic passageway. The previous owners constructed it after a series of terrible storms brought down the power lines. According to the real estate agent who sold Baba the house, the owners would go to my room whenever it thundered and keep watch over the door. In case the power went out, they wanted quick access to the roof, where they would be easily visible to a passing Medivac.

I jump as the door rattles, tearing me from the memory. Every instinct cautions me against opening it.

The taps keep coming. The twinkle lights around my ceiling vibrate, and one corner comes loose from its thumbtack.

And then—nothing.

I swallow, massaging my chest with the heel of my hand. "Hail," I say aloud. My voice rings in the newfound silence. "It must have been hail."

Someone knocks on the other side of the metal door.

I go perfectly still. Water drips from the rusted lip of the door, soaking the towel I'd shoved under it this morning.

Hail doesn't knock.

"Who's there?" Without taking my eyes off the door, I grope around for the heaviest item on my dresser. My fingers close around the long, gold aluminum perfume bottle Baba bought at the swap meet for my birthday.

Armed with my signature scent, I approach the door.

"Don't be mad," comes the voice on the other side of the door, and I nearly drop the perfume.

"Jesse?"

"Ding ding ding, she's done it again, folks," Jesse drawls. "Do you mind letting me in? These steps aren't exactly comfortable."

I hope the rain soaked him through. "Were you throwing rocks at my roof?"

A pause. "Maybe."

I make an aggravated noise. At least his confirmation eases my lurking paranoia that the thing has found a way to possess the weather.

To climb down here, Jesse would have had to scale our roof, push aside the thin copper sheet covering the steps, and maneuver himself into the opening. Extraordinarily dangerous in the best of weather, let alone in the rain.

I press my shaking fingers to my forehead. "This is a mean prank, even for you."

"Even for me?" Jesse's chuckle is sardonic. "Whatever could you mean?"

I flounder for a response that isn't *Everyone in town thinks you hate us* and come up blank.

The door hinges creak. "Let me in, Mansour. If I'm going to have my character assassinated, I'd rather be face-to-face."

Against my better judgment, I press my cheek to the door. This is the longest conversation I've had with anyone in nearly a month, and I hang on to every word. "I can't."

"Listen..." His tone shifts, almost gentling. It sets me on guard instantly. "I know. Okay? I know why you're afraid to open the door. I know what happened to Miss Diaz." A long pause, where I am viscerally aware of each beat of my heart. "I saw her eyes."

I gasp.

Tears blur my vision. I haven't told anyone about my visit to Masr since the aborted attempt with Alex, too afraid of finding myself yanked out of school and thrust somewhere I don't want to go. Of seeing Baba remove his glasses and wipe them on his shirt to hide his obvious apprehension, his flash of bone-deep sorrow.

How could Jesse know?

"If you know what I'm afraid of, then you should know why I can't open this door," I whisper.

"I'm saying it won't happen. Not with me."

I frown. He sounds so sure, so *certain*. I've been dealing with this for weeks, and he thinks he's cracked it in twenty-four hours? "It happens with everyone. Despite the best efforts of your superiority complex, you still count as everyone."

"Ouch," Jesse says cheerfully. "How about we test it? I won't move from the stairwell when you open the door. If it possesses me, just slam the door shut again."

"No."

I took a risk with Miss Diaz yesterday, and it ended with a pair of scissors in my arm.

"Mansour—Mina. I can help you." A short rap against the door startles me, and I pull back an inch. "Let me help you."

In the corner of my room, a single brown leaf drops from my calathea onto the carpet. The leaf has been dead for weeks, but I'd hoped it would recover the way my monstera usually did. It didn't make any sense to me how the rest of the calathea was thriving while an entire leaf had browned inches away; as if they weren't connected by the same roots, housed in the same blue ceramic pot. It might not have even felt the dead leaf finally fall.

I gaze at the corpse on the carpet and make a decision.

"Pull your jacket halfway down your arms," I order. If it possesses him and throws his giant body against the door, I need to give myself the advantage. "And tie your shoelaces together."

To his credit, Jesse doesn't argue, although I'm sure there's a sarcastic retort knocking on the back of his teeth. "Done."

Please don't let this be another mistake.

Bracing myself, I close my hand around the curved handle and pull the door open.

YASMINA MANSOUR
EL NOZHA, CAIRO
THREE WEEKS AGO

I held out my American passport to the man at the border control desk and answered his questions in perfect Arabic. Short sentences were the key to hiding my accent. They made it easier to obscure my hesitation over the correct plural of a word or a particular present tense form. I'd spent both flights practicing.

He glanced at my ID picture and then at me. "Welcome to Masr." The stamp pressed into the first page in my passport and released. His attention switched to the next person in line as he handed it back to me.

"Thank you so much" was one of those phrases without a direct translation into Arabic, so I offered the next best equivalent of a thousand thanks and skipped to baggage claim. I tried to resist opening my passport to marvel at the stamp. My first ever stamp. Plus, he hadn't charged me for a visa. All the websites said I'd be charged for one if I had an American passport.

I grabbed my bag off the belt and hurried out of the arrivals terminal. As soon as I set foot past the sliding doors, the air enveloped me, heavy and thick.

Whoa. I'd been warned about the smog, but it still took a second to adjust.

Bright fluorescent light washed over the street, where cabs and buses maneuvered around a crush of pedestrians headed to the sprawling parking lot below. My stomach roiled with nerves. What if my aunt had forgotten my arrival date? I didn't even know what she looked like. She could be any of the people milling behind the barricades across the closed-off street in front of the terminal.

I squeezed past jubilant families reuniting and tried to squash my uncertainty. Surely Khalto Safa hadn't forgotten to pick me up. She'd bought the tickets herself.

A hand fastened to my shoulder as a woman materialized from the crowd.

I jerked away instinctively. After a second, my jaw dropped, and I nearly blurted, *Mama?*

The same clever green eyes. Same tight curls pinned away from her round cheeks and angular jaw.

But this woman was flesh and bone. Living.

"Yasmina," Khalto Safa said. She studied my face, and I wondered if she saw pieces of my mother, too. "You're real. Huh."

I wasn't sure how to respond to that, so I settled for beaming. "I'm so glad to meet you."

She raised a thick black brow, switching to Arabic. "Are you certain you're Nadine's daughter?"

I blinked, trying to brush away my hurt. Everyone said I looked more like Baba than Mama, but I hadn't realized the difference was so noticeable. "Of course."

Khalto Safa started walking, presumably leading me toward the car. I dodged errant pieces of luggage, struggling to keep up with her. "Where are we going?"

Pyramids, pyramids, pyra—

"To eat," my aunt said. "How do you feel about duck?"

CHAPTER FIVE
PRESENT DAY

From his seat on the second step, Jesse waits patiently while I stare at him.

At this point, I could probably draw his eyes from memory. Steal Aida's sketchpad and re-create the sooty, unfairly long lashes around his dark brown eyes. The half-moons of exhaustion shadowing them. Two eyebrows that curve down at the ends and a cut at his jawline where he'd cut himself shaving.

It's dangerous, how misleading Jesse's looks are. On the outside, he might strike you as an angel. Elegant hands kissed by tiny white scars. Red knuckles chapped from the cold. A full, languid mouth. Effortlessly messy black hair most of the male student body would trade their spare kidney to replicate. Half the time, I think Jesse dresses like a rebel from an old sixties movie to overcompensate for how beautiful he is.

Most importantly, there isn't a hint of orange to be found anywhere in his indolent gaze.

Another full minute ticks by. Jesse raises his brows. "Does it usually take this long?"

Never. The thing keeps to a tight schedule. Carefully, I say, "I don't understand exactly how it works."

If he's immune, maybe other people are, too. Maybe Baba is.

Shaking the perilously hopeful thought loose, I cross my arms over my chest. "What do you think you know about what's going on with me?"

"I think I know a lot." Jesse shifts, long legs stretching over the steps. "Happy to break it down for you *inside*. These stairs are wet. My ass is numb."

I gnaw on my lip. What harm can he really do with his shoelaces tied and his arms stuck in his jacket?

One last time. I will try hope *one last time*.

"Alright." I throw out my hand to stop him when he rises. "Stick to your side of the room and don't untangle your shoelaces."

My room is barely bigger than an office. The options for hiding consist of my closet and under the bed, neither of which are particularly conducive to conversation. After a moment of thought, I push the dresser away from the wall and hunker behind it.

Jesse arranges himself at the farthest point in the room, which ends up being the head of my bed. The sight is so bizarre it's almost otherworldly. *Jesse Talbot* lounging in my bed, arms tangled in his jacket, the laces on his work boots clumped into a massive knot. He rests his head against the wall.

His shoes are on my bed, I think, aggravated. I'll need to wash the sheets while Baba's asleep.

The walls groan under the rain. "Start talking," I bark. Baba could be home any minute.

The command amuses Jesse. "Damn, who knew little cheer captain Mina Mansour had such a big bite?"

"Dance captain. For the last time, the cheerleading team is an entirely different extracurricular body. Different funding, different training, different rules—"

I cut myself off, shooting him my most scathing glare.

Jesse chuckles. "Bottle that glare back up, Sour Patch. You wouldn't want to hurt yourself."

Sour Patch?

It takes me a beat to piece it together. Mansour, Man Sour, ha-ha. What a comedian. He knows my last name isn't pronounced with hard vowels.

"Listen, if you're just plotting some elaborate joke..." My voice wobbles, and I stop to collect myself. I will not break down in front of him. He already thinks I'm softer than a charred marshmallow.

Heaving a disappointed sigh, Jesse tips his head to the side. "Well, if you're going to cry about it."

The side door rattles, hinges whining beneath the wind.

"You're cursed, Mansour."

I blink. "Sorry? I think I misheard."

"I doubt it."

Oh... oh, no. I glance at the door, gauging the distance between myself and the exit. I never put much stock in the rumors about the Talbot family, but that was clearly a mistake. A curse? Like in *Scooby-Doo*?

At my strained silence, Jesse's brows furrow. "Why are you acting so shocked? What the hell do you think that thing is?"

I wave my hand, accidentally knocking over a plastic bottle of strawberry champagne perfume. "I don't know, some kind of ghost? Demon, maybe?" Our family isn't religious, but I've watched enough horror movies to glean the general gist.

"Right. Look, can you come over here? I think it's safe to assume your curse doesn't affect me."

My cramping calves readily agree with Jesse. My whole body has gone through the ringer, and the thought of flopping on my queen mattress is very, very tempting.

"Have it your way," Jesse mutters. He maneuvers a hand into his pocket and pulls out a small, black object. With a flick of his wrist, a gleaming blade slides free. A switchblade.

I hurriedly check his eyes, but they're still a flat, flinty black.

"Use this. If it takes me, do what you gotta do."

Aghast, I sputter, "I'm not going to *stab you*!"

"Good. I'm not exactly in the mood to bleed out on a floral bedspread. But it's there if you need it."

Emerging from around the dresser, legs shaking like a newborn foal's, I hop onto the foot of my bed. When I refuse to take the switchblade, Jesse leaves it next to my hand. Up close, the force of his full attention is nearly too intense to bear. I try not to squirm.

"Do you wear sunscreen?" he asks, apropos of nothing.

Um. "Yes?"

"You have a lot of freckles."

I touch my temple, the freckle point of concentration. "I napped in the sun a lot when I was a kid." Mama thought it was hilarious. Though she named me after a jasmine flower, she wasn't expecting I would soak up the sun every chance I could.

"Huh." Jesse taps the handle of the switchblade. "Tell me what happened over spring break."

I play with the fringe at the bottom of my bumblebee sweater. A giant wad of apprehension sticks to the roof of my mouth, leaving my tongue flat and boneless. Outside, the storm howls. The paltry rays of sunshine from this morning are long gone. Ward residents will be unplugging all their appliances in case the electricity falters and fries their wirings. Calls will be made to family to check in, jokes exchanged about how this isn't a Ward Wailer, it's practically swimming weather!

Tucked away in a two-story house on Eighth Street, I glance at the rain and wonder why standing in a storm seems a thousand times safer than my own bedroom.

"You can't repeat it to anyone," I say. I can't believe I'm about to share my worst mistake with Jesse of all people. But I have to tell him, don't I? If there's even a chance he can help? If he knows about the possessions, maybe he knows how to stop them.

Jesse makes a crossing motion over his heart.

"Three weeks ago, I told my dad I was camping with a friend and went to Masr instead." At his puzzled frown, I clarify. "Masr means Egypt in Arabic."

Rather than lighten the weight pressed stubbornly over my heart, recounting the tale only lodges it deeper. I force myself to tell Jesse everything: how my parents left Masr when my mother became pregnant, how they never spoke about their parents or their childhoods.

"When people like Mr. Clay look at me, they see Masr. All my life, I was defined by a country I never even knew. Every time I asked Mama or Baba questions about our history, they'd change the subject." I tug on my fingers one by one. A habit I had developed to replace chewing on the ends of my curls. Before, whenever I would start pulling at my fingertips, Alex would gently take hold of my hand and draw my knuckles to his lips. "Baba hates Mama's side of the family. I mean, like, seriously despises the whole lot. Mama herself rarely talked about them. I think they're super rich—the kind of wealth that owns a fourth of the country or something."

Baba's bizarre anger to any mention of Mama's family only spurred my curiosity. Hatem Mansour isn't a man prone to dramatic fits of emotion. I've seen him show less reaction after getting doused by a cup of scalding coffee.

"My mom died when I was nine, during a visit to Masr. Her first visit." I still remember the day in brutal, painstaking detail. Trying to make a dress out of stained bed linens in the living room while SpongeBob played on the television. Fishing out the pink animal crackers from the bag and hiding the rest under the coffee table. I fancied myself a seamstress, using the measuring tape I found in the garage to snip and fold the linens into a ballgown.

I heard Baba make a sound from the kitchen. I'll never forget that sound. A hoarse, guttural cry, torn straight from the depths of his soul.

I rushed into the kitchen to find him on his knees, forehead pressed to the heels of his hands. He wasn't crying, wasn't breathing. He'd gone still as stone, utterly unresponsive to my nervous touch to his shoulder. The phone dangled from the cord, a tinny voice speaking on the other side.

"A car accident in Tanta, they said. Funerals work differently in Masr, so her body was prepared and buried the next day." In less than twenty-four hours, I went from having a mother and semi-functional family to asking Baba a question three times because he forgot I was in the room.

Jesse's still listening. I know I shouldn't, know it'll only make me seem unhinged, but the words rush out before I can stop them. "The thing is, my mom landed at Borg Alexandria Airport. I just don't understand how my mother was near Tanta unless she was on her way to Cairo. She doesn't even *like* Cairo."

I chance a glance at Jesse. I almost never talk about Mama, even to my friends. The pity rakes poison under my skin, makes me get overly bubbly and cheerful to compensate. Look at me, well-adjusted Mina Mansour. Save your sorries. Save your sympathetic smiles.

But pity isn't what I find lingering in Jesse's gaze. He waits for me to continue, a subdued understanding in his silence.

I forget sometimes, that under all the different rumors, is a single truth: Jesse lost his mother, too.

"I begged Baba to let me visit Masr. For years, I wondered about my mother's death, about the cousins and uncles and aunts I've never met. I wanted to walk into a room and not think about how the way I look affects everyone else around me. I wanted to sit at my mom's grave. I've always felt like there were two parts of me, two halves of my soul that have never met. Do you know what it's like when you can see an entire life you might've had stretched out in front of you? A life where—"

Where you aren't completely and utterly alone.

I wanted to impress upon Jesse that my decision to lie to Baba and book a ticket to Masr was out of character. Before spring break, I considered skipping class a cardinal sin. I ate my veggies and went to bed at a reasonable time. By all accounts, I was the perfect daughter.

"Last November, I got a call from an unknown number. It was a woman claiming to be my mother's younger sister. She knew details about Mama, about the history of her and Baba's marriage. She knew things nobody other than family would know. She offered to fly me out to Masr." I clear my throat. The excitement had been more than I could bear. I didn't stop and wonder why she had called me now, after seventeen years. After Mama had been dead for eight of them. I didn't wonder why she hadn't asked to talk to Baba, the way any normal adult would have. "I called her back the next day and accepted. I didn't tell anyone I was going. I knew Baba would never let me meet someone on my mom's side of the family."

The last sentence emerges in a shamed whisper. What a fool past Mina was. What a fool she still is.

A creaking from downstairs causes me and Jesse to freeze. "Yasmina? Are you home?" Baba calls. A replica of my own entry a few hours ago.

Panicked, I lurch off the bed and grab my door. "I'm home, Baba! I'm taking a nap, though, so please don't knock on my door."

"Are you sure? I bought your favorite for dinner." A worried pause. "Thai food is your favorite, yes?"

I've never tried Thai food. The nearest Thai restaurant is fifteen miles outside of Ward, and my car tries to pass into the afterlife if I drive it more than ten miles on any given day.

"Absolutely. Thank you!"

"Good, good. I'll leave it for you on the table."

I close the door, sliding the lock in place. I installed the latch myself a week ago. Baba still doesn't know it's there. Jesse finishes untangling his shoelaces and shrugs his jacket into place.

"Does it happen with your dad?" Jesse asks. He tips his head, and I realize that he's listened silently for the past twenty minutes. Cataloging, assessing. I still don't know why he thinks I'm cursed or how he knew about the thing, but he's got half my life story on a silver platter, and I know nothing new about him. A good negotiator, I am not.

"I don't know. We haven't been in a room together since I got back." Besides my newfound powers of avoidance, Baba is always at the university. We're glorified housemates.

Jesse jumps from the bed and begins pacing. Dressed in black from head to toe, he resembles a thundercloud creeping over my sunny yellow bedroom. His steel-toed work boots leave indents in my carpet. "Before I leave, tell me exactly what you've learned about this thing. How it works, when it appears."

I gesture at him to keep the volume down. Our walls are paper thin. "Not much. I'm usually too busy fighting for my life to jot down notes." No way am I showing him the journal.

"Mansour. I've seen you scribbling in that notebook of yours."

I balk. He's been watching me?

But Jesse has a strange look on his face, almost as if he regrets speaking, and I would rather not push for answers I'm not sure I want. If my fall from grace was obvious to even *Jesse Talbot*, then I don't want to think of how many curious eyes I've had on me since spring break.

I give him the recap without much emotion. "I can't be alone in a room with someone. That's the only part I know for sure. I was filling my car at the gas station and an attendant doused me in gasoline, so I think empty outside areas are also a no-go."

A hint of shock finally pierces Jesse's impeccable poker face. "Shit."

"Agreed." I replace the sopping wet towel under the metal door with a new one from the dresser. "I think it's getting stronger. What happened this morning, and with Miss Diaz, she—" I clear my throat. The words don't want to come, too horrible to usher into reality. "The thing shouldn't have been able to hold on to her after you arrived. It took way too long to leave her body."

I shudder, wrapping my arms around myself.

Whatever it is, it's getting stronger.

Jesse appears to arrive at the same conclusion. "First, we need to figure out what the hell happened during your trip. Collect intel on your aunt and the house. We need to find thc source before the solution."

"We?" I track his frenetic movements. "You're going to help?"

Jesse stops wearing grooves into my carpet, his features pained but firm. "Yeah, I guess I am."

CHAPTER SIX
PRESENT DAY

The bell rings, and I brace myself.

I've claimed my spot under the jacaranda tree, sitting on the side facing the cracked rubber running tracks. Behind me, backpacks hit stained tables and everyone still in PE shorts winces at the sting of the frigid metal bench against their skin. The chatter is less cacophonous out here by my tree, more of a comfort than an itch. I don't hear the strains of conversation reminding me of prom preparations and monogrammed graduation invites. I can pretend none of it is passing me by. I can pretend there is still a chance I'll get to be part of it.

Rainie, Aida, and Lucia enter the quad. Rainie tosses her backpack onto the table, mouth furled into a snarl as she talks. Probably complaining about Mr. Clay, who sprinkles passive-aggressive comments into his history lecture like racist seasoning. With her spiky red hair, sharpen-your-knives winged eyeliner, and unending supply of black clothes, Rainie Nguyen specializes in bringing her enemies to their knees.

Lucia reaches for Rainie's shoulder. Anyone else wouldn't dare touch Rainie in the middle of one of her rants, but Lucia Romano is the kind of girl who could befriend a ravenous wolf if you just gave her enough time. The third in a family of six, Lucia has years of crisis control experience under her belt. She wears sundresses with dancing ladybugs and a flower in her long hair. Her binders are covered in mismatched stickers, and she keeps colored tabs for her homework and class notes.

When I introduced rich, perky Lucia to Rainie, I worried Rainie would squeeze the life out of her. Rainie's reputation among strangers ranges from a wastrel (an insult from Mr. Clay that Rainie so enjoyed, she renamed our group chat) to a delinquent.

To everyone's surprise, Rainie developed a soft spot for Lucia. Lucia is the most well-protected senior on campus, because Rainie will use her three-inch spiked combat boots to stomp the stuffing out of anyone who breathes at her wrong.

Meanwhile, it took years of effort to convince Aida to open up to us. Aida, the quiet, reclusive artist had spent middle school as the only Black girl in our grade, and in a tiny town like Ward, where the Mr. Clays make it their mission to suck the joy out of every day, I didn't blame Aida for keeping to herself until high school.

The first time we had a real conversation was in the library. I was checking in the tattered third book in a paranormal vampire series, smoothing down the laminated cover before I slipped it into the return slot. Aida was sitting behind the circulation desk, and she'd tentatively asked me how I liked the twist at the end. We spent the next two hours passionately arguing the merits of the ending, and I'd sped read the rest of the series to give myself an excuse to keep coming back to the library. By our tenth argument, I had shored up the nerve to invite her to eat lunch with us.

"I don't know," she said, picking at the plastic spiral of her sketchbook. "I usually eat in the locker room."

I was aghast. "The *gym* locker room? With the shower mold and the smells?"

She grinned briefly. "That's the one."

She'd finally agreed to a trial lunch if I promised not to get angry if she decided to leave halfway through.

To my knowledge, she never ate in the locker room again. She still spends most of her free time sketching or reading, but now she doesn't mind doing it around us.

No one has ever seen Aida's art. If we even joke about glancing into her sketchpad, she'll slam it shut.

Aida glances over, and I quickly drop my gaze, blinking away the sting in my eyes.

I *will* get them back. I have to.

I spread my lunch out on the grass, brushing aside the jacaranda petals scattered everywhere. A legion of ants stir at the base of the tree, tiny black specks vibrating with anticipation.

"Never say I don't spoil you guys." I wag my finger. "We've got a turkey sandwich on the menu for today."

I'm peeling the rest of the plastic from my turkey sandwich when someone slides into a cross-legged seat in front of me. Whip-quick fear slashes across my insides, spewing a million scenarios that span the next two minutes. Most of them involve a rotting smell and orange eyes in a familiar face.

My apprehension fades at the sight of scratched-up work boots. It's just Jesse.

I snort, wadding the plastic into a ball. Just Jesse.

"Are you lost?" I ask bluntly. Seeing my friends has left me too raw—too likely to bleed under one of Jesse's casual barbs.

He peers at me with a distinctly unimpressed air. Then, to my shock, he grins. The expression transforms him, and for a split second, my mind goes blank of everything but one word: *whoa.*

Unfortunately, all my appreciation for his looks disappears the minute he opens his mouth.

"Damn, Mansour. I wish I'd known earlier you had such a mean streak. I might not have had to get up at dawn Monday through Friday to avoid running into you. Do you know how much sleep that adds up to?"

My jaw drops. I don't even know which part is most offensive. "You woke up early just to avoid seeing me on the way to school?"

He shrugs. "You kept asking how my morning was going. I ran out of answers."

"You mean you ran out of ways to grunt in my general direction." I figured Jesse wouldn't be a morning person, but it takes a staggering level of commitment to rearrange your entire schedule simply to avoid a few minutes of awkward small talk.

"I was worried you'd start in on the weather or how I slept last night," Jesse continued, undeterred by steadily climbing aggravation. "I once had a nightmare about you asking me my plans for the weekend." He shuddered.

When he pulls out a notebook, clearly intending to stick around for a while, I recover long enough to snap, "What are you doing?"

He makes a show of looking down at the notebook and back at me. "Take a wild guess."

"But you didn't even bring lunch."

Another nonchalant lift of his shoulder. "I'll eat when I get home."

I wait, but no luck. He's serious. Does he think I can actually continue eating my food while he has none of his own? I'm Masriya. My parents had drilled into me the etiquette of never keeping my plate full while someone else's was empty.

Sending a silent apology to the ants, I split my sandwich and hold the other half out to Jesse. "You can't help me on an empty stomach," I point out, preempting his refusal. If he thinks I'm acting out of pity or misplaced guilt, he might squash the sandwich in his fist.

Jesse nods sagely, plucking the sandwich from my hand. "So true."

I drop a sliver of my turkey onto the base of the tree, smiling at the rush of exultant ants.

"Whatcha writing?" I ask a few minutes later, not fully caring. The clouds are shining a pleasant silver, the turkey to lettuce ratio in my sandwich is perfect, and I have company. He could be scribbling more annoying nicknames to throw at me, for all I care. I'm just happy not to spend another lunch break idly feeding my ant army.

It occurs to me that I've never seen him sit with someone during lunch. The table at the far end of the quad serves as his island, severing him from the rest of us lowly creatures.

"I'm getting an outline ready," Jesse answers after a long moment. His pen rotates between his knuckles, slipping across surprisingly elegant fingers. "We need to find the patterns in the attacks."

"Outlining on paper?" I wipe a smear of mayo from the corner of my mouth. "Couldn't fit the typewriter into your backpack?"

Jesse shoots me a disparaging glance. "Anything can get copied off a computer. I don't want to leave a trace if this goes sideways."

The bite of turkey turns to sawdust in my mouth. I force myself to swallow. "Goes sideways."

Jesse's pen pauses over the page. The answer blooms in our silence, unfurling in black-tipped petals of possibility. *She loves me, she loves me not,* except now it's *she dies at a stranger's hand, at her father's, in a gas station, in a classroom.* The petals curdle into gray ash, but the sticky knob in the center of the flower reads the single, inevitable conclusion: She dies.

"Mansour, hey. Look at me."

It hasn't sunk in until now, how close I am to my own death. One misstep. One repeat of the mistake I made with Miss Diaz.

From behind the sheen of tears blanketing my vision, Jesse shifts uncomfortably. Unaccustomed to dealing with a weeping girl, I'd bet. If he plans to stick around, he better get used to it.

"We're gonna get this thing. I don't waste my time on lost causes," Jesse says. He doesn't shrink from my watery gaze, and his own is colored with such confidence, such unequivocal certainty.

For a dizzying moment, reality splashes cold water on my face, and I regard Jesse warily. He believed what I told him about my trip to my mother's childhood home without second-guessing, without even a moment of doubt. Why?

"I'm not a cause," I say, wiping my cheeks. "Why are you helping me, Jesse? Who *are* you?" Nothing makes sense anymore. Before Jesse waltzed in, at least I had an idea about how this thing operated. I could cling to a degree of control. But where does his immunity to possession fit into the picture?

I cross my arms over my chest. "Why can't the thing possess you?"

He stiffens. I wouldn't have noticed if I wasn't watching him so closely. "Maybe I'm a bad host. I always forget to ask if they want tea or coffee to go with my body."

"That's not funny." It is, a little bit, but I maintain my scowl. "How come you knew it wouldn't possess you? Did you feel it try? Has it happened before?"

Jesse rubs his forehead. Tiny scars mar his palm, crisscrossed over his skin. "God, of everyone at this crap school, it had to be the *homecoming queen* with the curse."

I ball my fists. "Are you making fun of me?"

"Not successfully, if you have to ask."

I snatch my backpack from the grass and shove to my feet. "Screw you, Jesse. You don't know me."

Storming away in a haze of anger isn't really an option in my situation. I stomp an embarrassing circuit around the quad, debating between the parking lot and the locker room to finish my lunch.

Jesse catches up. "What's your deal? I'm trying to help you."

"By mocking me? I'm already miserable in a thousand different ways that can't be avoided, but you? You *can* be avoided. So if you could just leave me to it, that would be great."

A deep groan tears out of Jesse, startling me. A long arm blocks my circuit around the quad. "Ditch your last class. I'll explain everything."

Some of the wind goes out of my sails. Despite my better judgment, I'm curious. Jesse and his dad are our town's biggest enigmas, and Jesse's strange immunity to possession has only added to my intrigue.

"I'm not ditching class."

Jesse rolls his eyes. "Yeah, wouldn't want to get a blemish on that perfect attendance record."

"My attendance record isn't perfect." I missed fifth period last semester. Rainie insisted we could go get lunch at the pizzeria across town and be back by the bell.

It's alarming how quickly Jesse gets me worked up. I'm a mellow person by nature, but every time he speaks, I switch into the worst version of myself. "Ditching class makes you truant. If I get a citation, I can't audition to be a speaker at graduation."

"Oh my gosh darn, a citation? What's next—a demerit?" He utters the last word in a scandalized whisper, and the urge to strangle him arrives fast and heavy.

I stare at my hands, utterly appalled. What is happening to me?

Something in my expression gives Jesse pause, and he sighs. "Whatever. Come to my place after school."

Jesse strides away before I can politely let him know that the only way he's getting me to visit his father's property is in a body bag. He hops over the fence separating the quad from the parking lot and lands on the other side in a slight crouch, unrolling his impressively limber body as he walks toward his truck. The lunch monitor spots him, but she must not be in the mood to deal with Jesse's particular brand of trouble. She turns away with a shake of her head. If there is anything living in Ward long enough will teach you, it's that not everybody can be saved.

I watch his truck disappear and nibble the end of my thumbnail.

Okay, going to Jesse's house. Decidedly not scary. Maybe his house will be fun creepy, like the Addams's family mansion. Or the funny haunted mansion from that Eddie Murphy movie.

I turn around, still trying to remember the name of the Eddie Murphy movie, and run directly into Alex.

"Oh!" I squeak at a pitch somewhere between parrot and bald tire spinning against asphalt. Behind Alex, Rainie, Lucia, and Aida watch us from the table. Aida's pencil moves over her sketchpad.

The despondent frown Alex has worn the last few weeks is nowhere to be seen. In its place lies pure disbelief. "Are you hanging out with *Jesse Talbot*?"

I should have figured the sight of Jesse and me together wouldn't go unnoticed. We don't exactly run in the same circles.

I've missed Alex so much. I can't help swaying closer to him. He's wearing a forest green sweatshirt with CANYON HIGH BASKETBALL spelled on the front. I'm sure if I tuck myself against his chest and press my nose to the spot where his sweatshirt meets his throat, I'll catch the scent of his cologne. A spicy, expensive mix I gave him for his seventeenth birthday.

"No. Not technically. Hanging out implies I'm seeing him for fun."

"You're *seeing him*?" Alex sounds like someone kicked him in the windpipe.

"No, no!" Frustration bubbles up. Nothing is coming out right. I haven't spoken to Alex in weeks, not since I stopped answering his texts. This isn't how I imagined our first conversation going. "Jesse is just helping me out with a project."

"What project? Talbot doesn't care about school."

The bell rings, saving me from an answer. I don't want to lie to Alex, but I can't exactly tell him the truth. Alex is a logical guy. He drives according to the speed limit, buys his teachers an end of the year thank-you gift, and uses the same brand of shampoo and conditioner he's had since he was fourteen. If I told him that Jesse was helping me break a curse, Alex would undoubtedly call Baba. Or 911. Neither option ends well for me.

I back away, half-eaten lunch gathered in the crook of my arm. "I gotta go. See you later," I say.

"Will you?" Alex replies, and he's lost all his steam. I can't stand knowing I put the wounded note in his voice.

I'm trying to fix this, I want to say. *I'm trying to put it all back together. Wait for me, please. Trust me.*

"I hope so."

CHAPTER SEVEN
PRESENT DAY

I've rarely spent much time thinking about what happens after we die. In many ways, I'm my father's daughter. I care about what's in front of me, what I can affect and change.

Lately, I can't stop thinking about the details of it. Whether my coffin will be brown or black. What recipes I should leave for Baba so he doesn't subsist solely on takeout.

What will people remember about me?

Ha. Like they'll remember anything other than how I died. If the thing successfully possesses someone to kill me, the murder trial will be the biggest scandal to hit Ward in decades. Especially if the murderer can't remember how or why they killed the former dance team captain and homecoming queen.

I halt at the gate blocking the Talbot property from the rest of the neighborhood. The house rises against the clouds like a headstone, nothing but gray paint and moldering walls.

My clammy palms almost slip from the rusted iron bars. As reluctant to grip the gate as I am to walk through it.

Closing my eyes is a mistake. Ice rolls down my spine, and suddenly, it isn't the gate beneath my hands, but a smooth banister. Steps carved into the darkness, leading me to an orange light spilling beneath the lip of a pale door.

Gasping, I drop my hold on the gate. A shudder crawls from the nape of my neck to the back of my knees, and I nearly drop to the sidewalk.

Damn it. Every time I see the door, the details shift. The elaborate carvings on the frame. The grain of the wood. The shine on the handle. Is it my memory playing tricks on me, or is something else?

I pull myself together and tug the gate open. The hinges scream in protest. Dead grass lays in matted brown patches across the front lawn, split in the center by the cracked concrete path leading to the porch.

I grimace. If Jesse's house was a person, it would be the kid on the playground who skins his knee and spends the rest of recess drawing with the blood. What kills me is how hard Jesse's tried to turn this hovel into a home. When the Talbots moved in, I would watch Jesse hammer at the front steps every winter. He'd set up his toolbox on the top step and stick the handle of a paint scraper between his teeth before crawling under the porch. I may know next to nothing about home repair, but Baba's ongoing battle with mold taught me that wood—especially wet wood—deteriorates dangerously fast. Every year, Jesse fights his house's slow slide into dereliction, and every year it drags him a little closer to the end.

Yet, he never seems to stop trying. There's not a single leaf left in the gutters. The grass—the living patches, at least—is always mowed and maintained. Baby branches poke out of plants potted along the far side of the gate, angled to catch every drop of sun. I touch a dented bird feeder dangling from a metal hook. Something in my chest squeezes painfully at the thought of Jesse all alone, waiting to refill a bird feeder that never ran empty.

I don't waste my time on lost causes.

"Liar," I mumble.

Too absorbed navigating the wooden steps, I don't notice the door open until my feet are safely planted on the porch.

Jesse leans against the doorframe, wearing a faded gray T-shirt and flannel. "Did you have a good trip? Four steps *can* be harrowing."

I huff. "I didn't want my leg to go through rotted wood."

Jesse scowls. Fantastic; I've been here two seconds and I've already injured his pride. "The steps are fine. I took care of them in October." He disappears inside the house, leaving me tripping over myself to keep up. No way am I being left alone anywhere on the Talbot property.

The door swings shut behind me. I shriek.

"Mansour!"

"Sorry, sorry! Did you see the door? Are those hinges heavy? How did it just—you know, actually, I felt a little bit of a breeze, so that probably explains how a million-pound door slammed shut on its own."

Darkness paints the inside of Jesse's house, and I blink until my eyes adjust. Two stairwells take shape in the gloom. One heads to the second floor, while the other descends below the house.

Morbid curiosity compels me closer. Could these stairs lead to the rumored Talbot mortuary? What if Mr. Talbot is down there with a body right now?

The same question floats to the top of my mind: *Is this what will happen after I die?*

Is this where I'll go when it kills me?

A shadow appears beside me, a hand clapping over my mouth in time to muffle my next shriek. Jesse's eyes are velvet black, darker than our surroundings.

"Wrong stairs," he says, ice cold.

When he retracts his hand, wiping it rather offensively on his hip, I blurt, "You smell like jasmine. And rain. Jasmine rain."

Jesse stares. "I do not."

"Oh, my bad." I forgot I was talking to the guy who dresses like a sixties gangster to cover up his ridiculously pretty features. "I meant motor oil and, um, danger?"

Jesse drags a hand down his face, giving me his back to climb the stairs to the second floor. "Hurry up. Wouldn't want you getting lost in the horror house."

"I wouldn't get lost," I mutter. When his footsteps grow fainter, I abandon any pretense of dignity and rush after him.

The door at the end of the hall lies open. I cautiously poke my head in.

Jesse's room is . . . not what I expected. I venture inside to inspect the bottle caps fighting for space in a chipped ashtray on top of his dresser. Books with foreign titles sway in a giant pile next to his bed, and torn envelopes litter the chair next to the window.

I pluck a black eyeliner pencil from inside a stack of empty Styrofoam cups. "This is how your get your lashes to look so luscious. The girls at school think you made a deal with the devil."

Jesse, who has been watching me peruse his bedroom with uncharacteristic patience, shoots me a wicked smile. "Don't rule it out."

I sigh. "You can't just say stuff like that when the kids at school are already scared of you."

He squints, as if waiting for a prolonged punchline. "Which is bad because . . ."

"Don't you want friends? You've lived in Ward for years and you're still—" *Alone,* I almost say, but I hold my tongue at the last instant. Jesse tolerates his time in Ward with gritted teeth and a clenched fist, never making any effort to leave a mark on this place. Is there somewhere else he considers home? Or does he think everyone in Ward is just too far beneath him?

My whole life I've done nothing but try to belong. If I couldn't be Masriya Mina, I'd take American Mina to her extreme. Homecoming queen, dance captain, leader of the Girl Scouts. In preschool, I'd write my name in the sandbox during recess and cry if another kid tried to wipe it away. *This is mine,* I would cry. *You can't just sweep me away.*

I desperately wanted to plant roots in Ward. What's wrong with Jesse that he's not remotely interested in doing the same?

"Sit down, Mansour," is all Jesse says. Mild, despite my insult. He points to the threadbare rocking chair by his window. "Let's get to business."

I plop myself into the chair. The eyeliner is still clenched in my fist. I'm keeping it. He doesn't deserve lusciously lined lashes.

A somberness settles over Jesse. "What I'm about to tell you can't leave this room. Do you understand?"

A strange, childlike urge to make myself as small as possible has me drawing my knees to my chest. What I want to say is *please don't tell me. I don't want to know. I have this terrible feeling I won't leave this room the same person I was when I walked into it, and I want everything to go back to the way it was. You have so much darkness, crawling in this house and inside you, and if you spread it to me, I'll never be the Mina Mansour I was.*

Instead, what comes out is a tiny, "I understand."

Jesse searches my face. Whatever he finds seems to satisfy him, and he takes a deep breath before he straightens.

"You aren't the only one who's cursed."

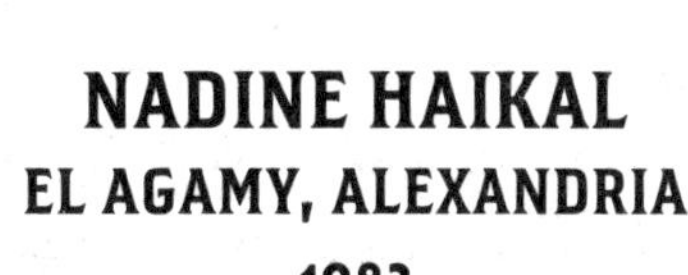

NADINE HAIKAL
EL AGAMY, ALEXANDRIA
1982

Nadine was the first to find the body.

She stopped just inside the gates, her backpack sliding from her arm to drop at her feet.

The body dangled below the balcony on the second floor, the wind snatching at its abaya and exposing the pale skin of its legs.

Nadine stood alone in the garden for long minutes, watching the hairstylist's corpse gently sway from the end of the rope. She didn't scream. She didn't make a single sound.

Truthfully, Nadine was disappointed. Nobody had been a bigger thorn in Teta's side than this woman. She'd been after the Haikal family for years, ever since her daughter's disappearance in 1977. The police hadn't helped—Teta made sure of that. Every avenue of justice the hairstylist sought had been a dead end. Janna's disappearance was simply one of many. Without evidence, the paltry investigation withered within a month.

The hairstylist hadn't quit, of course. She had pestered them continuously. Chased down their household staff, snooped through their garbage, even slept on the bench at the end of their road. Once, Nadine had found her waiting beside the gate, clearly intent on catching Nadine coming back from school. She had grabbed Nadine's shoulders and smoothed her calloused hands over Nadine's finely pressed school uniform. "It's okay to be scared of your family," she'd said with the balady accent Teta so disdained. "I won't let them hurt you if you tell me the truth."

Nadine had listened with a scared, uncertain expression until the hairstylist finished speaking. Then, she'd allowed her features to slide back into cold neutrality. "What truth do you want to hear? None of them will bring Janna back. Maybe you should focus on making sure your next child is less of a fool."

The hairstylist had recoiled, staring at Nadine like she'd never seen her before.

A slipper fell from the hairstylist's rigid right foot, landing in front of Nadine. With a vague curiosity, Nadine wondered what had finally broken the woman's spirit. After all those years, what was her last straw?

The gate creaked behind Nadine, footsteps squelching over the wet garden path. A head of wavy brown hair covered in butterfly clips appeared by Nadine's elbow. "Who's that?" Safa asked, sipping from her Juhayna milk box.

Nadine shook her head, drawing up her backpack. "Tell Mama to ring the sheriff," she said.

She crossed under the shadow of the hairstylist's corpse and spared her one final glance. When she lowered her gaze, she found the hairstylist's face leaning inches away from her.

Nadine's stomach dropped. Bulging, desperate eyes bored into Nadine's. The woman's neck dangled unnaturally, a thick bone protruding against her skin. Rancid breath slipped into Nadine's nose, souring her mouth.

Nadine had walked into one of the shadows. The imprints of time, as Mama called them.

"The shadow tricked you," Safa sang behind her. "What do you see?"

A tear trickled from one of the bloodshot, staring eyes. It trailed sideways over the hairstylist's face.

"Nothing important," Nadine said, and walked through the shadow.

CHAPTER EIGHT
PRESENT DAY

"*You aren't the only one who's cursed.*"

Rage vibrates in my chest. I fly to my feet.

"Are you making fun of me again?"

"Look, I'm fully aware of how this sounds." Jesse scrubs a hand across his jaw. "Just hear me out, okay? I listened to you, didn't I?"

"That isn't the same."

"True. You made me tie my shoelaces together and sit on icy metal steps first."

I scowl. A pointed reminder, but a fair one. Deflating, I return to my seat, but not without crossing my arms and setting my chin. If this is a prank, I won't saunter into it willingly.

Once he confirms I intend to stick around, Jesse's attention moves to the window behind me. Shades of silver curtain the sky as dense clouds swirl over our street. Unlike my window, Jesse's faces west, giving him a clear view of both of our driveways and the rest of the neighborhood. Wind slams the storm shutters on the aging houses. Down the street, Mrs. Khan's clothesline comes loose, whipping her nightgowns into a flower bed. Yusuf Ahmed runs out to his front yard in a bike helmet, securing the tangerine tree's branches together with strips of torn tarp. Our neighborhood is one of the oldest in Ward, and from here, I can see all its wrinkles and gnarled bones.

When Jesse steels his shoulders, I steel myself, too.

"My mother was the third child in a family of five and a registered nurse from Sarasota, Florida. In her entire life, she left Sarasota only once. She flew to New York on her twenty-sixth birthday to visit a friend from college. During her trip, she met my dad." Jesse picks at the fabric over his knee. "They hit it off, somehow. I guess a jaded New York mortician and a perky RN have more in common than you'd think. My mom went back home, but they kept in touch. Eventually, my dad followed her to Sarasota. They tied the knot, moved into a house with a white picket fence, got a Costco membership—the whole nine yards."

My throat tightens with trepidation. I hate the feeling of following a story I know doesn't have a happy ending.

"Fast-forward to three years later. My mom has spent two of those years trying to get pregnant, but nothing seems to work. When they eventually get tested, the results break my parents' hearts. They have pretty much zero chance of naturally conceiving a child, mostly due to something wrong on my dad's side of things. My mom was just... crushed. Dad says she didn't get out of bed for weeks. For some reason I'll never understand, she desperately wanted a litter of kids with her and my dad's DNA. To pass along her gallstones and my dad's bad back, maybe. I don't know."

Jesse chances a glance at me. I wipe my features clean. It wouldn't help to tell him I understand where his mother was coming from. I'd spent too many nights dreaming of what I'd name Alex's and my babies. How I hoped they'd have my hair and his eyes.

"Nothing works. They try IVF for two more years, but the cards are stacked against them. My dad wants to call it quits, but my mom... she has this idea. She'd worked in the maternity ward for most of her career, and she had heard stories. Outlandish superstitions, she thought. Patients who swore some spell or hidden force helped them conceive when nothing else worked. One night, my mom comes home and she doesn't speak to my dad. She walks right into the yard, sits in the dirt, and starts singing. Dad says he didn't have a clue what she was saying—it could've been English or ancient Greek for all he could tell, since she was muttering so fast and rocking back and forth. If my dad tried to touch her, she'd scream. She didn't move for twelve hours."

A frenzied energy grips the dark-haired boy, and he paces the limited length of his room as he speaks. His shadow follows him on the wall, rippling across his dresser and disappearing when he passes the mirror.

"My dad was about to call an ambulance when she finally snapped out of it. He swears she just stood up, dusted herself off, and asked if he wanted waffles or oatmeal for breakfast."

Jesse pauses and shoots me a doubtful glance. "Still with me, Mansour?"

I hesitate. "Still with you, Talbot."

One of Jesse's hands parses through his hair. The black locks fall like spun silk through his fingers, framing his agitated face.

"Nine months after my mom's episode in the yard, I was born, and my mother died."

My breath catches. I figured this would conclude with the truth of Mrs. Talbot's fate, but it still hits me harder than expected. "I don't understand. Did the treatments work?"

A caustic laugh. "Nope. The doctors called me a medical marvel."

The pieces won't come together no matter which way I fit them. Jesse must notice my struggle, because he heaves a sigh. "A couple of years after my mother died, my dad managed to translate a few sentences of what she'd been mumbling that night in the yard. It took him a long time; apparently, she'd been weaving together languages and dialects from all over the world. According to him, she'd convinced herself that she made a deal with some entity."

Jesse's shadow moves over his bookcase as he resumes pacing, flitting across the torn spines of well-read mystery paperbacks.

"To invite new life, she would need to usher out her own."

I try to swallow around the rock in my throat. "What does that even mean?"

"Apparently, not all of the stories in the Sarasota maternity ward are a crock of shit."

I pull my legs up onto the rocking chair, squeezing them into my chest. As much as the part of me that subscribes to a logical, ordered world wants to argue with Jesse, the truth is I believe him. I believe that eighteen years ago, a woman across the country had a desperate wish, and so she made a desperate decision. I believe something dark preyed on that desperation.

Where pain exists, predators thrive. Whether in El Agamy or in Sarasota.

"I'm sorry, Jesse."

Jesse props his shoulder against the window, pressing his forehead to the misting pane. "Yeah."

The light pours through the glass, fracturing around Jesse. The broken rays scatter his shadow across the wall. When Jesse pushes away from the window, his shadow re-forms once more.

And stays perfectly still as Jesse walks across the room.

Jesse is talking, but I don't hear a word. Every drop of blood in my veins turns to ice. The shadow moves, creeping over his water-stained ceiling. I watch, unable to blink, until it settles on the wall to my left.

"Jesse," I try to whisper, but my teeth are clenched too hard. His name is a barely audible hiss.

The shadow steps out of the wall.

I grab the chair's armrests, but my legs refuse to lift. I'm frozen, pinned like a moth in a glass case, helpless to do anything but watch as the shadow drifts to the foot of Jesse's bed.

Jesse passes in front of the shadow, momentarily blocking it from my view.

When he steps forward, a young boy sits on the edge of Jesse's bed.

Green-eyed, with curly hair the color of clover honey, he wears a rumpled gray and white outfit that looks straight out of a medieval movie set. The sleeves hang over his small fingers, and his suspenders are buckled into shorts that might've been made out of potato sacks. Beneath them are wool stockings that disappear into his flat, rounded shoes, which appear at least one size too large.

The boy smiles at me, revealing three missing teeth at the bottom of his mouth. He swings his short legs.

My knuckles whiten around the armrests. Despite the racing speed of my heart, my mind manages to cut through the haze to assess the situation with something approaching clarity.

I sniff, but the air smells the same. No trace of sewage or rot. The boy's unblinking, smiling eyes are green, not orange.

What *is* this?

A drop of blood lands on Jesse's gray rug. Another joins it, then more, until a river of red soaks through to the ground.

The boy's legs keep swinging.

It takes every ounce of my willpower to drag my gaze from the blood-drenched rug to the boy's face.

He continues smiling as blood drips from his eyes, coursing over his round cheeks. It flows from his ears and nose, running down his neck, his chest, disappearing into his uniform.

When he stands, the rug squelches beneath his oversized little shoes. He steps toward me, that eerie smile still fixed on his face, and covers the hands I've wrapped around the armrests with his own.

He feels *real.* Like skin and bone instead of the shadow he came from.

My jaw finally unlocks enough to force out a single question. "What. Do. You. Want?"

"Look what you did, Annie." A voice, older and distinctly feminine, slides out of his bloody mouth. "You almost wasted this boy. I found him running down the street, screaming for his papa. What if he'd gotten away?"

The blood has nearly coated the boy's entire face. When he brings it close to mine, I can barely see his features beneath it. "We have debts to pay, Annie. This life isn't free, and you cannot afford to have friends, my love. Not when it needs to feed."

Again, a blade of clarity temporarily cuts through the terror. *It.* The creature?

Tears slip from the corners of my eyes. The boy stumbles away from me, and his sob hits me like a fist to the chest. He finally sounds like a child, alone and terrified. His knees wobble as he trips forward and lands behind Jesse. He utters a pained sentence in a language I don't recognize.

With barely a sound, the boy's body melts into the floor.

My stomach roils. I can't breathe.

A shadow stretches behind Jesse once more when he steps toward me. The air thins, and time seems to restart with a shudder.

At last, my body thaws from its petrified curl. My limbs belong to me again. I can move my hands, my jaw.

With breath I shouldn't have, I unleash a blood-curdling scream.

CHAPTER NINE
PRESENT DAY

It takes nearly a full hour to calm down enough to tell Jesse what I saw.

"I don't get it," Jesse says from his cross-legged spot on the floor. He hasn't moved since I told him the shadow peeled away from him while he paced. "I was at the window, and then I crossed the room. By the time I turned around, you were screaming. It was five, ten seconds. You're saying all of that happened in ten seconds?"

I wrap my arms tighter around my knees. I wedged myself between his dresser and the wall, eliminating any chance of shaping my own shadow. "No, it was . . . three or four minutes, maybe?"

Jesse studies the thin shadow behind him. "So you think it stopped time?"

I wish I knew what to think. "It felt more like it pulled me out of time." I struggle to describe the sensation that washed over me when the shadow changed. "Almost as though we stepped into another room."

"Interesting." Jesse shoves an arm under his bed and withdraws the tattered notebook from our lunch in the courtyard. The spine falls open easily as he flips it to an empty page and begins to write.

I tilt my head back, briefly closing my eyes. "You never finished your story."

The scratching of pen against paper pauses. "Well, I *was* interrupted. Pretty rudely, by the way."

A reluctant smile cracks the stiff lines of my face. "Sorry. Next time, I'll wait until you're done to start screaming."

"That's all I ask."

The smile becomes a grin, and I open one eye to peer at Jesse. "Get on with it, Talbot."

The notebook balances on Jesse's knee as he leans against the bed's footboard, weaving his fingers together behind his head. "Where was I?

"Your mom had just passed. You think she made some kind of deal to bring about your birth." I open the other eye. "I still don't understand, though. Why do you think you're cursed? It sounds like your mom was the cursed one."

"I don't think my mom understood the terms of the deal. Curses are like termites. Once it burrows in, you're hard-pressed to shake it loose."

A ping on the other side of the room startles a squeak out of me. Jesse glances at his ceiling and sighs, reaching for a bowl layered with a dirty terrycloth towel and sticking it next to the dresser. A drop of water rolls across his ceiling and falls dead center into the bowl.

I chuckle. Jesse shoots me a hard look. "Something funny, Mansour?"

His waspish tone catches me off guard. "Every house in Ward has a bowl on standby for when the roof starts to leak. I was thinking about the ones I put out in our living room yesterday."

"Oh." Jesse shakes his head. "Sorry."

You would know that if you bothered to get to know anything about Ward, I wanted to point out. *You wouldn't feel like you were in a cage with the rest of us looking in on you.*

But I say nothing, because we're not friends, Jesse and me. Even calling us allies is a stretch.

Jesse crosses his arms over his chest, which is admittedly an excellent look for his biceps. He's not as built as Alex, but the lean strength in his body manages to exude far more menace.

"My mom's curse wasn't as simple as exchanging one life for the other," Jesse continues abruptly. "I wasn't born . . . whole. I had ripped away one soul, and as a result, I was born without one."

I blink. Wariness creeps over me again, the itchy paranoia that I'm being pranked. "Huh?"

"I don't have a soul, Mansour." He offers it without fanfare, the way you might tell someone you're a pescatarian. "That's why Miss Diaz stayed possessed after I showed up, even though you said it only possesses people when you're alone. It's why it can't possess me—there's no soul to attach to."

A thorn of uncertainty pierces my blooming fury. Jesse might still be a stranger, but I just can't imagine he would be cruel enough to compose this whole tragic tale about his mom simply to screw with me.

Which would mean he's telling the truth. Or he believes he is, anyway.

"If you were soulless, wouldn't you have showed symptoms by now? Symptoms aside from being a cranky loner with no taste in shirts."

"Symptoms like what? Stalking people in alleys and experimenting on animals?"

"For example."

Jesse mouth quirks. "I'll pencil it into the agenda."

Eventually, our smiles fade, and I swallow. "What does your curse have to do with mine?"

"Equilibrium," Jesse says softly. "One soul destroyed, one soul saved, and one soul earned."

He crouches in front of the rocking chair, dark eyes earnest.

"If I break your curse, Mansour, I think I'll earn my soul."

YASMINA MANSOUR
ALEXANDRIA
ONE MONTH AGO

My first week in Masr was a dream.

Our drive out of Cairo was terrifying. Cars weaving recklessly around bumper-to-bumper traffic, horns blaring every few feet. The thick smog choking the air, thickened by the cigarette swinging between my aunt's lips. But I was chronically positive, even if a bit scared and fighting a coughing fit.

When we'd unpacked at the hotel in Miami, Alexandria, I tentatively asked Khalto Safa about my other family members. "When do I get to meet my cousins? Or Teta and Gedu?"

A darkness stole across Khalto Safa, so venomous it sent me cringing back. "Your mother never told you?" Her laugh turned my stomach. "Your grandparents are dead."

"Oh. I'm sorry." I worried the edge of the bedspread, deliberating pressing her temper with another question. "Do we have any other relatives around?"

My aunt switched off the light. "None that matter."

Khalto Safa took me everywhere. I rode a camel around the pyramids, ate rice pudding on the thirtieth floor of a building overlooking the water, visited the mummies at the Cairo Museum, rode a buggy around the Citadel of Qaitbay in Alexandria. It was touristy and cheesy, but I ate up every minute.

I couldn't get over how time had splintered across Masr. Pieces of it forever frozen, ancient and majestic, while the rest raced toward the future. Restaurants overlooking the sphinx. Cyber cafés near the Alexandria Lighthouse. Suburban streets full of old, colorful buildings, some of which had little family-owned shops built into them. We picked up most of our snacks from those shops, since Khalto Safa hated the crowds at Fathalla, the main grocery chain in the area.

Khalto Safa had a tendency to act first, apologize second (minus the apologizing part). She had been complaining about my split ends daily, so I was only moderately surprised when the cab dropped us off in front of a blinking neon sign that read SAMIRA'S STYLES.

"Fine," I'd sighed.

I emerged from the salon with healthy curls, a wealth of information about Samira's sister's second divorce, and a long list of products to stop using on my hair.

On our second to last day in the city, Khalto Safa and I walked along the coast from Miami to Mansoura. Microbuses zoomed past us on the street, battling against yellow and black taxis and giant buses. I bought food from every vendor we passed. Grilled corn, cotton candy, fresca. Nothing was spared my curiosity and hunger. Khalto Safa had to drag me into the car before I could make a run for the guy selling Lotus crepes. I was squeezing lemon over my third cup of tirmis when my aunt, who dined exclusively on cigarettes, spoke. "The water used to be much cleaner," she said, flicking the ash from her cigarette out of the car window. *Her* car, which she'd apparently kept stored the entire time we were in the city. "I bet you think it's disgusting."

Her vehemence startled me. "What? Of course not. It's a little strange that they charge you an entrance fee, but I've paid for worse views." I intended the last part as a joke, but Khalto Safa's mouth tightened, as though I'd said the wrong thing.

"It never used to be so overrun," she spat, glancing at the crowds of people in the water.

I chewed my lip, unsure how to respond. What was the problem with more people going to the beach?

It wasn't the first time Khalto Safa had seemed irritated at my enthusiasm during the trip. I hadn't managed to pluck up the courage to ask her about visiting Mama's grave, although I'd nearly bitten my tongue in half when our cab passed Tanta on the way to Alexandria. The driver had been a nice guy—from the *aryaf*, which wasn't the name of any place I recognized. I'd asked Khalto Safa, and she'd responded with a little sneer. "The countryside. Can't you hear it in his accent?"

Which only further baffled me, because as far as I knew, seventy percent of Masr was the countryside.

Regardless, it was definitely not the time to ask about Mama. Not until I could figure out what I was doing to make her so angry with me.

I watched a child dart between stalled cars, knocking on their windows while they crawled through traffic. The box he cradled with his free arm contained dozens of plastic-wrapped packs of tissues. Twenty pounds each—less than fifty cents in American currency. I clutched a wrinkled fifty-pound bill in my palm and begin dramatically sniffling, just in case he came by Khalto Safa's window.

To my relief, he didn't approach Khalto Safa. She'd snapped at the last kid who came up to us trying to make a sale. The girl had returned the attitude right back. That little girl had a spine three times stronger than mine, because if anyone had told me I should be ashamed of myself in the tone Khalto Safa used, I probably would've cried until I fell asleep.

The children risking their lives to collect what amounted to a few bucks wasn't the only startling sight I'd encountered. In many ways, Alexandria was like any big city—luxury and deprivation wrapped around one another in an unbreakable coil. On the same street where we had lunch inside an iconic pink hotel in Mahatet El Raml, we drove past a man with one leg as he dug through a dumpster on a concrete island between two busy traffic lanes. Khalto Safa's Mercedes sped past a toktok driven by a boy who couldn't be older than thirteen.

And the *littering*. Khalto Safa had taken me to a juicery to try asab juice. Sugar cane, I'd later learn. Bags of mangos hung from the awning, and I took photos of the seller yanking long light green asab canes out of barrels and feeding them into a giant metal juicer. He poured the opaque yellow juice into two plastic bags and tied them shut around a straw.

One sip, and I nearly fell to my knees under the mango awning.

I finished the juice in minutes, but I held on to the bag for hours. Waiting to spot a trash can, any trash can. As soon as she realized what I was doing, Khalto Safa had huffed and snatched it from my grip, tossing it over her shoulder. It landed next to a dog with bald spots on its matted fur, sprawled out beneath a parked car. "Someone comes and picks it up," she'd said at my stricken face. "You take money away from them if you don't throw it."

I might be gullible, but I wasn't born yesterday. I started hiding my trash in my purse.

Despite Khalto Safa's . . . eccentricities, I was having a wonderful time. Every day was a new opportunity to disappear into the palaces of imagination I'd built in my head. Would Masriya Mina have been an artsy sort of person, working at one of the many cafés lining the streets, secretly dreaming of her big break? Would she have grabbed a fresh falafel sandwich from one of the street carts after school and made small talk with the owner before joining her friends at the library?

More than anything, I missed Mama. I couldn't help but wonder how much better this trip would have been with her by my side instead.

On our last day in the main city, we made our way into the enormous, glittering structure that was the San Stefano Mall.

It was the most beautiful mall I'd ever seen. Storefronts stretched on either side of long marble halls, winding across white banisters and rows of busy escalators. Towering pillars stretched from floor to ceiling, forming a cleft in each level. Families and teenagers streamed through the mall, and the smell of sizzling oil and fried dough made my mouth water.

"This is amazing," I breathed, zeroing in on a black leather bag with braided stitches. I'd seen several girls my age carrying it, pairing the purse with stylish outfits I could never pull off in a million years. I'd felt more than a little drab lately, having mostly packed jeans and fuzzy sweaters. Ward fashion did *not* hold up well in Alexandria.

Khalto Safa made a noise. "Really? You think *this* is impressive?" She rolled her eyes. "Don't condescend, Mina. I'm sure there's a thousand times better than this where you are."

I glanced at her to check she if she was serious. "Ward doesn't have a mall, let alone a *luxury* mall. I have to drive fifty miles up to Oregon to find one, and even then, they're usually just outlet stores. Maybe there are cooler malls in San Francisco or L.A., but the entire state isn't just those two cities any more than Masr is just Alexandria or Cairo." The words came out more heated than I planned. She'd been making these snide remarks since I landed, and I couldn't figure out *why*. She seemed determined to think my excitement was false, or worse—some kind of pity.

"Tell me about Ward," Khalto Safa said. It caught me off guard until she continued, "I want to understand why your parents chose that town in particular, if it's so unremarkable."

"I wouldn't say unremarkable, exactly," I hedged. I loved Ward; I felt protective of it and guilty for wanting to defend it.

My aunt sighed. She stopped at a kiosk and picked up a gilded lion-head lighter, flipping the heavy lid to test the flame. Satisfied with the fire dancing from the lion's jaw, she dropped a hundred and fifty bucks onto the seller's laptop and left, ignoring the confused glance he shot our way. "You can tell me about Ward while we get you some new clothes. It's embarrassing walking next to you in that outfit."

I instantly perked. She could insult me all she wanted if, in exchange, I'd get to walk out of here with shopping bags.

"What they say about earthquakes in California isn't completely true. We only get a handful of quakes every year. Barely even a quake, really. More of a shimmy," I start, subtly steering my aunt back to the shop where I'd seen the black purse. "Now, if we're talking fires and flooding..."

On the car ride to El Agamy, the signs of life disappeared with every mile under our tires. The ocean chased us, becoming bluer and brighter in the absence of families milling at its shores. A building with black scorch marks running up its left side leaned toward another building, this one with dangerously lopsided balconies.

"You and Mama grew up here?" I asked, momentarily distracted by the sight of a dog lying in the middle of the road. A dozen puppies clambered under her belly, nosing for milk. They were directly in our path.

I clutched the glovebox when Khalto Safa showed no signs of slowing. Before I could shriek a warning, she swerved, avoiding the pile of puppies by a bare inch.

"Yes," she said shortly. She lifted her lighter to her cigarette and tossed the empty box into the street. I watched it fall next to one of the puppies.

I pressed my cheek to the window, determined not to prove Khalto Safa right. Sure, El Agamy might not be as glamorous and fun as the rest of Alexandria, but this was where Mama grew up. This was her home.

Khalto Safa slowed at a speed bump the size of a small mountain. The car tilted backward, wheels spinning in the air as we climbed. The bottom of the car scraped the bump with a metallic shriek.

When the car crested the speed bump, I screamed.

Hundreds of children filled the road ahead of us. They wore uniforms that must have gone out of rotation decades ago.

The nearest child stood right at the car's front bumper, staring at me with big, mournful eyes. She was holding a long sandwich wrapped in plastic, and her crooked one-piece hijab slid partially down her face.

The back of the car rocked. Khalto Safa swore as the speedbump scraped the undercarriage a second time.

"Khalto Safa, what's—what's going on?" I choked out, unable to tear my gaze from the girl.

"What's going on is that someone decided to build speed bumps the size of a damn house in the middle of a fast-moving road 'for our safety' when all it does is screw up our cars and make them *less safe*!"

Ice water sluiced down my spine. She couldn't see them.

"I know it's not much now, but El Agamy is an up-and-coming area," Khalto Safa said.

A viscous black sludge poured from the little girl's mouth.

One by one, the children choked on the black liquid as it coated their chins, drenched their clothes. They were drowning, right here in the middle of the road.

"Your teta always talked about how busy El Agamy was before everyone made off to Marsa Matrouh and Marina. Everyone had a summer home here. We were a fun little trend for the rich and bored until they hopped to the next section of the coast. Ridiculous. If you think they did a number on El Agamy, you should see Abu Talat."

Khalto Safa's car sped forward, and just as her bumper reached the first girl, the children disappeared.

I screwed my fists into my eyes and shook my head. It was the weather change. Lucia mentioned her trips to Italy made her ears pop from the plane's cabin pressure even weeks after landing. Maybe my eyes were popping.

I took a deep breath, refocusing on the conversation. I dutifully did not point out that Khalto Safa could be the poster girl for the rich and bored. "That happened in California too, after the Gold Rush. People flooded the area and built towns to support them while they mined for gold, and when there was nothing left anymore, they abandoned it. We learned about them in eighth grade—they called them ghost towns."

Khalto Safa released a sharp laugh. "Ghost towns. I like that."

The car rolled into a narrow, uneven street. I held on to the console as we rocked from side to side, and my aunt spat another slew of expletives as the front wheel dipped into a muddy pond. "Runoff from the sewers," she growled. "New tenants in the house at the end of the road. Idiots built cheap pipes and turned our street into a toilet for the dogs. Not to mention the thieves have been stripping the copper from their wires, but don't worry—they would never try anything like that with our villa."

The crumbling junkyards gradually shifted to fading ivory walls. They climbed higher the deeper we went, eventually merging into a pair of soaring iron gates.

Once I finished picking up my jaw from the ground, I identified the vines snaking around the rusted metal as ivy and grape leaves. Mama had tried—and miserably failed—to grow grape leaves for mahshi in our old yard. Oddly enough, Baba managed to plant them with no problem the following year. Mama had joked her touch was just too toxic.

A sign with faded letters in Arabic and English reads RESIDENCE OF BAMBA HAIKAL.

"Your great-great-great-grandmother," Khalto Safa said.

"Wow." I stared at the sign. "That's a lot of 'greats.' "

Khalto Safa stayed silent, so I pressed on. "We don't really have those links at home. Our roots don't stretch too deep in Ward yet."

"At home?" Khalto Safa repeated, puzzled. An ear-splitting screech of metal shook the car's frame as the gates eased open.

A mansion torn from the pages of an old fable loomed above us. Ivory balconies wrapped around the second story of the villa, held up by looming white pillars. Stained glass windows glittered high behind them. To our right, a family of date trees rustled above a vast, overgrown garden. Neglect mottled the pillars and peeled the paint around the parapets, but there was no mistaking the house's mightiness. In a neighborhood of dust and bones, the Haikal villa was a vein of glory, thriving through El Agamy.

Entranced, I unclipped my seat belt, sticking my head out the window as far as it would go. The scent of overripe dates and pool bleach wafted over me just as something cold touched my cheek.

It fanned into the distinct shape of a hand. A scream flattened in my throat, leaking out of me in a trembling hiss.

I turned my head.

The little girl from the road leaned out of the back window, her sallow little face inches from mine.

Imshee.

She never moved her mouth, but the order rang as clearly as if it had been whispered into my ear.

Leave.

The girl disappeared as soon as the gates closed behind us.

"Welcome to the Haikal villa." Khalto Safa's voice washed over me as though from a distance. "Welcome home."

CHAPTER TEN
PRESENT DAY

Jesse stands, barely an outline in the dark. "Follow me."

I keep my gaze trained away from the shifting shadows behind him. "Where are we going?"

"Downstairs." He only gets a step to the door before I shoot to my feet and grab his arm. "What? Isn't downstairs where the mortuary is?"

A long pause. Jesse pries my fingers from his arm. "Stay close."

Silence cloaks the house, muffling the sound of my panicked breath. Mr. Talbot hasn't come home yet, but who knows when he might be back?

The stairs groan as we descend. When we reach the first floor, I come to a halt, rubbing the heel of my hand against my chest. "Does your dad own a defibrillator?"

Jesse leans against the banister and treats me to his signature eye-roll. "Who would he use it on? The corpses?"

"I hope you keep your sense of humor when I have a heart attack in about, oh, ten minutes."

Jesse sighs, shifting to the head of the stairs leading into the mortuary. "Come on, Mansour. I know you and your friends have gossiped about what's at the bottom of the Talbot house. Don't you want to finally find out?"

I pause, caught. "We don't gossip." Much. "We exchange pertinent social information."

He grins, his lips a vicious slash in the dark. "Consider this another piece of pertinent social information."

Before I can cobble together another protest, Jesse disappears down the stairs.

I linger next to the head of the narrow tunnel of stairs. Sweat beads along my forehead. The prospect of following him fills me with dread, but I can't stay up here alone.

My damp palm finds the banister and holds on for dear life. Just a set of stairs. Stairs aren't scary for anyone above the age of three.

A mocking voice drifts from the stairwell. "Do you need me to come up there and hold your hand?"

Unbearable, unmannered, smug little *jerk*. I put my other hand on the banister and begin my shuffling descent.

"I hate you, I hate you, I hate you," I sing.

A hums floats through the darkness. I pause, squinting in the direction of the sound. Is he . . . harmonizing with me?

I shake my head, too amused to remember my impending cardiac arrest. At least whatever's wrong with him is funny.

The temperature dips the farther we descend. I clutch the railing, trying not to wince each time a metal step whines beneath my weight.

After an eternity, the stairs flatten into a long hallway pulled straight out of the eighties. Faux wood paneling runs along one side, rounded doorways on the other. The long yellow bulbs lining the center of the ceiling emit a low buzz when Jesse flips the light switch. The tubes are scorched at the ends, flickering with the last of their life force.

I clutch my backpack a little closer and remind myself that if Jesse wanted to kill me, he wouldn't do it on his own property.

"What are these rooms for?" I nod at the doors.

"Storage, mostly. You could probably nick a lipstick or something if you want. We have stacks of the stuff."

Aside from the fact that I'm not eager to steal from the town mortician, "Why does he have stacks of lipstick?" I pause. "What does a mortician do, exactly?"

"The internet is free, Mansour."

Jesse turns to a door as nondescript as the other six we've passed. I hold my breath as he twists the handle, leading us into the belly of...

An office.

"Oh."

Jesse glances over his shoulder, arching a brow. "Something wrong?"

Since I'd prefer to cartwheel into an open flame than admit to Jesse I'd been imagining walking into a room of dead bodies, I merely lift my chin and follow him inside.

Compared to the rest of the Talbot house, the office is shockingly modern. A mahogany desk the size of three pianos consumes most of the room. Rows upon rows of polished wooden shelves line the walls behind it. A rolling drink cart in the corner holds dozens of expensive glass bottles, but only one tumbler.

A leather-bound book lies open on the desk. I inch closer, peering at what appears to be the anatomic image of a girl's spleen.

Jesse rounds the desk, dropping onto the plush leather chair. He adjusts one of the two giant monitors stationed in front of the keyboard. "This is my dad's study."

"Are we allowed to be in here?"

It's an absurd question, since the answer is *obviously not*, and Jesse does me the favor of ignoring it. "I've been doing some research," he says instead.

He stands, dragging the chair in front of his dad's desk to the other side. When I hesitate, he makes a show of dusting it off with his sleeve. "A throne for Her Majesty."

"Has anyone ever told you to pursue a career in comedy?" I ask, poking his arm away from the chair and perching on the edge.

"Not yet."

"Take that as a sign."

Jesse grins, as he always does whenever I say something especially mean. He seems to thrive on my bad attitude. "Noted."

With a swipe of the mouse, the monitors flicker on. The glow washes the shelves behind us blue.

Dozens of tabs open on the screen. More than I can count. It's a miracle his server hasn't completely crashed.

"I had to switch languages and click on some questionable links, but I finally found a thread about your family in El Agamy. I followed it down a rabbit hole that may or may not have been totally legal," Jesse says. "Have you heard of the Egyptian House of Archives?"

My brows furrow. "No." It comes out vaguely waspish. I hate it when someone asks me something about Masr and I can't answer. It makes me feel like a fraud.

If Jesse notices, he doesn't let on. "That's probably for the best," he mutters. "Can't be implicated if you don't know, right?"

An old article appears, fuzzy and scanned at a poor angle. "I had to put it through a PDF converter app," he says. "It didn't translate all of it."

"I can read Arabic." As long as the letters have the necessary tashkeel, I can usually figure out any words I don't understand from context. "But let me try the translation first."

NASHRA: NORTH COAST

FAMILY PURCHASES TWENTY ACRES IN WESTERN ALEXANDRIA.

The largest real estate purchase in Western Alexandria's history recently closed between Bamba Haikal and local municipalities. Government officials expressed their hope that the sale would catch the eye of commercial developers, leading to population and industrial growth along the shoreline. Is the tide changing for this beautiful and underutilized section of the Alexandria coast?

"Yeah, my aunt mentioned we've been in El Agamy for a long time," I murmur. I hadn't expected that to mean over two hundred years, though. "My however-many-great-grandparents must've been loaded."

"The wealth actually started with the first Haikal matriarch." Another swipe. A black-and-white painting fills the screen. In it, a polished older woman lounges on a velvet parlor chair. She stares at the artist unsmilingly, her hands folded over the rounded arms of the parlor chair.

Pain cleaves my head, sudden and vicious. "I know her," I gasp, and the pain grows teeth.

"Know her?" Jesse narrows his eyes. "Mansour, this woman is the Haikal family's first matriarch. She's been dead for over a century."

A woman kneels in a mud-covered road, her tattered gown blowing in the storm. Dirt streaks her arms and forehead. Lightning cracks above her. She rocks back and forth, lips moving.

I shake my head, rubbing my temples. The memory makes no sense. "Maybe I saw a picture somewhere in my aunt's house?"

The pressed suit and combed hair in the painting bear no resemblance to the bedraggled woman in my mind, but their eyes . . . the same flat, merciless brown.

"According to every article I could find, Bamba Haikal came into her fortune out of nowhere. She was an orphan without a home for most of her life. After she built the villa, the newspapers called her Sayida Bamba and vacationers started flooding El Agamy."

"Bamba means pink in Arabic." I offer the information seriously, as if it might contain a case-cracking clue.

"Good to know," Jesse says. The second opportunity he's had to mock me, and the second time he hasn't taken it. "Bamba was responsible for most of the development in El Agamy. She built her home there and worked with schools and business owners to draw families into the area. But then children started to disappear, and people got spooked. The trickle of life dried up, and El Agamy stayed mostly empty until Bamba died. Her daughters took up the mantle to develop the area into a place families would want to start their lives."

Jesse clicks his mouse, and a photo of a nauseatingly familiar villa replaces Bamba's picture. The paint is much fresher, and the garden appears to be in bloom, but it's otherwise the same.

"That's the house," I say. "The Haikal villa."

"I was afraid you would say that." Jesse swipes both hands through his hair, knitting his fingers behind his neck as he leans back in the chair. A stray lock of hair catches on his eyelashes, and before I know what's happening, I reach for it.

Jesse and I freeze. A dark gaze fastens on my face as I curl my fingers away at the last second. "Just a strand, uh, in your eyes."

Without looking away from me, he tilts his chin back, and the troublesome strand slides to his temple. "Better?" His voice sounds gravelly, borderline rough. I don't need a mirror to know my cheeks are warming.

"You were saying?" I clear my throat.

His lips twist, as though hearing a joke only he can understand. His gaze finally returns to the computer. "As I was saying, generations of Haikals lived in the villa Bamba built. Lots of them also left. There are Haikals scattered all over the world. The ones who remained in the Haikal house were constantly struggling to make their neighborhood a place where people wanted to live. Bamba's second granddaughter is quoted calling the tourists 'idiots chasing the next coast like a cat chasing the end of a string.' " Jesse snorts.

He clicks to the next picture. In it, the house has gone into complete disrepair. Weeds grow around the rusted gates, blocking out the sight of the wild garden behind them. The balconies lean dangerously forward. The villa seems smaller, too. Like it shrank into itself for perseveration.

"Cut to 1966. A Haikal daughter is born, and she grows up a little off. A little too polite, a little too quiet. After a decade of peace, children begin to vanish in El Agamy again, and the police are at a loss. There's never a struggle. Someone is hunting the children, and they're doing it with the kind of skill nobody has seen in centuries."

Jesse presses a button on the keyboard, and my mother appears on the monitor.

I stumble back, bumping my hip against the shelves. Mama can't be older than sixteen or seventeen in the photo. Her curls fall freely down her back, framing her slim figure. Her legs are crossed at the knee, hands folded politely in her lap. She gazes into the camera with an arrogant tilt of her head, as though she cannot comprehend that anyone viewing the photo could ever be worth her time.

"I don't understand." I rub my chest, striving for calm and landing on queasy. "You're saying my mom knew about the children disappearing?"

Instead of answering, Jesse draws up a list of images and converts them to midsize thumbnails. "This is your mom's house throughout the years. Look at the way it changes, and then look at the dates of the headlines I pasted underneath."

Dread builds in my chest, acid eating through my ribs and settling like a burning coat around my heart. My eyes slide off the screen, landing on Jesse. The terror must be plain on my features, because his gaze softens. The wheels of his chair squeak as Jesse rolls a little closer and says, "We can do this later."

"No." I don't hesitate. "There won't be a later. That thing—those shadows—" I square my shoulders and take a deep breath like Aida taught me, holding it for four seconds before I exhale. I repeat the action, inhaling for four seconds, holding it, and exhaling for the same amount of time.

I look at the screen.

The images of the villa go back at least a century. In the first set, it exudes an imminence reminiscent of a historical building, something powerful and timeless. Meanwhile, the headlines below it mark year after year of local children going missing. Vanishing into thin air, as far as the understaffed police can tell.

The years turn into decades, and the house begins to decay. The photo from earlier, with the rust-coated gates and shrunken pillars, captures it best. It reminds me of a starving lion, deadly despite the bones protruding from its golden coat.

The headlines tell another story.

Ahlan Wa Sahlan: Child Disappearances Hit All-Time Low

Nashra: Follow the timeline—tracking the vanished children on the western Alexandria coast.

Awdat il Nagah: Peace and Prosperity Returns to a Long-Isolated Neighborhood in El Agamy, known to Alexandrians as Makan il La'ana.

Jesse points at the last bit of the headline. "I couldn't translate that anywhere. What does it mean?"

It takes a couple of attempts to unlock my jaw. "Place of the curse. Cursed place."

I want to argue with Jesse that its normal for houses to deteriorate over time. They spring leaks that turn into mold; suffer termite infestations that force poisonous gas through every window and crevice; choke on gutters full of dead leaves and rain; wrinkle with fading paint and peeling walls.

As long as someone is there to turn the lights on, the house will survive. It may labor to breathe, rattling shutters and groaning in the night, but it will keep you safe.

That's what a home does. It guards you. It grows with you.

What it doesn't do is feed on you.

Disbelief builds in my lungs as I study the photo on the screen. The splendor it lost over the last two decades had resurfaced with a vengeance. Not a plant out of place in the trimmed garden. Freshly painted walls shine, cloaked behind fruit-laden trees and a soaring gate.

A hand grazes the side of my chin, gently turning my head to Jesse's. "Unclench your teeth, Sour Patch. I can hear your molars grinding."

My heart thuds, struggling to beat inside my tightening chest. "Five children go missing a year, and the house looks pristine. The disappearances stop, and the house starts to fall into ruin. I see the connection, Jesse. I understand the basic principles of a curse. What I still don't understand is what it has to do with my mom."

"You haven't looked at the last row of photos. You need to look."

"I *am* looking."

"Then you need to see, Mina."

My name—my first name—leaving Jesse's lips jolts me, tear off the thin layer of protection I'd plastered between myself and the photos on the screen.

It shoves me back into my skin. Back into my senses.

And I have no choice but to see.

The gleaming house, back in perfect condition.

The announcement, celebrating the birth of Nadine Haikal.

The headline beneath them, published eleven years later, that destroys everything I believe in.

Nashra: Janna Elshenaway—Third Child Goes Missing in Coastal Community.

CHAPTER ELEVEN
PRESENT DAY

It's three in the morning, and the shadow under the metal door hasn't moved.

I've been watching it for the last twenty minutes. Every time I think about sitting up or turning on the light, lead fills my stomach, pinning me in place.

Because I know it's watching me, too.

I can't explain how I know this shadow is an imposter any more than I could explain why fingernails grow outwards instead of sideways. Call it delusion, call it a rare moment of intuition, but I will swear on my life that I am not alone in my room.

The shadow under the metal door always shifts, moving with the moon throughout the night.

I want to call for Baba. I want to hear his footsteps as he lumbers down the hall. I want him to open the door and switch on the light with the hand he isn't using to rub his eyes. Just as he had when I was a child, I want him to sit on the edge of my bed and laugh at how silly I am to be scared of the dark. "Ya binty, what's in your head can't hurt you," he'd cajole, tapping my forehead. Back then, he would take me downstairs for a cup of mint tea, and we would watch *Sanawat il Daya'a* until one of us fell asleep.

But if I call Baba into my room, something much worse than a shadow will follow him inside.

My phone is under my pillow. I know who I need to call, if I could only convince my limbs to thaw. Some primordial instinct has locked them tight, trying to keep me frozen and invisible until the danger is gone.

Tears collect in my unblinking eyes. I have to call Jesse. I have to move. Otherwise, I won't just be playing dead. The fear alone will stop my heart.

I draw my phone out from under my pillow. The screen flickers on, harshly bright.

I can't unlock it without looking away from the shadow.

Saliva thickens on my tongue, syrupy with my rising nausea. *Count to three,* I order. *Count to three and look away.*

One. I maneuver my phone in front of my face,

Two. My thumb hovers over the bottom of the screen, ready to swipe.

Three.

I look down.

My thumb shakes as I pull up my call log and press on Jesse's number. He'd typed it in before I left his house.

It rings. I hold my breath, fixed on his name. (He saved it as "J. Talbot," probably to avoid giving me the idea that we're more than glorified business associates.)

Voicemail. The machine's robotic message passes too quickly, and I'm plunged back into the tomblike silence of my room.

"Jesse," I whisper. "There's something in my room. Please . . . please come."

I press the screen to end the call, and a weight settles on my legs.

When I was a kid, I heard this story about a guy who died from a prank gone wrong. His friends dressed up as kidnappers and abducted him from his dorm in the middle of the night, throwing him into a van headed for one of their houses. They dragged him into the yard and forced him to kneel in front of a tree stump. Trying to keep the laughter from their voices, they told him he would be executed. The poor guy was out of his mind with fear, sobbing and shaking and begging them not to do it.

They played him an audio of a sword being sharpened. In the back, another "friend" dunked a towel in a bucket of ice water. Then they forced him to count down from ten. At zero, they dropped the towel onto his neck.

The guy died immediately.

Ridiculous, isn't it? A person can't actually die just by *believing* they died any more than someone could live by believing they were still alive.

But when my legs are pinned beneath the weight on top of the covers and the seconds tick by like centuries, I can believe it. I can believe a mind can be convinced of something so thoroughly that it bends science and medicine and reality itself into compliance.

The shadow beneath the metal door has moved to my dresser. Back to normal.

And sitting cross-legged on the covers is my mother.

Her hair falls in a rippling black curtain down her spine. Bright green eyes rake over me with concern. "Why are you crying, habibti? Did someone at school upset you?"

Across her sweater, SAWYER ELEMENTARY MOM is embroidered in bold letters. Her jeans are distressed at the knees and belted low at her waist.

Mama scoots closer, and I'm too frozen to do anything but stare.

"Yasmina, what's wrong?" Tears collect in her eyes the longer I stay silent. "Did someone hurt you?"

This isn't real. This thing sitting on my covers is not my mother. It's wearing her clothes, and it even smells like her. The overpowering spice of her ninety-nine-cent bottle of Jordache tickles my nose. Longing surges through me, wrapping around my chest and wringing every last drop of air from my lungs.

"You can tell me, you know. I'm your mother."

I shake my head. It's the only action I can bring myself to take.

She studies me, searching for the lie. I know what she'll say next. We've had some version of this conversation a million times. Judging by the sweater, this one is from my last day in the fourth grade, when I'd come home with a bloody nose and a teacher's note.

"Yasmina, you are not weak." Her voice hardens, something cold and distant flashing over her features. "I did not bring you here to be weak. If someone hurts you, you hurt them back."

A distant thud draws my attention from Mama for a second. I glance at the roof, brows furrowing.

When I glance back down, her face leans inches from mine.

"What kind of home is this if you can't even fight back?" she demands. Her breath wafts across my cheeks. "If I can't protect you here, then what was the point of any of it?"

My fourth-grade self hadn't had a clue what she was talking about, and my teenage self isn't faring much better.

I force myself to hold her gaze. My lips tremble as I part them, my teeth struggling to unclench.

"You. Aren't. Real."

A fissure cracks Mama's skull open like a chisel taken to a statue.

"My mother is dead," I hiss.

Another crack, this time down her throat and across her chest. The tears spilling down her cheeks fall faster, a fountain without end. She wipes them away. When she lowers her hands, empty eye sockets stare back at me.

The metal door rattles. The sliding pieces of my mother's face rearrange into a gruesome grin.

"How did I die, Mina?" She bounces on her knees, pieces of her breaking off like glass and falling onto my bedspread. Blood pours through the cracks, winding through her in rivulets of red. Her voice deepens with each repetition, becoming an inhuman snarl. "How did I die? How did I die?"

"I don't—I don't know!" I scramble off the bed, clipping my elbow against the dresser. On the bed, her silhouette ripples and tugs.

"Liar!" she howls. The sound scrapes through me, knives hacking into my skull.

The shriek of hinges finally snaps me from the last of my shock, and I scream. I scream until it feels like my insides liquefy, rising like molten lava seconds from an eruption.

A cold hand closes over my mouth.

"Mansour!" Jesse growls. Rain dampens his hair, clinging to his cheekbones. Dark eyes roam over my petrified features. "Hey, hey, look at me! You've gotta calm down. Your dad—oh, crap."

Heavy footsteps thunder down the hall, headed straight for my room. "Mina!" Baba calls. "Are you okay? What's wrong?"

I push Jesse off and roll to my knees, crawling to the door just in time for Baba to twist the handle. The lock I installed strains, the metal bar bending as Baba pushes against it. "Yasmina!" he bellows. I can't remember the last time I heard him shout. "When did you get a lock? Open this door!"

I drag myself to my feet and rest my forehead against the door. "Nothing's wrong, Baba. I just had a bad dream. I'm so sorry to have woken you."

The lock strains again as Baba pushes open a tiny gap between the door and the frame. "You don't sound right. Let me in."

From the corner, I spot Jesse pushing the metal door shut. Is that how he came inside? Is he determined to slip off my roof and break his neck?

The door thuds, the gap widening as the lock struggles not to snap. "Mina," Baba snarls, and it hits me with the force of a truck.

For the second time tonight, my heart stops.

The fetid odor of rot and sewage slips through the gap in the door, curling into my nose.

"Mina, Mina, Yasmina," Baba sings, and bile surges into my throat.

It has him.

And it *can talk.*

"Jesse, come help me close this door!"

"Are the shadows keeping you company? We know how lonely you get, little Mina. So very lonely."

Jesse's shoulder joins mine, shoving against the door.

"Unless... uh-oh. Don't tell me you're scared of your own shadow," the thing that isn't Baba says, laughing. Ice sluices through my veins. "Your mother was never scared of her shadows. Then again, she rarely cared about anything long enough for its shadow to chase her."

The picture of Mama as a teenager flashes through my mind. Her cold smirk and flat stare.

"You don't know her!" I burst out, and I ram myself into the door over and over again. Pain explodes in my arm, but I would let the whole limb snap off before I let this thing keep talking. This creature in my father's body, this nightmare that's haunted me since I stepped foot in the Haikal villa—it doesn't get to tell me who my mother was. It doesn't get to eliminate the woman who raised me for nine years, who would drape me over her shoulders and spin us around until we were both dizzy and giggling, who would greet each morning by smoothing the furrow in Baba's brow and kissing his temple, who *loved me.* What right does it have to tell me she's not real?

I beat against the door until it's replaced by a wall of flesh and muscle. Jesse absorbs the blow across his chest before I can reel myself in. I gasp an apology as his large hand closes around my wrist. "Mansour, hey." His tone is firm, steady. It cuts through my panic like a ray of sun in a storm. "The door is shut. It's gone."

We wait in tense silence, listening for sounds on the other side.

I hated not knowing what it had done to Baba. The one time I stuck around to witness the thing leave a body it had possessed, the person had been staggering around, completely dazed. They hadn't remembered me, hadn't remembered a second of their possession. At the time, it infuriated me—there I was, bleeding and terrified, and the person who'd hurt me could scarcely remember why they'd walked into the room.

Now, their amnesia is a blessing. I hear Baba shuffling outside, probably disoriented, struggling to recall what brought him to my room in the middle of the night, and my only strength comes from knowing none of this will remain with him. He'll go to sleep with a faint headache, spared of any nightmares of a glowing door and orange eyes.

Eventually, the shuffling grows fainter as Baba returns to his bedroom.

Relief liquifies my muscles, and I sag into Jesse. His heart beats steadily under my cheek. Real and reliable, unlike everything else around me.

After a hesitant pause, Jesse's hand settles between my shoulder blades. He rubs soothing circles into my back, his breath a warm caress against the top of my head.

"You sure there isn't an easier soul out there for you to save?" I mumble. He smells divine, and I resist the urge to steal a deeper sniff of his collar.

A laugh rolls in his chest, rumbling against me. "I like a challenge."

After a moment, I draw back, the shock easing away enough to remind me that I'm getting too cozy with a guy who'd wake up early just to avoid speaking two words to me. He's being kind enough to comfort me—that doesn't mean he suddenly wants to be friends.

"Your arm is bleeding," Jesse says, zeroing on the clotted fabric stuck to my skin. "Come over to my place. I'll fix you up."

Since I don't plan on going back to sleep for the rest of my life, I nod. "Let me grab a jacket." I clear my throat, trying to rebalance myself. "By the way, we're going through the front door, in case you were planning to scale my roof a third time."

As I make my way to the closet, Jesse drops onto my bed. I pull out my fuzzy white jacket—the one Rainie says makes me look like a sentient cloud—from the hanger and draw it over my arms, yanking the zipper to my chin just in time to hear Jesse call, "Uh, Mansour? Is this yours?"

Jesse holds up my mother's journal, pinched between two fingers, open to the first page.

I'd had this journal for nine years. I'd bought a magnifying glass to study the texture of the pages, flipped through it in search of a secret notation or a hidden message more times than I could count. In all that time, I never found anything beyond bare, bone-white pages waiting between the photo of my parents and my mother's name at the front.

I gape at the pages open in Jesse's hand, inked in top to bottom with my mother's cramped, slanted writing. My vision darkens in the corners, hysteria squeezing a fist around my throat.

Jesse turns the journal back toward himself. "Is that a no?"

And there's really nothing either of us can do about it when my knees give out, and I slide to the ground.

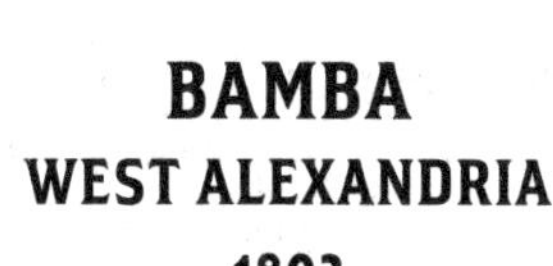

BAMBA
WEST ALEXANDRIA
1802

Bamba was tired of walking.

Night would fall soon, and she'd lost her blanket to the same woman who'd stolen her sleeping bench. On the bright side, she'd found a knife lying in the heaps of garbage scattered along the road out of the city. The dogs didn't appreciate her crawling under the bridge and competing with them for food, though, and long scratches lined her arms and legs.

The knife had helped her even the score.

Regrettably, the blade didn't have a handle. She'd already cut her palm twice, but at least she knew the next person who stole from her would deeply regret it.

The setting sun painted the road ahead in burnished gold, temporarily illuminating the miles of empty dirt and desert. The air wavered, soft and inviting, turning dust motes into shimmering diamonds. And the quiet—like a coffin lid had closed over Bamba, locking her in a living grave.

She should have stayed in the city. People who survived in the streets as long as Bamba had honed paranoia to an art. They were the ones who heeded unsettling rumors about places like these. Places where humanity had yet to leave its mark, where Masr was still ancient, its stories and superstitions pulsing hungrily beneath the rubble.

And what a floater never, ever did was sleep in those places.

Any other day, Bamba would have turned around and made the trek to an alcove she could shelter under until the shop owner chased her away. Gone back to the bridge and slit those vicious dogs open from stem to stern and curled into their furry pelts.

If only she wasn't so very tired of walking.

So Bamba trudged ahead, dragging her increasingly uncooperative legs, long after the sun sank into the horizon. Bamba had never experienced such a dark night. The air was different here No scent of horse manure left behind from the carriages crowding the city roads. Not a single trace of grease or cooking oil from the street carts selling chicken and beef shawarma sandwiches. She heard her every breath, loud as the whip of a cord. Her shuffling footsteps. She could feel her own heartbeat, hear her thoughts with more clarity than she'd experienced in years.

In the exact spot where she would later build her family villa, Bamba felt her soul for the first time.

She didn't like it. The shape of it was familiar in the worst ways, etched in too many scars that had once been open wounds. It took her back to evenings in the orphanage, listening to the girls in her room crying softly into their emaciated pillows.

While they wept, Bamba had seethed.

Those stupid children missed parents who had forsaken them. Abandoned them. Why would she turn their absence into heartache when she could turn it into hatred? A hatred she nurtured, branded into her ribs, scored in fiery red lines across every muscle and tendon. Some days, she thought that hatred might be the only thing keeping her alive. Other days, she knew it was only a matter of time until it burned through the rest of her.

Bamba didn't waste her tears mourning what could have been. Her parents hadn't liked her from the start. They were weak, easily frightened fools whose name would hardly last another generation before it faded into obscurity. What Bamba had wanted more than anything was to create a new family. A *strong* family, where lineage and home mattered above all else. Those children would be her stake in this world. They would keep her alive long after her time.

Bamba's laugh echoed in the vast nothingness of the desert. What a silly girl she'd been. Just as idiotic as the others. She had no anchor, no home. Nothing beyond the clothes on her back and the blade slicing into her hand.

Bamba's bare foot scraped a cluster of chiseled rocks. She hissed, stumbled. Dropping to the ground, she pulled the dirt-laden end of her torn abaya to her foot, trying to stem the bleeding.

As pain radiated from the wound, Bamba tilted her head back to search the fathomless sky. She thought of an old rhyme the matron at the orphanage would sing with a child strewn over her lap, just before she brought the paddle down on their behind.

Rocking in the dirt, Bamba sang, "Mama is coming, she's almost here, she's bringing toys and gifts!" The song drifted like a falling flower in the black meadow of oblivion. An unwelcome sound in this sinister desert void. She and the other kids had sung it to each other at the orphanage, and Bamba's mind settled on the silly rhyme any time she found herself ill at ease.

She hummed to the dark. "Do you know the girl named Bamba and what her Mama said to her? She said stand up, Bamba, move quick! Do you see what's coming? Do you see what's gone? Look up, Bamba, and move quick."

A horrible odor hit Bamba. She retched, leaning back, only for her elbow to descend into a stew of filth. Wet chunks clung to her, drenching her upper body.

Bamba tried to crawl without putting weight on her foot. She couldn't see her own arm in the darkness.

Frustration welled inside Bamba, blistering into rage. She deserved better than this. She hadn't survived beatings and starvation to be dismissed by Alexandrian aristocrats in tailored clothes and feathered hats, to be tossed from village to village. She was not a rat digging and dying in the dark. She was someone!

Wind howled through the desert, plastering Bamba's dirt-clumped hair to her neck. Lightning split the sky like a serpent's tongue, and in the brief glow, Bamba saw a hulking figure crouched by her legs.

A scream caught in her teeth. Bamba attempted to run, but her wounded foot gave out beneath her. Bamba groped for her knife, but it was gone. Most likely dislodged during her slow crawl into the desert.

The unmistakable scent of rot choked Bamba, so strong she thought it must be coming from inside her. Another lightning strike revealed the figure looming an inch away. Fetid breath mingled with hers.

YOU WANT TO BE SOMEONE?

Bamba whimpered. It was her own voice, silky and confident, coming from her head.

The rot intensified. Bamba had spent her thirty-six years living like a vulture, picking apart disaster sites for food or tools, moving around the carcasses of man and animal alike. In all those years, she had never come across a smell half as horrific as this one.

Before she could scream, the veil of darkness shifted, swirling around Bamba as it thinned into a ring of shadows. Through them, Bamba saw—

Bamba saw the impossible.

A grand villa with her name on the gate.

Servants opening the doors to her carriage, taking her gloved hand as she stepped inside.

The same people who would have spit on her in the street smiling across a gleaming marble table, snapping their fingers whenever Bamba's glass ran dry.

And children. So many of her progeny, filling the villa and eventually making their way through the world. They carry the Haikal name to the highest places, forge connections with powerful people Bamba would never have known existed.

DO YOU WANT TO BE SOMEONE?

This time, Bamba welcomed the voice.

"I do," she whispered.

CAN YOU PAY THE PRICE?

Thunder shook the sky, arrows of lightning arching inside the network of clouds. Bubbles formed under the murky water she knelt in. A small body rose to the surface, face down in the pond. A dead child.

Bamba's body finally defeated her self-control, and she retched again.

"What do you want?"

YOUR BLOODLINE FOR THEIRS. YOUR LEGACY FOR THEIR LIVES.

A rush of images flooded Bamba. Her back bent backward with the weight of the visions. Lineage after lineage severed. Families ended and uprooted. She would spin the destiny of thousands right into the greedy maw of the nothingness before her. In exchange, her own lineage would never end.

"What happens if they don't pay the price?" What if somewhere in her lineage, a weak seed sprouted in their garden?

IF YOUR DEBT IS NOT PAID, YOUR BLOOD WILL BE FORFEIT.

Breath icy in her lungs, Bamba stared at the dark shape. A small part of her recognized this offer for what it was. She had seen enough of the devil's handiwork to see through his bargains. This offer would permanently tie her bloodline to the altar of this day, to this very moment.

But she would *have* a bloodline.

Bamba offered one slow nod.

"I want to be someone," Bamba said softly. "Whoever it costs."

THEN SOMEONE YOU WILL BECOME.

The world exploded in a wash of blue as a bolt of lightning struck Bamba. Liquid fire raced through her.

A second bolt of lightning engulfed Bamba's mouth in rust. She was expelling her human weaknesses, the tender morsels of humanity she'd let the world prey on. No more. She was iron and fire. Burning. Molting.

It was the strangest thing. As Bamba's blood was tainted, doomed to pass from generation to generation of Haikal children, the rancid taste of death stung her throat.

And for the briefest instant, the lightning scorching inside her illuminated a curly-haired young girl in slippers and unusual clothes, staring at Bamba.

CHAPTER TWELVE
PRESENT DAY

The bell rings as the door swings open, blowing a gust of frigid air into the diner.

Loud conversation overlays the click of utensils against chipped ceramic plates. The back fryer hisses and sizzles. The smell of grease and melted cheese permeates the small space, sinking into the overstuffed vinyl booths pushed up against half-shuttered windows. Rain slides in rivulets down the glass, its gentle taps the only consistent sound in the cacophony.

"No better place to read the entries of a haunted journal than the Grease & Grind," Jesse remarks dryly.

"They have free refills on coffee and tea here," I mutter.

"The coffee is cinnamon-flavored sewage."

"Shhh." I point to the dented metal carafe single-handedly restoring my will to live. "She can hear you."

Jesse rolls his eyes.

Despite the early hour and the overwhelming smell of cheese, Jesse manages to draw the attention of half the girls who walk through the doors. I can't blame them. Were I not currently bottling a scream worthy of tearing through the earth's stratosphere, I'd probably take a second look at Jesse, too.

It's funny, in a bitterly ironic way—Jesse tries so hard to repel attention, but everything about him commands its own gravitational force. The oversized, tattered leather jacket molded around his broad shoulders. The windswept silk of his black hair, long strands falling onto his forehead and the bridge of his crooked nose. The permanent smirk on his full lips, probably stamped there the day he was born. He slings his arm over the back of the booth, sprawling with a casual confidence I couldn't pull off if I lived to be a hundred. His legs are set apart, one knee crooked to the side while the other leg stretches into my side of the booth.

I glare over the brim of my mug and kick his boot back to his territory.

Seeing how these girls react to Jesse just reminds me of how ardently he opposes any sense of attachment to Ward. He didn't *have* to be the school loner. Sure, he might be abrasive and sarcastic and a little too intense, but he could have found his people. And if not, his looks could have won him entry into pretty much any social circle at Canyon High.

"Ow," Jesse drawls, and proceeds to push his boot back between my feet. Neither of us has slept since the incident in my room. Heaven forbid Jesse allow a minor obstacle like sleep deprivation to stand in the way of irritating me to death. If a curse can't finish me, then by God, Jesse Talbot will.

He taps a finger against the tabletop. "About your dad—"

"I don't want to talk about my dad."

"Okay." He surprises me by moving on without argument. "What do you want to talk about, then?"

Reckless energy crackles through me, sparking from the depths of my grief. "Why do you hate it here so much?"

Jesse cocks his head. "Why do you think I hate it here?"

I tick each item off, trying to ignore my shaking fingers. "You've never said yes to a dance or a date, you turn away anyone who tries to be your friend, you push away every teacher that tries to reach out to you, and you never show up to functions for the school or the town."

"Hmm." Jesse sits forward, lacing his fingers together on the table. My skin tightens beneath his steadfast attention. "I had no idea you were so concerned about my community involvement."

The back of my neck heats. "Someone should be."

Jesse's lips twitch. He lifts a hand, mimicking me as he ticks off items on his fingers. "I've never been asked out by someone I want to say yes to, I *don't* turn away anyone who tries to be my friend, the fact that the teachers at Canyon have licenses continues to challenge my faith in our education system, and I would rather backflip into a deep fryer than show up for the town picnic or whatever."

"Wow." I fold my hands around my mug and raise both brows. "Do I get a drink with that crock of bullshit or should I use the coffee to wash it down?"

Jesse grins, ridiculously delighted by the swear word. He lowers his hands, folding them back on the table. "Any drink you want, Sour Patch."

My smile fades. I drop my eyes to the oil spots forming on the coffee's surface. "You turned *me* away."

It sits between us, a confession wrapped in thorns, too painful for either of us to touch. Had it not been for this curse, Jesse would have graduated from Canyon High without ever speaking more than a few words to me. He would have kept waking up early to cross the driveway and stayed sequestered on his side of the courtyard during lunch.

The waitress appears at our table just as Jesse opens his mouth. Though the dishes balanced on her shoulder teeter dangerously to the right, she swipes my empty carafe without pausing. "Refill?"

"No—"

"Yep!" I beam at her, and she winks before racing to the next table.

"Do you think my dad knew about Nadine?" I prop my chin on my fist as if we're in the middle of discussing the season finale of our favorite show. "Knew about her family?"

If Jesse is thrown by the sudden change in subject, he doesn't show it. "I doubt it."

"I think he knew. Why else would he refuse to talk about her family? He must have known. He must have. He let a murderer be my mother."

"Mansour..."

I wave him off, grappling for the strap of my backpack with the hand I'm not using to hold up my coffee. If I hear any concern in his voice, I'll lose it. Maybe I'm in shock or denial or a fugue state in between—I don't know, and I don't care. If he wants me to function, to keep swallowing the scream ringing inside me, then he needs to take his sympathy and drown it.

"Whatever is after me, it followed me from the Haikal villa." I draw out my mother's journal and slap it onto the table, directly next to a puddle of drying syrup.

The journal disappears before I can contemplate using it as a coaster. Jesse pulls it across the table, out of my mug's line of fire. Again, he wears an impassive expression, and I couldn't be more grateful for Jesse's disinclination to engage with any emotion that can't be worked out with his fists.

"You said this journal was blank before tonight?"

I follow the path of the rain trickling down the window. "Yup. I've combed through it a million times."

"So these entries appeared after you saw the shadow."

My gaze flies to Jesse and widens. I hadn't put the pieces together, but—"You think the shadows are linked to my mother's journal?"

A long exhale rattles out of Jesse. "It's one theory. Unless we contact your aunt, the journal is the only lead we have about breaking the curse."

I jerk as though I've been slapped. "Contacting Khalto Safa is out of the question." I try to imagine speaking to Khalto Safa knowing what I know, and a shudder runs through me. "She won't help me."

I reach for the journal, and Jesse doesn't resist when I draw it back across the table.

Inside the worn leather cover, my mother's name remains one of the few unchanged parts of the journal. I trace the letters, a bitter smile twisting my lips.

Nadine Haikal.

"Women rarely take their husband's last name in Masr," I tell Jesse. "It's not common practice. I never really thought much of it, her taking my dad's last name when they moved. I suppose I'm not surprised she wanted to leave Haikal behind."

I flip the page, turning to the first of three entries. It's two pages, and one of those pages is simply a list.

"Can you read it?" Jesse asks. I would bet every dollar in my pocket that if I glance up, I'll spot his hand hovering over his phone, ready to press open his translation app.

I sigh. "Yeah, but it's in rika'ah, so there's no tashkeel. It's harder to read without the grammatical support." No hamzas or kasras to help me out. My reading skills in Arabic are decent, but nowhere near sophisticated enough to read rika'ah with ease. Back when I was a kid, Baba and I would sit together every Saturday afternoon to work on my Arabic composition and grammar. I'd complain each time, because what do you mean I have to spend a chunk of my weekend reading about permanently down on his luck Goha and his donkey or trying to enunciate qaf and kaf? Now, I wish more than anything Baba had fought me harder when I turned thirteen and demanded to stop.

I fill my lungs with the scent of grease and burnt coffee, my nails digging into the laminated tabletop.

I already know the truth about her. It can't possibly be worse.

Clearing my throat, I begin to read.

AUGUST 17, 1977

The shadows keep following Safa.

Mama gets annoyed when I laugh, but it's hard to resist. They follow Safa to the store, to school, even to the shower. I'm laughing just thinking about it. Mama and I have tried to explain to her that the shadows will go away if she just stops looking at them, but Safa has always been so bullheaded. Wave a red flag, and she'll come running every time.

Mama thinks I need to be kinder to Safa. She says my sister holds grudges, and how I treat her now will determine how she treats me in the future.

I think she's just jealous that I fed the door the first sacrifice of the year. She thinks I cheat because I lure the children to the door instead of dragging them kicking and screaming like she does. No elegance to Safa's methods, and worse, it takes its toll on her. Why else would the shadows be hovering around, haunting her?

I wonder what she sees inside them.

The only shadow I've ever pulled was for Janna's mother, and it hasn't followed me since the day we found her body hanging outside. I see other ones lurking sometimes, but like Mama says—guide your eyes forward and point your feet straight, and they won't follow you. In her uncle's journal, he gives the shadows a bunch of names. A side effect. A tangle in time for every life we cut short. The stripped pieces of our soul for each child we feed to the door. Bla bla bla. If you ask me, they're just a bad aftertaste that needs to be spit out.

Anyway. Another doorwoman and her husband quit last week, and Mama hired a new couple this morning. The woman seems skittish, so I can already tell she's smarter than her husband, who's walking around like the only rooster in a hen house.

Let's see how long they last.

A tear lands on the faded blank ink and sinks into the page.

"They called the shadows side effects," I remark without looking up from the first page. "Do you think that means they're not necessarily part of the curse?"

Jesse considers. "Maybe. They seem more interested in scaring you than actually hurting you." To his credit, he picks up on my silent signal and doesn't address the tears collecting in the corners of my bloodshot eyes. "Plus, I don't see how it would benefit the curse to have these shadows hanging around, haunting the people in charge of keeping the curse alive."

I hear Mama in my head with crystal clarity, as though she's sitting beside me in the booth.

Everyone always underestimates guilt. They think fear is the fastest way to incentivize someone, but fear disappears when the danger does. Guilt... guilt never goes away. You can't undo time and fix your mistake. Guilt, ya eyun Mama, is a hole in the ground, and time is the shovel.

A shudder works through my shoulders, traveling to my knees. Mama died when I was nine—most of my memories of her have been worn away, the little details fading with each recollection.

This memory is pristine. Complete. It sits away from the others, as though its proximity might taint them.

"Mansour?"

I startle. Jesse leans forward, head tipped to the side as he scrutinizes my face. "You should go home. Sleep, eat—"

"She has around twenty or so time entries here," I interject, ignoring the absurd suggestion. How can I sleep when every shadow sends my heart plummeting to the ground? How can I force down a single bite? "Some of them are only a few minutes apart. Do you think she was keeping track of the shadows?" I shake my head. "She says they followed Khalto Safa a lot more than her. Why would she go hunting them herself?"

"She could have been trying to figure out their movements. When they come and go. How long they stay."

Why? I want to ask, snidely. *It isn't like she gave a damn about them or her little sister.*

Rage swells inside me, vaster and more unstable than any of its predecessors. It surges through my chest like a volcanic eruption. Reaching through time and space to devour my memories of Mama, burning through them with molten red fingers. In the ash, my mother's face appears as it had in the photo Jesse showed me. Cold and clinical.

A stranger.

The woman from my memories doesn't exist anymore. She never did. Nadine Mansour was a character, an actor reading lines from a script, and I was the only one who bought the act.

If only I could understand *why*. Why leave the villa and come to Ward if she had no issues with satisfying the demands of the creature? If she was so proud to be Nadine Haikal, why would she marry my father and become Nadine Mansour?

Why would she pretend to love me for nine years before going back?

Jesse raises placating hands. "We'll see what we can learn from the journal."

Appeased, I pull the carafe toward myself and pour a fresh round of murky black coffee. The bell over the door jingles, bringing in another blast of cold air. I lift the mug to my soon-to-be-frostbitten cheek.

"Mina?"

The mug jerks in my grip. Hot coffee spills onto my lapel, but I scarcely notice it.

Frozen next to our booth are Rainie, Aida, Alex, and Lucia.

I stare at them, stunned. Despite twenty-four hours of shadows and mortuaries and curses, somehow, their presence feels like the most unrealistic part of the entire ordeal. Figments of my imagination sprung straight out of my head and dropped in the middle of the morning rush at Grease & Grind.

"Well... this is a development." Rainie pushes bright purple strands from her eyes, cocking a hip. "So when you said you wanted to be left alone, you meant you wanted to be left alone by everyone except Future Inmate Number Twelve?"

Apparently, Jesse doesn't find insults as amusing coming from Rainie, because he raises a cold brow. He gives Rainie's tattered T-shirt and beige leather jacket a dismissive once-over. "You usually stop for breakfast after robbing a Hot Topic?"

Rainie opens her mouth, but Lucia wedges her elbow into Rainie's side. "Are you okay, Mina? You look... rough."

Her gentle concern pricks new tears in my eyes, and I wipe my nose with a napkin. Looking at Alex is out of the question; just having him this close risks unraveling me. "Just a long night, Luce."

Aida wraps her arms around her sketchpad, pressing it tight to her chest. She's studying Jesse with an intensity I've only seen her wear when she sketches.

Lucia fidgets with the bottom of her fuzzy cardigan. I would bet every hair on my head she's resisting the urge to pull me into a hug. "Well, we're going to be just over there, if you need anything."

Before Rainie can do more than curl her lip, Lucia ushers her away, Aida trailing behind them. Alex lingers by the table, and I force myself to look up. But his attention isn't on me—he's glaring at Jesse, pure murder glistening in his eyes.

"What did you do to her?" Alex growls.

Most people, when confronted with a fuming athlete slotted for D1 stardom, might take stock of the situation and decide it would be best to proceed carefully. Even if Alex couldn't win an outright fight against Jesse, he could cause some serious damage.

Jesse sets an elbow on the table, propping his temple against his fist. A lascivious smirk twists his full lips. "Nothing she didn't beg me for." It emerges low and husky, the meaning unmistakable. A flush of aggravation—and something else I refuse to examine closely—heats my skin.

Alex reddens. Before he can make a move toward Jesse, I catch his wrist, forcing his attention to me.

"There is nothing going on between me and Jesse. I promise you." I pray it isn't a wasted reassurance. It shouldn't be—I was Alex's girlfriend for three years. Surely that's earned me more credibility than the obvious jibe of a guy he doesn't even like.

Alex yanks out of my grasp. His glower burns me, loaded with a scorn I have never seen him aim in my direction. "Don't make any more promises, Mina. Haven't you broken enough?"

The waitress swerves out of Alex's path as he turns to storm away. He mutters an apology, polite even in his fury, and rounds the row of booths to the other side of the restaurant, where Rainie and the others have claimed our former Sunday table.

I knead the booth's cracked leather cushion to distract my hands from their urge to wrap around Jesse's throat. The current bane of my existence drops his chin on his open palm, watching me beneath infuriatingly long lashes, looking for all intents and purposes like I'm his favorite cable network and not ten seconds away from attacking him with a crusted ketchup bottle.

"You didn't have to do that," I say.

"True."

When my mask of rage refuses to crack, Jesse sighs, slumping back in his seat. "Don't be mad, Sour Patch. The guy just rubs me the wrong way."

"Awesome. With that C minus apology, I'm going to the bathroom," I snap. Hauling my backpack over my shoulder, I stride into the narrow hall behind the breakfast bar, where an abundance of thrift store artwork covers the yellowing wallpaper. Three doors face each other, dim beneath the single bulb dangling from a wire in the center of the ceiling. Two doors for the bathroom, and a glass door marked EMERGENCY EXIT: ALARM WILL RING at the very end.

Without a second's hesitation, I push the emergency door open and step outside. The only sound is the screech of the hinges fighting the door's weight. Grease & Grind hasn't fixed the emergency exit in years, not since a brawl broke out after our high school soccer team lost to Mount Shasta's.

I stride across the parking lot and onto the curb, where I come to a sudden stop. It hits me that I have nowhere to go. Baba should be at work right now, but it's entirely possible he'll take the day off to nurse his post-possession migraine. All of my friends are in the diner, probably dissecting me like a frog on a lab table.

The trees across the street rustle. A gray veil cloaks the sky over Ward, and through the lattice of clouds, a couple of watered-down rays of sunlight break through.

Beneath the trees, a shadow forms.

My chest ices over. The breath trapped between my teeth turns heavy, reshaping itself into a scream. I fix my gaze on the shadow, the instinct to run battling against the need to know what the shadow hides. If Jesse's theory is right, more of my mother's journal will reveal itself if I look into another shadow. If I let it manifest.

The street lays quiet. I can't bring myself to walk toward it.

But I know it'll come to me.

I close my eyes, and I wait. Mama's journal thumps like a heartbeat in the back of my head.

But it isn't a shadow that finds me.

A rough bag closes around my head, encasing me in darkness. Multiple arms haul me backward, and I only remember to struggle when the unmistakable shape of a car door bangs into my hip. I thrash, but it's too late—the door slams shut.

I don't stop struggling when the car screeches away, taking me with it.

CHAPTER THIRTEEN
PRESENT DAY

I roll around in the dark, my shoe connecting with a hard surface. "She's gonna break my car!" I hear a familiar voice complain. Aida.

"Mina, stop wiggling!" comes another voice. It's Lucia. "Ugh, I knew this was a bad idea."

"What other choice did we have? Talbot's hanging around her all the time now." My breath stutters. Alex.

"Well, what do you think he's gonna do when he finds out we kidnapped his girlfriend, smart guy?" The last voice, striking the perfect note between spite and boredom, can only be Rainie.

"She's not his—shut up, Rainie," Alex growls. "I'm not scared of him."

"We didn't have to put a tote bag over her head," Lucia continues. "Poor Mina. Your heart is beating so fast."

The screen over my vision lifts, and I blink until the shifting dots settle into Lucia's apologetic grimace. I'm strewn across her and Rainie's laps in the back seat of Aida's Honda Civic.

"Hi!" Lucia waves. "We're rescuing you."

"Rescuing me?" I struggle to sit up, and they release me, scooting until I sandwich myself between them. "From what?"

"I'm still pissed at you, but Talbot is a menace," Rainie says. "The hostage vibes you were giving off at the diner were hard to miss."

I gape. "There were no hostage vibes! Listen, you guys have got it all wrong."

The click of a seat belt comes from the front. Alex twists in his seat, angling his body into the back of the car. "Baby, please. We just want to talk. We're all really worried about you."

"I can't," I insist, but it's uncertain. Weak, just like my rapidly breaking resolve. Being around them is too addictive. Too long, and I might start to feel normal again. Like the old me, who never knew how blood tastes when it fills your mouth. How fear can grow so deep inside you it becomes almost boring, like a tumor you forget about until it's covered every surface it can reach.

Despite my protest, my resistance begins to drain. The familiarity of their presence, of sitting squeezed between them in the back of Aida's car while she breaks several traffic laws, settles me in a way nothing else can.

At least, until another smell replaces the scent of Aida's Vanillaroma tree freshener. One so faint, it's almost forgettable. It sneaks into my nose, metastasizes in my lungs.

Decay. Rancid, bloodcurdling decay.

It's here.

"You guys have to let me out. Let me out, please!" Can it possess someone if there's five of us in the car? I try to reach over Lucia to grab the door handle, but she bars my path, her arms clasping mine to my sides.

"Mina, it's okay!"

I think it's getting stronger.

What if it finds a way to possess everyone in the car at once?

I renew my struggles, but to what end? Aida is driving at her usual horrifying ninety miles an hour. Throwing myself out of the car would break more than my neck.

Lucia tries to cross my arms over my chest. "Mina, relax! We're just going to the drive-in theater. They're showing *Enchanted* tonight. You love *Enchanted*."

"I think she's having a panic attack," Rainie says, a hint of concern finally leaking into her voice. "Lucia, back off."

"Please, I have to go," I whimper.

Aida pulls to a stop in front of the ticket booth before Lucia can follow her sharp glance toward Rainie with an equally sharp retort.

Normal drive-in movie theaters don't open until six or seven in the evening, but thanks to Ward's suffocatingly dark winters, ours stays open around the clock. Aida drives past lawn chairs facing the giant plastic screen and honks at a couple trying to throw popcorn into each other's mouths.

As soon as she parks, everyone piles out of the car. Indecision holds me still. Spending time around my friends, even in public, flirts too close to danger for my taste. Jesse would surely disapprove. Even when he's reckless, he's smart about it.

There's nothing smart about testing the bounds of a curse while far away from the only person who can help me if it goes wrong.

"This wasn't my idea," Rainie says, startling me. The fading sunlight turns liquid in her eyes, a reddish tint reflecting off pools of hazel. "I suggested we just go for Talbot's car with a crowbar."

I groan, momentarily distracted. "Why do you hate him so much?" I ask. "You guys haven't even had an actual conversation."

Rainie blinks. "Who said I hate him? I think the guy's a hoot."

The sunlight in her eyes wavers, glimmering the faintest shade of orange.

I scramble backward, yanking open the door on the opposite side of the car. Rainie stares after me for a second, then shakes her head, as though waving away an errant thought. She emerges from the other side.

"C'mon, Mina. Sit." Lucia points at my usual seat, a lavender lawn chair with paisleys and pink-rimmed cupholders. "The movie's starting soon, and we need to talk."

The logical choice is clear. Break into a run and get the hell out of here. Call Jesse to pick me up and go wait for him somewhere crowded. Jesse, who's probably convinced I drowned in the toilet at Grease & Grind by now.

But logical isn't how I feel when Alex cups my face, thumbs sweeping over my cheekbones. "For me, Mina? Please?"

I swallow. Just a few minutes. A few minutes, and then I'll leave.

I let Alex guide me into the seat. My friends form a loose U in front of me, convening in a council of grim faces and crossed arms.

Of all people, it's Aida who breaks the silence. She folds herself into the chair to my right and asks, "So what's Jesse like?"

Anger steals across Alex's features. "He's a thug. You shouldn't be anywhere near a guy like him."

"Way to guarantee he's gonna be hotter than ever to her." Rainie shoulder checks Alex. "Jockstrap here has a point, Mina."

I can't blame them for coming down on Jesse. His reputation in Ward is well-earned, and he's done nothing to repair his image. "He's not a bad guy. Really," I add. "He's helping me figure some stuff out."

"The same stuff that's kept you away from us?" Lucia crouches next to my chair, her cardigan buttoned over a bumblebee sweater dress and knee-high winter boots. Earnest brown eyes peer up at me.

I rub the soft fabric of Lucia's sleeve and nod. "Exactly. Once I figure it out, I can come back. Things will go back to normal."

"What is this *stuff*, Mina?" Rainie drags her chair in front of mine and perches on the edge, elbows on her knees and fingers laced together like a detective across an interrogation table. "The sequence of events here doesn't make sense. You disappear for spring break without telling anyone where you're going, then you come home and basically tell us to go screw ourselves. What is going on with you?"

"And why do you think nobody but Jesse Talbot can help?" Alex adds.

They won't let this go. I need to give them something, or they'll just try again. This is the exact reason I was so harsh about pushing them away when I realized the curse had followed me from the Haikal villa—once they get the impression that I need their help, absolutely nothing in the world will dissuade them from trying to rescue me.

I flounder for a good lie and settle on a flimsy truth. "I'm . . . sick."

"Sick?" Lucia's eyes widen. "Sick how?"

"It's a kind of virus. Not contagious, necessarily, but still not super safe for me to be around people one on one. I spent spring break getting treated down in SF. Jesse is . . . he's immune, because he had it when he was a kid. He's helping me get better." Not a perfect explanation, but it covers enough that I'm simultaneously proud of myself and annoyed I didn't think of it sooner.

Rainie stares at me for a long beat. "That is such a load of—"

"Oh, Mina." Tears spill down Lucia's cheeks, and guilt stabs me straight through the chest.

"No, it's okay! Really. The virus will pass out of my system soon enough. I just don't want to risk any of you guys getting sick, and I knew if I told you the truth you'd never give me space."

"You got that right," Alex mutters.

"Please don't tell anyone. My dad doesn't know, and if the town catches whiff of this, they'll be knocking on our door at all hours of the day."

On the screen, the opening credits of the movie roll. I spot the attendants waving at people to shush and asking them to put their phones away. Mist curls between the scattered seats, drifting low over the grass. I pull my coat tighter around me, tucking my chin into my collar.

Alex, ever the rule-abiding golden boy, quiets down. "You're not making any sense. How can your dad not know?"

"I still don't see why you have to hang out with Jesse just because he's immune." Rainie shoots the attendant a dirty glare when he tries to shush her, and he quickly moves on.

"I'd say she traded up," Aida mumbles, and I make a mental note to figure out how long our quietest member has harbored a crush on Jesse.

The screen goes black. Two spotlights flicker to life on the edges of the field.

The camera pans out, and I sit ramrod straight in my chair. An image of a house appears where a cartoon Amy Adams should be.

The Haikal villa.

I raise a hand to my mouth as Khalto Safa appears on the second-floor balcony, a cigarette pressed between her red lips. She's young, twenty-six or twenty-seven. An older woman joins her on the balcony.

"Is she really coming?" Khalto Safa asks in Arabic. Ash drifts from the end of her lit cigarette, catching on the breeze. She and the old woman watch the street.

"So it seems," the woman clips. The frost in her eyes could revive the polar ice caps. "Is she bringing the brat?"

Khalto Safa laughs. "Hatem's brat? Of course not. When are you going to realize your precious Nadine is gone? Whoever drives through those gates is an imposter. I'm the only daughter you have left."

"Quiet," the woman—my grandmother—orders. "You still don't understand why it favors Nadine over you. Why Nadine's offerings were always accepted. Nadine sees everything, Safa. She sees the hearts that hurt from beating, the hands tired of lifting. The cleanest path to every end. She is meticulous. Crafty. You're a worthy attack dog, darling, but Nadine?" She smiles, the kind of smile a war commander wields over a battlefield littered with his fallen foes. "Nadine has always been a hunter."

Below, the gates creak open. Khalto Safa furiously stubs her cigarette on the ledge. "Your hunter has returned at last. Let's not keep her waiting."

Khalto Safa walks straight through my grandmother.

A shadow attaches itself to Khalto Safa's heels, trailing her as she ventures into the house.

The camera pans to the villa's entryway. I ignore my friends' outstretched hands as I lift myself from the chair. My mother is at the Haikal villa. My mother, who supposedly died in a car wreck in Tanta during this visit.

The woman stepping onto the Haikal property grounds resembles my mother in appearance alone. There's a hardness to her, a detachment, as though someone chiseled life into a statute. Her heels click against the granite steps, echoing between the peeling pillars.

At the top, she halts. A cold finger of dread traces along my neck.

"Bad girl." My mother tsks, her back to me. "You cheated."

Slowly, Nadine Mansour turns around. Except she's not Nadine Mansour. She's Nadine Haikal, a stranger.

And her eyes are a bright, glowing orange.

I trip over the chair, a cry tearing free from my frozen mouth. My mother watches me from the screen, head tilted in idle curiosity. Rot burns my nose, strong, so strong. How hadn't I noticed the scent growing?

It was toying with me. Distracting me while it gathered strength.

A shadow slinks across the grass, gliding over the lawn chairs.

"You don't belong here, little one," Nadine says. "Bad things happen to little ones here."

Ignoring the shouts, I break into a run. A crunch draws my gaze to the ground, and bile sticks in my throat at the sight of stark white bones protruding from the grass. Small, bloated gray hands jut from the dirt, scratching at my ankles.

The other shadow. It caught me.

Before I can reach the attendant's booth, the ground disappears under me. I plunge into the duck pond, water rushing into my mouth as I gasp.

Black sludge bubbles to the surface of the pond, bursting like pus from an open sore. I roll out of the pond, crying out when one of the small gray hands snags a lock of my hair.

"Yasmina, little Mina." Nadine's taunting voice follows me as I run, a childlike singsong ringing in the night. "Mama's waiting for you to run back home."

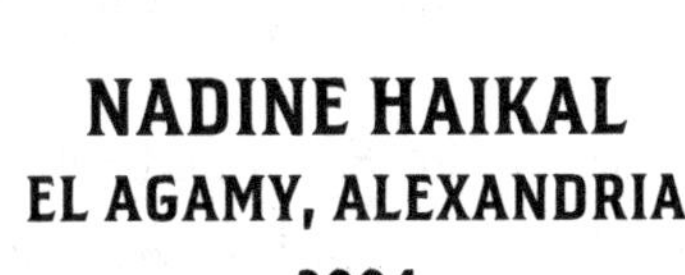

NADINE HAIKAL
EL AGAMY, ALEXANDRIA
2004

There was a child growing inside Nadine. Hatem's child.

Hatem didn't understand why she wouldn't leave El Agamy to live with him in his quaint loft by the University of Cairo. "I have plenty of space for you and baby," he had pleaded. "You won't need to go back to the villa again."

Nadine could never risk him learning the truth about her. About the Haikal family.

About the debts they owed.

Nadine turned in her bed, laying a palm over her flat belly. Soon, she'd begin to show. Her mother would be thrilled. A pregnant woman doesn't raise suspicion when she enters a daycare or school grounds. They could fulfill their quota early this year.

The only appealing part of using her pregnancy to bring home more offerings was how angry Safa would be. Safa was too lazy, too vicious. She didn't take the time to win the children's trust the way Nadine always did.

Nadine knew what would happen when this child entered the world. Her mother would lay the baby at the door. They would watch it wriggle in its blanket, waiting to see if the orange light would leak under the door's lip. If the light would spread over the infant, sending the Haikal women to the ground, or if it would leave the baby alone.

"It rejected your brother," Nadine's mother had shared one afternoon. Nonchalant. "We sent him off to live with my cousin in El Mansoura. The ones it rejects will never be strong enough to fulfill the debt. They only exist because of *our* strength. Their lives, their wealth, their comfort—it begins and ends here."

For the longest time, Nadine hadn't understood what that meant. She'd always known she had relatives all around Masr and the rest of the world. She'd been jealous of her brother, this mysterious sibling who had grown up without bloodying his hands in the Haikal family debt, but who unknowingly reaped all the benefits throughout his halcyon life.

It wasn't until Safa turned sixteen and failed to bring any children to the door for a full year that the truth had exploded out of Mama.

"If we fail, it isn't just us who pays the price. Every single member of Bamba's bloodline—people you've never even met, their children and grandchildren—will die."

Nadine studied the ceiling. This child would be half Hatem. Half the man with smudged glasses and perpetual ink stains under his nails. The man she thought she might love. But it would also be Nadine's offspring. A child born from the woman responsible for a third of the disappearances in western Alexandria.

Would it be worse for the child to be chosen and live out their life in the Haikal villa, wrapped in the luxury Bamba had secured with their lives? Or worse for them to be rejected and have their fate tossed into the hands of Haikals like Nadine and Safa?

Whatever happened, this child would not bear their burdens alone.

Nadine closed her eyes and dreamt about a curly-haired little girl with brown eyes and her father's wide, open smile.

CHAPTER FOURTEEN
PRESENT DAY

"The last four years we have spent at Canyon High have set the foundation for who we will become," I read. Jesse watches me pace from his perch on the train's platform, idly playing with the zipper on his jacket.

"Too passive," he calls out. "Also, corny."

I stop. Scowl, rereading the introduction. I pull the pen out of my hairband and make a note to rephrase.

The wind howls between the six abandoned shipping containers on the train tracks. The train holding them lies in front of a long row of warehouses, most of which have been empty since Ward's economic collapse in the eighties.

The train tracks are also the site of Ward's most notorious massacre. In 1997, six men highjacked a passenger train on these rails and slaughtered every single person onboard, including the conductor. As the story goes, the engine propelled the train past half a dozen towns before it finally rolled to a stop in Ward. They say on stormy nights, you can hear the train's phantom whistle, the hissing and screeching of the brakes grinding to their ultimate stop.

"Should I replace 'who we will become' with 'who we are'?" I tap the pen against my lip. Auditions for graduation speakers are next Wednesday, and so far, I hate every word I've written.

"If this is your revenge for my comment at the diner, consider it carried out successfully." Jesse hops to the ground. The stones beneath the tracks crunch under his boots. I think of child-sized bones sticking out of the earth and shudder. "You said you wanted me to show you how to fight."

"I also want you to help me with my speech. I can contain multitudes. A plethora of motives."

"A *plethora*, huh?" Jesse plucks the pen from my grip and flips it between his fingers. "Cuddling with your thesaurus again?"

My entire search history contains the phrase "synonym for—," but I scowl at Jesse anyway. "Are you calling me dumb?"

"No." He tucks the pen back into my hairband, and I momentarily freeze as his jacket brushes my arm, the heat of his body radiating across the diminishing space between us. "I'm calling you a maniac."

"The auditions are in a little over a week. I haven't even started practicing my delivery yet," I despair.

Jesse fixes himself into the path I've been pacing, leaving me no choice but to look up from the draft of my speech. His brows appear an inch away from disappearing into his hairline. "Sorry, did I hallucinate the conversation where you said that you were attacked less than twenty-four hours ago?"

"It wasn't technically an attack." The worst damage was to my sleep, which eluded me all night. Oh, and the utter destruction of my favorite pair of shoes, thanks to the mud in the duck pond.

Two new pages had appeared in my mother's journal, but they were useless. Just more random times and dates. At least it had confirmed Jesse's theory about the shadows somehow being connected to the journal. "Besides, I can't ask the graduation committee to give me an extension on account of my curse. Life goes on. I'm not losing any more of my senior year to this."

"Right, right. Can't lose your senior year, but you're just fine with losing your life."

I turn to leave. I've had my dose of browbeating for the next century thanks to Alex and the others. Jesse can mock me all he wants—I'm just not sticking around to catch the live act.

"Wait!" Jesse cuts in front of me, sending stones skidding into my ankles. "I'm not saying you shouldn't go on with your life. Just prioritize. This thing . . . Mansour, do you understand how much power it takes to do what it did at the drive-in theater? And this is the warm-up. If you don't focus, you're gonna have to read your speech from six feet under."

A few days ago, a line like that would've had me in tears. Now, I glare at Jesse, lips pursed.

"Alright." I tuck my paper and pen beneath one of the tracks. "Teach me to defend myself."

Jesse shrugs off his jacket and tosses it carelessly to the side. A long-sleeve thermal covers his arms, catching on the waistband of his jeans. "Put your dukes up, Sour Patch."

We circle each other. The wind ruffles Jesse's hair.

Compelled to break the rising tension, I ask, "Do you usually fight girls at creepy abandoned train tracks?"

"Nah, I'm a creepy warehouse sort of guy." Jesse crooks his fingers. "Swing at me."

I jab halfheartedly in his direction. He knocks my arm away with a flick. "Mansour."

"I'm trying." I jab again. The opportunity to pry into Jesse's life is much more compelling than hitting him. For now, anyway. "Seriously, though, Jesse. Where do you go to have fun? I've never seen you hanging out anywhere. Not at the drive-in or Don's Donuts or any of the festivals."

Jesse moves in a swift strike, wrapping an arm around my waist and cutting my feet out from under me. I shriek as I careen backward, grabbing handfuls of his thermal. His arm tightens, keeping my back from hitting the rocks. "Definitely not Don's Donuts," he says, his face heart-stoppingly close to mine. My breath stutters. Every thought in my head temporarily offloads to make room for just one.

He's so ridiculously pretty.

I smack at his chest until he straightens, setting me back on my feet.

"It's not going to work," I huff, dusting off my blouse. I'm wearing black leggings under white shorts and a pink peplum blouse. An outfit more fitting for a trip to the mall than a haunted train track.

"What?"

"You're trying to piss me off so I won't ask questions. It's your pattern."

Jesse blinks, nonplussed. I punch his shoulder. "Point."

"Point," he concedes. He lifts a brow, an action of his I've come to associate with the need to proceed with extreme caution. All of Jesse's limited range of emotion is contained in that arched brow. "Paying attention to my patterns, are you?"

"You might be out of practice, but there's this social phenomenon where you notice things about people you spend time around." I extract a strand of hair from my mouth, keeping a close eye on Jesse's hips. It might bruise his ego to hear it, but sparring isn't much different than dancing. The body always has a tell, and Jesse's lies in his sharp, narrow hips.

"Oh yeah?" Rocks crunch under Jesse's boots. The energy between us shifts, so subtly it takes me a full minute to notice. "Or are you collecting gossip on the school freak to carry back to your friends?"

I frown, lowering my fists. "Of course not." I kick a pebble at his shin.

"Besides, if I was going to gossip about you, I'd start with your abysmal taste in T-shirts."

Jesse laughs. A startlingly rich sound. Momentarily dumbfounded, I realize I've never heard Jesse laugh before. Not a real laugh, anyway. It seems to surprise him, too, and he schools his features quickly.

"Since my personal life is keeping you up at night..." He braces his hips, and I lift my arms just in time to block his swing. "My dad needs a lot of help around the mortuary. Between the small matter of being soulless and the dead bodies, I don't have a whole ton of time for fun." He lifts a shoulder, as though he didn't just utter one of the saddest sentences I've ever heard.

The setting sun spears through the clouds. Gold glints off the landscape of metal around us. A gust of air hits the train with a mournful rattle.

A shadow moves behind one of the train's windows, and my heart leaps into my throat. I watch for a face to form behind the glass or bloody fingers to press to the cracked pane. But the clouds converge again, casting the train in gray.

"Did they ever catch them?" I murmur, unable to tear my attention from the window.

"Who?"

"The people who did it. The murderers."

Jesse glances at the train. "Two of them. Nabbed them trying to pawn some of the stolen jewelry. But the leader was never found."

A horrible thought claws forward, born from the abyss in the human brain that collects the ugliest and scariest parts of reality. The crater where our fears leak out at night, conjuring killers in every creak and demons in the dark.

"What if they're still in there?"

Jesse drifts closer to me. Worry tightens his mouth. "Hey, are you alright?"

"What if their souls are trapped, Jesse?" I stare at the window until my eyes burn. "What if the passengers never left?"

And then they come, a battalion of terrors marching into truth, pulling me under. *What if my mother never left the house, what if I never left the house, what if I'm still there and it's toying with me, letting me die slowly behind that door in a room of crawling walls while my reality rots into dreams, and it's feeding on me as I die, savoring me like a meal it's been denied for too long—*

My entire body jerks. The door. The door, the door, *the door—*

Cold hands frame my face, easing my gaze away from the train. I become aware of Jesse's thumbs sliding over my cheeks, catching stray tears.

"Hey, look at me." Dark eyes bore into mine. "You're okay. You're safe."

I take a deep breath, filling my lungs with the icy burn. I focus on the feel of Jesse's hands, firm and unyielding. A frost has invaded deep behind my ribs, consuming every molecule of warmth inside me.

Jesse's breath brushes my ear, drifting against the crook of my neck. "Think of something good."

Nothing is good. Nothing has been good in so long. Except...

"My dad... he tried to make me French toast this morning," I whisper.

"Tell me about it."

"I do most of the cooking at our house. Even before my mom died, I was the one who made sure he was eating and taking his blood pressure meds. But then I stopped nagging him a few weeks ago, and I think he's convinced himself that I got fed up with him for being so absent. So scattered." The fugue of dread lifts from me, inch by inch. "I came downstairs after he left for work today, and the smoke alarm was in the sink. Breadcrumbs and milk *everywhere*. But there on the counter was a perfect plate of French toast and a bottle of sugar-free maple syrup. He always uses black molasses honey, so I knew the syrup was for me. After I ate, I went to clean up and throw away the napkin. I found ten pieces of burned toast in the trash." My voice hitches. "He emptied our bread drawer trying to make me French toast."

Jesse tips my chin up. "This isn't forever, Sour Patch. We're going to crack this. Your dad will still be there when we do."

When my breath stabilizes, he pulls away, raking his hair against the breeze. My cheeks warm. Another Mina Mansour breakdown, served farm fresh and ready.

Jesse clears his throat and resumes his fighting stance. "Have you given any more thought to getting in contact with your aunt?" He gestures for me to put my fists back up.

"Absolutely not."

"Why do you turn green every time I ask about your aunt? What happened at the end of your trip? When you got to the villa." Jesse blocks my weak blow, shoving a finger into my shoulder. "Point."

I kick at him, only for him to hook his foot under my knee and yank. I fall onto my side, landing on a pile of pebbles. "Hey!"

Jesse looms over me, a dark silhouette against the tumultuous sky. "A toddler could lay you out. Hit me like you mean it. I can take it." A private smile plays at the corner of his lips. "And answer my question."

Pushing back to my feet, I snap, "You sure are making a lot of demands." My punch manages to graze his arm.

When I swing, Jesse catches my wrist, drawing me to him. I cage my breath when my chest bumps into his, my wrist still held fast in his grip. This close, every beautiful shade of brown in his eyes comes to life. Layers of sunshine and honey swirling in the gaze of a boy who would hate to hear what I had just thought about his eyes.

"Finish your story," he murmurs. He studies me, his lips close enough for his breath to brush my forehead. Once again, my heart performs a complicated flip in my chest and misses the landing, plummeting straight to my feet.

He shouldn't be looking at me like that.

I use the leverage to drive my fist into his solar plexus. Jesse releases me with a grunt, and I finally smile.

"Fine." Last I left off, Khaltò Safa and I had just arrived at the Haikal villa in El Agamy. "Strange things kept—"

YASMINA MANSOUR
EL AGAMY, ALEXANDRIA
ONE MONTH AGO

Strange things kept happening on the Haikal estate.

They started small. A mascara wand going missing from the dresser drawer. A pile of cobwebs on a pillow I'd dusted hours earlier. At exactly four in the morning, a bunch of crows perched in the date trees would start to scream. In the streets, the stray animals would join the call, dogs howling and cats shrieking. I didn't know how anyone could sleep through the din.

The house itself existed in a state of suspended disintegration. Doors creaking on their hinges; an ecosystem of spiderwebs stretching over arches and in every high crevice; slanted tiles shifting beneath my feet. Every banister leaned dangerously to the side, as though aiming to separate itself from the stairs it supported.

"Try not to leave your room at night," Khalto Safa said, stirring sugar into her tiny cup of Turkish coffee. Doing so ruined the pretty foam layer I'd watched the housekeeper spend five minutes developing, but I stayed silent, picking at the surface of the kitchen table. The housekeeper's young daughter clung to her mother's ankle and stared at me. "Parts of the villa are very old, and I don't want you wandering somewhere unsafe."

"Which parts?"

Before she could answer, her phone lit up with a call. She licked the spoon and set it next to her coffee. "I'll be right back."

As soon as my aunt left, the housekeeper yanked her daughter off the floor. "I told you never to come into this house," she scolded. "Go to your father."

The girl burst into tears and scampered out the back door. The woman avoided my gaze, pouring boiling water into a tea glass.

I chuckled uneasily. "I guess *you* know where the unsafe parts of the house are."

The kettle jerked, sending water splashing on her abaya. She ignored it, whirling to face me. "You speak Arabic?"

I blinked. "Yes, of course. If you're feeling generous, you might even call me fluent." When she didn't laugh, I awkwardly pressed on. "I've just been speaking English because Khalto Safa seems to prefer it. I'm Nadine's daughter. Mina. Sorry, I didn't catch your name."

The housekeeper materialized at my side in an instant. A hot hand covered my elbow. "Run. Get a car in town and don't look back. There is nothing safe in this villa."

I laughed again, expecting her to join me, but she was dead serious. Her horror-stricken eyes fixed on mine.

"My husband will get you out. How—" She glanced through the door, but my aunt's voice was still far away. "How old are you?"

"Seventeen?"

"Has she tried to take you to the third floor yet?"

Apprehension skittered down my spine. I pulled away from the woman, backing away from the table. "What third floor?" The house ended on the second level.

She clutched her chest, a spasm of pure terror shaking her frame. Terror for *me.*

"Your mother ran away from this house for a reason. You should never have come here."

Khalto Safa's return abruptly ended the conversation. The woman sprang to the counter, stacking our breakfast onto a gilded tray with trembling hands.

"What's wrong?" Khalto Safa asked. I was still standing. "Hamida, what is it?"

"Nothing, ya doctura." The tea glasses shook in the woman's hand. Her fear was real. Fear of Khalto Safa, fear for her daughter. Misplaced as it might be, I couldn't help but be rattled by it.

I reclaimed my chair. "Nothing."

Khalto Safa and the housekeeper's warnings spun in my head later that night. Sleep refused to come, and every attempt at a distraction failed miserably. The wi-fi signal barely reached this bedroom.

I'd left the window cracked to air out the musty smell of the furniture. I moved to close it and reconsidered. Khalto Safa had said I couldn't explore the *villa* at night, but my room was fair game, wasn't it?

I rifled through the dresser and nightstand, unfolding old receipts and compiling a stack of stray buttons. Not exactly hidden treasure, but it beat staring at the ceiling and counting sheep. I stuck my arm under the bed, sweeping my palm across the dusty floor.

A sharp, flimsy object collided with my hand.

Delighted, I pulled it out from under the bed, sitting on my haunches to evaluate my new prize. A plastic tiara. Coated in a fine layer of dust, a band of pink fuzz went around the tiara's edge, and fake gemstones bedazzled the crown's arches. Someone's kid must have forgotten it. One of my cousins, maybe?

In the mirror, I fixed the tiara over my hair. The curls bunched up under the tiara's forked teeth, stretching the band to its breaking point.

Bored again, I roamed the room. If I would be staying up anyway, I might as well watch the sunrise from one of the balconies on the northern side of the villa. Technically, it wouldn't be breaking Khalto Safa's rule. I wasn't planning to wander, just walk in a straight line to the balcony.

I shut the door behind me as quietly as possible. From our travels, I knew Khalto Safa slept lightly.

The second floor of the Haikal villa could swallow my house in Ward three times over. I knew my bedroom was on the garden side and the balconies were on the pool side, but I hadn't considered how tough it might be navigating a villa in the dark. I crept past a sparkling clean kitchenette, dragging a hand along the wall for balance. At this rate, the sun would be fully risen by the time I reached the balcony.

I mentally smacked myself for leaving my phone on the nightstand. I could have used the flashlight to guide my path.

Another ten minutes of wandering later, and I was still winding up in one of the ten million seating areas scattered throughout the second floor. I leaned my forehead against the wall, releasing a sigh as I accepted the inevitable. Maybe the sunrise would be better from my window. Besides, there were a ton of mosquitoes on the balcony, and what if I encountered the creature those birds and animals howled at every night?

I trudged back to my room in defeat. Halfway there, my foot met hard resistance, nearly hurtling me to the ground. I cried out, stumbling against the blast of pain in my toe. I landed on my knee and clutched a wrought iron baluster for balance.

As soon as the pain cleared, bewilderment followed. How did I get to the stairs? I was almost certain I'd been walking straight, and the stairs leading to the bottom floor were to the left of my room.

In the gloom, long windows took shape beneath the high ceiling. Twisting intricate patterns crisscrossed the stained glass. Those windows . . . I had seen them when I'd entered the property, but I hadn't come across them until now. The first hints of dawn seeped through, tinting the walls a soft orange. The light spilled onto a set of spiral marble steps.

I stopped breathing. These stairs hadn't been here before.

With an uncomfortable jolt, I realized I was still kneeling. My throbbing toe forgotten, I rose.

Before me, a set of spiral steps emerged from the wall.

My muscles relaxed as a wave of tranquility washed over me. Every bit of alarm faded, suffocating beneath a heavy quilt of calm.

Mesmerized, I took one step up, then another. I wanted to see what was at the end of the stairs. I *needed* to see.

A door appeared at the top of the stairs. Unlike the rest of the mansion, it retained its pristine condition. Gold hinges hung on the gleaming white door, matching the interwoven gold patterns crossing vertically down its center. Playful accenting danced on the carved panels on each side.

With a dizzying sort of clarity, I understood that this door was ancient. Older than the pyramids I'd climbed. Older than Stonehenge, the tombs in France, the temples in Turkey.

Only three steps separated me from the door. The smooth surface was missing a handle, but I knew it would open. If I stood close, if I touched it, the door would open for me.

A ball hit me square in the back.

I blinked, tearing my gaze away from the door. A Barbie head landed on the ground next to me. At the foot of the stairs, watching me with stricken eyes, was the housekeeper's daughter.

Before I could move toward her, the ground dipped. I keeled to the side, grabbing the banister for support—but it was gone. The stairs, the baluster, the door. Vanished.

I looked up to find myself kneeling on flat carpet, surrounded by couches shrouded in gray sheets. My palms facing up on my thighs.

"Yasmina! What are you doing?" Khalto Safa's voice slapped me harder than a physical blow.

I shook my head, trying to clear the strange fog that had descended over me. "I was trying to find the balcony. I wanted . . . I think I wanted to see the sunrise."

Wasn't I looking for someone? I had the vaguest memory of a child, but the harder I tried to chase it, the faster it fled.

"The sun rose an hour ago," Khalto Safa said. "I told you, don't wander the house at night without me. I'll take you where you need to go myself." She lit a cigarette, tightening her robe around her slim figure. I used the wall to pull myself upright. A sharp pain in my toe pierced the haze. Why did my toe hurt?

The orange tip of Khalto Safa's cigarette bobbed between her lips. "Where did you get that?" She was staring at my tiara. A strange, wild light brightened her eyes.

"Uh, I found it. Under my bed." I extracted the prongs from my curls and held the tiara toward Khalto Safa. "Sorry, do you know who this belongs to?"

Dark satisfaction wove around Khalto Safa. With the hand holding the cigarette, she pushed the tiara back. "Consider it yours."

CHAPTER FIFTEEN
PRESENT DAY

The trees sway toward the empty highway, forming dark parentheses on either side of my car. Clouds swirl overhead, thinning the farther I get from the center of town. The university sits at the westernmost border of Ward, only a hundred yards or so from crossing into the next town over.

I eye the leaning trees. No way those trunks are structurally sound. It looks like a single ambitious squirrel could break most of them in half. I can't imagine how Baba drives on this highway at night, nothing but his headlights to spear through the dark of the surrounding woods. It's only late afternoon, and I already want to turn on my high beams.

Tightening my hands around the wheel, I resist the urge to make an illegal U-turn in the middle of this highway. I've only visited Baba on campus once before, when me and Mama surprised him with a cake on his one-year anniversary as an associate professor. I remember being eight years old and struggling to choke down my giggles while we waited for him in his office. How Baba had laughed when he saw us and swung me into his arms, proceeding to introduce me to his colleagues as "the secret boss." Mama cut the cake and passed plates around to his co-workers. The three of us went to eat in the courtyard while I daydreamed about enrolling at Baba's university and seeing him all the time.

I park in a garage not far from the campus library and switch off the engine. A headache stirs to life between my temples.

After our meeting at the train tracks, Jesse had gone off with Mama's journal to see if he could decipher the lists of numbers. I'd told him I was going home to work on my speech a little more. If I had mentioned my plan to visit Baba on the edge of town, he would have insisted on tagging along. And if I had added that I plan to confront my father about his marriage to a serial killer, he would have slashed my tires and stolen my keys.

The last thing I need before this conversation is another distraction, and Jesse . . . Jesse is one hell of a distraction.

I close the car door behind me, flinching at the echo in the parking garage. I made the right choice leaving Jesse behind. He brings out a side of me I don't recognize; someone who doesn't think through her words ten times before she speaks or constantly shift her presence to accommodate someone else's. Someone who can be brash and irritable and snide, who probably would never have been voted homecoming queen.

The worst part is that I think she might be the version of me I like the best.

An ache blooms through me as I cross campus. Kids my age lounge on blankets laid out on the grass. The campus bookstore bursts with harried students, their coffees angled in the crooks of busy arms while they toss cookies and scantrons into their basket. Someone passes me a flyer as I head toward a row of booths lined up on either side of the walkway. Flyers and stickers are shoved into the hands of the students scurrying to the other side.

If this curse wins, I will never be a college student. I'll never enroll here, never major in something practical so I can guiltlessly minor in Performance Arts.

I'll never . . . *be*. Right now, I feel like the first draft of my graduation speech: strong foundation with lots of room for improvement. The beauty comes later—in the first revision, the second, the third. The person I've dreamt about being lives in one of those revisions, and the thought of never meeting her fills me with a nameless grief.

I dodge a guy on his scooter. He throws an apology over his shoulder, and I shake myself off. The curse won't win. We're making progress, Jesse and I. We have a plan.

According to our shared location tracker, Baba is in the library. I walk past the sliding doors and shiver at the blast of unnecessary air-conditioning.

A pretty older woman with silvering hair and a pair of square glasses perks up at the circulation desk.

"Do you know where I can find Professor Mansour?" I ask.

Her forehead furrows. "Oh, um, his office is—"

"No, not his office. I think he's somewhere in the library, but it might take a while to check three floors."

"Are you one of his students?"

"I'm his daughter."

She brightens instantly. "Oh, hello! It's so nice to meet you, Mina." When I blink, she hurries to explain. "Sorry—Hatem speaks about you so much, it feels like I already know you."

I offer her a smile and wonder if perhaps it isn't the books drawing my father into the library for hours every day.

She sticks out her hand. "I'm Noura."

I shake Noura's hand and try to push aside a thought that's both comforting and awful.

At least he won't be alone if I die.

Noura leads me across the library floor, dodging stray book carts and chairs like an obstacle course she's practiced to perfection. "Hatem comes in between his classes to work on his research. The professors in the rooms next to him always hold their office hours while he's trying to focus, so he avoids the noise here."

Definitely not the books.

"Mm-hm."

We climb the stairs to the second floor, past shelves full of weathered books with cracked canvas spines, their titles too niche and grandiose to invite much traffic. The farther we go, the dustier the shelves become, until we find Baba at the single table wedged between the emergency exit and the last shelf, a bottle of water at his elbow and an explosion of papers around him. His glasses sit backward on his hair, the rounded ends curving against his earlobes instead of around them. At some point, he'd touched his face with inky fingertips, smearing a constellation of ink across his cheeks.

Tears spring to my eyes, proving the other reason I couldn't bring Jesse along.

My father destroys me. He has always been terribly, desperately human. Mama was larger than life. Someone who could walk into a disaster and neutralize it without skipping a beat. I never worried about her, never wondered if she'd remembered to eat dinner or refill her prescriptions.

I don't know when loving Baba started to feel like I was holding my breath, waiting for the universe to give me permission to exhale.

He glances up, a ready smile at his face, and visibly startles at the sight of me. "Mina!" He shoves his chair back. It slams into the shelf, and he struggles to stand in the tight crevice. He switches to Arabic, a clear sign he's panicked. "What is it? Are you okay?"

"I'm fine, Baba," I say, amused and a little sad. He would've been less surprised if someone showed up at his table with a hunting rifle. I'm an intrusion in this slice of life he's carved without me.

The seed of a headache from earlier has grown, and I hide my grimace before Baba can see it and call 911. His reactions to my pain have ranged from staying up all night to check my breathing after I coughed a few times at dinner to blasting through ten stoplights to get to the ER because

I threw up chunky blood (also known as Twizzlers, six packs of which I'd snuck to my room and devoured at the ripe age of ten).

"Can you take a quick walk with me?" I ask Baba.

He glances at his mess of papers and then at Noura, who waves away his concern. "Just leave it, Hatem. I don't mind, and no one else is coming back here."

With Noura's blessing, Baba follows me out of the silo of shelves. We go down the stairs without speaking, and only when we've stepped out of the library and into the quad does he break the silence.

"Let's get you something to eat," Baba says.

I open my mouth to protest and think better of it. He's tapping his loafer and glancing over my head, clearly excited to show me to a food spot nearby. This campus is his home. He spends far more time inside these buildings than under the roof we'd once shared with Mama. Here, he's not Hatem Mansour, widow and single father. He is Professor Mansour, a man with a crush on a nice librarian and research that keeps his days busy.

As angry as I am, I can't bring myself to ruin it for him. I want him to think of me here. When he does, I want him to remember it warmly.

"Sure."

Baba tugs on the sleeves of his blazer while we meander across campus and clears his throat. A bittersweet fondness tugs in my chest. Serious conversations have never been Baba's strong suit.

Students shuffle around us, headphones on and gazes aimed at the ground. Laughter rings in the distance, sweetening the air.

"Why have you never taken me to Masr?"

The setting sun breaks through the clouds just in time to illuminate Baba's features slackening in surprise. Years have passed since the last time I asked him this question.

"You were busy with school and your friends. Your dance team." He looks away. "I didn't want to disrupt your plans."

In one burst of light, the lamps across campus flicker on.

And behind every person we pass, a shadow appears.

Regular shadows. Normal, physics-approved shadows.

I tear my gaze away and stop walking. "Or you didn't want me to find out you married a monster."

Baba also stops, turning to face me. He crosses his arms over his chest. "Excuse me?"

I had a plan. I was going to wait until we were seated somewhere private, ask him how his day was going, and *then* demand to know why he'd made vows to a serial killer. "She was in the news, Baba. They'd investigated her family for *decades*." I shake my head, disgust warring with anger. "You married Nadine Haikal knowing exactly who she really was."

When I say Mama's maiden name, Baba jerks as though I've shot him. Horror fills his brown eyes to the brim and overflows.

"Yasmina. What did you do?"

I threw my arms out. "I did *something*, Baba! I didn't just hide myself in books and libraries and pretend everything was fine! I knew Mama's death wasn't normal. I knew someone was lying to me, but I never expected—" My voice breaks. "I never expected that person to be *you*."

"What. Did. You. Do?" In two strides, Baba is in front of me, hands on my shoulders. "Tell me!"

The force of his anguish clamps my jaw shut. If I tell him I snuck off for two weeks and met Khalto Safa, he might actually suffer some kind of collapse.

"Just random research, Baba. I found articles about El Agamy and saw Mama's picture in one of them."

Relief floods Baba, and his hold on my shoulders turns gentle, apologetic. He sighs. "I'm sorry, Mina. I can't imagine what kind of shock that must have been for you."

Guilt forms brambles in my throat. "I just want to know why you didn't tell me the truth about her. About her family. Are they why you wouldn't take me to visit Masr?"

Baba drops his hands to his sides and glances around, his ever-present worry of drawing attention overtaking every other concern. He gestures for me to resume our walk toward the food truck. "None of the garbage you read is true. Your mother's family just had a bad reputation, and they didn't treat her well. She barely escaped that house."

His watch gleams as he scratches the prickly hairs along his jaw. "My family didn't believe Nadine. They thought she would ruin me. They actually tried to have her arrested the first time I brought her home."

At my raised brows, he adds, "Reputation means a lot to families in Al Qalyubia. It doesn't help that some of them—my family included—tend to be on the superstitious side. They keep track of news from other small towns, like the ones in El Agamy, and the Haikal family had been on their radar for a while. At best, Nadine and her family were victims of a terrible curse. At worst, they were legacy murderers. Neither possibility really appealed to my parents."

I couldn't remember the last time I heard my father speak so much in a single turn. I didn't dare breathe, confident he'd clamp up if I did.

"They forbade me from marrying her. When I ignored them, they disowned me. Well, not in the sense they do here, with legal paperwork and the like. They said—do you remember what ghudub means?"

"Disappointment?"

"In a sense, but stronger. When you have incurred a parent's ghudub, you've basically broken their hearts and forsaken yourself as their child. After I married your mom, they didn't want to see me anymore. Your mom's family hated her for leaving the villa. When we realized you were on your way into the world, we wanted a fresh start. A new beginning."

We reach the end of the short line for the burrito truck, and Baba lowers his voice. "When you were nine, your mom started . . . seeing things. Hearing voices. She would be doing small tasks, unloading the dishwasher or sorting the mail, and go stiff with fear. I tried to get her to talk to someone. Our insurance covers therapy, but she refused. Then one day, I woke up to a note at the bedside table that she'd gone on a trip to El Agamy and would be back soon."

When we reach the window of the truck, Baba orders without pause, a rare confidence shining in his voice. I listen to him with a small smile. Maybe this is where Baba's true self hides: in the small traditions he deems sacred, the routines he follows without fail.

I wonder if my mother was the greatest risk of his life, and now he does not remember how to play it anything other than safe.

We go off to the side to wait for our orders. The gravity of our conversation seems ill-suited to the cheerfulness of the colorful truck and the smell of grilled chicken and steak.

"Did they know about me?" My voice is small, the question emerging from a wounded place I'd nearly forgotten about.

"Who?"

"Your family."

"No, ya noor eyni. They didn't know about you." A sheen passes over Baba's eyes, and in another light, I might think they were tears. "How could anyone know you without loving you?"

Damn it. Damn it and *damn him.*

Baba pulls me into his arms when I start to cry.

"I didn't want to take you to Masr because I was a coward. Not because of you. Never because of you," he says fiercely. "You are my proudest achievement, Mina. The best part of my life. I didn't want to risk them hurting you with their rejection. I didn't know what I would find if I tried to get in contact with them, and I was too scared to try. You're braver than I've ever been."

His fingers tighten around my shoulders. "And your mother's family is dangerous. They have connections everywhere. They'll do anything to get their way—bribe, threaten, and worse. Your mother and I were worried they'd track us down if we brought you for a visit."

Our order number is called, but Baba doesn't budge. "None of that is an excuse. After you graduate, I'll take you to Masr. We'll spend the entire summer there, and we'll make it a tradition to go visit during your school breaks. I'll show you the beautiful country you come from."

For so long, I dreamed of Baba offering to share Masr with me. Of us taking summer trips to Masr the way the Ahmads did, of having little stories, anecdotes, and memories that could form a bridge between my two worlds.

If only he had tried earlier.

If only he wasn't too late.

I pull away from Baba, dragging my sleeve over my face. A blotch stains his button-down in a display of false advertising from my waterproof mascara. "They called our order."

Shooting me another concerned glance, Baba approaches the truck. While he grabs the grease-stained paper bag, I collect myself. The headache from earlier has only gotten worse, and it won't help if I dehydrate myself by crying out every ounce of liquid in my body.

Baba leads me to one of the tables behind the food truck and settles down, handing me my spicy chicken burrito along with a cluster of napkins and a Dr Pepper.

"Did you know you have eight middle names?" He takes a giant bite out of his carne asada burrito, squeezing sour cream all over his fingers.

"Eight? Seriously?"

"Well, they're not on your birth certificate, but you should know them." He wipes his mouth. "Masriyeen—and probably other North Africans and Arabs—kept excellent record of family lineages. For the longest time, the best way to do that was with certain naming conventions.

So my full name is Hatem Galal Hani Omar Kareem Gad Gabar Afifi Mansour. My father's name was Galal Hani Omar Kareem Gad Gabar Afifi Mansour, and his father's name was Hani Omar Kareem Gad Gabar Afifi Mansour, and so on."

I peel the foil off my burrito and try not to show my giddiness. Perhaps it's silly to think that my eagerness could cause Baba to shut off again, but I have plenty of experiences that say otherwise.

"So my full name is Yasmina Hatem Galal Hani Omar Kareem Gad Gabar Afifi Mansour?"

Baba beams. "Exactly. Now, your Gedo Galal might not be my biggest fan anymore, but when I was growing up, he taught me everything I know about books. When I was twelve, he took me to the Ma'rad il Kitab in Cairo—they call it the Cairo International Book Fair nowadays, and I want to take you to it next January—and I bought the biggest book on beetles I could find."

"Beetles? Seriously?"

He laughs. "Seriously."

We eat our burritos in the sun's fading glow, and for a few blissful hours, there are no shadows between Baba and me.

CHAPTER SIXTEEN
PRESENT DAY

I have never had to pee so badly in my life.

The class goes quiet when I raise my hand, and I try not to fidget. I haven't made a peep in class in almost a month. "Yes, Mina?" Mr. Frank asks, a hopeful note in his voice.

"May I use the restroom, please?"

"Oh. Yes, certainly. Take the key with you."

I shoot out of the room, the key-shaped bathroom pass clutched in my sweaty palm. The huge copper key barely fits in my pocket. Mr. Frank made it unwieldy to discourage students from trying to steal and copy it. Mr. Hale, the hall monitor on duty this week, despises his job and despises anyone who makes it even a smidgen harder for him.

The school has four levels, with the administrative offices occupying the first floor. The third level has been under construction for over a year, mainly due to Canyon High's abysmal lack of funding. It remains off-limits to students, but the warning sign hasn't stopped anyone. Thanks to Rainie's graphic description of what eating freezer-burned sushi did to her, I know for a fact the plumbing works up there.

The third level is also my best shot of not running into anyone in the bathroom.

I rush up the stairs. Traffic cones block the top step, and a sign taped to the wall cautions me away. I crane my neck to check for any faculty members on my heels before I skirt the cones.

The area behind the cones unfolds into a colossal health hazard. Stacks of wooden planks line walls riddled with black scratch marks. Flakes of white powder drift from the rim of abandoned paint buckets. The rooms have been boarded shut. I grin at Rainie's initials carved into the board on my right.

At the far end of the hall, a blue tarp hangs over the unused stairs to the fourth floor. Beneath the tarp, a pair of work boots tap against the unfinished tiles.

I roll my eyes. Of course he'd be here. He hasn't picked up my calls since yesterday.

Though I'm about as silent as a drunk raccoon as I make my way around the obstacle course of nails, tools, and boxes littering the floor, Jesse's boots don't budge an inch. I could be a teacher coming to catch him in the act, for all he knows.

What is his central nervous system made of? Steel and sarcasm?

I pull the tarp aside and immediately start coughing as smoke envelops me.

"Fancy seeing you here." Jesse exhales plumes of gray. I stare at the small pile of ash by his elbow.

The ghost of Khalto Safa rises in the smoke, her red nails tapping the ash from the end of her cigarette.

"You smoke?" The wisps of white curling from his nose trouble me. Baba might not be the most attentive father in the world, but he'd certainly know if I started smoking. He'd at least *smell* it. "Does your dad know?"

The look Jesse offers can only be described as insulting. "Sure, Mansour. He buys me a pack from the gas station every day."

I purse my lips, wishing I had a better gauge on sarcasm. I never used to think my struggle to detect it was a problem, even though Rainie would always tease me about being too earnest. *You're so painfully sincere, Eenie Meenie Mina. It makes you easy to trust, but also easy to prank.*

I snatch the pack of cigarettes by his backpack and give it a shake. "Your dad does *not* buy you cigarettes."

A smile stretches around the cigarette dangling between his lips, and I loathe the shiver that runs through me at the sight. "You got me, Sour Patch."

Jesse leans back against the stairs. He flicks the cigarette to the tile, twisting his boot over the lit end.

Mastering the art of minding my own business continues to prove impossible. "How long have you smoked?"

I am well aware that the last thing Jesse wants is to be interrogated on his life choices. In the best of circumstances, people think I'm too much—too competitive, too sensitive, too literal. With others, I've learned to amend myself to suit their taste. Cracked the code on how to be nice and palatable, no matter who stands across from me.

None of those rules seem to apply to Jesse. With a few words, he can pare me down to the core, to the truest version of myself, and the truth is I don't *get him*. He found out I was cursed, and instead of running in the opposite direction, he started taking notes. He hangs out in haunted train yards and lives above a mortuary. I'm not sure how he has any energy to get through the day, considering the only grocery in his fridge is a month-old lasagna.

He treats his life like it's a plant he never remembers to water but can't quite bring himself to throw out. Yet he has the audacity to tell me to prioritize the curse over prom or my graduation speech. To take care of myself.

I might be cursed, but Jesse Talbot is a walking tragedy.

I repeat the question, and his eyes narrow. "Why do you care?"

An excellent question. Why should it bother me how little regard Jesse has for his own well-being? We're business associates. As soon as I get my curse broken and he gets his soul, our paths will diverge again. I'll forget all about this. All about him.

But as Jesse studies me, his unkempt black hair mussed around his ears and a tear at the bottom of his profanity-ridden shirt, I can't convince myself of a future where I forget him.

"Because I need you," I say. "For the curse, of course."

Velvet dark eyes brush over my face like a caress. Jesse's lips quirk. "Of course."

He stands abruptly, sending me back a step. "No need to hunt me down, by the way. A text would have sufficed."

I roll my eyes. My bladder howls, reminding me of our original mission. I barely clip out, "Come stand guard in front of the bathroom," before dashing off.

"You say the sweetest things to me," Jesse calls, following at a leisurely pace.

To my immense relief, I haven't been misled about the plumbing. The toilet flushes without trouble, and I wash my hands in front of the brand-new rectangular bathroom mirror. I have been up here for so long, Mr. Frank and the others are going to think I ditched. Worse—they might think I have diarrhea. Freaking Jesse and his death sticks.

A knock on the door startles me into dropping the paper towel. Jesse murmurs a single word that drops the temperature in the bathroom to the negative degrees.

"Incoming."

Incoming? Who—

"Talbot! Again?"

Oh no, oh no, oh *no.* Mr. Hale.

"How's it going, Ron? Lovely weather we're having, isn't it?"

I shake my head, once again marveling at the pure steel in Jesse's spine.

Steel, spite, and sarcasm: the ingredients responsible for Jesse Talbot's chemical composition.

Meanwhile, I'm about to puke my lunch into the sink, and Mr. Hale hasn't even seen me yet.

"Why are you standing outside the girls' bathroom?"

"Seemed strange to stand inside."

"Is there someone inside the bathroom?" A pause. "Move aside, Talbot."

"'Fraid I can't, sir. Wouldn't look great for you sneaking into the student bathrooms, would it? On account of us being teenagers and all. I'm saving you from yourself."

God. Jesse has really done it now. Mr. Hale's fragile temper is as fundamental to Canyon High as its poorly weeded lawns, and Jesse just verbally slapped him into overdrive. I have to intervene. Jesse can't take the heat for me. It's not fair.

"This is your last warning. You can't hide your delinquent friends."

When Jesse answers, his tone changes, losing the mocking edge. "Mr. Hale, I'm serious. I can't let you in. Someone's been puking in there, and it sounds real rough. Can you go get the nurse?"

Right. The second Mr. Hale leaves to get Ms. Sorben, Jesse will stow me in the empty stairwell or hide me under a pile of wooden boards. Mr. Hale must come to the same conclusion, because he scoffs. "You must take me for a real fool. That's it. I'm going in."

I rush forward. If Jesse assaults a teacher, he'll get expelled. Possibly arrested.

"Mr. Hale!" I boom, tossing open the door. Mr. Hale and Jesse are nose-to-nose, and both startle at my appearance.

"Mina? What are you doing up here? With *him*?" Mr. Hale looks aghast. "Mina, this behavior isn't like you."

I glance at Jesse, expecting to find him gathering up these Good Girl

Mina morsels to tease me over later. But Jesse's lips are pursed, a hand fisted in his pocket.

"Someone had an accident in the downstairs bathroom." The lie falls from my tongue like water, smooth and almost thoughtless. "I wanted to get back to class quickly, so I came up here. I'm sorry."

"Oh. Well, I suppose I understand. You always follow the rules, don't you? Sweet little Mina and her perky ponytail." Mr. Hale giggles. Jesse and I glance at each other.

The smell hits my nose with the force of a truck, sending me back a step.

No! It can't be here! Jesse's with me—I'm not alone with Mr. Hale. How is it here?

The harshest truths carry the worst timing, and each one hits me like a bolt of lightning.

Ms. Diaz was still possessed when Jesse rescued me, and Jesse is immune to possession.

It doesn't count him as a person.

He was telling the truth about his soul.

Jesse's nostrils flare. He understands what the smell means.

He understands we're out of time.

Mr. Hale's voice changes, becoming deeper, harder. A million echoes scraping together to form a single, hollow sound. "Do you break the rules like your Mommy did?"

I raise my arm, but it's too late. Mr. Hale's fist catches me in the jaw, smashing me against the door. It swings open with my weight, and I crash to the ground.

In seconds, he looms over me, blotting out the weak light. "It didn't have to be so bad, Yasmina," Mr. Hale croons. His orange eyes widen in mock sympathy. "It doesn't have to this way at all."

The single bulb bursts, shooting electric sparks over Mr. Hale's head. I cover my head with an arm and curl my knees into my chest.

I vaguely register the sounds of a struggle. Mr. Hale is the PE teacher and football couch. He can bench higher than I can count. Even Jesse's quick fists won't be able to deter him.

I should get up and try to run. If I leave, it'll evacuate Mr. Hale, leaving him dizzy and confused, with no memory of nearly murdering two students. If I leave, Jesse stands a chance.

But my bones refuse to loosen. My teeth clamp together, as rigid as every muscle in my body.

So it's a surprise that while I hold myself still, the ground beneath me begins to move. The floor undulates, rippling like water sloshing in a tub.

A small, cold hand brushes my face. I gasp, finally kick-starting into motion, but I'm too late.

Another little hand grabs my ankle, dragging me into the darkness.

Bright blue waves lap at my feet. Freezing, despite the sun shining overhead.

On the other side of the beach, a group of children chase an inflated ball while their mothers lounge on plastic beach chairs. I'd passed them on my way here and counted no fewer than three trays of cheesy macarona bechamel and two platters of tightly wrapped mahshi korumb.

Despite the pockets of chaos, the beach in this neighborhood of El Agamy is the quietest one yet. The part of the coast me and Khalto Safa visited near San Stefano had been chock-full of people. The activity and chaos had been thrilling in its own way, but the quiet soothes me. I can hear the water rush and retreat. Listen to the distant sound of children's laughter.

Someone sits on the sand to my right, and I count it a miracle that my heart doesn't up and quit right then. I'd let the rhythmic sound of the waves lull me into a kind of hypnosis.

A pretty woman settles on top of a torn beach towel. A blue scrunchie with almost no elasticity remaining fights for its life to keep her thick curls wrapped in a bun. She seems younger than the streaks of white in her hair would indicate, her round face and soft features placing her somewhere in her thirties.

"Sorry," she says, her gaze rapt on the water. "I didn't mean to startle you. Hey, you! Come here!"

I jump. It takes me a second to see the shout isn't aimed at me, but at a little girl playing in the water.

"Is that your daughter?" I still didn't know why this lady chose to sit next to me when seventy-five percent of the beach is empty, but honestly, I don't mind the company.

"That's my little headache, yes." She softens her words with a wan smile, and I join her in a laugh.

I dig my toes in the sand and watch the stranger's daughter run from the waves as they crash onto shore. Her shrieks of delight ruin any semblance of peace and quiet, but I find myself smiling each time she sprints to and from the water.

"She's such a friendly girl. It's a shame how lonely it is for her out here," the woman murmurs. "When her father and I moved from Ain Shams, we really thought she would be happier. It was a big adjustment—I grew up in Cairo, and I never cared about living near the coast. This neighborhood isn't the busiest, but the schools were strong, and we were only a few blocks away from the hustle and bustle in Hannoville. Her father could drive her to school on his way to work instead of putting her in a microbus and asking the driver to keep his eye on her. She could play outside without us worrying about creeps or reckless motorcyclists. It would be a quieter life, but a safer one."

I gesture to where the families still play in the distance. "I'm sure it'll happen. The community here seems really strong. She might just need some time."

She doesn't bother glancing toward the other beachgoers. "They won't be here for long. Sooner or later, one generation or the next, they'll leave. Chased out by the very thing that keeps the rest of us trapped."

I raise my brows, but she's distracted again, calling for her daughter to stop wading so deep in the water.

On the other side of the beach, the families disappear.

"They buy up our homes, and then they abandon them," she continues. With a sharp tug, she pulls her hair free from its bun. Cascades of wavy amber hair fall past her shoulders. "They leave these rotting shells behind, and the rest of us stuck inside them."

"I'm sorry, I don't understand." The wind picks up just as the clouds converge over the sun. "Who abandons the homes?"

"The ones with other choices. The ones who might be missed." She pulls a strand of her hair from her mouth. The waves creep higher and higher up the shore, nearly reaching my ankles.

"But not all the people who stay are good."

Sand flies into my eyes as the wind turns vicious, kicking mini sandstorms along the waterline. I shield my face and try to get up, but my body refuses. My limbs remain fixed beneath an immovable weight.

"Some of the ones who stay don't care about a good or honest life. They just care about an easy one. A life without hardship. A life with all the resources they can spend, all the power they could need." A tear drips down her cheek, and an odd red rash circles the bottom of her throat. "They make us mortal so they can be everlasting."

The waves crash, soaking my clothes, and something hard bumps against my foot.

I lower my hand, still blinking out grains of sand. Everything inside me curdles, withering until I'm nothing but a whimper in the void.

The woman's daughter lies at my feet. Bloated, eyes empty and staring. Dead.

"Janna always trusted too easily."

I lift my horrified gaze to see the woman's neck snap into an impossible angle right at the spot where the red rash—*rope burn*, the functioning part of my mind whispers—covers her skin.

"Then again," she says, blood oozing from the corner of her lip, "in the end, I suppose you did, too."

It's only when Janna grabs my hand, dragging me into the next wave sweeping toward us, that I remember I can scream.

CHAPTER SEVENTEEN
PRESENT DAY

I open my eyes to Jesse's face hovering inches from mine, his phone's flashlight inches from my face.

The tense lines of his face melt in relief. He utters a low oath and sits back on his haunches. "God, Mansour. You nearly killed me."

My gaze slides past Jesse and lands on a figure sprawled out by the first stall. Mr. Hale.

"Is he okay?" I whisper.

Jesse snorts. "He's fine. After you vanished, the thing started shrieking. I saw the orange drain out of his eyes before he collapsed. I checked his pulse, but I'm pretty sure he's just sleeping."

"Pretty sure?"

Jesse groans, scrubbing the heels of his hands into his eyes. "Positive. I am absolutely positive that Ronald Hale is in perfect condition and only in danger of catching a strain of whatever bacteria lives on this bathroom floor. Now, can we talk about you *disappearing*?"

Bile burns in my throat. I maneuver around Jesse, trying to pull myself off the ground. A strong arm comes around my waist as I stumble, helping me to my feet.

"You're shaking," Jesse murmurs, his hold tightening.

"It was a shadow." I chuckle without a trace of humor. "We must have missed it coming inside."

Jesse's pause lengthens, and I glance up, curious despite myself. Through all of this, he hasn't panicked or flipped out once. Meanwhile, my fingers ache from holding tight to the seams of my sanity. I am one stiff wind away from scattering.

I wish we could split the difference. My heart, a little steelier. His, a little softer.

"But you said the last shadow turned into a version of your mom." His fingers flex on my hip, a distracted motion.

"It wasn't my mom this time." Without meeting his gaze, I pull out of Jesse's arms and head to the door, checking for any movement. "Each shadow shows me something different. The last one transformed the entire drive-in theater. This one . . . took me somewhere."

I skirt the traffic cones at the head of the stairs and take the steps two at a time, eager to put as much space between me and the last twenty minutes as possible. As soon as we land on the second floor, a wave of noise crashes into us. Students stream through the halls, relishing the seven-minute pass period before our last class of the day.

Jesse keeps easy pace as I stride into the crowd. "Where did it take you?"

They leave these rotting shells behind.

"I don't want to talk about it." I push my hair out of my face, fighting to regulate the air coming in and out of my mouth. My lungs struggle to expand for a full breath.

"Can I have my mom's journal? I'll translate the new entry and call you later today to go over it."

He fishes the leather journal out of his backpack and passes it to me, a frown tugging at his mouth. "We should talk about what just happened. I think your mom was right about the shadows being a side effect. They're connected to the curse, but I don't think they're necessarily on the same side."

An invisible tourniquet cuts off my airways. "Later," I manage to force out. "I need to be alone for a while."

I snatch the journal from Jesse and take off in a run.

I remember leaving the parking lot and picking a random direction to start walking. Walking and walking, long after my breathing slowed and my toes began to throb inside my sneakers.

By the time I realized I'd walked to the haunted train, I was already climbing inside.

I wanted to be alone. Far away from Jesse and Baba and Mr. Hale. Far away from the people I kept inadvertently hurting.

Ward's rumbling skies finally make good on their threat, opening in sheets of freezing rain. The world outside disappears under the curtain of rain washing over the windows.

I pick at the moth-eaten cushion. How long did it take them to clean the blood from these seats? How rancid must the bodies have smelled after being left to swelter and putrefy for days?

Those people were going somewhere. They packed their bags and chose their most comfortable sweaters. They probably arranged for someone to pick them up at their stop and spent their last hours excitedly picturing the face of the person they were waiting to see.

If they knew they would die, would they still have bothered fixing the scarves around their necks? Packing snacks for their children?

I've always thought life was long and death was quick, but what if that's not true? Death isn't exiting a door and locking it shut as you go. What if when you die, you leave the door cracked behind you?

What if just a few inches away, those passengers are sitting right next to me, as alive as they were the moment they boarded the train?

The battery on my phone sends out a despair signal. Notifications flood my screen, all of them belonging to Jesse.

I lay my cheek against the chilly window, curling my knees to my chest. The train seats aren't particularly comfortable, but at least they're cushioned. Outside, the wind howls, whipping the phone cables between the leaning utility poles.

I should open my mother's journal. Another shadow means a new entry. There might be a clue, some miniscule detail that'll help me and Jesse figure out our next steps.

But it isn't my mother's memories I want to understand today.

It's my own.

YASMINA MANSOUR
EL AGAMY, ALEXANDRIA
ONE MONTH AGO

Khalto Safa left shortly after dawn on my last day in El Agamy, promising to return by dinner. She wouldn't say what business required her urgent attention. Pressing her wouldn't lead to anything pleasant, so I watched the gates close behind her with a mixture of relief and worry.

She had to come back, right?

I tried to spend my last day productively. I finished some required summer reading for AP Lit. Planned the meals I'd make for me and Baba during the new semester. Plotted how I'd convince my friends to forgive me for ditching them without a word.

By sunset, Khalto Safa hadn't returned. I pushed off the couch and checked the gate for the millionth time. The lock hadn't budged an inch. No way Khalto Safa could've come back without going through the gate, not unless she'd developed supernatural climbing skills and scaled the walls surrounding the estate.

What if she didn't come back tonight? Who would drive me to the airport tomorrow morning?

Viscerally aware of the darkening sky, I ventured across the second floor, turning on the lights as I went. I even found the switch for the crystal chandelier hanging above the center of the hall. It lit up like a star, the teardrop diamonds dangling in long strands from the center, creating chess patterns on the walls.

Triumphant, I placed my hands on my hips. There. They could probably spot the house from space with all these lights.

I veered to admire my handiwork and bumped into one of the side tables. A mirror propped on the table tipped forward. I caught it just in time and quickly righted it.

"Watch where you're going," I told my reflection sternly. The chandelier glowed behind me, casting my features in a soft bronze. With my hair loose, I looked like a character out of one of those gothic novels Mrs. Lawrence kept asking us to read. Little did Mrs. Lawrence know that apparently the secret to gothic-era hair was to anxiously pick apart your curls until they formed a cloud of tangled frizz around you.

My campaign to distract myself from Khalto Safa's prolonged absence (*She'll be back. Of course she'll be back. Just because my mother never came back doesn't mean Khalto Safa won't come back*) led me downstairs, where I continued flipping light switches and wreaking havoc on the estate's electric bill.

A breeze brushed my skin as soon as I stepped outside. I always forgot how freezing it was inside the house until I emerged into the lovely summer evenings stretching over El Agamy.

These balmy nights were one of the rare times I remembered others lived in this quiet little neighborhood. I'd gone for a walk the day before and spotted families lounging on plastic chairs out in the street. One family nursed a small bonfire as the father roasted a basket of corn, much to his squealing children's excitement. Another family passed around a tray full of glass cups, filled nearly to the brim with dark red tea.

The third family I'd passed had been my favorite. The boy and girl were older, maybe around my age, and had been splayed out on square cushions arranged on the porch. The guy had his nose buried in his phone, only looking up when his mother kicked his shoe and pointed at a ginger cat trying to discreetly sneak into the street. The girl had a striped bandana tying her curls back from her face while she read. Her wide-rimmed glasses were fogging from the steam curling out from the mug at her elbow. While I'd hovered in the street like a creep, the father had ventured onto the porch with his laptop in one arm and a deck of cards in the other, clearly planning for an evening spent with his children and the full moon.

The mom had run outside to catch the cat and smiled at me as I passed. I nearly cried at the thought of my mom in some other life, cradling our family cat while I read a book on the porch.

I toyed with the idea of going for another walk before discarding it. The streetlamps weren't the strongest in this neighborhood, and tonight's moon was hidden beneath an opaque screen of silver.

Not that the light in the Haikal garden was any better. I rubbed my arms, wandering further into the overgrown thicket. Yellow grass crunched under my shoes. Rutab were scattered beneath the trees like forgotten gemstones. The only illumination came from a small string light dangling above the tall bushes. Leafy vines crept over the walls separating the garden from the street, winding tight around the perimeter. In the daylight, I might've said they were shielding us from the outside.

I wiggled a finger between the tightly woven branches. The date trees rustled above me, whispering with the wind.

At night, it was hard not to wonder if perhaps these plants weren't protecting us from the outside, but penning us in.

The breeze carried over a flurry of whispers from behind a row of prickly rose bushes on the southern wall of the garden.

"The girl flies back tomorrow. Safa will have to leave to take her to the airport. We will be waiting inside when she returns," said a familiar voice in short, gruff Arabic.

I pressed my palm to the vines as I moved closer. Were they talking about me and Khalto Safa?

"You know as well as I do that girl is never leaving this house."

I made out a figure standing by the edge of the wall, speaking into a gap in the bricks.

The housekeeper.

"It's not safe inside," the person behind the wall urged. "Hamida, I know you're scared—"

"Not safe inside? It won't be safe anywhere in El Agamy!" Hamida smacked her fist against the brick. Blood scraped over her knuckles. "It's happening again! Why else do you think she brought Nadine's daughter here? She's going to pick up where her mother left off. She won't have a choice." A dry sob left the housekeeper. "The house has been in ruins for years. Safa is sick. I thought, *finally*. Finally, the curse of this family and their horror house will finally end. Our children will be safe again. Families can grow old here without fear."

A dry leaf snapped underfoot. The sound cracked through the air, and the housekeeper whipped around. I froze, plastering myself to the wall. She couldn't see me through all these bushes, could she?

I held my breath.

Finally, the housekeeper murmured something to the person waiting outside. As soon as she left the garden, I bolted for the house. Dates split against my heels, a chunky mash oozing behind me.

I paced inside my room. What was the housekeeper talking about, picking up where my mother left off? Picking up with what?

And what did she mean, my aunt was sick?

It took an hour until I stopped waiting for the housekeeper to storm my bedroom. I opened my window, hoping to catch a sound. Any sound. I'd settle for shouting and car horns, at this point.

I missed mainland Alexandria. It had thrived in the night. Groups hanging out by seaside cafés, watching soccer matches in twenty-four-hour restaurants, driving beach buggies in country clubs.

Not here. As soon as night deepened, the entire neighborhood withdrew.

I watched prom proposal videos at top volume to chase away the quiet. Everything was packed and ready for my flight tomorrow. I should've been restless with nervous energy, thinking of fake stories to share with Baba. But America felt far-off and unreal, like an idle daydream I'd indulged in a little too long.

The house was heavier tonight. The dust motes seemed to swirl slower. Every groan and creak stretched for centuries. I played with the curtain by the window, searching for the moon behind the clouds. For some reason, I felt confident the moon would chase away the danger. If the moon emerged, then Khalto Safe would come home. Hamida would swing by with a smile and explain she'd been pranking me with that scene out there in the garden, and did I fall for it? The air would move normally again, releasing the villa from this smothering stillness.

The gates cast shadows over the still road, and a sense of danger dragged icy fingers through me.

I was on the wrong side of those gates.

The more the hours ticked by, the less effective the videos became at calming me down. The silence grew, layers upon layers. Suffocating.

This room used to be Mama's.

The thought came out of nowhere. I sat up, bedsprings creaking beneath me. Time became as thin as a thread, unspooling around me in a single, unbroken line.

In a million years, I wouldn't be able to explain how, but I *knew* my mother had slept in this bed. Paced around these floors. I could see her imprint in flickers, like the corners of an unfinished memory, or a shadow in the corner of my eye.

At four in the morning, the birds started to scream.

I groaned, throwing my legs over the side of the bed. Every damn night. I could set my watch to the sound. The other animals joined, a mixture of frenzied howling and shrieking grating inside my ears. "What is it?" I mumbled. "What are you all screaming at?"

I pushed my feet into a pair of fuzzy slippers and slipped from the room. A warm glass of yansoon might help me sleep.

Darkness cocooned the second floor. Strange—I hadn't heard Hamida come up, and I'd turned on every light in this villa the minute the sun set. I groped around the wall for a light switch.

Nothing. The light switch had vanished.

My slippers shuffled across the marble floor. I kept waiting to bump into a loose suitcase or an armchair, but my feet navigated the terrain without encountering any obstacles.

A peculiar notion crossed my mind. Perhaps my mother had walked these floors so often, she had worn a groove into the energy of the air itself. I was walking her steps, guided by whatever imprint she left behind.

I collided with a hard barrier. I reflexively reached for my toe, then stopped. What was I doing? I hadn't hit my toe.

I straightened, and the darkness roiled.

A set of wide steps materialized in front of me. A banister ran along the side of the short stairwell, supported by white balustrades shaped like hourglasses.

My muscles tensed for only a second before they eased. The fear that had been coiled in my chest since I stepped into this house evaporated. My worries drained away. None of it mattered anymore. None of it could hurt me anymore.

At the top of the stairs, a door appeared.

Everything was going to be okay.

I reached for the banister, my arm operating of its own accord. As soon as my palm settled over the smooth metal, my entire body seized. Electricity ran burning currents inside me, scorching through my veins.

Come to me, Mina, sang a sweet voice. Mama. *Oh, I've missed you so.*

I couldn't speak. The electricity burned off the wetness of my mouth, leaving my teeth loose and brittle.

But I could still climb.

With each step I put behind me, my breath came easier. The burning eased, promising sweet relief if I could only reach the top step. Promising more of my mother.

My beautiful, beautiful daughter, she sighed. *My greatest joy. The piece of my heart that lives outside my chest.*

I reached the top step and stood in front of the door.

White and ornately decorated, it sent childlike joy washing over me. Terrible things couldn't look this beautiful. This door would only take me to equally beautiful places. It could take me to the mountains at the world's first snow; the Nile's marshes before the floods; the earth's finest flower as it unfurled its petals to the sun. This beautiful door could take me to my old house in Ward, where the languorous melodies of Mohamed Mounir filled our living room while Baba tried to cook Mama dinner on her birthday.

A perfectly round silver knob bloomed in the corner of the door.

I could travel to any other life behind this door. I could live any variation of the lives I had dreamed of.

I was reaching for it when something slammed against me.

NO! Mama screamed. *NOT MY DAUGHTER!*

I rocked back on my heels. Static burst in my ears. I cried out as nails scraped against the inside of my head, and the villa disappeared.

A woman in rags knelt in pools on a pitch-black road. Head bent, clumped hair hanging in her narrow face. Thunder split the sky, washing the world in blue. Even without any other signs of civilization around us, I recognized the bumpy path leading to the Haikal estate.

Lightning blasted into the water around the woman's legs, and she jerked. Light emanated from her bones. Her head snapped up.

Black blood ran down the woman's face, oozing from her scalp, her ears. She rocked back and forth, dirty nails scraping against her throat and collar. She resembled someone. Who?

The glow illuminated another shape in the muddy water. A small body floating on its stomach.

The lightning struck again, and her eyes flew open.

Bright orange eyes stared directly at me.

I slammed back into my body, finding my hand already wrapped around the door handle.

A wail came from behind me, so real I almost turned around. *She's not finished yet! She needs more time!* Echoing around me, over and over, a bottomless plea stretched through space and time.

"Mama?" I whispered.

Every molecule of me ached. I could rest behind the door. I could finally get some sleep. Maybe Mama would be there, and she would untangle my curls and call me a real Masriya. Maybe the Masriya Mina was in there, and she could tell me how to become her.

I twisted the handle and pushed the door open.

The world went white.

CHAPTER EIGHTEEN
PRESENT DAY

I wake up to a loud clattering noise.

Ouch. My neck twinges from the awkward angle of my head. I'm frozen stiff, too rigid even to tremble.

Another noise strikes a bright match of terror inside me, but the flame sputters out before it can properly burn. I'm too tired. I just want to go back to sleep.

The train groans with new movement. Footsteps pad against the carpeted ground.

Maybe it's the other ghosts. They've banded together to welcome me to the afterlife. Any minute now, a kindly old man with an open, bloody gash across his throat will hold out his hand and tell me to hurry along.

"Mansour, you here?"

Oh good. It's Jesse. I can sleep if it's Jesse.

The egregious clomp of his boots stops. The seat next to me depresses, and a stream of curses follows shortly after. "Mansour, hey! Can you hear me?" He shakes my shoulder. If I had the willpower, I'd tell him to quit it.

"You're freezing. Shit, *shit,*" Jesse swears. A knuckle passes gently over my numb cheeks and neck. "How long have you been here?"

I make a feeble attempt to protest as my body is dragged onto the other seat and then onto Jesse's lap. He unzips his jacket and tucks me tight against his chest, closing the leather around my quaking body. Warmth envelops me instantly. "Unbelievable. I went around asking people if they'd seen you, you know that? You made me *talk to people*."

I rub my cheek against his soft cotton shirt. Jasmine and rain. The signature scent of the boy who wouldn't have glanced twice at me a week ago. The boy who's currently saying some stuff about hypothermia in a livid tone.

The warmer I get, the harder it becomes to control my shaking, but Jesse's arms simply tighten around me. He jumps when I press the cold tip of my nose to the dip where his throat meets his collarbone. I should tell him that I finally remember how I got home. I remember the housekeeper's daughter patting my face to wake me up. Crouching next to me in the middle of the floor where I had sprawled out and calling for her mother, who ran up the stairs and blanched at the sight of us. She'd shouted at her daughter to get out of the villa and then helped me to my feet. "Are your bags packed?" she'd asked. When I nodded, she swiped open her phone and tapped on the screen. "Good. Your ride to the airport will be here in fifteen minutes."

"J-J-Jesse?" I slur.

"Yeah?"

"I h-hate t-trains." Whoops. I was supposed to tell him something else. What was it?

His low laugh brushes against my forehead. "Duly noted."

My eyes drift shut. Lulled into a trancelike state by the steady rise and fall of Jesse's chest. Jesse keeps talking, and I do my best to focus, hoping it'll distract me from the unpleasant tingle of blood returning to my toes.

"You also hate the color beige, greasy cheeseburgers, the spelling of any word with 'gh' in it, the smell of cigarettes, and the rain. You order takeout on Fridays and leave the delivery person thank-you cookies in disposable containers. I am regularly forced awake in the middle of the night by you setting off the fire alarm—which I'm guessing is thanks to the warehouse of candles you've got squirreled away in your room—and the way you parallel park is bloodcurdling."

I'm collecting the energy to argue about the poor ventilation in my room and the oversensitive fire alarm when everything he said registers. I wedge open one eye to squint at him. "You g-got all that from a w-week?"

Jesse sweeps his thumb over my brow, gazing down at me with an unfathomable expression. "I've been your neighbor for years, Sour Patch. I know you think I didn't like you, but that doesn't mean I didn't notice you."

Jesse is only saying this because my brain currently resides in a puddle of soup. Easy to bank on me not remembering. I tighten my fingers in the fabric around his waist, pressing myself like a brand against him. I want to get warmer, fast. Get my brain back in fighting form.

The closeness has the opposite effect. My muscles slacken, one by one. A primitive part of me registers the safety in Jesse's arms and relaxes. Fully relaxes, in a way I haven't in too long.

"I'm hard to ignore," I joke, basically handfeeding Jesse the opportunity to break the tension. The elephants in my stomach have begun to perform a complicated dance worthy of a gold medal, and Jesse's steady gaze isn't helping.

But he doesn't take the bait. If anything, the corners of his eyes tighten, and he sounds pained when he whispers, "You are."

I study Jesse, startlingly clearheaded for a minute. "You're being too nice."

"Aren't I always?"

"No," I retort, but I sense the lie as soon as I say it. Jesse might be surly and occasionally rude, but he's also been patient. He's been thoughtful. He—

"You talked to people," I say slowly. "You talked to people until you found me."

He finally looks away, rolling his eyes to the ceiling. "Don't remind me. Worst experience of my life."

My torso has thawed enough for a laugh to break free. An actual laugh, when moments ago I'd been prepared to tragically freeze against the window.

What good is a soul if someone like Jesse Talbot doesn't have one?

He is angry—always, always angry—but it's an anger he never directs toward anyone it might harm. An anger he seems to have forged, link by link, into chain metal standing between him and the rest of the world.

I wish I knew how to convince him that the world was worth it. That it was worth putting down his armor and standing in the sun.

"Mansour?" Jesse sweeps the hair from my forehead, his hand coming to curl around the side of my face. His other arm remains tight around my middle, preventing me from tumbling off his lap. "You're spacing out again."

My fingers tighten on the collar of Jesse's jacket, and before I can think about it too long, I draw his head down toward mine.

Too fast, and *way* too clumsy. He pulls back in time to avoid smacking into my nose, but my death grip on his collar keeps him from straying too far.

Any remaining lethargy evaporates like mist in a hundred-degree day, and I suddenly wish I'd been right about the train ghosts finishing me off.

What was I thinking? Jesse hadn't so much as *glanced* at someone for longer than half a minute since he moved to Ward. The one time a girl had shored up her courage to ask him to Sadie Hawkins, he'd shut her down. Politely, I'd heard, but thoroughly. Afterward, the whispers had been vicious, and they hadn't stopped until someone started one about Jesse preferring the romantic company of corpses to that of the living. Jesse had tracked down the guy who started the rumor, a mouthy athlete with a superiority complex, and allegedly filled his car with yellowjackets.

The students kept their speculations about Jesse's love life to themselves after that.

And here I was, just grabbing the guy and going for it like a character in those '90s sitcoms Lucia loves.

Dark eyes swimming with amusement roam over my face and the blush scorching over it. "Were you trying to kiss me, Sour Patch?"

"Please don't talk." I pause. Squeeze my eyes shut. "I'm sorry. I didn't mean to make you uncomfortable."

Laughter rumbles in the chest I'm currently plastered against. I try to wriggle out of his arms, but he only tightens his hold. "Wait, wait. *I'm* sorry. I didn't want to ruin the moment, but you were about to use my head to break your own nose."

Well, the angle might have been a little off, but... "I was delirious. Possessed. This train is haunted, you know."

"Oh, we're blaming the spirits now?"

"I'm not blaming—would you just let me go?"

"Do it again."

I stop wriggling. Jesse watches me closely, not a trace of humor left.

At my bewilderment, he traces the curve of my chin with his thumb. "Do it again, Mina." Low and husky. Heat scorches the back of my neck.

My heart judders like a motor struggling to kickstart, and I desperately wish I had any frame of reference to rely on. Kissing Alex had been easy, simple, about as unnerving as a sunny day.

He hadn't held my eyes like he might cease to exist if I looked away. He hadn't touched me like he wished he could fuse me to his bones.

I grab Jesse's collar with both hands, the soft leather bunching in my fists. My breath emerges in stops and starts, and Jesse's brows begin to furrow, concern overtaking everything else. Always concern, and always for me.

Business colleagues. So many lies out of such a beautiful mouth.

"Mansour, you don't have to—"

I slant my lips over Jesse's, cutting off whatever unnecessarily honorable words he'd been about to offer.

For a second, when Jesse's lips stay slack beneath mine, I commit myself to wandering into the woods to live among the frogs and fish forever. It's the only rational solution. The trees will keep my secrets, and I can wither away in humiliation.

I pull back a fraction, resolved on my new life plan, and Jesse finally reacts.

I gasp as he swings me upward. My legs dangle over the side of the seat, my torso angled to the right. The mild discomfort of the position quickly wanes when Jesse grabs my arms and pulls me flush against him, smothering my next gasp with a kiss that reaches the very tips of my newly thawed toes.

The next few minutes pass with the hazy cadence of a fever dream. I rake my fingers through the waves of Jesse's hair, my nails sliding over his scalp. He fists the fabric at my hip, holding on to my blouse so tightly that no iron or steamer has a hope of smoothing out the creases he'll leave.

Before today, I would have sworn that I've been kissed. That I've known what it's like to want someone so badly, you can scarcely breathe through it. *Kissing is fine*, this Mina would have said. *I just don't quite see what all the fuss is about.*

What a silly girl.

"Mina," Jesse groans, the single word so decadently tortured. It's raw, stripped of any sarcasm or imperiousness. Just bare Jesse, and it goes through me like a shot of adrenaline.

I crawl higher on his lap, my mouth moving to the long column of his throat, determined to wring out a million more of those sounds.

Except as soon as I lean forward again, the solid body beneath me vanishes, and I find myself alone in the seat.

Jesse bows forward in the aisle, gripping the seats on either side of him while he catches his breath. "Damn it, Mansour. Damn it."

"Did I do something wrong?" It comes out wobbly and a little frightened, but the whiplash has temporarily knocked my pride away.

"*Yes*." A beat passes before Jesse finally looks at me. "No. No, you didn't do anything wrong. It's my fault."

"Your fault for what?"

"That shouldn't have happened."

The looming threat of tears abates, replaced with indignation.

"Why not?" I don't appreciate being yanked around like this. Eighteen is too old for him to have the emotional maturity of a soccer ball.

"You're seeing someone, Mansour. Or you will be, when we get rid of this curse. I'm not interested in being a rest stop on your journey back to your boyfriend."

Taken aback, I stare at him openmouthed. He thinks I'm planning to get back together with Alex?

Which . . . isn't an unfair assumption, considering I pretty much said so the minute I told Jesse about the curse.

Jesse just shakes his head and fixes his collar. "We should go. It'll be night soon."

The train creaks with his departing strides. After a couple more stunned seconds, I get to my feet and glance across the empty seats.

"I hope you enjoyed the show," I mutter, and I let myself imagine I hear a ghostly laugh trailing behind me.

CHAPTER NINETEEN
PRESENT DAY

At the grocery store, I push the cart's useless wheels down the frozen foods aisle. Given the month I've had, comparing the price of bread and debating between Swiss and cheddar feels deliciously normal. Just another boring Saturday afternoon at the market. Any minute now, Lucia will come around the corner, pushing a cart with Aida crouched inside. Rainie will pretend not to know any of us but keep an eye out on the store attendants, just in case someone decides to give us trouble. I would arrange my groceries around Aida and try to sneak peeks at her sketchpad.

God. I miss them so much. They were my family. The only people I had here.

I roll my shoulders back and tighten my grip on the cart. There's being melancholy, and then there's being melancholy in the middle of the pasta aisle. I can already hear the gossips of Ward reporting back to their friends: "Did you see Mina Mansour crying in front of a box of discounted fusilli? Odd, right? Maybe... oh no, do you think her credit card declined?" Before you know it, the entire town shows up with lasagna because my dad must have lost his job, we're losing the house, and we can't afford $1.25 fusilli.

I push the cart into the cereal aisle and contemplate the wisdom of texting Jesse a third reminder that he better be at my house by six thirty for dinner. When I floated the idea past him after the train incident, he'd protested. *Apparently*, he has food at home. Where, I'm not sure, since my quick peek through his kitchen cabinets revealed exactly one expired bag of instant mashed potatoes and a jar of chili that should've been refrigerated after opening.

I told him I wouldn't talk about my mother's journal entries unless he joined me for dinner, and he agreed to a free and nutritious homecooked meal like a martyr surrendering to the guillotine.

I throw a package of feta cheese into the cart with a touch too much force. The joke's on Jesse. There's nothing to discuss. The newest entries are just about as useless as the previous ones.

The last entry said: The shadows are its vulnerability. They come with the curse, but they cannot be controlled by it.

The one before it was longer.

From 1640 to 1710, the curse lived in Germany. Small, impoverished town. High child abandonment rates. There, a destitute and orphaned street sweeper invited in the curse. Overnight, he had a home, grander than every home in that desiccating little town. A town full of children nobody would miss. Years passed, and his family grew. In those conditions, the curse should have been thriving. But for some reason, it didn't. The house was falling apart. This family was starving the curse, even though they suffered along with it. The last birth announcement I could find was of a daughter. A little girl born in the house and abandoned shortly after by her mother, who walked into their family lake and drowned herself. The father lived across the country and returned for the birth of his child. He managed to rescue the baby and took her back to his city, leaving the house empty.

Four days later, fifty-eight people were dead. It took the newborn last.

The entire bloodline had been wiped out. The debt hadn't been paid, and the curse collected. But why not eliminate the lineage earlier, when they were feeding it one or two kids a year? Why wait until then? The timing didn't make sense, until it occurred to me that if the child hadn't passed the test

She'd stopped there. Her ink had bled around the last letter, as though she'd been interrupted while writing and dug her pen in.

I suppose I should be as interested as Jesse is in determining what "test" the journal means. I should wonder why she thinks the shadows don't necessarily obey the curse, since they're clearly a package deal.

Except, I can't convince my mind to unwrap those questions. I can't bring myself to read my mother's words and experience anything other than the throbbing betrayal that's lived between my ribs since the minute I found out who she truly was.

I told Jesse about my last night in the house. About opening the door. When he asked the inevitable, I had no choice but to face the answer.

I don't remember what happened after I opened the door.

I toss a box of chocolate granola into the cart with excessive force, shoving my cart around the corner. It slams into a solid resistance, sending a basket flying out of someone's hand and emptying its contents onto the floor.

"Oh, I'm so sorry!" I rush to the ground, scooping as many items as I can carry.

Spiked combat boots enter my field of vision. Purple stripes weave across the leather in the style of an artist I happen to know. Those boots are older than time itself, though you wouldn't think it at first glance. Every year, Aida paints over the fading patches. Every year, Lucia gives Rainie a new pair of boots for her birthday, only for Rainie to stubbornly hold on to this decaying pair.

My gaze travels up ripped camouflage pants and pepper spray dangling from a belt loop. Past a skintight black shirt and a red choker. I stop at the impassive face of my former best friend.

I stand slowly, halfway convinced I've conjured her through wishful thinking alone. "Hi."

Rainie stands a few inches taller than me, but after so much time with Jesse, everyone under six feet seems downright diminutive. "Hey."

I unload the mess in my arms back into her basket. "You dyed your hair again."

Purple fingernails tuck locks of spiky red hair behind Rainie's ear. "Yep. Went on a Manic Panic binge at three in the morning."

"It looks great."

Shoppers shuffle around us, bumping against my cart. Rainie's knuckles tighten on the basket's handle. "Thanks. I should get going."

Disappointment crushes the tendrils of hope Rainie's appearance planted. "Oh. Yeah, of course. Sorry for knocking over your basket." I wrap my arms around myself, turning to the cart. I don't want her to see me tear up. I understand her position, I really do. They'd tried to talk to me at the theater, and I caused such a catastrophic scene that the staff had to pause the movie until I confirmed I hadn't hit my head when I fell into the pond, and no, I have no "litigious intent," whatever that means.

Understanding doesn't make it hurt any less. Rainie was the first real friend I made in Ward. I've known her since we were in the third grade, when she nut-punched a boy for asking if my parents rode to America on a camel. She's the person who comes over when I'm sullen and weepy on Mother's Day and rips the family album out of my hands so we can binge cheesy action movies.

Watching her hate me for the last three weeks broke my heart. I don't think I can watch her walk away again.

"Don't cry, Mina," Rainie says, sighing.

I whirl around. Rainie hasn't moved from her spot. She aims a lopsided smile at me. "Remember our deal. I get to pick the music every time you cry. I'm probably up by like sixteen car rides."

I cover my sniffle with a cough. "I'm not crying."

Rainie rolls her eyes. "Sure, and I don't have a tattoo of a scarecrow on my thigh." After weeks of pointed glares, her exasperation warms me to the core. Exasperation means she cares. It means she hasn't written me off.

No earthly force could stop me from throwing my arms around her in a crushing hug.

She goes back on her heel, gruffly patting my shoulder. "Okay, alright. C'mon." She pries me away. "Get it together, Eenie Meenie Mina."

I groan. "Please do not revive that horrible nickname. I have enough of those going around."

"Oh?" She raises a pierced brow. "Do tell."

"Absolutely not. You don't need any more fodder."

"Okay, I'll guess. Minatour, Mina-ty Fresh—"

I grin, shaking my head as she recites an increasingly ridiculous list of nickname options. We meander around the store, and I keep piling items into my cart to avoid the inevitable checkout line departure. Rainie regales me with the latest drama at school, and I soak it up eagerly. Life exists outside this curse. Life didn't stop when I fell off track; it's still moving, still marching forward, and if I stay tuned to the beat, I might have a chance of catching up if this curse breaks.

When. When this curse breaks.

At the checkout line, Rainie browses the gum selections. The girl hates chewing gum nearly as much as she hates fruit-scented perfumes.

She's lingering. Could she be as reluctant to leave as I am?

I pay a staggering amount at the register and load my cart with the bagged groceries. I clear my throat, trying to think of something to say that doesn't sound as desperately pathetic as *Does this mean you like me again?*

At the exit doors, I stall, pretending to peruse a barrel of persimmons, but this time it's out of caution. Rainie might follow me to the car if we walk out together. Fewer people in the parking lot means a higher chance of winding up alone.

"We're going dress shopping tomorrow," Rainie blurts, eyeing the persimmons like they're about to grow teeth and jump her. "Come with us."

I blink. "For prom?"

"Ugh. Yes. Lucia insisted. We're driving up to Klamath Falls."

My brows hit my hairline. "You're leaving the state to go dress shopping? Who *are* you?" Much like Ward, Klamath Falls straddles the border between Oregon and California, except Klamath sits on the opposite side of the line. Most folks in Ward just drive down to Redding for their big shopping sprees.

She kicks my shin. "I'm buying my outfit from a thrift store. Lucia's the one terrified of repeating the red dress incident. A couple of girls wear the same dress at MORP one time, and she loses her crap."

I ache to accept her invitation. A day away from journals and curses and haunted houses, worrying about the neckline of overpriced dresses and arguing over where to eat dinner... the wanting hollows me out. "I don't think I can. Klamath is kind of far."

"It's less than two hours." Rainie crosses her arms over her chest, scuffing her shoe against the linoleum. At this rate, Aida's gonna have to repaint the boots within the month. "Are you gonna make me say please? Fine. Please, Mina. Come with us to buy stupid dresses for stupid prom." Rainie picks at her lower lip, a nervous habit I haven't seen her whip out since the sixth grade. "Lucia would love it. Probably spend half the ride crying on your shoulder. She misses you."

I know what Jesse would want. He'd tell me to square my shoulders and let her down gently. Remind me not to follow my heart when my head knows better.

"We all miss you," Rainie confesses on an exhale, and my heart calls the game.

"What time are we heading out?"

At eight the next morning, I trudge out of the house to a street shrouded in fog and a stoic Jesse leaning in front of my car. Half obscured beneath the fog, his boots crossed at the ankle and his hands jammed in his jacket pockets, he seems more suited for roaming the marshes. A character conjured from the pages of a tragic gothic tale.

"Good morning," I chirp.

"According to who?" Jesse pushes off the car and does a double take at my ankle-length lavender trench coat. His languid perusal slides over me like a caress, igniting heat low in my belly.

"I spoke too soon," he says somberly.

Flushing, I poke his arm. "I'm wearing clothes underneath it. Everyone knows you wear easily removable clothes if you're spending the day trying on dresses."

"I can assure you everyone does *not* know that." He runs his thumb over his chin, staring into the distance. "Huh. Maybe school dances aren't a complete waste of district funding."

"If you're here to talk me out of going, it won't work. I've planned the whole day out." I tick a finger for each point. "Rainie's picking me up last, so Aida and Lucia will already be in the car. I won't let any of them follow me into the dressing room or walk into an elevator or bathroom with me."

"You're not even going to prom, Mansour. Why risk it at all?"

I tighten the belt on my coat. "Who says I'm not going?"

Jesse pushes his hair back, the locks spilling like ink between his fingers. The fog outlines him in silver and white, elevating him from stunning to ethereal. A stray urge to trace his lovely face and smooth the stress from his tightly wound muscles confounds me. Jesse's still the same untouchable enigma. The walls of hostility between him and the nearest living creature haven't changed. When it comes right down to it, I still barely know him.

What happened in the train was a situational glitch. A survival exception.

When Jesse speaks, it's quiet. Grim. "Are you so desperate to get back to your old life? To leotards and crowns and your two-bit boyfriend?"

I tilt my chin up, studying his stony features. "I thought you wanted me to get back with my two-bit boyfriend."

"I never said that, and you know it," Jesse says. "It's not about what I want."

"Then if it's about what I want, let me go with Rainie, because I want to forget any of this ever happened. I'm so tired of being tired, Jesse. I want to go to prom, worry about how I'm going to control my curls under my graduation cap, have summer picnics by the lake." When his expression only grows harder, I try again. "I'm not as tough as you are. I faint at the sight of blood and cry at those car commercials where the whole family goes on a road trip together. If I stop hoping that I can get my old life back, then . . ." I shake my head, staring at the shrouded street behind him. "I won't let it win."

"I see," Jesse says, frostier than the ice under our feet.

Headlights emerge from the mist, and a baby blue Jeep swings into my driveway. Rock music spills from inside the car as Rainie rolls down her window. From this angle, Jesse remains out of Rainie's sight. "Mina!" she hollers.

"Be careful," is Jesse's flat parting statement. He jumps the fence between our houses, disappearing before I can say goodbye.

Shrieks assault my ears as soon as I open the car door. "Mina!" Lucia wraps her arms around my shoulders, and I cough as the scent of citrus envelops me. "I can't believe you're here!"

"Hey, Mina." Aida pops her head between the seats, shooting me a small smile.

Rainie reverses from my driveway, and I scramble for my seat belt. Aida kicks her feet onto the dashboard, balancing her sketchbook on her lap. The baby blue Jeep belongs to Lucia, given to her as a birthday gift last year, but she hates driving it. Rainie tames the four-wheeled beast with ease, although she regularly complains about the color.

I lean forward to poke Aida's side. "You put beads in your braids."

"Mr. Clay called my braids distracting, so I figured I'd show him exactly how distracting they could be."

"Ugh, that bastard. We were talking about Hiroshima on Thursday, and he kept glancing at me," Rainie growls. "I genuinely don't think our history teacher knows the difference between Japan and Vietnam."

Lucia grimaces in sympathy. She and Alex are the only white members of our group, and they've listened to our complaints against awful teachers over the years. Mr. Clay gets the gold ribbon in his category, though. Of everyone I've ever angrily journaled about, Mr. Clay has received the most entries.

I roll down the window and inhale deeply. The wind whips my curls in every direction, and I scrounge around my coat pocket for a hair tie.

"Do not even think of playing your music," Aida warns Rainie. "I get to pick until we hit the border, and I choose Ludovico Einaudi."

"I will drive this car off a bridge," Rainie replies.

"We aren't going over any bridges."

"I'll find one."

Rainie enters the highway, flooring the car into the empty lane. Streetlamps fight a losing battle against the fog, and Rainie flips her high beams every time we switch lanes. Lucia reads out the directions, straining against her seat belt to peer through the windshield. Aida taps her marker against her sketchbook, watching the trees fly past us in blurs of green and brown.

I relax into the seat, watching them repeat the same patterns we've had for years.

Before we cross the border out of Ward, Rainie swings into the gas station. I follow them into the store, my heart beating at double speed when I realize we're alone with the attendant. Three others in the store should be more than enough, but the curse is getting strong. Less bound by the rules I've grown accustomed to. Each minute inside the gas station store passes like an eternity, and I hover by the donuts until Rainie and Lucia finish checking out.

Lucia pulls out the snacks as soon as we return to the car, handing out Corn Nuts and M&M's like a junk food fairy godmother.

Muttering something about mileage, Rainie reroutes us back onto the highway. Lucia tosses the rest of the snacks on the seat between us and spreads the empty plastic bags over the car's floor. "To catch the crumbs," she says.

"You know we're gonna get lunch while we're there," Rainie points out, pausing to snarl at a weaving trucker.

"I like gas station food. Makes me feel like we're on an adventure," Lucia says. She smiles apologetically at the same trucker.

The music changes, a slow song filling the car. Lucia sings along to the Italian lyrics, and I catch Aida's raised brows in the rearview mirror. Equally impressed, I elbow Lucia lightly. "Someone's been practicing."

She laughs, but it trails off into a sigh. "My dad has been so weird ever since my nonna died. He and my mom only speak Italian in the house, but he never cared if I responded to them in English. Now, he says it's like watching our heritage die before his eyes when I struggle to put together a sentence or haven't heard of some famous poet he grew up reading. The other day, he said each generation after me would lose more and more of their identity as Italians, like a dishrag being wrung out with the next set of children, until the only thing we knew about being Italian is what other people told us."

Rainie whistles. "Yikes. That is *harsh*."

"I get it, though," she says softly. "I memorize popular songs because it's the only time I speak Italian without stuttering, and my mom always plays them around the house. I spent twenty minutes arguing with my cousin the other day because I told her Italians like spicy food, and when she asked me where I got that from, I was too embarrassed to say I saw it online. I watch videos and follow the news; I *try*. I really do. But at the end of the day, it still feels like I'm trying to crowdsource my own identity. Like I'll never be able to reach one hundred percent, and my dad will be right."

"Yeah," Aida says, her pencil paused over her sketchpad. I wonder if she's thinking of her mom, who nearly cut contact with Aida's older sister after she married a guy without "a lick of Ethiopian in him." Aida's nieces don't speak Amharic. It grieves Aida's mom endlessly. "We understand."

"My mom literally could not care less," Rainie says. "She doesn't listen to me no matter what language I talk to her in."

Lucia squeezes Rainie's shoulder.

I wonder, if I look around, how many shadows would be filling this car. How many of them trap these moments of heartbreak, haunting us with fleeting reflections of who we might have been.

Lucia's dad is right about one thing: It won't be the same for our kids. We might not be able to pass along all the stories, we might mix up the details of some traditions, but we will pass along a new kind of strength. For better or worse, our children won't grow up like this, frozen on the threshold between two worlds. They won't be made to feel like they're on the outskirts of their own identities, afraid to venture too far into one side and lose sight of the other.

"Do you think we're the kids our parents imagined we'd be when they were young?" Lucia murmurs.

They won't ask questions that break your heart, because you know exactly what kind of guilt inspired it.

We aren't spare parts of an identity or uneven pieces struggling to fit anywhere they're placed. We will never be fully one or the other, but we can be something third. Something new and special and just as whole as those who came before us.

The song ends. Rainie thumbs a button on the steering wheel, and it starts playing again.

"We're way better than they could have imagined. You're co-captain of the varsity soccer team and head of the spirit committee. You bake for *fun* and don't suck at it. You're so freaking sweet, it's like being friends with a walking root canal." Rainie takes a bridge too fast, and we collectively lean to the left as she rounds the bend. "You're a whole person, Lucia. You're not a fragment or a *dishrag*." Her tone brooks no argument, and it brings a small smile to Lucia's face.

"Now, finish serenading us with this depressing-ass song," Rainie orders.

A green sign signals the end of Ward's perimeter. THANK YOU FOR STOPPING BY, it declares. Spray painted an inch beneath it, in rebellious black, are the words "DON'T COME AGAIN."

NADINE HAIKAL
EL AGAMY, ALEXANDRIA
2004

The baby was due one month from today.

Nadine paced her room, rubbing circles into her protruding belly. They were leaving for California tomorrow. Hatem had booked their tickets, gotten their visas. He'd shown her photos of a tiny house in a town called Ward.

Nadine knew the burst of productivity had as much to do with their new family as it did with losing his other one. Getting disowned by his parents had hit Hatem hard. He wouldn't let Nadine apologize, told her over and over that "they just don't know you like I do" and promised they'd come around once they had some time.

The personal distaste of Hatem's parents meant nothing to Nadine. Her mother and Safa were the real danger. They had no idea what she was planning. No idea they were losing one of the last Haikals capable of feeding the curse.

It was all set. Every loose end tied. So why couldn't she shake the feeling that she'd miscalculated?

Hatem might have the advanced degree, but nobody strategized like Nadine. For her fiancé, she let herself seem soft and sweet, a small-town girl dreaming of far-flung shores. With time, she hoped to become that woman. The soft Nadine Mansour.

But until then, she was still Nadine Haikal, and she would bet her right arm that something was amiss.

An hour before dawn, the animals began to howl. A flicker above her bed stopped Nadine mid-pace. The air warped, folding open like the spine of a book. A girl took shape, perched on the edge of the bed. She frowned at the window and covered her ears.

Nadine froze. The girl phased in and out, her movements stitched together with unsteady thread. Tight curls fell past her shoulders, and she had brown freckles by her temple.

A shadow? But—why was she so blurry?

"Who are you?" Nadine demanded. Her heart beat a frantic staccato, warning her away from the specter, but Nadine was not easily intimidated.

The girl shoved her feet in a pair of slippers at the door and squeezed outside, closing the door with a click behind her.

A sharp, piercing pain shot through Nadine's stomach. She gasped, catching herself on the wardrobe. What on earth? The pain blossomed into agony, and she doubled over.

Nadine stumbled to the mirror, shoving her blouse up to expose her stomach. As she watched, little hands took shape beneath the thin layer of skin covering her womb. Pushing. Scratching.

Nadine coughed, spattering the mirror in red flecks. Engorged red veins formed over her belly, pulsating ropes of flesh throbbing an inch high.

Another cough. Blood ran down Nadine's chin, syrupy thick.

The baby. Something was wrong with her baby.

Nadine limped outside, leaving wet red handprints in her trail. Where had the girl gone? She needed to follow the girl.

"Nadine?" her mother gasped. She caught Nadine as she stumbled, laying her gently onto the ground. "Safa! Get over here!"

Her mother smoothed the sweaty hair from Nadine's forehead. "Darling, it's time. Your child is coming."

Nadine shook her head, arms wrapped protectively around her middle. "No, no. No, it's too early. She's not finished yet. She needs more time."

Pain ricocheted through Nadine. She screamed, clawing at the marble floor. A nail snapped, but she didn't feel it. The pain in her stomach was a vortex, subsuming all else.

The baby couldn't come now. They were leaving for California tomorrow. Nadine would give birth to this child far away from her mother and sister. Far away from the door and that horrible orange light.

Safa knelt at her feet, laying out towels and pots. The sight of a baby blanket with a paisley pattern sent Nadine rolling to her side, vomit bubbling forth and mixing with the blood in her mouth. Her daughter couldn't be born here. Her mother would lay her daughter—*Hatem's daughter*—at the door on the third floor. If Nadine's daughter passed, her family would never let her leave this villa. Nadine's daughter would be marked for life, as surely as Nadine was marked.

A million wails shredded the inside of Nadine's brain. She tossed her head back and forth, trying to expel the heinous noise. They belonged to the parents of the children she'd offered. The mothers of the kids she'd laid at the door. Their howls would mix with her baby's birth cries.

Safa shoved Nadine's knees apart. The towels went under her hips. A maniacal glee shimmered in her sister's black gaze.

"Take a deep breath, Nadine," Safa said. "This will hurt."

CHAPTER TWENTY
PRESENT DAY

Jesse hasn't replied to any of my calls or messages, so I've resorted to setting up camp on the living room couch and peering out the window every few minutes. He'll have to leave his house eventually, right?

Steam curls from my mint tea. A quilted throw blanket Lucia thrifted for my fifteenth birthday covers my legs. My journal lays open over my knees. Every entry since the curse has been dark and depressing, so I filled five pages with the joy of yesterday's shopping trip. I described watching my friends' faces light up when they found their favorite dresses; Rainie and Lucia's argument when Rainie flipped the price tag and tried to return her dress only for Lucia to offer to pay the difference; Aida's little smile as she ran her fingers along the stitched bodice of her pink mermaid gown.

I grin into my shoulder. No attacks, no orange eyes, no rotting smell. For a whole day, I got to pretend none of this was happening.

A car speeds by, headlights shining through the window and trailing across the living room like a pair of yellow eyes. They illuminate Jesse's car parked in his driveway. I know he's home, and I know *he* knows I'm home.

Setting the journal aside, I open the window and offer my hand to the punishing bullets of rain.

I have never minded that Ward is a stagnant place. A collection of dots on a map for tourists to skim past on the hunt for somewhere better. A town where the dust never stirs.

Even when I dreamed of living outside Ward, part of me knew it would never be anything but a dream. I couldn't abandon Baba. He had no family here, no hobbies, no true friendships. Not even his wife's tombstone to visit. On our anniversary last year, I told Alex my doubts, and he laughed. He thought I was joking. His parents had existed before him. They would exist after. I didn't know how to explain that the day my father left Masr for me, he reached into the future and changed it. He created a debt I would pay, lovingly, forever. He left for me, and I will stay for him.

Still, I don't mind the dream. Reality can't cast its shadows there. In it, a phantom version of me gets to live a thousand different lives. Golden lives full of sunshine and colorful gardens. Lives where I go to Masr again and sip fragrant espresso at one of the cafés facing the endless blue of the Mediterranean Sea. Where I meet Baba's side of the family and show off the paltry local knowledge I'd acquired during my first visit.

It is safe to rest my hopes there, in these dreams where no shadow stays.

A knock comes at the door, startling a yelp out me. I forgot to keep watch over the driveway, but it couldn't be Baba. Baba would just use his key to enter, and he isn't due home for another hour or two.

Another knock. "It's me. Open up."

If I knock over the journal and nearly overturn my tea in my rush to get off the couch, well—nobody needs to know.

I throw open the door, belatedly remembering that I'm supposed to be annoyed with him for dodging my calls.

Rain drips from the awning behind Jesse. The porch light we've been meaning to fix flickers petulantly over his head. It glows over the length of the boy on my porch, his mouth pulled into a tired half-smile.

"Hey, Sour Patch."

"I'm about to sour-punch you," I tell Jesse, fiercely determined not to find his smile charming or the wet hair plastered to his forehead endearing. "Where have you been?"

The half smile becomes a full grin. My heart performs a complicated flip in my chest. Jesse is always handsome, even in his brooding, solitary hours, but a smiling Jesse?

My grip on the door tightens. I avidly observe the awning behind his head.

"Sorry, honey bun. Did I miss the kids' bedtimes?"

I try to slam the door in Jesse's face, but he catches the frame with one hand and pushes it back with mortifying ease. "I love it when you get all huffy," Jesse says, leaning over the threshold. "So un-cheerleader-like of you."

"For the last time, I am *a dancer.* It is a different set of rules, a different coach, a different training regime, a whole other competition track—"

I stop myself midway through the sentence, recognizing the trap too late. Shaking my head, I throw out, "Jerk. What are you going to do when you get your soul back and half your personality disappears?"

Regret hits me as soon as I say it.

Jesse's mouth drops open. So does mine. We stare at each other for a full thirty seconds.

Before I can profusely apologize, Jesse bursts into laughter. He doubles over, heaving like he's about to hack out a lung. He laughs for so long, my remorse melts back into irritation, and I put my hands on my hips.

Another minute ticks by. "Let me know if you're almost finished or if I should go grab a snack while I wait."

Jesse straightens, wiping at his eyes. When he speaks, his voice rasps with poorly suppressed delight. "Imagine how well we would've gotten along if you'd just been yourself all these years."

"Who else do you think I was?" I say tetchily.

Jesse sighs. Studies me. "Never mind. I take it back. We would've killed each other before sophomore year."

He steps closer. The edges of his jacket brush my bare arms. "Or," he murmurs right by my ear, "I might have fallen desperately, pathetically in love with you."

I freeze. Another joke?

I search, but there is no malice in Jesse's features. No indication he's playing games with me.

"Big words for a guy who basically threw himself into oncoming traffic when I kissed him," I say hoarsely. A little teasing to show him the kiss in the train doesn't have to sit between us like an unpinned grenade.

Except there's nothing joking about the way Jesse's jaw tightens.

My mouth goes dry when his hands cup my face, his thumbs light as a feather on either side of my cheekbones.

"Yasmina Mansour, hear me well, because I'll only say this once. Actually, that's a lie—I'll say it as many times as you want to hear it. As many times as it takes for you to believe it." Jesse's voice drops, his breath caressing my parted lips. "If you still want to kiss me after we break this curse, I am all yours."

I stop breathing.

"I thought it was obvious, but I forgot who I was dealing with," Jesse continues, a hint of frustration seeping into his tone. He catches one of my curls and wraps it around his knuckle. "When you're not stuck with me anymore—when you have every option available to you again, including Mama's Boy—I'll know that when you kiss me, it's not just because I'm the only one left."

Frustration boils inside me. He genuinely thinks he's some kind of placeholder for Alex. How am I supposed to convince him that I haven't given Alex more than a passing thought in weeks?

The temptation to argue is overpowering. So what if Jesse's the only one I can be around right now? I had wanted to kiss him because he was *him*, not because he was there.

The fact that it was the best kiss of my life, well . . . his ego doesn't need the stroking.

I stay quiet. Even if I know he's wrong, he doesn't. Jesse, who tries so damn hard not to care about anything and winds up caring more than any single person should, is offering me the chance to hurt him. For the first time, Jesse Talbot isn't hiding that he cares.

"I'll hold you to it," is all I say, and the relief on Jesse's face makes me doubly glad I didn't try to push.

He steps back. The mood shifts, a stiff formality replacing his warmth. "You should go get your coat."

I eye the rain pouring behind him. I have exactly zero desire to leave my comfortable nest on the couch and step into the deluge. "Why?"

"We need to go to the mortuary. There's something I need to show you."

CHAPTER TWENTY-ONE
PRESENT DAY

"Stop staring. It won't bite."

Despite the reassurance, I'm not sure where Jesse thinks my attention would be better directed if not at the corpse in the middle of the room.

Painfully bright lights wash over the cavernous mortuary. Silver faucets gleam behind three enormous sinks, two of which are filled to the brim with what smells like lemon and bleach. Five metal slabs, including the one currently occupied by a dead body, are lined up in perfect symmetry in the middle of the room. A tiny drain perforates the center of every slab, the coils rusted red. On the other side, tightly latched lockers cover the wall.

Cold and clinical, Elias Talbot's mortuary leaves no doubt that this is not a place where the living belong.

The vent above the sink rattles. A whoosh of cold air hits the top of my head.

Jesse waves a hand. "Just the AC. He keeps it cold in here."

Of course. For the bodies.

I lean against one of the slabs, trying to school my features into neutrality. Boredom, even. A dead body just a couple of feet away? Okay, and I had chicken parm for lunch, so now we have two facts nobody cares about. A freezing basement mortuary where the only sound is the hum of the machine that sanitizes the tools Mr. Talbot is going to use on said dead body? Please.

I am *not* going to think about it.

From behind a desktop roughly the size of small television, Jesse says, "The faster you get over here, the faster we can leave. My dad's software doesn't let me extract information on a hard drive, and if I try to email it to myself, he'll get the notification on his phone."

I think the corpse was a woman.

"Why did you use your dad's computer to begin with?"

"His database."

I wait for him to tack on the rest of the sentence, but he presses a button on the keyboard without glancing up.

"Congratulations, you just won first prize for THE most useless answer!" I applaud politely.

Mirthful eyes flick up from beneath his lashes, his lips twisting in a reaction I now recognize as him locking in a laugh before it can break free. The sight is enough to ease a few of the knots tightening in my belly. It's strange, not having to hold back my thoughts before I speak or edit my words to make sure they're the best fit for the person hearing them. I've spent so much of my life moving through the world as though I need to compensate for taking up space in it. As though everyone whose life I entered was owed the best version of me, and the best version was who *they* wanted. Jesse, though... none of my calculations work on Jesse. I can't figure out which Mina he wants, so he just gets the Mina that *is*.

"Remember when I told you my dad spent a few years trying to figure out what kind of deal my mom made in Sarasota? Well, he needed access to a ton of information, and he found a way to compile a search engine with a database of articles he pulled from across the globe. The database only covers twelve countries, but he scoured them from head to toe. Every region and locality, every newspaper, periodical, bulletin, or police report.

It took him years to put it together." Jesse chuckles, though there's no humor in it. "All that work only to find out my mom's curse originated on the west coast of Florida."

I inch around the slabs, sticking close to the wall. Jesse watches me, brow arched, looking torn between amusement and exasperation. When I finally reach his table, he kicks a stool toward me. "Glad you had a safe voyage."

I huff, settling onto the stool. "You know, I think you should rein in the sarcasm a little considering I haven't screamed even once at the DEAD BODY."

"This *is* me reining it in," he says. "If I rein it in any more, I'll end up on one of the slabs."

I aim a kick toward his stool and wince when my toe slams into a metal leg. "That isn't funny!"

He flashes a smile so wicked it would make the devil flinch. "Last one, I promise."

Right, and someday I'll be able to watch *Assal Eswed* without sobbing at the ending. I shake my head. It only occurs to me after Jesse returns his attention to the monitor that the knots in my stomach have almost completely disappeared.

"I figured out what the numbers in your mom's journal mean." Jesse purses his lips. In an unusual turn of events, he seems to be struggling for words. "When your mom found out she was pregnant with you, I think she started researching the curse."

The glow from the monitor casts the sharp angles of Jesse's face in a ghoulish blue. The knots return with a vengeance. "And? What did she find?"

"She found other families who had struck deals like the one Bamba made. She traced the curse all over the world." Jesse angles the journal toward me and taps a line of numbers with his pen.

"Once I found this family, it was easier to figure out what she was looking for."

He presses a number on his keyboard, and a series of paintings show up. On one of them, an unsmiling set of parents stand behind two somber young children. The palace around them is nothing short of grand, rendered in hues of red and gold.

"This was a military general's family in the Ottoman Empire. He was nobody. No wealth, no reputation, no well-to-do family. Then out of nowhere, he's appointed to a top political position in the region. He builds a mansion so spectacular, the townspeople start mistaking it for a royal post. But soon after it's built—"

"Children start to disappear," I finish, unable to tear my gaze from the man in the uniform.

"Yes. It continues for six generations." Jesse points to the line of numbers in my mother's journal again, to the left of the dates. A simple ו marked the generations.

"What happened after the sixth generation?"

He taps the keyboard again, and a translated black-and-white headline fills the screen.

Mass Deaths of Demir Family: Eshak Palace in Ruin

"When the curse finishes with a family, it doesn't just end. It eliminates every living member of that family and destroys the host home. Look at your mom's markings—each of these rows is a place where the curse traveled and the number of generations it lasted. Families across the world: Germany, Portugal, Libya, Nigeria, New York. Your mom traced at least a dozen. The longest the curse lasted in a family was nine generations." He swivels back to the monitor and hits the arrow. Another image loads, this one a black-and-white photo of a large family posing in front of a beautiful countryside estate, their smiles aimed at the camera and each other. In the corner of the screen, Jesse has pinned a row of scanned newspaper articles under the heading "*Possibly Linked Disappearances.*" I might've gathered the energy to make a crack about how if Jesse showed this amount of discipline with his schoolwork, he might be graduating as valedictorian instead of Aida.

But my eyes fall on the photo of a small boy at the bottom of the screen and freeze.

"I know him." My voice echoes between the mortuary's sterile walls. "That's the boy I saw in your room—the shadow!"

"Him?" Jesse enlarges the photo, and I nod, tears pricking my eyes. The headline is in French, but thanks to a language app and a two-year obsession with *Anna and the French Kiss* in middle school, I can decipher "missing" and "dead."

That smiling family had killed him.

How many children has this curse taken? How many lineages has it ended at the expense of maintaining its favored one?

"I wonder why the shadows showed you this kid in particular," Jesse muses.

I swipe a tear from under my eye before Jesse can see. "I don't know. Who took the curse on for this family?"

"I couldn't find records tracing back to the origin, just that the first recorded owner of the estate came into wealth suddenly and held on to it for decades. This thing, this curse... it always picks someone broken down, no money or family. They have nothing, and then the curse gives them everything."

"And in exchange, they get to take away everything from people who have nothing." The bitterness leaks into my voice, and Jesse finally glances over, brows knitting in concern.

I don't look at him. "Did the curse always end the same way?"

Silence follows.

"So it is going to kill me," I say dully. "I'm not useful to it, and Khalto

Safa is sick. When she dies and there's no one left to satisfy the conditions of the curse, every Haikal in the world dies with her."

"No." The harshness startles me, and I find Jesse's boot at the bottom of my stool, his burning gaze inches away. "I didn't bring you here to show you how you're going to die, Mansour. Your mom had a plan. She was trying to find a way to break the curse without, you know, killing Bamba's entire bloodline. I'm guessing she used your dad's access to the National Archives to find some of these dates."

"Why would she think she could end it? She has a younger sister who seems pretty happy giving the curse whatever it wants."

Jesse watches me for a minute. The scent of acetone and alcohol wipes tingles in my nose. "Do you not remember what the housekeeper said the night you saw the door?"

Why else do you think she brought Nadine's daughter here?

The house has been in ruins for years.

Safa's sick.

"Your aunt is dying, Mina."

I weave my fingers together to stop their trembling.

Jesse keeps going. "She's probably been sick for a long time. She called you when she did because her time was finally running out, and she knew there would be nobody left to satisfy the curse."

"But why?" I gasp. "She could have just found someone else. Why would she bring me to that house knowing what it meant?"

Jesse flips the pages of the journal, back to the very first entry we read at the Grease & Grind.

Mama thinks I need to be kinder to Safa. She says my sister holds grudges, and how I treat her now will determine how she treats me in the future.

"Spite," Jesse says, simply. "She despised your mom. You were the best way for her to get her revenge."

Impulse propels me before sense can catch up, and I grab Jesse's hand. I hold tight, breathing hard. I don't care if he doesn't hold my hand back, I just need to feel another person, to remember I'm alive, I'm alive, *I'm alive—*

To my relief, Jesse's hand closes around mine, warm and strong.

"After Mr. Hale attacked us, I saw a woman on the beach," I whisper. "She was talking about how our family had made a name for itself by destroying others. How they'd destroyed the vulnerable community around them and built a legacy with its bones."

They make us mortal so they can be everlasting.

"No wonder Khalto Safa was so angry. No wonder the curse won't let me go." I release Jesse's hand, wrapping my arms around myself. "My mother cheated."

"Cheated?"

I'm too numb to cry. Too numb to do more than laugh through cold lips. "She killed all those kids... ruined so many families, and she thinks that's not going to catch up with her? She thinks she can marry my dad and move away and pretend none of it happened?"

No wonder Baba's family had disowned him for marrying her. No wonder he'd let his fear and conflict-aversion prevent him from making amends and decided the easiest course of action was to pretend the past never existed. In that sense, he and my mother were alike.

"There's something else."

I close my eyes. I'm not sure how much more I can bear before I lean over and puke on Mr. Talbot's equipment.

"The curse... I don't think it's trying to kill you. I think it's trying to drive you out of Ward." Jesse's fingers brush my cheeks, skimming over my closed eyes. "Mina, when you opened the door, I think you took the test. You must have passed, because it wants you back. It wants you out of Ward."

My heart stops.

"Why would you say that?" I shoot off of my stool. "Why would I have passed the test? You think I'm capable of—you think I could *ever*—"

"That's not what I meant." Jesse rises, kicking the stool between us to the side. "I don't know how it decides who passes and who fails. Who has to be an active participant in the curse and who just gets to go off and live their life without seeing the cartoon anvil hanging over their heads."

"I can't deal with this, Jesse," I say, my voice cracking around his name. "I'm not built to handle this much death. To handle any of this. You were right, you were right about me being nothing but an airhead social butterfly, that's what I'm good at, that's what I can *manage*— "

Jesse's hands move to my face, fingers pushing into the curtain of my hair and tilting my head up. I grab his wrists tight, just in case he tries to draw away. He waits until my breathing slows to speak. "Did I ever say it was *easy* being a social butterfly?"

"Airhead social butterfly."

"Airhead social butterfly," Jesse amends with a curl of laughter. "That's a damn difficult job. You care about things. Miss Diaz, sports, dance routines, contestants on that unspeakable dating show. Your friends and father." He moves close. For a second, we stand in a vast nothingness, the only spots of color in an endless void. If these shadows can truly mark moments, I hope this one earns a red thumbtack. Securing us here, forever, even as the rest of the world marches forward.

"You care about things, too," I say. If I'm not careful, I might admit to Jesse I've discovered his secret. How he cares more than any of us. About crooked porch steps and quarreling drama students. About his father.

Maybe even a little about me.

Jesse catches a tear beading in the corner of my eye with his thumb. "You're a terrible liar. We'll have to work on that after we figure out this curse crap."

Despite the cauldron of despair bubbling in my stomach, I manage to laugh. "Stop trying to corrupt me."

Jesse's smile becomes a full-fledged grin.

"Never."

A bang from above freezes us in our tracks. A door slams shut, and Jesse releases a string of profanity vile enough to make a pirate's ears bleed. "My dad is home."

Jesse slams a button on the computer, closing out the open screens.

Panicked, I say, "You can't let him come down here. It'll just be the three of us, and after Mr. Hale—"

I can't let Jesse fight his own father if the thing takes Elias. Not to mention our cover would be blown, and Jesse's dad would probably force his son to stay away from me. One curse on Jesse's plate is bad enough, and adding the girl next door's might be too much for Mr. Talbot to handle.

"I'm aware," Jesse grinds out. "I'll go upstairs and tell him my truck's engine is busted. When you hear the door close, turn left for the kitchen and sneak out the back door. There's a hole in the chain link fence you can fit through."

Inanely, I think, *So that's how he got to the front door without crossing the driveway.*

Without waiting for my input, Jesse unlocks the door with his thumbprint. He grabs a clipboard from the rack and uses it as a doorstop, forcing the door slightly ajar. "Don't let the door shut," he says. "Only my dad and I can open it."

"Trust me, I won't. Getting stuck in here would be the final nail in the coffin." I laugh nervously. "Get it?"

Jesse stares at the ceiling for a long beat. When he lowers his gaze, it's unbearably soft, his panic temporarily shoved to the wayside. "Yeah, Mansour. I get it."

Jesse disappears, leaving me alone in the mortuary. Without the computer to focus on, ignoring the corpse on the other end of the room becomes impossible. I fiddle with Mr. Talbot's tools, but the knives and stitching equipment gross me out. The air conditioner clangs to life, shaving another few of my nerve cells to the nub.

Why hasn't the upstairs door shut yet? What's taking so long?

I tug curiously at the red handle of one of the metal lockers on the far wall. The latch catches, refusing to open. I try a blue handle. It unclicks easily. There's no one lying inside, thankfully. I hastily shut the locker door.

After accidentally inhaling a few too many chemicals, I hop onto a metal slab and lie back, tucking my hands neatly by my sides.

Wedding rehearsals, graduation rehearsals, why not death rehearsals? I'm more likely to die than graduate at this point, aren't I?

Jesse's dad will be the one who cuts me open, probably. He'll have no choice.

I turn my head to the large rectangular mirror reflecting the length of the mortuary. My hair spills over the side in a black wave.

If Jesse's research proves true, if my mother really was trying to break the curse... that would mean there was a solution. A way to survive.

In the mirror, the sheet-covered corpse on the other end of the mortuary sits up.

CHAPTER TWENTY-TWO
PRESENT DAY

My heartbeat slows. Subsumed under a tidal wave of terror so potent, I can taste its sour tang under my tongue. I lay still on the table for six seconds that stretch out into eternity. In those six seconds, a reel of disjointed thoughts flick through my mind like credits at the end of an old movie.

I should've gotten the second cartilage piercing on my seventeenth birthday instead of waiting for my eighteenth.

Who will take care of Baba when I'm gone?

I wish I'd adopted a hamster. Everything would suck so much less if I had a hamster.

And finally: *I miss Mama. Monster or not.*

The white sheet slides from the corpse as it stands, revealing the pale, puffy, and very naked form of a middle-aged woman. A long line of stitches runs from her throat to her pubic bone. The thin lines of a tattoo twist over her hip, unreadable under the peeling flecks of skin. The flap of her skull curls at the edges, where it's been surgically carved into a U-shape above her neck.

Where was the rot smell to warn me? The orange eyes? Bluish veins coil over the dead woman's white eyes. It's almost as if the thing simply plucked the nearest human-shaped entity in the room to control.

Jesse was right. It hasn't just gotten stronger; it's gotten strategic.

The corpse stands between me and the door. Slowly, I slide off the metal bed. Maybe if I injure it and run, I can make it to the stairs before it recovers.

Can you even injure the dead?

Limbs stiff with petrified flesh move toward me. I spring into action, grabbing a handsaw from Mr. Talbot's workstation. Shrieking at the top of my lungs, I swing the saw without aim. In my frenzied grip, the saw meets it mark, gouging a gash across its chest. The would-be fatal wound doesn't slow it down.

The corpse grips my arms, knocking the saw loose, and hurls me into the door. I collide against the solid surface. A loud snap rings in my ears.

No.

The clipboard lies in pieces by my legs. The doorstop Jesse used to prevent me from getting locked inside—gone.

I'm trapped in a mortuary with something that wants to kill me. Something I can't kill.

Horror rises inside me like volcanic lava. I crawl under the metal slabs, skittering away from the clawed fingers swiping for me. My chest heaves, my need for air stronger than my aversion to the chemical odors wafting off the body. If I can evade it long enough for Jesse to come check on me, I might make it out of here.

A hand closes around my ankle.

I shriek as my writhing body slides into the light, dragged forward by a preternatural strength. I kick the corpse's chest as soon as I'm close enough, but it grabs my ankles and twists me onto my stomach. My head wrenches back as it grabs a fistful of my hair. At the desk, the computer suddenly flickers to life.

The image of my mother as a haughty young woman returns.

"Just because she gave you what you wanted doesn't mean I will," I snarl, terror and pain brewing into the most potent spite I've ever experienced. "Neither you, my mother, or Teta Bamba get to make my choices for me."

A black substance beads at the edges of the monitor and runs down the screen. The dead woman kicks me in the stomach. Hard.

Pain explodes in my middle. I cough wetly, struggling to stand and crashing to the ground again. It reaches for me, and I yank two handfuls of its hair. They tear easily in my grasp.

The computer screen warps like plastic left in the heat. In place of my mother appears the same sad young girl with the half-eaten sandwich. She watches with mournful eyes as the corpse slams me into the lockers. A rusted hinge slices my shoulder blade, leaving my blood dripping down the smooth panes.

A young boy replaces the girl on the screen. Child after child, watching me with accusation and despondency.

The corpse hurls me into Mr. Talbot's tool table, and dozens of forensic instruments shatter with the impact. Scissors and tweezers fall to the ground, their edges colliding with the tile in the sound of windchimes.

A searing agony knifes through my leg. Against my will, I glance down at my thigh and release a strangled cry. A shard of glass the size of my palm sticks out from my upper thigh, broken off from the beaker I'd smashed.

The corpse approaches, and my fury gets the better of me. "Why are you doing this?" I shout. "What do you want from me?"

I yank out the glass with a sob wrenched from my very soul. I wait until the corpse gets close and shove the shard deep into the side of its neck. A dribble of dark liquid seeps from the wound, dripping lazily onto its shoulders.

It doesn't falter as it dispassionately grabs my hair and drags me across the floor of the mortuary. I manage to swipe a pair of scissors from the ground and hack at the body's legs and arm, anything I can reach. Its grip doesn't budge.

The corpse slams my head against the table again. The thin skin at my temple breaks. Blood trickles down the side of my face. The scissors clatter to the ground, freed from my limp grip.

By the time the corpse pulls its arm back for the third time, I'm deadweight. Floating somewhere above it all. I barely register when it suddenly drops me or when its dismembered arm flops to the ground.

Jesse drops beside me. His mouth is moving, and I think he might be shouting, but my ears buzz too loudly to decipher his words. A face as lovely as his should never look so upset. I try to find my mouth to tell him as much, but it floats out of my reach.

From what seems like a great distance, I hear Jesse call, "I'm bringing her inside. You have to stay in a different room!"

Arms gently lift me from the ground. My head lolls to the side, and I absently note that I'm bleeding onto Jesse's jacket. "Sorry," I slur. Keeping my eyes open is getting harder. I think I tell Jesse I'll buy him detergent for the stain. He makes a noise like I've just run a knife through him.

"Don't worry about my goddamn jacket," Jesse growls. "Open your eyes, Mansour. You have to stay awake, okay?"

I'm getting tired of finding myself in situations where I need to stay awake. Why can't sleep be the answer for once? A nice, long sleep. Full of happy dreams and pillows that never get hot.

"I shouldn't have left you down here," Jesse continues. It takes me a second to identify the undercurrent in his strained voice: guilt. "If I thought there was the slightest chance—it animated a *corpse*—"

"Not your fault," I mumble. Jesse takes the stairs two at a time. The motion jostles the wounds on my temple and thigh. My whole body feels like a giant, throbbing bruise. The corpse hurled me around the mortuary, and my fading adrenaline is bringing the pain home to roost.

"It's not even that bad, Mina," Jesse says lightly. "Just a little bleeding here and there. Barely worth a second look."

Jesse lays me down in a cradle of blankets and pillows. His bed. When he moves to leave, a spurt of terror gives me the strength to grab his hand.

"I just need supplies to fix you up. I'll be right back," he promises. A quick squeeze. "Stay awake, little cheerleader."

"Dancer," I groan. Jesse grins briefly, and I let him go. He won't be long. He always comes back.

Time moves sluggishly. I imagine Mama leaning over me, a familiar pucker of concern in her forehead. Anytime I was sick, Mama would become inconsolable. She'd hover over me like a dragonfly, flitting around my bedside until I was all better.

Jesse returns between one blink and the next. "Good. You're awake," he says. He sets a white kit next to my leg and bites his bottom lip. I'm unduly fascinated by the action. "I'm gonna need to cut off your pant leg."

"Okeydokey," I say, yawning. Wasn't I sad a minute ago? What was I sad about? I'm too tired to remember.

The scissors neatly slice the denim, exposing the weeping wound on my thigh. Jesse sucks a breath in sympathy. He removes a syringe from the kit. "Some local anesthetic. I have to suture this."

I start to drift. Jesse flicks my knee. "No sleeping. Come on, tell me about your new and improved graduation speech. Tryouts are coming up." He maneuvers me onto my back, brushing aside the curls crusted to the blood on my temple. "Or maybe you want to talk about prom. Did you end up finding a dress with your friends?"

The cloth he wipes against my forehead comes away red. I stare at the ceiling. My thoughts drift, flakes in a snow globe the world won't quit shaking. "Don't make fun of me, please," I whisper. My nose tingles, the telltale warning of tears. "I know I'm not going to make it to graduation. I probably won't even survive until prom." The dance is this weekend. Four days away. A lifetime in curse years.

Jesse's incensed face fills my vision, looming above me. "You're gonna read your speech to that panel in two days because you *will* be at graduation. Where's your prom queen spirit?"

"Homecoming queen."

"For now. I doubt this bruise will be gone by the weekend, but you'll still get your crown, even after ten rounds with the dearly departed." Jesse dabs at my temple, cleaning it for the gauze. He's so meticulous, so careful.

Wasting more of his effort on another lost cause.

After he finishes, he ties off a trash bag and pauses. "I'll be back. Don't go to sleep."

I grunt. Whether or not I go to sleep is beyond either of our control at this point.

Jesse disappears outside. My head settles deeper into his pillow, and I breathe in the scent of his shampoo and fresh detergent. Closing one eye at a time doesn't count as going to sleep, right? They're just so heavy.

Voices filter from the hall. "You can't come inside. It'll possess you the minute you're alone with her."

"Then come with me," says a brusque, irritated male voice. My eyes fly open. Elias Talbot. "She needs professional care. She's probably got a serious concussion."

"I can take of her myself," Jesse answers. I almost smile. Always so stubborn. "Besides, the thing doesn't care if I'm in the room, too. I'm an exception."

A long pause. "The 'thing'? I thought you said it was a curse."

A shiver races down my aching body at the ice in Mr. Talbot's voice. "You've got a girl bleeding in your room right now. The damn high school homecoming queen. Do you understand the danger you've put her in? As soon as you realized she had a problem, you should've alerted me."

"I didn't need your help."

"Clearly," Mr. Talbot seethes.

"Dad—"

"No! This isn't your job, Jesse. You're going to get yourself killed protecting the neighbor's daughter. We've given up too much for you to treat your life so carelessly."

When Jesse speaks, it's quiet. Almost inaudible. Craning to listen helps ward away the sleep creeping up on me. I'm eavesdropping purely for my own health. "I didn't ask you to give anything up. You and Mom made a choice. All my life you've been making my choices for me, and I've let you. Mom decided she would rather I be born without a soul than not born at all. You decided we would live in this nowhere town and try to fit in with people I can barely stand. But you can't convince me to trust anyone else to protect Mina Mansour. Not this time. Not her."

"Ah, so that's it. You think helping her will earn you your soul."

"It's not about that anymore."

What?

Mr. Talbot sighs. "What is so special about this girl?"

I prepare for Jesse's glib remarks on my dance prowess or the unstable social hierarchy at Canyon High.

"Do you remember when we moved to Ward? No one in town would talk to us. They were afraid, and rumors followed us everywhere. But our second week here, I looked out my window, and I saw Mina mumbling under her breath outside our fence. She was holding a tray of homemade baklava and trying to figure out how to open the latch without putting down the tray." Jesse's soft laugh is music to my ears. "Eventually, she just used her nose to push the latch up. Anyone else would have given up or just put the tray down. She didn't stop until she was at our door, baklava in tow. And when she knocked, I didn't answer."

He was in the house? I remember the day clearly. Nosing the latch open like an overeager puppy and tiptoeing up the dodgy porch steps. Rocking on my heels as the doorbell echoed inside the house.

"Why not?" Mr. Talbot asks, grudgingly curious.

The words seem heavy on Jesse's tongue, reluctant to hit the open air. "Because. Because she's the kind of person who tries to talk to the loneliest person at a party. She cares so much it should be a crime. I knew the second I opened that door, the second I let myself accept any of her kindness, she would be done for. She wouldn't give up on me or put herself first—she would hold on even if I pushed her away, even if I completely broke her."

I turn my cheek into the pillow, tears dripping from my nose. The girl Jesse's talking about is gone. He only let himself get close to me once I was already broken, once there was nothing left to damage.

"You don't break people, Jesse. I raised you better," Mr. Talbot says, in a hard tone that brooks no argument.

This time, Jesse's laugh is cold, spreading through me like morning frost. "You did. That's the problem."

The door creaking open punctuates Jesse's statement, and he closes it before I can catch a glimpse of Mr. Talbot.

We stare at each other. Jesse tips his head back, exposing the long column of his throat. "Any chance you didn't hear that?"

"It was really good baklava," I say. "I ground the pistachios myself. You missed out."

An old sadness flits over Jesse's features. "I know."

He straightens, the moment gone before I even realized it was there. "We should get you home. Your dad will freak out if he notices you're gone."

Panic cannons through me, whiting out my mind. "No! No, please, let me stay. Don't leave me alone again." I start to cry in earnest.

"Whoa, hey. You can stay. Of course you can stay. I'll text one of your friends to call your dad and tell him you're spending the night with her. Sound good?"

I sniff. "Okay. Text Lucia. Baba likes her best." She always patiently listens to his rants about the flaws in higher education.

"Done," Jesse says, tapping out the keys on my phone. "You're good to go. I'll monitor you throughout the night, but try to stay awake for just a little longer."

The long day comes crashing down on me. Staying conscious becomes a feat of epic proportions. Dimly aware of Jesse rummaging in his closet, I peel open one eye when he strips off his bloody shirt, revealing miles of smooth skin. Without the obstruction of clothes, a tattoo I've only caught glimpses of reveals itself fully for the first time. Small black and white flowers blooming from an elegant stem trace the curve of his bicep.

"An orchid," Jesse says in response to my shameless staring. "Dad says it was my mom's favorite."

"Pretty."

Though I've never been to Europe, I imagine the slopes and divots of Jesse's body resemble the statues housed in the world's grandest museums. It suddenly seems like a crying shame that Jesse hides his beauty behind aggressive T-shirts and a beaten leather jacket.

When he moves to his dresser, still shirtless, I press a curious hand to his bare stomach.

Jesse freezes. I trace the taut line leading from his abdomen to his waistband. His skin feels soft, delicate velvet overlaying hard muscle. Before I reach the groove of his hip, a firm hand closes around my wrist.

"You are incredibly concussed," Jesse remarks flatly. I wiggle in Jesse's hold, aiming to map out the sinuous motions of his back, starting from the sharp points of his shoulder blades.

"Nuh-uh."

To my disappointment, Jesse tugs a shirt over his chest. He flashes a smile a touch too sour to be sincere. "Lose the head injury, and I'll let you touch whatever you want."

I flop back against the bed, scooting to make room for Jesse. At his hesitation, I pat the empty space. "No, you won't," I say, despondent. "You're afraid you'll break me."

He lays down stiffly, keeping a good foot of space between us.

"I'm stronger than I seem, you know."

Jesse's head turns on the pillow. "I don't think you're weak. That's not what I meant."

"Then what did you mean?"

He pinches the bridge of his nose, running his fingers to the furrow between his brows. "Hey, weren't you telling me about the dress you bought?"

I brighten instantly. "Was I? Oh, it's so lovely. Out of my budget, though. Baba will be mad, but maybe they can bury me in it. Kill two birds with one stone."

Aghast, Jesse says, "I can't tell if you're joking."

I describe the dress to Jesse in excruciating detail. Excruciating because I know the reality: Most guys simply don't want to hear a detailed breakdown of sequins versus flared sleeves. Alex would politely chime in with an "Oh wow!" every now and then, but I had no doubt he was mentally planning out his gym schedule. Jesse, on the other hand, couldn't be paid to be patronizing. He's been bluntly honest since the moment I met him.

The fact that he doesn't say a word while I go on and on about a prom dress confirms my fears.

He's afraid I'm a goner.

I force myself to settle in the moment. Curl my toes in the fuzz of Jesse's black comforter. Listen to the ticking clock until it syncs with the rain pattering against his window. Even the bruises, throbbing beneath my skin, ground me. I'm clutching at the present the way a child holds on to blades of grass. Watching as who I am permanently transforms into who I was. Who I will never be again.

"Why didn't you like me?" I ask. A flash of lightning through the window illuminates the wall of newspaper clippings and photos on Jesse's wall. The headlines on the mortuary computer flash through my mind, and I look away. "I mean, before all this started. Why didn't you like me?"

"Who says I didn't like you?"

I scrunch my face in disbelief, wincing when the action pulls at the wounds in my temple.

Jesse props his back against the headboard. The same restless, anxious energy from the train vibrates around him. I've learned to recognize it as Jesse carving out a window in the walls he carries inside himself. Small, easy to brick over. But a window, nonetheless.

"I don't know how to explain it. Do you remember freshman year, when it started to rain during lunch? Serious rain, practically Ward Wailer levels. Everyone was running for cover and screaming. You, being a menace to society and all, climbed on top of the lunch table and laughed. And because you're Mina Mansour, everyone stopped running. They started climbing on lunch tables, too. Dancing and cheering." Jesse glances at me, and his inscrutable features waver with something almost . . . soft. "You bake desserts that take hours for strangers you've known for minutes. All your friends would defend you to the death, and you would do the same for them. You tear up when you see burned French toast in the trash, 'cause it means a lot to you that your dad tried so hard to make it. It's not that I didn't like you, Mansour." Jesse tips his head against the wall, fixing his attention on a mustard water stain. "I just didn't get you."

I trace a paisley pattern onto the bedsheet. "And now?"

"Huh?"

"Do you get me now?" I can't bring myself to look up. At some point, Jesse's good opinion of me stopped being a trophy I could add to my collection. Jesse has seen me unravel. Seen me furious and broken and hopeless. His opinion of me won't be based off a shiny veneer. It'll be based on the real me. The real Mina, whoever she is.

Two fingers coax my chin up, bringing my gaze to Jesse's. A small smile curves his lips. "Even less."

I pinch the nearest body part I can reach. Jesse yelps, prying my hand away from his thigh. He dissolves into laughter, and the pressure in my chest eases a little. "See? A few weeks ago, I never would've thought you're the kind of girl with crab pincers for fingers."

Jesse settles into bed, drawing the cover over his waist. He reaches for the light and stops short.

"It's okay," I murmur. "You can turn it off."

Night envelops the room. Jesse turns on his side, facing me. I fold my hands under my head, grateful the bruise on my temple and thigh are on the same side of my body. I can't turn over, but at least I don't have to lie flat on my back.

Movement rustles from Jesse's side. He draws a pillow into the space between us. I ignore a spark of hurt. He's just being thoughtful. A divider pillow is way less awkward than waking up tangled around each other.

"How about me?" comes the quiet, intense question just as I'm settling into sleep. "What did you think about me?"

For one mean, petty second, I almost say, *I didn't.* It's not the truth, but the words would cut Jesse too quickly for him to see the lie in them.

"You scared me."

He doesn't say anything for a long moment. His chest rises and falls, and I find myself slowing my breath to match his.

"Do I still scare you?"

I lay my fingers on the pillow between us. I hate this pillow, I decide. Why does he think we need it? As though I need a pillow to stay away from Jesse. As though I might reach out to him otherwise, do something silly like rest my head on his chest and curl myself like a quotation mark around him.

Jesse is still waiting for an answer.

"Even more," I whisper.

A dark shape watches me from the ceiling.

To my right, Jesse sleeps. His even breaths dissolve in the deep, drowning silence. A lock of black hair lies over his temple.

The shape scuttles out of view. I keep watching Jesse, ignoring the pulse pounding in my ears. Half of me wants him to wake up and switch the light on. Watch him rake a hand through his tousled hair and squint irritably at the ceiling.

The other half wants him to stay as still and quiet as possible.

I can sense it behind me. Staring. The hairs on the back of my neck stand on end. My pains fade, replaced by a clarity only visceral fear can induce. A primordial instinct warns me against turning around and looking at the shadow.

Baba used to talk about common beliefs of the supernatural when he taught World Mythology. For instance, hunters never stalk their prey after sunset. When the night takes hold, the rules change. The balance of power between prey and predator disappears.

And there are hours of the night where the lines between realities become blurred. Where some believe time itself thins, becoming little more than a thread looping through the eye of God's needle.

The knot in my gut, the cold sweat on my palms. Familiar warnings. They happened in the villa every night, right before the animals began to screech.

I can feel the shadow breathing against my hair.

It wants me to turn around.

The clock on Jesse's wall ticks loudly. It won't leave until I face it. Until I let myself see.

With a shaky hand, I smooth the lock of hair away from Jesse's forehead.

"I can be brave, too," I say to the pillow between us.

Drawing away, I turn to face the cavernous darkness behind me.

"Don't take her! Safa, give her back!" it screams in my mother's voice, and time weaves through the needle.

NADINE HAIKAL
EL AGAMY, ALEXANDRIA
2004

"Don't take her! Safa, give her back!" Nadine screamed. Her sister ignored her, wrapping Nadine's daughter in the paisley blanket. Nadine tried to move. Hot pain razed through her.

Their mother accepted the crying bundle from Safa. She smiled down at the infant and said, "I hope it picks her. She has your grandmother's freckles." A ringed finger smoothed the baby's hair from her forehead. "A little freckle cluster, right on her temple."

Nadine curled against the tile, the residue of blood slick between her thighs. Everything inside her howled, demanding she stop them from taking her child. They couldn't do this. She had paid Bamba's debt her entire life. Ruined family after family, inflicted this very same agony on other mothers. What was the point if her own daughter wouldn't be spared?

"Get up, Nadine," her mother sniffed. "This behavior is unbecoming."

"Love has made her soft. Look at her. Probably thinking of her little graduate student in his sweater vests," Safa sneered.

Nadine glanced up sharply. Safa laughed. "Oh, did you think we didn't know who the father was? How the mighty do fall. Have you forgotten who we are, sister? Who we serve? You had no chance of running away with him."

"Spare the girl," Nadine ground out. "Spare my daughter, and you can take Hatem."

Even Nadine's black heart shivered at the callousness of her offer. She loved Hatem, yes. More than she thought possible. But she would also hand-feed him to wolves if it meant keeping her daughter.

"What would we do with him?" her mother asked, perplexed.

"Maybe we can show him exactly who his sweetheart really is. How do you think Hatem Mansour will react to learning that his rosy-cheeked love is the Terror of El Agamy?"

While Safa spoke, Nadine closed her hand around the scissors by her knee. Safa had used them to cut the umbilical cord. Nadine hid the scissors in the folds of her gown.

"Don't worry. It rarely rejects Haikal women," her mother said. She smiled down at Nadine. "The three—maybe four—of us in this house are its last agents. The only ones capable of repaying Bamba's debt. It needs us. I'm not angry with you for trying to run, ya umri. But you must understand that wherever you go, it will find you."

Nadine's mother flicked the switch, pitching the second floor in darkness. "No!" Nadine cried out. She groped for the wall.

In the center of darkness, a set of steps materialized.

Her mother's robe swirled around her ankles as she walked, carrying Nadine's daughter toward the steps. Safa followed eagerly, barely sparing her older sister a glance. In moments, they would lay the baby down at the door. The orange light would spread over her newborn in the test most Haikals had taken to determine their role in preserving the family line. If the child was chosen to serve the curse, then she would never be safe again. If she failed the test or failed to take it, then her life would be in the hands of the only people who *could* serve the curse: Nadine, Safa, and their mother.

As her mother ascended the stairs, a figure appeared beside her. The curly-haired girl in the slippers. She glanced back briefly, and Nadine's heart stuttered.

She had freckles on her temple.

The girl vanished, but Nadine was already moving. Any earthly pain took a back seat to the determination blazing through her. She crossed the floor, scissors held in a tight grip.

Nadine shoved Safa aside as she raced up the steps. The baby wiggled as Nadine's mother gently deposited the bundle on the ground. "Mama!" Nadine shouted. "Stop!"

At the door, Nadine's mother turned, the beginnings of a disapproving frown on her face.

Without a second of hesitation, Nadine plunged the scissors into her mother's heart.

The moment stretched for eternity. And as Nadine watched blood soak into her mother's robe, a chilling thought struck her. Evil was built into the bones of the Haikal villa. Like toxic dust motes floating on the stagnant air, it settled on the nearest breathing surface and *corroded.* Layers of tragedy and pain and loss. How long had Nadine been buried beneath them?

Bamba's deal didn't give Haikals roots or a legacy. It gave them chains.

Her mother stumbled into the banister, staring at Nadine with disbelief. Safa screamed. More tragedy to whet the house's appetite.

Nadine had ruined countless lives at the threshold of this door. She wouldn't let her child be next.

Nadine scooped up the baby and yanked the scissors from her mother's chest. Blood spurted onto the tile, a growing pool that dripped down the top step.

A macabre grin split Nadine's mother face as she collapsed. Her tongue flicked over red-stained teeth. "My favorite daughter. So cold, so compassionless." A laugh gurgled wetly in her chest. "You are an artist of cruelty, Nadine. Your child will be the worst of us. Worse than Bamba herself."

As much as Nadine wanted to bolt down the stairs, heedful of her dangerous proximity to the door, she couldn't help herself. "I'll raise her to be kind. Gentle, like her father. She won't be anything like us."

Twin rivers of blood streamed from her mother's nose. "Oh, you foolish girl. A beast cannot raise a butterfly."

Safa rushed to their mother. Nadine pointed the scissors at Safa, and her sister glared at Nadine with unmitigated hatred. A shiver of unease traveled down Nadine's spine. Safa was savage. Shallow and eagerly violent. Nadine had done her a grievous wrong tonight, and it would not be forgiven.

She and Safa would find one another again. Their story would not die here today.

"You and me," Safa whispered. "We will end in blood."

Nadine gripped her whimpering child against her chest. A hollow smile sprang to her lips. "A Haikal can only end in blood."

Her feet trailing red tracks on the steps, Nadine left a dead woman in front of the third-floor door.

If she had known what would happen to her daughter in seventeen years' time, Nadine would have turned around. She would have gone back upstairs and shoved the scissors into Safa's neck, over and over until the blades snapped against bone.

But Nadine didn't remember the girl in the slippers. Not for nine long years.

CHAPTER TWENTY-THREE
PRESENT DAY

"How do you know it wasn't a dream?" Jesse asks, drawing his boot up onto the seat. He balances on the back of the bench, his boots landing next to my thighs. The morning breeze batters us, coiling around my puffy pink sweater and seeping through the seams. Brown leaves shake loose from the trees whispering above.

"I could feel it. It was like I was in the house with them." I draw my sleeves over my knuckles. My cheeks redden from the cold, and it isn't lost on me how completely out of place I must seem next to the harshly gorgeous, leather-clad Jesse. Neither of us bothered to attend class today ("Maybe miracles *are* real," Jesse said when I announced I was ditching, proceeding to dramatically fall to his knees in the middle of the sidewalk), but Rainie had threatened to show up at my house if I didn't show proof of life. Meeting them for lunch in the school quad was our diplomatic middle ground.

There was no question of whether or not Jesse would join me. The incident in the mortuary had clearly spooked him more than he was letting on, because he hadn't left my side since this morning.

Teta—Nadine's mother—was wrong, I think bitterly. Mama raised a butterfly after all. Iridescent and empty-headed, fluttering desperately after others. I foolishly landed on Jesse's shoulder, and he's borne the weight of my problems ever since.

"So you're saying your mother killed your grandmother at the same door that opened during your visit? And you still don't remember what you saw behind the door?"

"You think I wouldn't tell you if I remembered what was behind the door?" I snap. The bandage on my head shifts, and I smooth the sticky edges back down. "Sorry."

"Don't worry about it." Jesse's knee knocks into my shoulder, and I glance back to find him frowning. "You know this isn't forever."

I almost laugh. In what world would anyone think Jesse Talbot would be the one encouraging *me* to be more positive?

Nadine Haikal was a completely different person than Nadine Mansour. When my mother left my grandmother to die in front of that accursed door, she'd left her old self behind, too. Two dead women, but only one kept going to start a new life here in Ward.

"I was born the same night my grandmother died." I'll never forget the seething hatred in Khalto Safa's eyes as she stared at my mother. But she didn't stand a chance against Mama, not then. Not until Nadine Mansour flew to Masr nine years later.

"I was right, wasn't I?" I ask. Toneless. "My mom didn't die in a car accident in Tanta. Someone hurt her."

A Haikal can only end in blood.

"Or some*thing*," he murmurs.

What I can't understand, what I've been unable to stop thinking about since my dream, is why Mama went back. She willingly returned to Khalto Safa and the Haikal villa, despite the fate she must have known awaited her.

Why?

Reading my mind, Jesse taps his backpack. "At least the shadow means we have another entry in your mom's journal. It might give us more answers."

"For once," I mutter.

The bell sounds, scattering my attention to the flood of students entering the quad.

"The graduation speech tryouts are at one today, right?" Jesse asks.

I narrow my eyes. "Yes. How did you know?"

He hops off the table, dusting himself off. "You've only forced me to listen to you practice half a dozen times. I checked to see when my torment would end."

"Well, you don't have to worry. I'm not trying out, so you won't have to listen to any more speeches."

Jesse ignores this momentous news in favor of tapping at his phone. "I'll see you after tryouts."

"Didn't you hear me? I'm not trying out."

He strides away. Over his shoulder, he calls, "One o'clock!"

He must have helped himself to an extra scoop of delusional this morning.

As soon as Jesse hops the fence, my friends emerge alongside the flood of students leaving for lunch. Lucia spots me first, and her features slacken with surprise before rearranging themselves into a beaming smile. Rainie is busy with her phone, maneuvering without looking up, but Aida maintains a hand on her shoulder to prevent her from walking into a beam.

Lucia throws her arms around my shoulders, nearly knocking us to the ground. "I am so, so glad to see you. When Rainie said you were coming, I didn't believe her."

Aida takes a seat across from me, spreading her lunch in its usual configuration. From left to right, it goes drink, meal, dessert, sketchbook.

"Lucia, could I see Mina's shoulder for a sec?" Rainie says.

Lucia and I exchange a bewildered glance. Rainie isn't exactly the hugging type.

The instant Lucia's arms are back at her sides, Rainie pinches my shoulder.

"OW!" I holler. "What was that for?"

She pinches me again, this time right next to my armpit. I flail, smacking at her torso.

"Why did Talbot text me to say you're not planning on going to tryouts?"

My jaw drops. That traitor!

"What?" Lucia gasps. "Mina, you've been wanting to speak at graduation since we were freshmen."

"I would blame Talbot, but I don't think this one's on him," Rainie adds. "What's the deal?"

"You love speeches. You're practically a walking three-part structure," Lucia agrees. "What changed your mind?"

"How about you guys leave Mina alone?"

Three heads swivel to Aida. She doesn't flinch, intent on sticking her straw into her strawberry banana juice box.

"Do *you* think she should skip tryouts?" Rainie crosses her arms over her chest.

"I don't care about tryouts. I don't care about graduation, either." The straw successfully impales the container, and Aida immediately clamps the end between her teeth.

"But Mina does," Lucia argues. She turns back to me. "At least, you used to."

I dig my knuckles into my eyes, leaning my forehead against the flat of my palms. In an academic sense, I understand why my abandonment of a long-held dream frightens them. I understand why they would see it as more evidence of some fundamental shift.

"But I don't, though," I say. "I don't care anymore."

I can't tell them the only reason I'm here is to maintain appearances for Jesse.

"Oh," Lucia whispers. She looks crestfallen. Rainie sets her phone down on the table and watches me, an inscrutable furrow in her brow. Only Aida doesn't react. She squeezes the bottom of her juice pouch until the thing is completely desiccated.

"Stop giving me the puppy dog eyes." Resigned, I cross my arms on top of the table. "If it means that much to you guys, I'll try out."

Lucia whoops, but Rainie's stare continues to bore into the side of my head. I brace myself for another round of questioning, but Alex's arrival effectively quashes that conversation.

Alex slides into the empty space opposite me. "Hey."

I straighten. The sight of my golden-haired ex brings with it a twinge of nostalgia, but nothing else. I broke up with Alex as a preemptive measure against the curse. Leaving him was awful, but I knew it was temporary.

Now, it may as well be a gulf between us instead of a rickety lunch table.

"Hi." I give him a small smile.

I hope he'll remember me fondly after he leaves Ward.

"What happened to your head?" Aida asks, bluntly asking the question everyone's thinking.

I touch my bandaged temple. The lie flows easily, water gliding over a timeworn stone. "Let's just say trying to stargaze from your roof is a bad, bad idea."

All of them except Alex buy the lie instantly, shaking their heads and muttering about my ridiculous impulses. After all, it wouldn't be the first time I'd taken advantage of the metal door to sneak to the roof and people watch.

Despair bursts in my chest. Have I always been such a talented liar? What else did I inherit from my mother?

A beast cannot raise a butterfly.

I'm the child of the Terror of El Agamy. That's what Khalto Safa called Mama.

Alex leans forward, his forearms pressing on the table. "Be honest. Did Talbot do it?" He gestures angrily at the bandage.

"Dude!" Rainie explodes.

"Alex, honestly." Lucia sighs, exasperated.

Aida pinches the bone in Alex's wrist, nearly earning herself a knuckle to the nose.

I wait until they fall silent. "Jesse would never hurt me," I say coldly.

"Because he's such a paragon of stability and calm?" Alex shoves his lunch away. I've only seen him this upset a handful of times. "Wake up, Mina! He has a disciplinary folder the size of France."

"So what?"

Alex's lips part. He stares at me as though I've announced my intention to dance buck naked in a pit of gators.

"Do you want to rehearse your speech?" Lucia interrupts, visibly quivering under the tension. She handles confrontation about as well as Rainie manages small talk.

"Not really. Can you believe prom is this weekend?" I say, rerouting Lucia's attention to her favorite topic.

The tactic works. Lucia launches into the game plan for Saturday, starting with the driver she hired to pick us up for dinner. "I made a reservation at Hathaway's for six, so don't be late."

Rainie cuts Lucia off. "Hathaway's? Isn't that the Italian restaurant with forty-dollar meals?"

"Oh, don't worry about the cost. My folks already paid for everything," she says.

On cue, Alex and I exchange a familiar glance of exasperation. I look away quickly. It's too easy to forget I'm not part of the group anymore.

"I can pay my own way," Rainie snaps. "Just don't force us to eat at hoity-toity restaurants."

At this point in the argument, Lucia would usually sigh and pull out her phone to make the requested change. To my surprise, Lucia's lips purse into a blazing line of determination. "If I didn't plan prom, nobody else would. I asked you a dozen times where you wanted to eat, and you just blew me off. You don't get to complain after the fact."

"Maybe I would've paid more attention if I knew our options were starvation or bankruptcy."

"Give it a rest, Rainie," Alex groans. "Can't you just say thank you and move on?"

I've known Rainie longer than any of them. Telling her she's overreacting is the equivalent of throwing gasoline on a forest fire. Before she can try to French braid Alex's earlobes together, I press a quelling touch to her shoulder. When her glare lands on me, I hold steady against it. We communicate in terse silence.

"Fine. Thanks," Rainie grunts at last. The table lets out a collective breath.

The conversation flows seamlessly. I stand outside the tide, occasionally wading in with a comment or chuckle. In a few months, they'll be attending the senior banquet and walking the stage to accept their diplomas. Brimming with excitement at the prospect of steering their lives to new horizons.

I smooth the torn corners of the graduation speech I'll never get to give and try to be happy for them.

At the bell, Aida says, "I'll walk with you to the admin building, Mina." She hoists her backpack over her shoulder.

Lucia grabs my arm. "We'll see you on Saturday, right?"

I squeeze her wrist. "Try and keep me away."

Cheered, Lucia wishes me luck on the tryout and dashes to her class across campus. Rainie elbows Alex, but he shakes his head, retreating into the current of students headed for sixth period.

"I'll make sure he's less annoying on Saturday," Rainie says, sighing. "Are you bringing Jesse?"

I scoff. Jesse attending a school dance is beyond even my formerly vast scope of optimism. "Jesse wouldn't be caught dead anywhere near prom."

"Shame. Would have loved to see someone force Talbot into a tux." Rainie runs off at the warning bell, leaving Aida to walk with me toward the admin building.

"Don't you have physics right now?" I ask.

Aida is jittery, restless. She shudders, scanning our surroundings with a care that skirts close to paranoia. "Can't you feel it?" She rubs her arms, nails biting into the creases in her elbows. "It's always near you. Waiting. I don't know how you can breathe."

I go still. Aida pays me no mind, focused on the dull brown of the admin building ahead. Lunch monitors mill around the quad, ushering loitering students toward their classes.

"Aida, what..."

Without slowing, Aida reaches into her backpack and pulls out the battered sketchbook. At the building door, she pivots. "Here. Take it." The sketchbook hits my chest.

She may as well have handed me a grenade. I hold the sketchbook at arm's length, gaze flying between it and Aida. "Are you seriously giving this to me? You haven't even let me take a *peek* in all the years I've known you."

"My sketches aren't always safe," she says cryptically. "If you're not meant to look at them, they can hurt you."

"Aida." I massage my forehead. "What the absolute living hell does that even mean?"

"It means these are for you. Just for you." Aida's gaze strays a few inches to my left before she blinks hard.

"Do you see them, too?" I whisper. "The shadows?"

She tangles her fingers in the gaps of her crocheted sweater, as if she doesn't know what to do with her hands now that there's no mysterious sketchbook between them. "I always see shadows, Mina. Always have, always will."

Before I can give voice to the myriad of questions rushing for freedom, Aida continues, "I've felt something attached to you since spring break. Aida I thought I was imagining it. But the drawings..."

Dread curls in my belly.

"Whatever this thing is... it's so angry. Beyond any menace I've ever felt." Aida draws a ragged breath. I can hardly comprehend the fact that Aida *knows.* Not everything, but enough. "Every second, it moves a little closer to you." Faintly audible, she whispers, "I can barely tell where it ends and you begin anymore."

"My mom." I swallow hard. "Did you feel it around my mom?"

Aida flinches, as though struck. After a minute, she offers a reluctant nod.

Aida had only met my mom once before she died. On a random Tuesday in the fourth grade, Mama came to pick me up after school. She'd stepped out of the car to wave me over from my perch beneath the jacaranda tree. Aida, who had yet to befriend anyone other than the librarian, had taken one look at my mother and screamed her little head off. She'd thrashed and wailed until Mrs. Watts carted her off to the nurse's office.

I'd forgotten about it until now. All Mama did at the time was shake her head in disapproval and mutter something about the chemicals in our school lunches.

The curse had claimed my mother. If Aida could sense it over me now, it could only mean one thing.

The curse claimed me when I opened the door. It added me to the row of Haikals bound to serve it.

I slide my speech over the front of Aida's sketchpad. "You should get to class," I say quietly. "I'll see you at prom."

"Will you?" she whispers.

My teeth click shut. Heartbreak swims in Aida's eyes, and from her, it's more than I can handle. I hurry into the admin building, heart racing sickeningly fast against my ribs.

The tryouts are being held in the counselors' conference room, and I peek through the window to make sure I won't be alone with anyone. Principal Bess lifts her head at my entrance. Her blond brows rise. "Miss Mansour."

Miss Diaz beams. "Hi, Mina!"

The other two teachers haven't had me in their class, but they've clearly kept up with the drama. *Is that the captain of the dance team who quit without warning? The one with dropping grades and a ruined social circle?* "Are you here for the graduation speech tryouts?"

I nod. Miss Diaz gestures at the seat near me, and I slide into it quickly.

"Go ahead, Mina," she encourages.

I unfold my speech and smooth the edges of the paper. Damp spots form on the margins, softening beneath my sweaty palms. I can't bring myself to look at Miss Diaz. Yet another person whose life I almost torpedoed.

I tuck my curls behind my ears and take a fortifying breath. "My name is Yasmina Mansour, and I'm auditioning to speak at graduation for this year's class of seniors."

As soon as I start to read, my nerves settle. I've rehearsed these lines a dozen times. Before spring break, I was mumbling them in my sleep.

My imagination drifts, and I picture myself standing behind a podium in May, facing the students I grew up with as we gather for the last time. Rainie would give me a standing ovation, partly out of pride and partly to spite the school event coordinator one final time. Lucia would wipe her tears on the dangling sleeves of her robe. Not because my speech is especially moving, but because Lucia tends to get stuck in sad moments. She needs someone like Rainie to pull her loose and remind her to keep moving.

Aida won't clap. Instead, she'll aim a secretive smile my way. The Aida version of shouting at the top of her lungs.

If we were still together, Alex would command the basketball team to stand on their chairs and sing my name in an embarrassing, wonderful display.

Jesse wouldn't attend graduation as a student. He'd ask them to mail him his diploma and use the money he saves on graduation regalia to buy another slew of bizarre T-shirts. But I like to think he'd still come to hear me speak. He'd linger by the edge of the bleachers, twirling his car keys around his index finger.

And best of all, Baba would be there. He'd be in the front row, holding bags full of those cheesy grad gifts they sell in the parking lot. Despite his deep disdain for speaking to strangers, he would tell everyone within earshot, "That's my daughter" as soon as I came onstage.

In the torn, rumpled page of my graduation speech, a bright future unfurls. One where everyone I love is happy and whole, and I'm around to see it.

When I finish, I find tears glistening in Miss Diaz's eyes. Even Principal Bess's reserved frown falters.

"It's a little too personal," one of the teachers says. "Graduation speeches should generally be relatable to the whole student body."

"It's not an ad for car insurance, Linda," Miss Diaz returns.

"Thank you for coming in, Miss Mansour," Principal Bess interjects. "We'll get back to you with our decision shortly."

I close the door behind me to the tune of Miss Diaz saying, "I know her grades have dropped, and she's been acting a little strange, but—"

Outside the admin building, rain plinks against the crooked awning. The quad has emptied out, with only a handful of stragglers taking shelter from the rain beneath the canopy enveloping the lunch tables. In the sea of gray cement and grayer skies, I stick out like a sore thumb in my bright blue coat, its bronze buttons shinier than a polished coin and matched to the pink sweater underneath. Paired with my striped leggings, it's an outfit Rainie once referred to as the manifestation of a twelve-year old's Pinterest board.

As soon as I step out from under the awning, water soaks into my hair, dripping against the back of my neck. I walk fast, barely watching where I'm going. Aida's sketchpad weighs heavily inside my coat. All I want is a warm shower and a blanket three times the length of my bed.

Mid-shiver, I slam directly into a firm body. I careen backward, my ankle twisting painfully beneath me, but a quick grip prevents me from cracking my head open on the concrete.

Jesse frowns down at my ankle, still holding tight to my arm. "We've gotta set up some kind of traffic signal around you."

"Or," I growl, shaking him off, "you could start watching where you're going?"

Like a switch, my aggression summons Jesse's wicked smile from its storage unit in the depths of hell. "Maybe I *am* watching where I'm going."

Despite the fact that my toes have surrendered all feeling and the moisture in my hair has unleashed my frizz quicker than sticking a fork in an electric socket, I still summon the energy to glare.

"I know what you're doing."

Jesse clicks his tongue. "Don't have a clue what you mean, Sour Patch."

A raindrop runs down his cheek. Shoring up my courage, I step close to Jesse and catch the raindrop with my thumb. In the same movement, I sweep the skin over his cheekbone, trailing my fingers over the regal line of his jaw. A shudder goes through Jesse, and my stomach tightens. So many invisible fault lines in this contradictory, beautiful boy. One tiny shift, one wrong collision, and the quake would break him apart.

And here I am, pressing. Trying to see what it would take to break him. Gouging, piercing, looking for the cracks in the layers of protection between him and the world.

My fingers travel as far as his throat before he seizes my wrist.

Rebuke burns in his eyes, disappointment close behind it. He swallows.

"I get it, Mansour. I understand how it feels to be furious with the world. To want to lash out and claw back some of what it's taken from you." His grip on my wrist softens, and he twines his fingers with mine for half of a heartbeat. With the same hold, he tugs me closer. Even a drop of rain would struggle to squeeze between us, finding itself trapped between my pounding heart and Jesse's.

"Don't turn me into collateral damage," he murmurs. "If you want to hurt me, choose another way. Choose something I can recover from."

He releases me and steps back, tucking his hands into his pockets. "How did it go?"

It takes a minute to process the array of shame, confusion, and disappointment clashing inside me. "The audition? It was fine."

Jesse seems prepared to press for more, but his gaze catches on something over my shoulder. His features slacken in disbelief. "Unbelievable," he snarls, with such menace that I nearly step away.

When I try to turn and see what he's glaring at, Jesse grabs my coat's lapel. "C'mon, let's get out of here." He pulls me forward, holding on to my coat like a leash.

"Wait!" I swat at his arm, wriggling in a futile effort to dislodge him. What doesn't he want me to see? "Jesse, let go!"

As a last resort, I pull my arms out of the coat, leaving him with an armful of empty blue cotton. I spin around. Squinting through the gray haze cast over the half-drowning campus, I search for the culprit behind Jesse's sudden rage.

Nothing out of the ordinary. Everyone is in sixth period, so only the athletes mill around the quad.

The basketball team runs laps on the track fenced in next to the parking lot. Tucked behind the bleachers, Alex puts his arms around a tall blond I vaguely recognize as Diane Rigmore.

"Huh," I remark. I probe around for any hurt and come up empty-handed. My relationship with Alex seems like a relic from a lost age. Honestly, I'm glad he moved on. The girl he was waiting for doesn't exist anymore.

Jesse, usually eerily adept at reading my mind, misses the mark by a mile. "He's been going around playing the heartbroken puppy, you know that? And then he pulls this crap with you? In front of everyone? The little prick."

Pushing my coat into my arms, Jesse stalks toward the fence.

NADINE HAIKAL
EL AGAMY, ALEXANDRIA
2013

On a late Thursday afternoon, Nadine Mansour stepped out of Borg El Arab Airport in Alexandria and nearly fell to her knees.

People bustled around the motionless woman, throwing their bags in taxis and greeting their loved ones. Busy, distracted. They didn't stop to appreciate the magnificence around them. The setting sun's trail of blazing red, like a thumb dipped in paint dragging across the sky's clear canvas. The dry breeze, wrapping around her in a welcoming hug.

Tears tingled in Nadine's eyes.

She was home.

"Ma'am, do you need a taxi?" a boy in a cheap button-down and poorly knotted tie asked. He couldn't be older than eighteen. He offered a gap-toothed smile, likely hoping to charm the peculiar tourist away from the shiny cabs lining the airport's exit.

The thought entered Nadine's head, so familiar yet so foreign: *He would make an easy target.* Young, nervous, shy. He was too old, of course. Kids his age left too many tracks for the authorities to follow.

Nadine swallowed hard, clutching the necklace hanging between her collarbones. Mina had made it in art class out of beads and string, and she'd danced when Nadine put it on. She loved dancing, her daughter.

I'm not that woman anymore, Nadine reminded herself. She did not strategize and scheme as easily as a fish breathed underwater. She did not look at a person and immediately identify their weakest points of attack.

She was not Nadine Haikal anymore. She'd left her for dead nine years ago, and Nadine Mansour was only back to finish the job.

"Yes," she said. "I'll pay you to drive me to El Agamy."

The boy hesitated. "Which part of El Agamy? Sorry, I only ask because some of the roads wreck my tires."

"Don't worry." Nadine lifted her chin. "I'll show you where to go."

In the car, Nadine folded her hands in her lap and gazed at Alexandria. The beautiful city she'd longed for in her childhood. The buildings had grown higher, the beaches more cluttered, but the rest was the same.

What if she had raised Mina here? Would her daughter be one of the little girls sitting on the concrete benches along the sidewalk, watching the waves crash below and buying cotton candy from the street-cart vendors rolling along the shoreline?

What a silly thought. Yasmina Haikal would've spent her life in the Haikal villa if she'd passed the test, just like her mother and aunt. If Mina had failed, Nadine didn't know if she would have been strong enough to hand the baby to Hatem while she remained behind.

Nadine rarely thought about her. The daughter who never was. The other daughter she might have raised in the Haikal villa.

"Wait!" Nadine called suddenly, startling the driver into slamming on the brakes. She rolled down her window and rummaged around her purse. "Hey! You with the tiaras!"

The street vendor pointed at himself. Nadine nodded. He pushed his two-wheeled cart to the edge of the sidewalk, and Nadine gestured at a bright pink tiara. "How much?"

"Fifty pounds, ma'am."

Nadine rolled her eyes. He was fleecing the seemingly rich lady in the private car, but she wasn't exactly in a haggling mood. She held out the money and accepted the plastic tiara.

They resumed driving. "For your daughter?" the driver asked.

Nadine swept her thumb along the rhinestones studding the cheap crown. "She wants to be a princess when she grows up."

The boy laughed. When Nadine didn't join in, it trickled into an awkward cough. "She sounds very special."

Nadine slid the tiara into her purse. "She is."

Beads swung gently from the rearview mirror. The driver tapped the steering wheel, black flecks of its leather peeling under his nails. Static hummed over the radio, tuned to a twenty-four-hour Um Kalthoum station.

Traffic thinned out the farther west they drove. They passed the salt lakes, stunning streaks of pink whirling over their surface.

When last Nadine lived in El Agamy, this stretch of the highway had been silent as a tomb. Not anymore. The neon lights of a shopping center flashed to her right. Cars vied for a spot in front of three-story restaurants. Parents waited to pick up their children from a private academy across the street from a deteriorating public school. Tailors and cafés and mechanic shops, crammed within feet of each other.

If Nadine needed any further proof that Safa had weakened, here it was. El Agamy—the parts of it outside their neighborhood, at least—thrived. The parasitic influence of Nadine's family had waned, reviving the blood flow of the dying creature they'd preyed upon for over a century.

An insatiable hunger, that was the Haikal villa. Never satisfied, never finished. It consumed the life around it. Left behind half-built homes and partly paved roads like grave markers of humanity.

Signs of civilization disappeared as they approached the villa. The driver gritted his teeth when Nadine pointed to the slim opening leading to her street. Probably dreading the damage to his tires. If Nadine were a better person, she'd offer to get out here and walk.

The car rocked, buffeted by uneven slopes of dirt. It crested over a speed bump, and Nadine inhaled sharply.

Hundreds of dead children blocked the road ahead. Many in outfits and hairstyles nobody had seen in centuries. They stared at Nadine. Baleful. Furious.

Several of the ones in the front Nadine recognized. She'd fed them to the curse herself.

At the helm stood Janna, still clutching her feeno sandwich.

As Nadine watched, the little girl's pale lips mouthed one word.

Irga'y.

Turn back.

Nadine tore her gaze away from the lives she had stolen. Of course the shadows had followed her here.

Only one life mattered to her now, and she was trying to learn a handstand in a stormy town thousands of miles away.

"Drop me off around the corner," Nadine said.

The driver glanced at the mangy packs of dogs patrolling the abandoned lots. He pulled over next to a shuttered dukan. The *K* in *Kamel's* dangled upside-down. "Oh, is this a surprise visit?"

"No." Nadine opened the car door. "They're expecting me."

CHAPTER TWENTY-FOUR
PRESENT DAY

I balk, checking over my shoulder to make sure I haven't hallucinated the last forty seconds. What does Jesse think he's doing? Even if Jesse is taller, Alex has at least twenty pounds on him, and he trains religiously.

Jesse grabs the chain link and jumps the fence in one swift move. A few of Alex's teammates stop running as Jesse crosses the track.

The fog of shock finally lifts. "Jesse!" I shout. The wind whips my voice away. I sprint for the fence. By the time I reach the chains, the last patch of dry clothing on my body has succumbed to the downpour. Ahead, Jesse reaches Alex, who breaks away from Diane with a scowl.

I grab the nearest player. "Greg, help me up!"

Greg raises his hands instantly. "Uh—"

I channel some of Rainie's ferocious command. "Don't just stand there! Pick me up!"

Alex's teammate grabs my upper arms and swings me over the fence. My shoes land in soft mud, and I suppress a howl. Jesse is *so* dead.

To my shock, Jesse knots his fist in Alex's jersey and slams him into a bleacher. Diane covers her mouth. She flees for the admin building, and I push my legs harder. If a staff member catches Jesse accosting another student, he can kiss walking at graduation goodbye.

With a flying leap, I throw myself onto Jesse's back hard enough to dislodge his grip on Alex's shirt. My arms wind around his neck, my legs sticking out on either side of his waist. "Stop!" I pant against his ear, not even caring how gross my labored breathing must sound. He deserves it for making me run in the rain.

Alex straightens, getting right up in Jesse's face. Blood smears his bottom lip. "What the *hell* is your problem?"

"Taken too many basketballs to the brain, kiddo?" Jesse bites out. "Give it a guess."

"You scared Diane!"

Neither acknowledge my very real presence on Jesse's back. I climb higher, hooking my chin on Jesse's shoulder. "Hello!" I shout.

Nothing. Not even a glance.

Jesse bites down on his knuckles with mock concern. "Oh no, I scared Diane? Do you think she'll ever recover?"

When I start to slip for the third time, Jesse finally grabs my elbows and hauls me upward in one powerful motion. I squeak, barely remembering to grab onto the front of his jacket. He winds his arms under my knees, giving my legs an anchor. I'm plastered to his back like a five-foot-two koala, arms welded around his shoulders and neck.

I ignore how nice his hair feels against my cheek, even damp and rumpled from the rain.

"Did you forget you have a girlfriend?" Jesse spits. "Or did you lose that inconvenient tidbit behind Diane's tonsils?"

Alex's mouth opens, speechless, and I use the opportunity to shout directly into Jesse's ear. "I don't care about Diane!"

Unfortunately, I'm successful in grabbing Jesse's attention just as I notice the red stain spreading over my pant leg. I must've reopened my wound while I was running.

Uh-oh.

Dizziness slackens my muscles. I slide off Jesse and crumple to the foam blacktop. Alex exclaims my name. Jesse shoulders him aside, crouching at my side.

"Why is she bleeding?"

Jesse ignores him, gently palpating the bruise on my thigh.

"It's barely bleeding," he mutters. "Not nearly enough to cause disorientation."

"She faints at the sight of blood, douchebag," Alex snaps. He wipes the blood from his mouth with the edge of his sleeve.

I close my eyes, tuning them out in favor of counting the raindrops falling onto my cheeks. My stomach settles. Without moving, I say, "I could've been asleep under six blankets right now."

A thumb sweeps away the water lingering in the hollow under my eye. "How do you feel?" Jesse asks.

"How do I feel?" I swat his hand away. "How do I *feel*?"

The boys glance at each other, momentarily forgetting their antipathy in favor of shared confusion.

"Here's what's going to happen." I push myself onto my elbows, carefully avoiding the red patch on my thigh. "In about fifteen seconds, I'm going to get up and start walking. If either of you so much as twitches in the other's direction, I'll ask Greg if I can climb onto his shoulders and use him as a human battering ram. I think I could make a solid case to a judge that my actions were a public service. Jesse, do you think if Alex was cheating on me, Rainie, Aida, and Lucia would have let it slide? Do you think *I* would have let it slide?" I move my glare to Alex. "Can you finally start telling everyone we broke up? People are going to accuse Diane of being a homewrecker, and she doesn't deserve that."

Slapping away their efforts to help, I pull myself to my feet. Diane emerges from the admin building, the school secretary on her heels. "Alex," I grind out. "Get your girlfriend away from here."

"She's not—"

"Alex!"

He leaps into motion, heading straight for Diane. Jesse and I rush in the opposite direction, around the theater building and behind the teacher's parking lot. I don't let myself relax until we've cleared the gym.

My chest heaves with exertion. Alex better have used his good boy charm to explain away Diane's accusation. I can't stand the idea of Jesse getting in any more trouble, even if he deserves it. What was he thinking?

At the student parking lot, I veer from Jesse, giving him my back as I stomp toward the crosswalk.

Jesse follows. "You can't walk home with a bleeding leg and a concussion."

I ignore him. I walked here just fine this morning. I'll just sit on the curb if I start to get woozy.

Jesse tries again. "Mansour."

I press the yellow crosswalk button. The stop sign changes to a small white figure.

"Why are you upset? I thought the ball jockey was cheating on you. Turns out I was wrong. No harm done."

I whirl around. "No harm done? You could've gotten suspended!"

"I thought he was cheating on you in front of the entire school," Jesse repeats curtly.

"Why do you *care*?" I yell. My frustration echoes in the empty parking lot. "You could've, I don't know, asked me before you stormed off. God, don't you get tired of being angry all the time? You don't even try to change. Anger *burns,* Jesse, and you're so distracted by the smoke that you don't realize it's eating away everything good inside you!"

A vein pounds in Jesse's forehead. "You're assuming there was anything good inside me to begin with."

I throw my hands up. "Unbelievable. You are *so* dramatic, do you know that? Oooh, I'm dark and damaged, world beware. *I* am literally descended from a family of killers, but I still pour my cereal before my milk like everyone else."

Jesse's face does a complicated dance, like he can't decide whether to laugh or trip me into a puddle. What he eventually settles on looks a lot like remorse. "Look, I'm sorry. I didn't mean to freak you out, and I'm well aware your friends would have torn the guy to shreds if he was actually disrespecting you. I just . . ." He studies the sky, seeking answers behind the gray veil permanently cloaking Ward. "I don't have a lot of experience with this."

"With . . ."

He lowers his eyes to mine. They're pained, clearly struggling against some revelation. "Caring about someone. I don't think I'm doing it right."

The pause that follows lasts a century. Holding on to my anger becomes impossible, and it settles into a warm and familiar exasperation. I've already seen countless examples of how Jesse acts when he cares about something. Dedication doesn't do it justice. Up until now, most of what he cared about revolved around curses, home improvement projects, plants, and a bird feeder.

I sigh. "You can just ask next time."

Relief loosens the tension in Jesse's shoulders, and he gestures at his car. "Let me give you a ride. Please."

I pull at my soaked clothes. "Sure. Say goodbye to your seats."

"They'll survive."

The truck door opens with a whine of metal. Jesse arranges me on the leather seat, buckling me in as I begin to shiver in earnest. I'm still holding my coat balled up in my lap.

As soon as he hops into the driver's seat, he twists a dial on the dashboard. Hot air coughs out of the vent. The engine turns, and my back hits the seat as Jesse peels out of the parking lot.

The rhythmic *fwip-fwip* of the windshield wipers joins the pattering rain. Trees blur past the window. Ward lies empty and silent around us.

"You've given up."

I go still at Jesse's softly uttered accusation. He stares at the rivers of water sluicing down the windshield.

"I've had to listen to you rehearsing your graduation speech thirty times. Suddenly you don't care? And your bonehead shacks up with someone else and it rolls right off you."

"Diane is sweet."

"Admit it. You don't think you're gonna make it."

"What if I just don't want Alex anymore?" The words fall free before I can stop them. "What if I want someone else?"

If I had several years of my life to spare, Jesse's silence would have shaved them right off. His face smooths into a terrifying blankness.

"Don't mess with me, Mansour. I'm not some puppy you can lead around by the nose if you bat your eyes and promise them a dance at the ball."

My jaw hangs open. "I'm not—I wouldn't—I'm not messing with you. I haven't thought about Alex since . . . you know. Since the train."

Jesse doesn't respond. Why did I expect anything else? He cares about me—okay, great. But acting on his feelings? Bridging the gap between longing and having?

There's a reason I lived next to Jesse for four years without knowing a thing about him. A reason everyone at school trades rumors and theories about the Talbots like daily horoscope readings.

We've been trying to pull Jesse into our world, but Jesse Talbot has always existed in the shadows. The way I feel—the way I could swear he feels, in those moments when his gaze settles on me and lingers—demands light.

And Jesse refuses. He's just passing through, after all. A relationship, an *attachment*, would just be a chain around his boot.

"Forget Alex," Jesse says. "Do you believe you'll survive this curse?"

Ah, there it is. The real question at last, yanked bloody from the heart of Jesse Talbot.

The least I can do is reach into my own and extract the same. The horrid truth, as terrible to his ears as it is bitter to mine.

"I'm sorry, Jesse."

Jesse twists the steering wheel. The truck skids to the left, missing the turn onto our street. We speed onto the one-way lane leading into the forest around Ward's border. In a single move, the truck fishtails off the road and onto an empty dirt trail. I grab the car handle above me as I swing from side to side.

As soon as the tires stop, I unbuckle my seat belt and slam out of the truck. "What the hell was that?" I holler.

"My bad, I thought you weren't scared of dying anymore!" Jesse rounds the truck, heedless of the mud soaking into his boots.

My flinch gets to him, wiping the sneer off his face. "So that's it? All this progress we've made, all the work we put in, and you're ready to let the curse win?"

I laugh, wild abandon careening through me. "What progress? You saw my mom's journal. Nobody has been able to break the curse! Not my mother's family, not the other families she was tracking. This curse is ancient."

The rest comes pouring out of me. "Besides, how would it be fair if I survived while the children they sacrificed didn't? How is it fair that my mother can wreck an entire community and expect not to answer for it?" I spread my arms. "I'm the consequence, Jesse. I'm fate finally catching up to what they've done."

The clouds writhe, streaks of white promising a storm to shake every window in Ward. The forest unravels in every direction around us. Long shadows shiver under the roiling clouds, shifting beneath the howling gale. If the storm grows, we'll have a bona fide Ward Wailer on our hands.

Jesse seems to realize the danger at the same time. "Get in the truck. We'll talk about this at my place."

"There's nothing to talk about."

Jesse responds, a short and sharp statement, but I don't hear it. I don't hear the wind howling or the metallic rattle of the rain hitting the truck.

A woman watches us from between the trees. Warm brown eyes catch mine, and a wide smile spreads over her angular face. She wears jeans we thrifted in San Francisco on my seventh birthday, the words *Sugar High* bedazzled in red across each of the pockets. Her hair hangs loose by her shoulders.

It's the hair that convinces me. Not a drop of rain touches her; not a single strand sticks to her face or neck.

Mama beckons me.

Without taking my eyes off her, I ask, "Do you have the journal with you, Jesse?"

"Yeah, it's in the back. What—"

"Don't follow me."

Mama slips into the gloom of trees, and I break into a run.

It takes twenty minutes after I run out of the woods to realize the shadow is leading me back home. I lost sight of it a couple of blocks ago, but its path is unmistakable.

I stop to catch my breath and push the sweat-soaked hair from my forehead. I briefly entertain the notion of texting Jesse, but there's no point. As soon as he finishes searching in the woods, he'll head straight to my house. If I call him now, he'll demand I wait.

But we're out of time. The answer to how to break the curse might be in my mother's journal, and we won't know if I don't look into the shadow and unlock another entry.

There is a bitter irony in finding myself chasing Mama's shadow yet again.

I spent years wondering what happened to her. Looking out into the audience after a dance competition and scanning for her face like a broken reflex. Wishing I could hear her voice in the morning, feel the soft press of her palm against my forehead when I'm sick, lay my head on her lap when my heart weighs me down.

Which version of my mother was true? Which Nadine am I chasing?

By the time I reach my house, every inch of my body aches. I ease open the front door. "Baba?"

No answer. I figured as much. His car isn't out front, but sometimes he parks in the garage when it storms. I toe off my shoes and shake the rain from my coat. The house lies dark, and the shadows stay still when my gaze glides over them. It's here—I can feel it. But which one is it?

After a minute of waiting, I flip on the lamp by the couch. If it wants to play coy, fine. I'm not going anywhere.

I draw my phone from my pocket and plug it into the charger. The battery died shortly after Jesse's confrontation with Alex, and I gape at the texts lighting up my screen.

Lucia:

AIDA OVERHEARD MISS DIAZ TALKING ON THE PHONE

MINA

YOU GOT IT YOU GOT IT YOU GOT IT

Rainie:

congrats you lil nerd!! classic

I scroll through my notifications, stopping at an email from Principal Bellis at the bottom. My hands shake as I thumb it open.

★ ⮌ ⋮

Dear Ms. Mansour,

Thank you for attending graduation speech tryouts today. Canyon High School would be honored if you would speak at this year's commencement ceremony. Our school celebrates its 45th graduation this May...

I got it.

I got it?

I GOT IT.

They want me to speak at graduation. Me, Mina Mansour, will stand behind a podium and address hundreds of parents, students, and teachers on one of the most memorable days of our lives.

I find a pad of blue sticky notes on the mantel and hunt for a pen. Baba will be upset if I tell him the goods news late, but I can't exactly share it in person. Leaving it in a note seems more personal than a text message. Baba always goes straight for the kitchen when he gets home, so I'll put the note on the fridge.

Between one blink and the next, everything goes black.

Power outage. Crap. I figured we'd get one with the Ward Wailer, but it got here faster than I expected.

Oh no. What if Jesse is still in the woods? He must be on his way back by now, right?

I stumble in the general direction of my phone, relieved I remembered to plug it in. It should have just enough battery for me to use the flashlight to rummage around for the storm kit in the garage and call Jesse. Assuming they haven't been moved because Baba decided to add new shelves at three in the morning while listening to his old lectures. The man brings nocturnal productivity to a whole other level.

I step in a patch of wetness and wince. Great. A leak must've sprung earlier.

Making a mental note about the spot, I pat the entryway table until I find my phone. The screen flashes open. Twelve percent. Not good.

I press the flashlight on, the stream of yellow knifing through the dark. The light sweeps over the floor as I pivot toward the garage. It crosses the wet patch I'd stepped in.

A streak of red stops me in my tracks.

"What the..." I move closer to the carpet and glance at the ceiling. Why did the water look... rusty?

I fish a tissue out of my pocket and pat the ground.

When I turn the tissue over, I nearly vomit.

Blood.

My heartbeat slows. I can hear each individual beat, pounding against my ears.

"You're home."

The flashlight swings up, illuminating two figures in the living room.

One is Baba. Slumped on the ground, his body propped against the other side of the couch. Blood blooms from three tears in his sweater vest, and a sticky red wound seeps at his temple.

"You were very rude, Mina," a chillingly familiar voice says. "Why did you leave without saying goodbye?"

From the couch, Khalto Safa smiles at me with bright orange eyes.

NADINE HAIKAL
EL AGAMY, ALEXANDRIA
2013

The black gates scraped open as Nadine approached. Behind them, her childhood home sprawled out in all its sullied glory.

Nadine stood for a moment, taking it in. She never thought she'd be back here. For years, she'd dreamt of this villa. In those dreams, she'd walked these grounds as she once had, its ruler and purveyor. The monster at its helm.

Shadows hadn't stalked her then. If they tried to follow, Nadine would cast them aside without a second glance.

When you don't question your own soul, Nadine had discovered, shadows have nothing to anchor to. What regrets can they become, when the world is as you will it? What hopes can they manipulate, if no dream is beyond your reach?

That was the trouble with having a daughter like Mina and a husband like Hatem. Their love shined a bright light on all the gaping holes of Nadine's soul. It forced her to reckon with the rot inside of her.

The minute she began to doubt, the shadows found her.

Nadine climbed the wide marble steps, pausing at the front door.

The Haikal grounds had fallen into disrepair in Nadine's absence. Ravens perched at the top of the pillars, ruffling their wings in the evening breeze. Branches snapped beneath her shoes, shed from the overgrown date trees swaying high above her.

Someone had left the gate ajar.

Irga'y. Janna's warning circled, scraping around Nadine's skull.

She shouldered the iron-wrought door open. Her footfalls fell like claps of thunder against the marble. From her purse, Nadine extracted the taser and knife tucked into her purse. Acquiring a gun in Masr was extremely difficult under the best of circumstances, and Nadine didn't have the time to find people who'd sell one to her.

As she walked, the memories assaulted her. Eager children, following Nadine up the stairs, never to return. Children from struggling families. The ones police wouldn't dig too deep for, whose parents would feel the loss most acutely. For those who had nothing, children were their greatest gift. Their loss fed the curse best.

Nadine's grip on the banister spasmed. She couldn't let herself get lost in the past. She was a different woman now. The lives she'd taken could never be returned. The least she could do was make sure no more were lost to the Haikal debt.

On the second floor, Nadine found Safa lounging on an armchair, a book balanced on her lap.

"My beloved big sister," Safa said without glancing up from her book. The only light was a single lamp by her elbow. "Welcome home."

Nadine ran her finger along a shelf and inspected the dust. "So it isn't just the outside of the villa falling apart. Can't hack it on your own, Safa?"

Safa tutted, slinging the book aside. In her late twenties, Safa radiated an untamed beauty. The long, black curls Nadine and her daughter shared tumbled down her sister's back, much sleeker than the last time Nadine had seen her. Nimble, deceptively delicate hands folded over Safa's knee. "Surely you didn't come back just to ask ridiculous questions?"

"I saw the newsletter those women started. 'Mothers for Missing Children'," Nadine mused. "You never did know how to cover your tracks."

Safa stood, flicking her fingers dismissively over her shoulders as she pulled on a cardigan. "We both know it'll lead nowhere. Let them have their fun. Tell me, how is America? Your daughter would be nine now, right?" Safa trailed her hand over the high-backed chairs in the sitting room. "Was she worth our mother?"

Nadine kept her gaze fixed on Safa, avoiding the whispering shadows snaking over the walls. She could never predict what she would witness by looking directly into one. In this moment, she had a feeling it would be her mother, blood dripping from the end of her robe and pooling around her bare feet. A pair of scissors protruding from her chest.

"Our mother made her choice," Nadine said. She should end this pointless conversation before it went any further. Safa was sneaky, manipulative, and Nadine was out of practice. She moved toward Safa slowly, rounding the empty armchair.

"It might have spared your daughter, you know. If she had failed the test, Mama would have let you leave with her. If she had passed, we could have been a family." Safa neared Nadine, the hatred in her green eyes tainted by a sorrow Nadine understood too well.

Nadine pictured Mina climbing up the stairs, a child trailing behind her. Doomed to feed the curse until her dying days.

Her grip on the knife tightened.

"I made my choice, too," Nadine said. She swung the knife toward Safa.

In a flash, the second floor pitched into darkness. Safa's light laugh rang out in the empty. "You've been gone too long, Nadine."

The shadows grew louder, whorls of black dancing in the night. Nadine heard snatches of Mina's voice, Hatem's, her mother's, Janna's. Calling her name. She left the knife raised, edging back slowly. If she could get the wall behind her, it would be easier to anticipate an attack.

"My daughter is nothing like us," Nadine snarled. "She would never pay our debt with the blood of others."

"Are you sure about that?"

In the center of the floor, a staircase appeared.

One of the shadows darted close to the banister, and as Nadine watched, a girl took shape. It took Nadine a minute to place her, and when she did, terror raked its claws across her spine.

It was the same curly-haired girl in slippers Nadine had seen the night she'd escaped.

The girl glanced over her shoulder, and Nadine gasped at the freckles on her temple. They were—but it couldn't be—

"Mina?"

The teenage version of the child Nadine had left at home climbed the stairs. Nadine forgot about Safa, about the shadows. Her daughter was heading for the door. The same door Nadine had narrowly saved her from nine years ago.

Nadine ran for the stairs. The banister burned under her touch, and she recoiled with a cry. The shiny marble steps wavered, a mirage undulating in the dark. Filthy water poured down the steps, a murky tide pounding against Nadine's legs. She held her breath against the dizzyingly foul odor and climbed a step. Her foot slipped. With a splash, she tumbled into the stairs.

Small, gray hands shot out of the filth, grabbing at Nadine. "Mina!" she shouted. The girl didn't turn around. Nadine threw her knife aside and slapped away the hands. She grabbed the banister, gritting her teeth against the agony sizzling from her burning flesh. Mina couldn't open the door.

Nadine reached the top of the stairs. She grabbed the girl's shoulder, but her hand passed straight through her. Panic choked Nadine. "Mina, listen to me. Hear me, somehow. Do not open this door. Turn around."

The girl reached for the handle. Orange light crept from the bottom of the door.

"Ya umri, please," Nadine pleaded. She beat her raw fist against the door. "*Don't take my daughter!*"

The girl disappeared. Nadine whirled around. Where was Mina? Had she opened the door?

Behind her, Safa leaned against the banister. She kicked aside Nadine's knife and withdrew a small pistol from the inside of her cardigan. "Mama warned you. Wherever you go, whatever new identity you build, it will follow."

"It won't follow Mina," Nadine said fiercely. "It never touched her. She's safe."

"It hasn't touched her *yet*." Safa raised the gun almost lazily, aiming for Nadine's forehead. "Open the door, sister."

Nadine balked. "What?"

"Go on. It's time to face your mistakes." When Nadine didn't budge, Safa smiled. "Or I can shoot you where you stand and have a flight booked to Ward, California, before your blood's gone cold."

Not a drop of compassion tainted the clear pools of cruelty in Safa's eyes. Nadine had underestimated her sister. Experience and time had sharpened Safa's brute savagery into a deadly art, imbued her with Nadine's skills of deception and their mother's ruthlessness.

"How do I know you won't go to Ward even if I open the door?"

"Because your daughter will come to me. The worst I can do in Ward is kill her. If I wait, your Yasmina will find her way to this door. To the test." Safa shook her head, gazing at Nadine with amazement. "You don't see the irony, do you? You fed this curse well, Nadine, and you never thought twice about the lives you devastated. Why do you think your daughter deserves to be spared when theirs weren't? That girl is your debt, and fate will always come to collect what it is owed."

"She's innocent."

Safa offered her an inscrutable smile. "Aren't they all?"

Her sister gestured with the gun. "On with it, now."

Nadine had fed dozens of children to the door behind her. Watched as unadulterated horror tore across their faces, breaking their young minds in two. Between getting shot and opening the door, Nadine would die by gun a million times over.

But she also knew Safa would make good on her promise. If the vision of the curly-haired girl was just a trick, then Mina would be safe in Ward. At least for a while.

It wasn't much of a choice. Safa had her gun, and the house wasn't on Nadine's side. It wouldn't let her escape a second time.

Nadine took one last, long look at Safa. The baby sister she'd held in her arms the night Mama laid her at this exact threshold. It spared Safa, and Nadine remembered feeling a mixture of relief and despair. Despair, because another Haikal would be consigned to repay Bamba's debt. But at least Nadine wouldn't be expected to shoulder the burden alone.

She turned around. The white door shone, gold hinges gleaming. An invitation. A handle appeared from the door's frame, round and untarnished.

Nadine's hand closed around the handle. Her corrupted soul shuddered, shrinking away at the nearness of such a consuming evil. She would never get to see Mina grow up. Hatem was like a stone in a river: reliable and steady, but averse to any kind of forward movement. He wouldn't bring Mina to Masr out of fear of confronting their families. He might never even speak of Nadine again, shying away from the pain of her memory.

As for Nadine, this was what she deserved. The doomed tapestry she had sewn for herself with each grieving parent and broken family, now settling over her like a corpse shroud.

Nadine twisted the handle and pulled the door open.

A bright, searing orange light blinded her. She blinked, adjusting, and what she saw made every horror, every pain and tragedy she had ever encountered seem like a paltry sentence in the page of a children's book. Nadine's careful, calculating mind unraveled. Spools of her sanity curdled like hair brushed against an open flame.

Nadine Haikal screamed, and screamed, and screamed.

The door slammed shut behind her.

CHAPTER TWENTY-FIVE
PRESENT DAY

I stare at Khalto Safa, and an absurd thought strikes me: *We're going to have to move again.*

We've ruined the heart of this house like we did our old one. Nourished its bones on dread and loneliness. On my father's blood, slipping between the floorboards and into the house's waiting mouth.

Blood. A dizzy fog steals over me, and I yank my gaze from the puddle. I won't faint. I can't.

"He's alive," my aunt reassures me. Khalto Safa cups a slim hand around her lighter, the *snick snick snick* of her thumb against the wheel cacophonous. The spark finally catches, and she lowers the tip of her cigarette to the precarious flame. "Don't look so frightened, ya habibti. I just want to talk."

"How did you find me?" I sneak a glance toward the shoe rack, where I'd tossed my purse. Jesse's switchblade is still in my bag.

She rolls her eyes. "Your father's photograph is on the university website. I didn't even need to pay to find your address. It's rather alarming, how accessible all your information is."

Khalto Safa picks up a strand of thick, glossy hair and twirls it around a ringed finger. Her skin glows, unnaturally smooth and pristine. Every part of Khalto Safa dazzles, and now I understand that this perfection is part of the curse's bargain. Anyone who looks at her wouldn't think twice about her intentions. She is too beautiful to doubt—too stunning to suspect.

Mama had always look normal to my eyes, but how lovely must she have been when she was the Terror of El Agamy, feeding the curse and reaping its benefits?

Khalto Safa crosses her legs, folding her hands over her knee. If it weren't for the unnatural orange glow in her eyes and the repugnant odor wafting off her, she'd be the most elegant person to ever enter Ward. "I know you have questions about your mother. About the Haikal villa. I can answer them for you."

"I have all the answers I need." I slink an inch back. Her reptilian gaze tracks the motion.

"Fantastic!" She claps her hands once. "Then you must be all caught up on what happened to your mother eight years ago."

I go still. An icy finger of dread drags down my throat. Reason insists that trusting anything she says is a mistake. Khalto Safa is a consummate liar. A *murderer*, worse than almost everyone in her family. Only poison falls from her lips, as naturally as the ash flaking from the end of a burning cigarette.

But if anyone knows what really happened to Mama during her visit to Egypt, it's Khalto Safa.

"She died in a car accident."

A ghastly grin spreads over Khalto Safa's face. A black shadow darts from the fireplace to the kitchen wall. Another swirls beneath my feet, causing me to stumble backward.

"I'm afraid not," Khalto Safa hums. She beams at the shadows. "Would you like to see?"

She crooks her finger, and the shadows rush to me. Vying for attention. Snippets of sound leak from the swirling pockets of black. I screw my eyes shut.

"They won't hurt you, Mina. They just want you to see."

"What *are* they?" Mama had studied the curse's movement over centuries, and she still hadn't found an answer for these shadows. "What do they want?"

Khalto Safa's laugh rings like music. "They don't want anything, habibti. Every legacy needs a record, and these shadows keep ours. Our shame, our regret. Our choices. If it weren't for Bamba, we wouldn't exist. Every scar we leave on this world creates a shadow."

Breath drifts over my cheek. I need to open my eyes to see an attack coming, but the shadows are all around me. Disaster waits in any direction I turn. The only choice they've left me is to decide how much I can bear.

"Open your eyes, ya umri," my mother's voice whispers, and I obey.

Standing inches away is me.

Or a version of me. One more beautiful than I've ever been—more beautiful than I can bear. Shadows lick at her edges, slipping tenderly through her shiny curls.

I hold my breath, unable to shrink away. Khalto Safa moves to stand by the other Mina. "There's still a chance for you to have everything you've ever dreamed of. Come with me. Come back to the Haikal villa and claim the legacy your geda Bamba built for us."

"Legacy?" I bark a harsh laugh. "Bamba stole her legacy." Even from her own bloodline. Our lives were hinged on this curse; our existence tied to the debt Bamba opened in our name.

Khalto Safa rolls her eyes. "You spoiled little child. Don't you understand that it takes sacrifice to build something great?"

The other Mina curls her lip. I hold perfectly still as Khalto Safa uses razor-sharp fingernails to lift my chin. "Bamba accepted this debt because she wanted to be someone. She wanted power, and this bargain is power. Everyone is born with a debt, Yasmina. Every choice has consequences, and sometimes, we are asked to pay for the choices others made. It isn't fair. It isn't just." Her eyes soften as she studies my face. "All we can control is our own choices. Our own fate."

I've heard that before you die, the world around you sharpens. Isolating sounds, smells, sights. A last bright imprint of the life slipping away, burned on the inside of your fading eyes.

Orange light rings the halo of shadows. Spreading inward, reaching for me.

Hot breath moistens my neck. I whirl around, fists raised to protect myself from the other Mina, and stare directly into the shredded face of my mother.

Bloody slashes the width of my thumb gouge across every inch of Mama's face and neck. Half her skull is missing, the indents around the hole suggesting teeth marks. Her eyes melt, sludgy orange rivers dribbling down ravaged cheeks. She opens her mouth, revealing a swollen, pocked tongue. Tiny creatures wiggle on the roof of her mouth.

A scream catches in my throat and expands, choking me slowly.

"When your mother returned to the villa, she never planned to leave." Khalto Safa regards the monstrous version of my mother without flinching. "She knew I was sick. She knew that if there wasn't anyone willing to serve the curse, it would claim every Haikal life still roaming the earth. Including yours."

Khalto Safa sighs, scratching her eyebrow with a thumb. The cigarette's red tip comes alarmingly close to her hair. "You were my last hope, you know. When you passed the test, I was ecstatic. I thought... I thought it might go differently." She perches on the arm of the couch, and the orange drains from her eyes. The glimmer of ethereal perfection wavers. For a split second, Safa Haikal just looks like a woman. A tired, ill woman.

Passed the test?

"Khalto Safa—"

"It's time to make a choice, Yasmina," she says.

The shadow ring bursts upward, forming a column of smoke with me in the center.

The world goes black.

When I open my eyes, I am on the ground.

Kneeling.

Shadows wreath the inside of my house, hanging over every surface like a widow's shroud.

A dark shape materializes in front of me. In seconds, the stench of rot and exposed sewage thickens in my nose, slithering wetly to the back of my throat.

There have been several times in the last few months that I've experienced terror. Too many to count. But if someone summed up all the fear I've lived through, tallied up every scream and whimper, collected each stone of dread in my gut—it wouldn't come close to this. Every awful moment would still pale in comparison to the visceral terror swallowing me whole.

I have seen this creature before.

In another time. Another place. Another Haikal.

As it had the night I witnessed my grandmother's death, time thins around me. The shadows slither over the floor, brushing over my skin.

YASMINA MANSOUR.

My lungs seize, collapsing beneath the wrecking ball of a scream hammering in my chest.

It's my own voice.

I CAN GIVE YOU WHAT YOU DESIRE MOST.

I try to unclench my teeth, but they won't stop chattering. A shadow wraps itself around my neck, and I hear the faintest echo of Rainie's voice.

"Come see what I wrote, Mina!" the phantom voice calls. *"Quick, before Mrs. B comes out!"*

Second grade. Rainie had to give herself a red card after Mrs. B saw the string of profanity she'd written in chalk on the playground.

YOU CAN HAVE A LIFE. YOU CAN HAVE THIS ENTIRE TOWN.

The dark shape leans, and before I can faint, heat explodes in my head.

And finally, I understand what my mother's journal meant.

The shadows are its vulnerability. They come with the curse, but they cannot be controlled by it.

The shadows pin us to reality. They show us what was, and most importantly—what could have been.

The curse shows you a dream. It shows you what could still be.

Under its touch, a life unfolds before my eyes like an unraveling roll of thread . I see rain pounding our house, but not a drop makes its way inside. The roof, finally fixed. Baba sitting on the couch, reading the newspaper while a pile of pistachio shells gathers on the coffee table.

In my room, the metal door is gone, as are the yellow stains on the ceiling. It's been transformed into a space I couldn't have designed in my wildest dreams. Colorful and cozy, a place I could dance or study or lounge inside for hours on end. Our house wouldn't be a villa, but it would be the envy of everyone in Ward.

The thread turns, and I see Jesse leaning against his car, boots crossed at the ankle. Waiting for someone.

In front of him is a small dance studio bearing my name. *Mina's Moves,* a name so incredibly silly that I fall in love with it immediately. I watch myself run out of the studio with a large bag and light up at the sight of Jesse. He slings my bag over his shoulder before pulling me in for a long kiss, laughing when I playfully shove him away to gesture at the sweat on my face.

Another twist of the thread, and I'm in Alexandria. Sitting on a thick carpet while a pretty woman braids my hair, both of us fixed on the television, where the soap opera we've been tuning into daily after dinner plays the mid-season finale. She's my aunt, my father's second cousin. Baba comes out with a tray of tea, passing me one while he pretends not to be avidly watching the soap. He hands the next two cups to his mother and father, who argue with my cousins about their grades and the upcoming nightmare of senior year exams. Another cousin splashes sharbat over a tray of hot kunafa, the sizzle of syrup on hot shredded dough momentarily distracting everyone.

The thread could go on forever. It could show me every moment of my life until the day I die, and I know it would show me the most beautiful things.

For the first time, I understand why Bamba cursed herself. How she didn't look hard enough through the mirage to see the monster behind it.

I want it. I want that life more than I want my next breath. When I passed the test, the curse gave me the ability to make my fantasy a reality. It put the power of choice in my hands—a power and burden not every Haikal bound to the curse gets to claim.

I open my eyes, and in front of me is the third-floor door.

My muscles finally unfreeze. I throw myself back, away from the door.

I CAN GIVE HIM HIS SOUL.

I yank my gaze from the door to the monster. I don't need to ask, and it doesn't need to explain. We both know whose soul it means.

"And the cost?" I whisper.

As one, the shadows rise, filing into neat formation.

The room blurs, and before me appear dozens of children. Each shadow melts into one of the lives lost at the hands of Bamba's curse. The price paid for the deal she struck so long ago.

In front of them stands the little girl with the feeno sandwich. The daughter of the woman on the beach.

YOU WILL WANT FOR NOTHING. THIS HOUSE AND THIS TOWN WILL BE YOURS.

I stare at the little girl's mournful eyes, and her mother's words ring in my ears.

. . . not all the people who stay are good.

It wants me to carry on Bamba's curse. To live out my dreams by the anguish of the families I destroy. Another small town to feed on, more families with little to their name to steal from.

I wish I could say I didn't consider it. I wish I could say there wasn't a second where I imagined accepting. That I cast aside the life it offered with force and certainty. That I immediately looked past the thread to the cruel hand unspooling it.

At the top of the stairs, the third-floor door cracks open. Orange light spills down the steps, creeping closer. Reaching for me.

CAN YOU PAY THE PRICE?

The life it offers is beautiful. It's beyond what I might have dared dream.

Which is why when I speak, when I utter the single word that puts scissors to the thread, it leaves my throat bleeding.

"No."

Jesse has a soul. Whatever he says, whatever *it* says. He has more soul than anyone I have ever known. Jesse's problem is not the lack of a soul, but the excess of one.

At the bottom of the stairs, Khalto Safa appears. She climbs the steps, her fingers gliding over the banister. She glances back at me, then to the children still gathered around us.

"Foolish girl," she whispers. "You could have *lived*."

The door opens wider, and Khalto Safa slips inside.

"No!" I shout. I struggle to my feet. "Wait!"

Small hands grab onto my clothes, my ankles, restraining me as I try to chase the door. The children converge around me as I weep, and for the second time, everything goes dark.

CHAPTER TWENTY-SIX
PRESENT DAY

I rouse to gentle hands smoothing my hair.

"Mina, binty habibty." Baba cups my face, pushing away the tangles of my curls. "Can you hear me?"

He sounds so worried. I should open my eyes and let him know there's nothing left to worry about.

A gruff voice cuts in. "She needs to see a doctor. I'm quite confident she had a preexisting head injury."

"What?!" Baba's exclamation finally jolts me the last few inches into wakefulness, and I pry open my eyes to the unlikely sight of my father and Elias Talbot looming over me.

I struggle to sit up, kicking my blankets into a heap at the foot of my bed.

"It's okay, Mina. You're safe." Baba helps me prop myself against the headboard. "How do you feel?"

I stare at Elias Talbot's face for longer than anyone would consider polite. He doesn't look much like his son—where Jesse's hair falls in midnight waves of black, Mr. Talbot's is a light brown. He's shorter than I thought he would be, standing an inch below Baba. In his jeans and button-down, he looks more like an accountant than a mortician.

Except... he has Jesse's eyes. The same dark, piercing stare cutting through me like an unsheathed knife.

"Baba, are you okay?" I search his head for wounds. "Where did she hit you?"

Baba's brows furrow. "Where did who hit me?" He glances at Mr. Talbot worriedly.

"It's normal to lose time after a head injury." Mr. Talbot presses a thumb to my eyelid. "Look up, please. Good. Now try to look at your toes."

He gives a few more instructions before I'm seemingly cleared. "My son found you and your father collapsed in the living room, Miss Mansour. We were hoping you could tell us what happened."

Jesse found me?

"Where is—" My voice peters out before I can finish, too hoarse and weak. I clear my throat. "Where is he?"

"Right here, Sour Patch."

Leaning against the doorframe, Jesse smiles wanly at me.

Elias Talbot's lips thin. "Shouldn't you be home?"

"I wanted to check on her."

"You've checked. The mortuary sinks won't sanitize themselves."

"Is he in trouble?" I ask Mr. Talbot. "He shouldn't be. He only came to check on me because he thought I was in danger."

"In the middle of a storm," Mr. Talbot points out.

Baba nods. "A Ward Wailer."

Oh, great. They've teamed up.

"Can I talk to Jesse alone?"

Baba's face darkens. A long, tense minute passes. Jesse eyes my dad nervously, but he doesn't know Baba. This entire situation reeks of my father's least favorite perfume: conflict. It's too much trouble to argue with me, and most likely now that he knows I'm alive, he'll get his laptop case and drive back to campus for the rest of the day.

Baba bursts into laughter, grabbing my dresser to steady himself.

Professor Mansour snorts—an actual snort—and doubles over while he struggles to catch his breath.

Straightening, Baba wipes the corners of his eyes, still chuckling softly. "Ala gusity, Yasmina Mansour."

My jaw drops the rest of the way open. I can count on one hand the number of times Baba has spoken Arabic in front of strangers.

He's angry. No, not just angry. For the first time I can remember, my father is *furious.*

"Over his dead body," Mr. Talbot translates for Jesse. When Baba and I glance at him in surprise, he shrugs. "I'm a mortician. Part of the gig includes knowing the different words for corpse."

"Glad to see you're well, Miss Mansour. We'll come visit when you feel better," Mr. Talbot says. He takes his son by the elbow, steering him out of the room. Jesse doesn't resist, letting himself be led away without a single glance back.

It's for the best. No need to irritate our fathers further, right? It would be stupid to feel hurt over him following the rules for once.

Later, we can figure out how I'm still alive. I was the last Haikal who could feed the curse, and I'd said no.

Why hadn't the curse come to collect yet?

In my fugue state, the consequence of their departure doesn't settle over me until Baba leans over to fuss with the pillows behind me.

For the first time since I visited the Haikal villa, Baba and I are alone.

Anxiety tightens cords in my stomach. My nostrils flare, anticipating the odors of sewage and rot.

One tense moment slips into the next. Baba is speaking, but I'm fixed on his brown eyes.

His wonderfully *normal* brown eyes.

I grin, a wild laugh bubbling in my chest. Maybe it's over. Really, truly over.

I survived. The curse didn't win.

"Oh, by the way, I booked our tickets," Baba continues, sniffing the cap of my water bottle suspiciously before passing it to me. "We leave for Masr a week after you graduate."

I accept the bottle without thought, waiting for the punchline. Baba continues to fiddle with the items on my dresser, organizing them without a single iota of precision.

"Really?" I don't dare breathe. This kind of hope is life-threatening. Too much weight attached to such a fragile hook, waiting to crush me at Baba's command. "You'll take me to meet your family?"

I scoot over as Baba perches on the bed. When his arm goes around my shoulders, I curl into him without a second thought. Despite the tears I've already shed, more of them gather against my eyelashes, dripping onto my cheek.

"You'll meet everyone, and they'll get to meet you," Baba murmurs into my hair. "They live in Ain Shams, near where I went to university. We'll visit el balad, where *I* used to spend my summers. Your gedo built an istiraha there when I was a kid for people to gather and spend time together outdoors, and I used to love roasting corn after dinner while your aunts embarrassed me at card game after card game."

Istiraha sounds like raha, which means rest, so istiraha probably means rest place. I'm about seventy percent sure, but I'm not about to distract Baba into giving me an etymology lesson.

"I also got us tickets to the new museum in Cairo." Baba grimaces slightly, a world of opinions in that single action, and joy fills me at the realization that I'll get to spend a summer seeing Masr through Baba's eyes. Learning how to love it the way he does and maybe helping him love it in ways he didn't before.

We don't mention Mama, and for once, I'm grateful for it.

"What if they don't like me?"

"They'll love you, Mina. It would be too hard not to." Baba laughs suddenly, and says, "Yalahwi. I'm going to have to buy *so many gifts.*"

I pat Baba's arm and smile up at him. "Leave that—and your credit card—to me."

Three days go by without a word from Jesse.

Baba happened to see the bandages from my encounter with the corpse in Mr. Talbot's mortuary, and it triggered a parental meltdown the likes of which I'd never seen from my father. He called the school to arrange for someone to bring me my homework, flipped out again when he learned I'd accrued several truancies over the last two weeks, and decided I would be staying home until a) I healed and b) he could "trust a single word coming out of your mouth."

For the first time in his professional life, Baba takes time off work to camp on the living room couch and ensure I don't sneak out. Part of me wants to rage at him. He practically authored the book on absent fatherhood, and now, when I need him to tune out of my life more than ever, he decides to dial back in?

The larger part of me, however, wakes up with a ridiculous smile on her face when she smells burning bread. Despite knowing he has the attention span of a fruit fly, Baba refuses to microwave pita bread. He insists on sticking it straight onto the stove, where it inevitably catches on fire when he gets distracted. Dinners watching *Ertugrul* while Baba grumbles about historical inaccuracies, yet yelping when I close the screen after a four-episode binge. Evenings doing our work quietly in the same room, the tap of our keyboards the only sound for hours.

It's everything I wanted.

Two days after the confrontation with Khalto Safa, Baba hands me a steaming glass of red-tinted tea. When I wrap my hand around the middle instead of taking it by the handle, he hisses between his teeth. "Your fingers, ya mama!"

"Oh, sorry." I quickly switch it to the other hand and let Baba examine my fingers. "I feel fine, I promise." Too fine, actually. I flex my fingers in bewilderment. Grabbing onto a glass cup of boiling liquid should've hurt, even if just a little. I haven't felt much sensation in my hands and feet since yesterday, but I don't want to worry Baba. My tangle with Khalto Safa might have caused some nerve damage.

He grabs his laptop off the coffee table and drops onto the couch. "We don't get to watch *Ertugrul* until we've gotten some work done. Go grab your backpack. I forwarded you your assignments. Spanish seems especially time sensitive, so I'd prioritize finishing that one first."

I groan. "Baba, it doesn't even matter. I'm graduating in two weeks."

"Not if you fail Spanish."

"I'm not going to fail!"

"Now say that to me in Spanish."

I glare, and he rewards me with a triumphant smirk. "Get moving."

I stomp upstairs, taking care to hit every step as loud as I can. As soon as I walk into my room, I beeline for the window and check Jesse's driveway.

His truck is still there. Three days, and it hasn't moved an inch.

Why hasn't he called me back? I've even left the metal door in my room unlocked every night since Khalto Safa's visit.

I've considered the grim possibility that Jesse simply doesn't want to see me anymore. Without the curse forcing us together, am I back to being the Canyon High social butterfly he can't stand?

The thought cuts deep. I can't imagine going back to a world where Jesse isn't one of the best parts of my day. A world where I walk past him hammering at his porch and don't say hello, because he frightens me and I'm not accustomed to being disliked. Where I forget what it's like to just be myself around someone.

A world where he looks at me and my heart doesn't ache.

I turn away from the window with an aggravated exhale. At least Rainie, Aida, and Lucia have gone back to calling and texting me like the month of separation never happened. Prom is tomorrow night, and they've been begging me to come with them.

I'd thought about it. After all, I bought my ticket months ago. I have a dress. Prom was something I'd looked forward to for years. Baba has even given me a pass for the evening so long as I come home by eleven o'clock sharp.

But even though life continues to march forward, I'm still stuck.

In my sleep, the orange eyes follow me. I see shadows that aren't there in the corner of my eye, urging me to acknowledge them.

She knew that if there wasn't anyone willing to serve the curse, it would claim every Haikal life still roaming the earth. Including yours.

I don't understand why the curse hasn't taken me. Mama, Khalto Safa, and Teta were the last ones able to serve the curse until I opened the door. Until I passed the test.

When I said no, I broke the bargain. I dropped the Haikals' end of the deal.

So why am I still here?

CHAPTER TWENTY-SEVEN
PRESENT DAY

The next morning, I wake up to a text from Jesse.

Meet me at Lake Lasem, it reads. **Let's have a picnic.**

I reread it five times, double-checking it came from Jesse and not an eerily manipulative spam number. Since when does Jesse willingly attend a picnic, let alone initiate one?

. . . **why?** I text back.

The response comes instantly. **Heard you nailed the graduation speech audition. Figured we're due a celebration.**

The corners of my mouth turn up in a reluctant smile. I hadn't gotten the chance to give him the good news. The Canyon High grapevine works its magic once again.

Another text lights my screen. **It might take your mind off prom.**

I hesitate. I want to demand an answer for his radio silence over the last four days, but it won't do any good over the phone.

Okay, I type out. **See you in an hour. I'll bring sandwiches.**

I tiptoe to the kitchen, and after a cursory investigation of the fridge, I whip up a couple of cream cheese and cucumber sandwiches. Baba hasn't woken up yet, so I leave one of the sandwiches on a plate for him and scrawl out a note.

Gone to prepare for prom with Lucia, Rainie, and Aida. Enjoy your day off guard duty and go hang out with Mr. Talbot or that cute librarian lady. Love you!

I hate to lie to him, but if he knew I was going to meet Jesse, he would flip out. Or worse, call his new best friend—Jesse's dad—to tattle.

After packing the sandwiches and a couple of juices into a basket, I head upstairs to get changed. It takes longer than it should to make it up the steps. The numbness in my hands and feet has traveled to my calves and crawled up to my shoulders. I promised myself I'd tell Baba if it got worse, but he's been so *happy*. We FaceTimed with his parents, who didn't seem at all suspicious or wary of me. Teta Maha gushed about how much I looked like her mother, while Gedo Galal complimented my Arabic and grilled me about my grades. I've gotten a flood of friend requests from cousins and relatives on my dad's side, and I've spotted Baba wiping his eyes and smiling down at his phone more times than I can count.

He may not have died from the Haikal curse, but he was a victim of it, too.

I toss open my curtain. Sunlight floods my room, the golden hues of a sunny day brightening my walls and bedsheets. I grin until my cheeks hurt. It wasn't too long ago I'd sat by my jacaranda tree at school and dreamt about a picnic by Lake Lasem.

It's the first sunny day we've had in weeks, and I refuse to waste it. I pull on a red polka dot sundress, adjusting the straps around my shoulders. The skirt twirls around my knees when I move, light as a feather. Thanks to Ward's endless winters, the dress has been taken off the hanger a grand total of two times. I draw a white cardigan over my arms and clip a tiny glass dolphin necklace around my neck.

Staring into the mirror, I twist the necklace between clumsy fingers and try to swallow around the rock in my throat. Mama bought the dolphin for me when I turned seven. She'd gone to a conference with Baba in Santa Barbara and delivered it to me inside a cerulean glass case.

This little basha couldn't wait to find you, she'd said in a co-conspiratorial whisper. *He leapt right into my hands.*

I turn away from my reflection. Someday, I'll make my peace with never having truly known my mother. Love is difficult to suffocate. It fuses to your bones, fills your veins, coils around your mind. At best, extracting it leaves scars. At worst, you don't survive it.

Maybe when I'm stronger, I'll bury my memories beneath the truth of who she was and hope it extinguishes that persistent voice that whispers:

She was terrible. She was a villain.

But she was mine.

The trees whisper as I walk between them, branches rustling in the warm breeze.

The only parking near the lake consists of a three-car dirt lot, so I parked near the tourist center. Baba would have too many questions if I came home with mud splattered over the tires.

I try to move carefully along the path, avoiding the trenches of mud left over from the Ward Wailer. Not an easy task in the best of times, but with half my body numb and leaden, I keep forgetting how to shift my weight against the dirt.

The sun pierces through the trees, casting twisted shadows along the path. They stop my heart for a good minute.

I shield my face against the sun, grumbling a laugh. Of course, it would be in the brightness that I'm most afraid. Shadows don't exist in perfect darkness. They can only be created in the light.

I pass warning sign after warning sign, most of which have met the unfriendly end of a bottle of spray paint. I don't need to read past the graffiti to know they're warning hikers away from this side of the lake. Even during the day, Lake Lasem poses a real threat to anyone unfamiliar with the path. The most careful Ward locals have stumbled off the ledge on the south-facing side of the lake. One wrong step, and you're free falling sixty feet into the water. In the winter, if the drop itself doesn't kill you, the temperature of the lake will.

I'd bet my last dollar that Jesse picked this spot to avoid the crowds on the other side of the lake. Canyon High tradition dictates a pre-prom picnic by Lake Lasem, which means half the school is probably camped a few miles north.

I walk for what feels like an eternity before I find him.

Sitting against a slim redwood, his arm slung over one crooked knee, is Jesse. He doesn't notice my arrival. I stop short, drinking in the sight of him.

He looks . . . exhausted. The dark circles under his eyes have only sunk deeper. The light tousle in his hair has officially upgraded to messy, as though he's been shoving his hands through it at all hours of the day. He rolls his head back against the tree, bloodshot eyes fixed into the distance.

Deep in thought, he doesn't notice my approach.

"You can't be mad at me for being late," I say. "I hiked a mile to get here. In a *dress*."

Jesse doesn't raise his head, but a single sardonic brow arches. "The parking lot is over there." He gestures vaguely behind him. "It's a five-minute walk."

"I didn't want to get mud on the car."

His lips hitch into a small smile. "Ah, the great Yasmina Mansour finally falls prey to parental wrath. Celebrities—they're just like us!"

Rolling my eyes, I settle next to Jesse on the blanket, placing my basket next to his. "If skulking around train yards doesn't pan out, I'm glad you have a career in mediocre comedy to fall back on."

Jesse's smile graduates to a full-blown grin, but it doesn't spark the same warmth in my belly as it usually does.

He isn't looking at me.

"Your dad still pissed?" he says.

I study Jesse's profile for a minute before turning my attention to the lake. "No, he doesn't usually stay mad for long. He's just hovering. Guilty conscience, I think. He hasn't paid this much attention to me since I was a kid. Lot of years to catch up on."

We gaze out onto the lake. I rearrange my dress around my legs as a I draw my knees to my chest. Closing my eyes, I tip my chin toward the sun, soaking in the warmth.

"You've been avoiding me," I murmur.

A pause. "Yes."

I swallow. No beating around the bush, I guess. "Why?"

"I needed time to think. To process . . . everything."

"Since when do you need time to—"

It hits me like a clap of lightning.

One soul destroyed, one soul saved, and one soul earned.

My eyes fly open. "Your soul. Jesse, did—do you know if—"

Wasn't that his mother's deal? He helped me break the curse. He saved me.

"I don't know." Jesse rakes a hand through his tortured hair, still avoiding my eyes. "Souls don't tend to send you a confirmation receipt once you've earned them back."

I twist onto my knees and overbalance, dropping like a sack of sand onto the blue crocheted blanket Jesse spread on the grass. Jesse immediately grabs my shoulders and hauls me upright. "What the hell? Are you okay?"

"I'm fine. Just a cramp." It's my turn to avoid his eyes. I can't tell him about the numbness yet. For once, I want to focus on *him*. "Stop with the quips and the sarcasm, Talbot. You helped me break the curse. You saved me. Those were the terms of your mom's deal."

A look of pure devastation flashes across Jesse's features, there and gone in a blink. It's heartbreak in its most human form, and it shakes me to my core.

I touch his arm. "Jesse, what's wrong? What is it?"

Jesse curls away, and to my shock, tears gather in his bloodshot eyes. "I'm so sorry, Mina. I—I didn't break a damn thing."

From under the basket, Jesse withdraws my mother's journal. I recoil so hard I nearly overbalance again. I forgot he still had it.

"A ton of new entries appeared after you ran out of the woods. I didn't mention it because after everything you've been through, you deserve a break. I figured it would be better to translate them on my own and bring the journal to you if there was anything worth discussing."

I flip through the entries with a single finger, ensuring Jesse doesn't notice the clumsiness in my hands. Scanning my mother's writing alongside the pages of Jesse's notes, I'm struck by the sheer dedication it must have taken to compile this. They span *years*. Attempt after attempt to find ways to break the curse, to end the debt without ending the entire lineage.

The last entry is dated the day before she left for the Haikal villa.

It can't be broken.

It can only end.

I'll give her as much time as I can.

I look up at Jesse, hands shaking so violently that his notes slide out of the journal and scatter around the blanket.

Khalto Safa's voice rings in my ears. *When your mother returned to the villa, she never planned to leave.*

"When she found out Safa was sick, she went back," I murmur. "She was going to stay in the villa and feed the curse until she died, just so I could have a life."

I shake my head, tears clinging to my eyelashes. I couldn't tell what tore me apart more: knowing how fiercely my mother must have loved me to make that kind of sacrifice, or understating that the monstrous part of her, the Terror of El Agamy part, had never disappeared. She would have killed so many more children, destroyed more families, just to keep me alive.

The journal tumbles from my weak fingers.

"There are Haikals mysteriously dying all over the world," Jesse says in a broken whisper. "The first deaths started three days ago."

I lean back, tipping my face toward the sun. I stare until my eyes burn. When I close them, the sparks behind my eyelids rearrange themselves to look like Baba. Rainie, Lucia, Aida, Alex. Like the initials we carved under our lunch table freshman year. My favorite latte at Espresso Yourself. The tooth I buried in the yard of our old house. Mama's spiteful pomegranate tree that tries to die every winter.

I'm sitting against the towering jacaranda tree, watching its petals float on the breeze. Marveling at the bumps running beneath the concrete where its roots disappear deep, deep below.

Khalto Safa's last words drip like poison.

Foolish girl. You could have lived.

When I open my eyes, no trace of tears remains. Jesse is on his knees, hovering above me. The sun crowns his head in a fiery halo, his black hair rippling across it like an eclipse.

I slide a palm over his chest, knotting a fist into the soft fabric of his shirt. The other hand curls around the collar of his jacket. "I was going to ask you to come with me to prom, you know."

Jesse lets me tug him to the ground, bracing himself on his elbows above me. A thumb brushes the length of my brow, sweeping over the sensitive skin of my temple. "I would have said yes."

My laugh tapers into a long sigh. "Liar."

Large hands frame my face, drawing my gaze up. "I would have said yes," he repeats firmly. "I would have gone anywhere with you, Mansour."

A tear beads in the corner of Jesse's eye, and the muscles beneath my hands coil, as though he's about to pull away. I tighten my grip. "Everyone leaves Ward. That doesn't mean much to me." I wipe his tear with the heel of my hand and wish I could feel it. "Would you have stayed?"

The numbness reaches my chest, paralyzing my lungs. I struggle to hide my flagging breath.

Jesse waits until I'm looking at him again. "I would have stayed. I might've even been convinced to plant a fruit tree in the yard."

I laugh, half humor and half heartbreak, and if my heart wasn't slowing beneath the poison traveling through me, it would have cracked. Jesse Talbot finally did it. He finally set down roots in Ward. Left a mark on this town, a handprint in the ground saying *I was here.*

He cared.

Jesse sweeps my hair from my cheek and lowers his head, pausing with his lips a hairsbreadth from my own. "Can I—"

I silence the rest of the sentence against my mouth, arms winding around Jesse's neck as he finally, *finally* kisses me like he did the day in the train. If my toes were still capable of sophisticated movement, they would be curling inside my shoes. Heat races through me, and for the first time since Khalto Safa's visit, my body acts in a way I understand. I arch into Jesse, clutching the back of his jacket as his hand slides to the small of my back and presses me against him.

It's perfect. The curse would have given me this if I'd let it. A lifetime of Jesse's lips on my throat. Of him holding me desperately close, each press of his fingers against my skin a promise and a claim.

When the numbness reaches my chin, I force myself to pull back. I'll need my vocal cords to say what I need to, and I don't know how much longer I'll have use of them.

I put my hands on either side of his face, forcing his gaze to mine. "I want you to listen carefully, because I think it'll be hard for you to remember much about today, but I need you to remember this: You broke the curse, Jesse. My soul is mine again. Your mom's curse didn't say anything about saving a life."

I tighten my hands when he tries to look away. "I might have said yes if it weren't for you. I might have brought this curse to Ward and started the nightmare all over again." With every passing minute, the numbness sinks deeper. Soon, I'll lose even the ability to lift my limbs. "We ended two curses, Jesse Talbot. Be proud of that."

"Said yes?" Jesse rears back. Disbelief paints his features in broad stripes. "Mina, did it—did it give you the choice?"

I roll to my knees with difficulty. Jesse steadies me, and it finally appears to dawn on him that my clumsiness isn't normal. I press my lips to his cheek, leaning my forehead against his hair. "Of course it was a choice. It has always been a choice."

I want to be someone. Bamba had said, so many generations ago. *Whoever it costs.*

"Take care of Baba, please," I rasp. "Have him kiss Teta and Gedo for me."

I lift my head and prepare my body. The body I'd spent so many years training, strengthening. The body of the former dance team captain that, with any luck, still has enough juice to outrun the mortician's son.

I memorize Jesse's face, tracing each lovely line.

"Tell him I fell," I whisper.

By the time his head snaps up, I'm already running.

"*Mina!*"

I sprint past the abandoned picnic baskets, full of food we never shared. Past the crochet blanket I didn't get a chance to ask about. Past the warning sign four feet from the ledge. With each step, the numbness spreads, billowing like a toxic fog through my joints.

Unlike Jesse, I grew up in Ward. I know every tree, every footpath, every cliff. His shouts grow fainter as I weave toward the steep eastern trail, ignoring the signs posted along the path. Mud from the Ward Wailer slicks the narrow, descending path between the high crags of the lake. My lungs scream, fighting to push against the thick weight surrounding them. If I slow, if I even entertain the thought of stopping, I won't make it another step. I'll die right here, out in the open, the curse claiming the last Haikal a mile away from dozens of celebrating teenagers. Right next to Jesse Talbot, the boy shrouded in rumors and darkness, who would be given the benefit of the doubt by no one and arrested faster than he could say, "It was the curse!"

I didn't ask Jesse how the others had died, but I imagine it was identical: a slow suffocation, as though the breath of life the curse granted us was slowly leaking from our lips.

I thought breaking the curse would kill the Haikals instantly, but I was wrong. It was killing us off in order. Death took three days to reach me because I am the last of them.

If there is any blessing to the numbness, it's that I don't feel pain when my foot slips. When I slide down the trail, rocks tearing against my clothes and skin, I only feel relief.

Because at the end of the trail, rushing toward me, stretches the endless blue of Lake Lasem.

Sinking into the lake isn't much different than falling into a dream.

The numbness conquers the last inch of sensation left in my body. My lungs exhale the remaining tendrils of air inside them and ice over.

The water closes over my head. The lake's gentle fingers drag my cold body down, down, down.

In the dark, hundreds of small bodies take shape. The sad girl with her sandwich. The boy from Jesse's room.

They sink with me, countless bodies rippling beneath the surface of Lake Lasem. Children stolen from the tide of life, leaving broken hearts stranded on shore. This creature—this monster's greatest evil comes from the gouges it leaves in the tapestry of time. Lives it unravels, legacies it unbuilds. It ensures the survival of a few at the cost of many.

They make us mortal so they can be everlasting.

My hair billows around my face. I think about Jesse. If he'll stay in Ward to help his dad after graduation. If he'll spend more years hammering at his porch, keeping his deteriorating house together out of determination and pure spite. If he'll leave Ward and never look back.

The children swarm me. Soft hands press against my cheeks, clutch my arms and ankles.

At the bottom of the lake, a light appears.

Bright and golden, it pierces through the darkness. The children cling to me. We barrel toward the light like shooting stars.

It engulfs us, and the world turns white.

I flail, burning, when a firm hand grasps mine.

The touch scorches, but I hold on tight. The lake churns, launching us forward.

The grip on my hand tightens and pulls.

I gasp as my head breaks through the water. The sun beats down from its perch in the clear blue sky. Warmth chases back the chill on my skin, and I gaze out at the unmistakable coastline of Alexandria. Laughter drifts over from the shore, where families lounge beneath leaning umbrellas, plates of food balanced on their knees. Children chase each other on the edge of the beach, tossing balls of wet sand and ignoring their mothers' shrieks.

I blink at the figure leaning over me, blotting out the sun. Slowly, their features slide into place.

My eyes. My mouth. My freckles.

My face.

"The food is getting cold. Amu Amir ate the last piece of macarona bechamel," the other Mina says. "It's time to get out of the water."

The children rise behind me, cheeks flushed, smiling. Alive.

She doesn't let go of my hand, and together, we walk to shore.

EL AGAMY DAILY NEWS

اخبار العجمى اليومية

The long-isolated corner of the western Alexandria shoreline is dusting itself off for another influx of visitors this Sham el Niseem.

The wave comes after a record-breaking year of new real estate purchases and developments across the sleepy region. The spike in population has brought sorely needed foot traffic to local businesses and the languishing tourist market. To accommodate the newcomers, municipal authorities took a closer look at the safety of structures in older neighborhoods of El Agamy, where the buildings have stood empty for decades.

Their investigation was due in no small part to the catastrophic destruction of the home in Kadir Abaid, the most desolate neighborhood in El Agamy. The initial conditions of the collapse made it too dangerous for authorities to excavate, but a later search determined nobody was home during the collapse.

The listed owner, Safa Haikal, has not been found. Authorities have been unable to find a living next of kin.

The Haikal villa has stood nearly as long as El Agamy itself. The stories about them stretch from coast to coast, generation to generation. For years, the Haikal family has been blamed for the lack of growth or tourism in the area. Despite countless legal investigations, nobody has ever been able to produce concrete evidence of any crimes committed by the Haikal family.

You can read more of the Haikal family's reputation in Abir Hanafi's *Local Legends* section and make up your own minds.

Superstition or slander, truth or tall tale—without a house to investigate or a living Haikal to interview, the question of what really took place in that villa may never be answered. The whispers about its bloody history, the talk of curses and strange lights in the window....

It will all be just another ghost story.

ACKNOWLEDGMENTS

Writing these acknowledgments is tough, because there's so much I want to say about this book. About El Agamy, which I had a whole enemies-to-lovers arc with as a teenager and through my early twenties, because I was loyal to "central" Alexandria, where I'd spent middle school and several childhood summers.

I've loved horror for as long as I can remember. As the eldest cousin at family gatherings in Masr, I grew up being tasked with distracting the kids while the adults talked. What better way to do so than by inventing a terrifying story about what would happen to them if they ever dared enter the empty apartment on the third floor of that one creepy building? Or a story about a bride that never makes it to her wedding and comes back as a spirit to seek vengeance on all who wronged her?

Those summers of stories eventually led to the summer of 2021 in El Agamy. I was staying up late to accommodate the ten-hour time difference between me and my virtual externship, trying not to think about the book that would later become my adult fantasy debut fighting for its life in the query trenches. Pacing beneath the locked third-floor door (behind which was nothing more than chicken coops and my rampant imagination) and listening to the animals outside start to howl.

In the midst of those long nights, *Where No Shadow Stays* was born.

Mina's story took hold of me and would not let go. A haunted house. A cursed legacy. An impossible choice.

While creating Mina's journey in the Haikal villa, it occurred to me that the questions—behind the places time hadn't touched, behind every rusted gate and hollow building—were my favorite part of horror. They were the heart of the story; the *why* of the haunting. The desperate pursuit for answers against the inevitability of the ending. The history in every brick and shingle of a haunted house. Horror was the perfect medium to explore the idea of how some actions reach into the future and tangle the very threads of time, manifesting themselves into each generation like a curse.

Thank you for picking up *Shadow* and diving into Mina's story. There are so many people who helped usher this book into your hands.

Eternal gratitude to my agent, Jennifer Azantian, who went to bat countless times for this book. Many thanks to the team at Holiday House for their hard work and vision for *Where No Shadow Stays*. Marcela Bolívar, the ethereal, gorgeous cover you created had me spellbound from the moment I laid eyes on it.

To Ream Shukairy, who writes powerful, devastating, unapologetic books and inspires me to be braver every day. I do not know how I would function in this industry (or life) without you. Maeeda, thank you for offering the most level-headed advice and never giving up hope that our writing retreat will happen.

To Jess Parra, my honorary aunt. I would have gone off every deep end known to science if it weren't for your friendship. Thank you for the podcasts, the brunches, and for reminding me how to love this book. To Abby, who is the most nonchalantly hilarious person I've ever known. Thank you for reading the earliest draft of this book and tolerating me hovering over your shoulder for a few weeks. (Sometimes I was just hovering for the soup). To Kate Dramis, Ruth Y., Bisman B., and Chelsea Abdullah: I can't believe I have such absolute icons in my life.

To my family. Always to my family, who hold me up whenever the brass knuckles of life try to knock me down and make me so unbelievably proud every day. And Hanan, I adore you for reading (and proofreading) this book twice and staying up to finish even when you had to be up early. You carved time for this book into your horrifying schedule, and it meant the world.

To every reader, bookseller, and librarian who has welcomed my books into their shelves. I am so grateful for each and every one of you. I can never thank you enough for the enthusiasm, encouragement, and love you've shared with me. Some of you don't even gravitate toward horror, but you took a chance on *Shadow* anyway. I could write an entire novel about what your words and kindness have meant to me. Thank you for being here.

الحمد لله والشكر لله